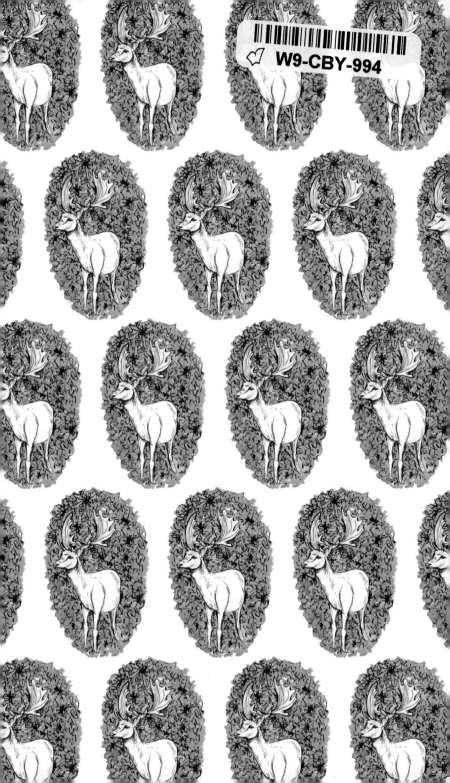

The

King Arthur
Case

ALSO BY JEAN-LUC BANNALEC

Death in Brittany
Murder on Brittany Shores
The Fleur de Sel Murders
The Missing Corpse
The Killing Tide
The Granite Coast Murders

The
King Arthur
Case

—◆ **A BRITTANY MYSTERY** ◆—

Jean-Luc Bannalec

Translated by Peter Millar

MINOTAUR BOOKS
NEW YORK

First published in the United States by Minotaur Books, an imprint of St. Martin's Publishing Group

THE KING ARTHUR CASE. Copyright © 2020 by Verlag Kiepenheuer & Witsch. Translation copyright © 2022 by Peter Millar. All rights reserved. Printed in the United States of America. For information, address St. Martin's Publishing Group, 120 Broadway, New York, NY 10271.

www.minotaurbooks.com

Designed by Devan Norman

Endpaper art by Ella Johnston

Library of Congress Cataloging-in-Publication Data

Names: Bannalec, Jean-Luc, 1966– author. | Millar, Peter, translator.
Title: The King Arthur case / Jean-Luc Bannalec ; translated by
    Peter Millar.
Other titles: Bretonische Geheimnisse. English
Description: First U.S. edition. | New York : Minotaur Books, 2022. |
    Series: Brittany mystery series ; 7 | "First published as Bretonische
    Geheimnisse in Germany by Verlag Kiepenheuer & Witsch." |
Identifiers: LCCN 2021052247 | ISBN 9781250753083 (hardcover) |
    ISBN 9781250753090 (ebook)
Subjects: LCGFT: Detective and mystery fiction. | Novels.
Classification: LCC PT2662.A565 B73513 2022 | DDC 833/.92—
    dc23/eng/20211029
LC record available at https://lccn.loc.gov/2021052247

Our books may be purchased in bulk for promotional, educational, or business use. Please contact your local bookseller or the Macmillan Corporate and Premium Sales Department at 1-800-221-7945, extension 5442, or by email at MacmillanSpecialMarkets@macmillan.com.

First published as *Bretonische Geheimnisse* in Germany
by Verlag Kiepenheuer & Witsch

First U.S. Edition: 2022

10 9 8 7 6 5 4 3 2 1

à L,
à mon ami Helge

Just being alive today is seriously dangerous.

—BRETON SAYING

The

King Arthur Case

The First Day

Val sans Retour! We're here, boss, the Valley of No Return."
Inspector Riwal's eyes lit up. His entire face beamed.

Commissaire Georges Dupin and his little team at the Commissariat de Police Concarneau had made good time; it hadn't taken them much more than an hour. Dupin had driven, as usual completely ignoring the speed limit. His angular Citroën might be aged but it was still remarkably nimble; traffic cameras had flashed twice. Riwal and Kadeg, his two inspectors, sat in the back while Nolwenn, his indispensable assistant, sat next to him on the armchair-style front passenger seat.

Dupin had initially been somewhat reserved in his attitude toward Nolwenn's "grand idea" of merging an unfortunately unavoidable trip the commissaire had to make into the Forêt de Brocéliande with an "office outing." But Nolwenn was determined. Even Kadeg, who usually had to be coaxed into something, found the idea to be excellent.

It was already two years since their last office outing, Nolwenn had made a point of reminding them, when they had gone to the north-westernmost point on the coast, and if Dupin was honest, it had been very enjoyable. His reservations had more to do with his official business, which had to do with his last case, in the early summer of that year, when he had made a deal with his old Paris police friend Jean Odinot. The deal was in the police "gray zone" in which Odinot had provided Dupin with important information, and Dupin in return had made clear he was ready to look into an unsolved case for the Paris police. Dupin didn't want to shirk: it was a matter of honor for him to fulfill his part of the deal, and, in any case he would have done so for Jean Odinot even if there wasn't a deal involved. No, Odinot wasn't the problem, the problem was the Paris police. Back then, after his "resignation"—a "suspension" for seriously and unfortunately very publicly insulting the city mayor—he had sworn that never again in his whole life would he have anything to do with the Paris police. Odinot's comment when they spoke on the phone yesterday that it was "a completely absurd matter" they were chasing up had added to his motivation.

"Brocéliande." Nolwenn had pulled a thin volume out of a provisions bag that would have sustained all of them for several days in the wilderness. "'Brocéliande! What stunningly precious memories were summed up in a single word! The whole of Europe in the Middle Ages pronounced it only with the deepest reverence. The sole remaining kingdom of the fairies. It was here that some of the most wonderful creations of fantasy were played out, creations that had moved the hearts of men.'"

It really was Dupin's first excursion into the Forêt de Brocéliande—or Forêt de Paimpont, as it was known more prosaically—the biggest forest in Brittany. The biggest, and above all, the most famous. Not just in Brittany, but obviously all of France and all of Europe. It was undisputedly the heart of fantasy in Brittany, the most magical of all its fairy-tale sites. The legend of all legends. Which meant something amid Brittany's wealth of legends. Dupin had taken it for granted that Riwal and Nolwenn would be even more eager travel guides than usual on this trip and would come out with a knowledgeable commentary, and was determined to be totally calm.

"We'd do best to park by the Church of the Holy Grail. That's the ideal starting point," Nolwenn said, and nodded to her left.

Everything here hinted at the spectacular. The signs at the edge of the road pointed to the Church of the Holy Grail, Lake Lancelot, Merlin's Steps, the Tomb of the Giants.

"Seventy-seven hundred hectares of forest!" Riwal had undone his seat belt, and was leaning toward them. "Woodland and heath, full of lakes and ponds. The proud reminder of the vast forests that back in Celtic times covered all of Brittany. It's shaped like a sleeping dragon. You can make it out from the air! The seemingly irrelevant name comes from *broce,* for *forêt,* and *liande,* for *lande,* the strips of heathland. But the real meaning of the words derives from the Celtic: the Fortress of the Other World." Riwal sat back briefly, only to lean forward again and continue more emphatically: "Endless Celtic-Breton legends are set here, the craziest stories from down the millennia. But the forest reached its greatest fame through King Arthur and his Round Table. And as you know"—a purely rhetorical finesse to increase their attention—"Arthur is of huge importance for us Bretons! He stands for one thing in particular: resistance! One of our proudest virtues!" Riwal's pathos reached a new height. "The very core of our being. Resistance as in standing up for the highest of ideals, the very principles of Arthur's rule: equality, brotherhood, and kindness. It was we Bretons who believed unwaveringly in Arthur's return, who have put our unbreakable trust in him!"

"Nobody even knows really if Arthur even existed," Kadeg muttered, looking indifferently out the window.

Riwal was not about to let himself be embarrassed.

"The legend *itself* and its powerful influence are unquestionably true!" he said. It was a typical Riwal statement. "The strength and force of his aura! Nonetheless there's an increasing number of scientific indications that there is a real figure behind all the fantastical stories."

Nolwenn joined in: "And a whole host of stories about King Arthur and his world are set in this wood."

The tiny village in the so-called Val sans Retour, the Valley of No Return, at the far western edge of the wood, was called Tréhorenteuc. It consisted of a few solitary houses to the left and a plowed field on the right. Dupin could already see the church, and the cemetery diagonally behind it. There was no doubt that it was an enchanting little place with a lot of atmosphere. The last quarter of an hour's drive since leaving the Route Nationale had led them through the sort of landscape Dupin liked. Gently hilly in all shades of green, matching fields, surrounded by ancient stone walls, meadows, wild woods, winding roads, and pretty villages. A unique blend of culture and nature. Brittany's inland, the "Argoat."

Riwal stuck his head between the front seats again. "In the first French version of Geoffrey of Monmouth's *Historia Regum Britanniae*, from the middle of the twelfth century, the forest where the adventures of Arthur's world took place was clearly located in Brittany. The author of the story of Arthur's world was Chrétien de Troyes, who lived from 1135 to 1188. He came from Champagne."

"Not bad! A good basis for top-class fantasy stories!" Kadeg seemed pleased with his joke.

But Riwal continued all the more determinedly:

"Chrétien took the reports from the *Historia*"—Riwal particularly emphasized the word "reports"—"but also ancient Celtic stories, initially just the orally transmitted accounts about Arthur and his Round Table. There are five books by Chrétien, and for the past two weeks they've been lying on your desk, boss."

The commissaire made a point of staring straight ahead. He had seen the fat volumes but never lifted one of them up.

"As usual," Riwal continued, "there are adaptations as well as rewriting and endless popular reworkings of the material at the highest literary level. You need to think of the whole of Arthurian literature like a rogue patch of ground gone wild, with things sprouting up all over the place. It is"—and here Riwal got completely carried away—"a story that goes on forever, the material inexhaustible, reworked over and over, unending."

"Just stop here, on the right, by the side of the road," Nolwenn interjected. "That's perfect."

"The other thing I left on your desk is an edition of the famed Lancelot and the Holy Grail cycle, which is one of the most important elements of the Arthurian legend. Tales of young Arthur, of Merlin, the greatest magician of all time, of the fairy Viviane, Arthur's half sister Morgana, of Lancelot, and Yvain, the lion rider. You have—"

"We're there."

Dupin had brought the Citroën to a stop behind another car. It was less than twenty meters to the church. He turned off the engine, opened the door, and got out. The others followed him.

He stopped and took a deep breath.

Even here, in the heart of Brittany, the weather was fabulous.

The forest was situated almost exactly in the middle of the north and south coasts, the Bay of Biscay and the Channel, Vannes and Saint-Malo. It was often cloudy. Today, however, was a phenomenal day. It was mid-August, a peculiar time of the year: summer with melancholy undertones. Residents were surprised when the weather turned, sending bleak, violent, monstrous clouds racing along the heavens; it got stormy and wet and, unlike how it had been two weeks earlier, the wind suddenly ripped the leaves from the trees. All of a sudden the mood was different. The light was milder, softer, velvety, especially around noon.

You could put a date to the day when the weather changed. Not that there weren't any more summer days; of course there were some between now and the end of October, days of summery warmth and occasionally even heat, but even those were not the same as earlier. Nonetheless, there wasn't even a hint of fall in the air today. The thermometer in Concarneau had climbed to a remarkable twenty-seven degrees by the time they set off just after one in the afternoon. Even now the sun was still burning hot. The sky was still bright, a satisfied glorious blue.

"Let's go over our plan for today," Nolwenn said. She was bursting with energy. They had gathered behind the car, with their bags and day packs from the trunk. "The inspectors and I will meet with Marie Line at the Maison des Sources. You have your rendezvous now, Monsieur le Commissaire, and can meet up with us afterward," she said, and wrinkled her brow. "But it shouldn't be later than four."

Dupin had agreed to meet Fabien Cadiou—the man he was to interview on Odinot's behalf—at two thirty. He hoped it wouldn't last longer than an hour and a half.

"We can find maps, books, and everything else we need at Marie

Line's, and also get a bite to eat, savory and sweet delicacies." Nolwenn had already told them about the Maison des Sources over the past few days; it was a little coffee shop with a bookstore and art gallery attached.

"I imagine you'll want to drink a *café* after your interview. Then we can start with today's excursion, the first stop being the Church of the Holy Grail." She nodded with her head toward the church and continued: "Then the Valley of No Return, also known as the Dangerous Valley and the Valley of the False Lovers."

"The most important thing about the valley," Riwal said, dropping his voice deliberately as the expression on his face changed, "is not what you see, but what you feel."

"Scandalous! Stealing our beach just like that!" Kadeg threw the newspaper he had been reading during the journey into the trunk with a sour face. His indignant outburst stripped Riwal's emotional discourse of its effect. "I think we should sue," he added.

But no one responded. For the past week the Breton newspapers had been full of it: the Corsicans—normally well received in Brittany—had been using photos of a Breton beach in a brochure intended to depict the unique beauty of the Corsican Mediterranean coast. The Bretons had cursed up a storm—but deep down they were filled with pride: the Mediterranean beaches were advertising with pictures of Brittany, because Breton beaches looked more Mediterranean.

"Between seven and half past, we'll head for the hotel. We have a table reserved for dinner at eight thirty," Nolwenn said, dismissively ignoring Kadeg's outburst.

Nolwenn had spent ages discussing the choice of hotel with Riwal, and in the end they had chosen La Grée des Landes in La Gacilly, primarily of course, because they wanted to try the restaurant, which was highly praised. For good Frenchmen, which of course, the Bretons also were—at least as far as this went—the choice of restaurant was the most important factor. From there they could start their plans in earnest.

"Fabien Cadiou's house isn't far from the Maison des Sources, boss. Three minutes from here, no more. We can walk a part of the way together before you turn off. *Allons-y!*" Riwal said. He had already set off, well prepared, with his outdoor clothing and shoes that would have been good enough to scale Mont Blanc. Even the blue backpack matched. Kadeg was wearing jeans, a T-shirt, and a thin jacket in military green, with a large *S* on the shoulder for Salomon, Kadeg's favorite brand. Nolwenn was as dazzling as ever.

Riwal turned around to face Dupin and said, "Like I told you before, boss: Fabien Cadiou is a real luminary! He's one of the world's leading Arthurian experts."

Dupin didn't go into that; he had tried to ignore the fact that Cadiou was involved with the Arthurian legend.

"Did you remember to order me a vegan meal, Nolwenn?" Kadeg said just at that moment. The inspector and his wife, a martial artist from Lorien, had recently converted to veganism. Dupin didn't mind per se, but what did get on his nerves and those of everyone else and regularly drove them mad was Kadeg's excessive zeal. Kadeg always turned everything into a mission.

"What I'm up for today is a large fricassée of snails with parsley butter." Riwal walked on, speaking without the slightest touch of irony or provocation. "Followed by a *carré d'agneau* in an herb and forest nut crust." Obviously he had gone over today's menu scrupulously. You could almost hear him licking his lips.

They were quiet for a while.

"And tomorrow," Nolwenn broke the silence, "the program looks like this: in the morning we visit the Fontaine de Barenton, the famous spring with its miraculous water from Paimpont, more or less at the heart of the forest, then—"

Riwal had come to a sudden stop. "You need to go that way, boss," he said, and indicated a wide gravel path that turned right from the road. "It's about three hundred meters. The old manor lies right at the edge of the forest. The Maison des Sources is—" The inspector turned, and with a brief nod at the houses, continued. "—just on the right there in front of us. You can't miss it."

Dupin saw a stone wall at waist height with a thick clump of hollyhocks behind it and an old reddish stone house.

"Pink granite," the commissaire stated. He had paid particular attention to this stone ever since his vacation on the Côte de Granit Rose.

Riwal was quick to reply:

"Slate, if I might correct you, boss! Red slates, not granite. The stone in the forest is slate, both gray and red. Even the Val sans Retour, where one or another individual has gotten lost, has been carved out of red slate. The unusual amount of iron in the stone confuses the compass, and human senses too. Do you know why the slate is red?"

Dupin shook his head with a sigh.

"Seven faeries," Riwal was already explaining, "lived with their treasure hidden at the bottom of the lake. They had sworn to one another never to let humans see them. The youngest of them broke the oath and showed herself to a young man riding along the edge of the lake. Her sisters decided to kill him, to prevent people discovering them. The youngest of them got into such a rage that she cut her sisters' throats in their sleep, made a magic potion out of their blood, and brought the young man back to life. People say that the murdered sisters' blood was soaked up by the slates for seven days, which gave it the red color."

Dupin left the asphalt road. He wasn't in a mood to comment on the story.

"See you later, then."

"Like I said, four o'clock at the latest, Monsieur le Commissaire," Nolwenn called out.

"At the very latest," Dupin mumbled, and increased his speed. The gravel under his feet crunched.

The path led around an old laurel bush, and all of a sudden the view opened up. There lay the famed forest: gentle, curving hills; imposing, thick, hard, and impassable. A breeze surrounded him, not exactly cool, but not friendly either. It seemed to swallow up all the light. In contrast, the fields and meadows that rose slightly toward the forest were in bright sunshine. The grass was a glaring, almost blinding green. They clearly belonged to the ordinary world, they were real, clearly on this side, whereas that could not be said about the forest.

Dupin shook his head. "Nonsense," he said out loud. He had probably already heard too many stories about the great magic forest. It was a wood, just a wood. Nothing more than that.

* * *

A few minutes later Dupin was standing in front of the old manor. Red slate; large, elegant blocks; tall, imposing; three floors and a steep dark gray roof. An old compact structure that made it look almost like a tower.

It was just as Riwal had said. The house was right on the borderline, one half in the meadow, the other into the forest.

Dupin walked past the house on the left, then belatedly saw a grand square courtyard behind it, enclosed by a tall, neglected stone wall. It smelled murky, earthy, woody, damp. And it also felt notably cooler.

The wall gave the air of something enduring. It seemed to communicate that nothing could force its way in from the forest wilderness that began just a meter away. No doubt there were all sorts of wild animals—boars, stone martens, badgers, barn owls, otters, beavers—who in this magic forest could grow to unimaginable dimensions. There would certainly be strange tall poisonous plants you could get trapped in.

Dupin saw a wooden shed in one of the rear corners, next to it a Citroën SUV, impressively dirty on both sides. The trees were climbing in an unruly fashion over the wall and into the courtyard. The sun would have had to be at its zenith for its rays to reach into the yard. Only then would it get really bright here.

Dupin turned his eyes toward the wide stone steps that led up to the manor's wooden entrance door. A simple bronze plaque below the doorbell declared: *Blanche Cadiou—Dr. Fabien Cadiou.* And below, a second sign read: *Brocéliande: Le Parc de l'Imagination Illimitée.*

The forest didn't just swallow up the light, but, it would seem, the noise of the world as well. It was as quiet as a mouse.

Dupin pressed the bell, looking around. To the right of the entrance stood a blue table with five chairs on the gravel around it, each the same blue as the table. They looked new. There was a curious object on the table, a vessel of some sort, in an unusual shape.

Dupin rang again. Waited. Glanced at his watch. He was punctual. The appointment had said Wednesday, half past two, at Fabien Cadiou's house.

Dupin rang a third time.

Then he took a few steps back from the house.

"Hello?" He looked up. Three windows on each floor. One on the second and one on the third were open. "Monsieur Cadiou? Commissaire Dupin here, Commissariat de Concarneau. We have an appointment."

His words had hardly faded away before he suddenly heard a strange sound and turned quickly on his heel. A sort of scraping, scratching. He caught a glance of something white scurrying along the wall, mostly obscured by leaves.

The next moment it had vanished as if it had melted into thin air.

A cat?

"Goddamn!" Dupin exclaimed. Where was this Cadiou?

The commissaire noticed how tired he was. He needed a *café*. Two. Claire and he had sat up until half past two unpacking cardboard boxes. Lots and lots of cardboard boxes. His life, her life all in cardboard boxes. Downstairs in the living room of their new house that they had rented that summer. A house in common, in a breathtaking spot, a stone's throw from the little sandy beach of Plage de la Mine d'Or, with a view of the sea and the wide bay. They had opened two bottles of white wine during the course of the evening, and emptied both. They kept having to look for the glasses behind cardboard boxes, and Claire had to tell him the story of every object she unpacked. Dupin smiled at the memory. In the meantime, it had gotten dark, and they went for a quick swim. The water was an incredible twenty-one degrees. It seemed as if the whole summer had been stored in the Atlantic. They would be able to swim for a few weeks yet, tomorrow too. But first they had several dozen more cardboard boxes to unpack. Dupin had planned to be back at home tomorrow afternoon.

He shook off the reverie and walked farther around the house.

"Monsieur Cadiou?"

To the right there were steps down to the cellar, to the left a very narrow hallway, then three steps and a door that happened to be open.

"Dupin here, we have an appo—" Dupin's phone rang. He took it out of the rear pocket of his jeans.

"Yes?"

"Where are you?" The voice on the other end of the line sounded even more annoyed than his own.

Damn! Dupin hadn't checked the number. Something that always backfired on him. It was the prefect! Locmariaquer.

"In the magic forest. The office outing. Remember?"

As far as Dupin's little police mission went, more accurately the favor he was doing for Odinot, the prefect naturally knew nothing. He hadn't even the faintest idea that Dupin had had anything to do with clearing up the criminal events on the granite coast the past summer.

"There's trouble outside some bakeries in Concarneau."

Dupin didn't react.

"Butter! It's about butter. There are hordes of angry people on the streets."

There was a war between the wholesalers, producers, and the distributors. About prices. Not just in Brittany but the whole of France, over the dramatically rising export of French butter, which brought in more attractive profits than the domestic market. As a result, butter had become scarce in recent weeks, to the extent that lots of bakeries, restaurants, and little supermarkets had run out. There was no butter in tens of thousands of households, and a general "butter crisis" had broken out. When it came to butter consumption, France was the undisputed world champion (far ahead of the Germans in second place). But naturally that hit Brittany particularly hard, where the situation was considered a state of emergency and had reached crazy levels, obviously helped by the media. At the beginning of the week there had been a report that a man from Vannes had offered a half pound of semi-salted for €250 on the internet. And it wasn't a one-off. There was an end-of-the-world feeling in the air: A baguette without butter? Crêpes even? A *gâteau Breton*? Better to die!

"I think our colleagues will handle it," Dupin replied in a relaxed tone.

"It could erupt to a general state of unrest! It only took a shortage of bread in 1789!"

It was the general mood, Dupin knew; it wasn't just the prefect's hysteria.

"If the revolution breaks out, we'll be back, Monsieur le Préfet. You can count on us."

"But—"

"We're just in the Church of the Holy Grail." The church was a good excuse. "I have to go."

Dupin put the phone down. He had to deal with things here and be at the Maison des Sources by four, where he could get a *café*. And before that he wanted to call Jean Odinot. He was nervous about getting it all done.

"Monsieur Cadiou!" Dupin called again, now back at the front door. He shouted louder than before, and above all sounded more impatient. "I'm down here!"

With those words he entered the narrow corridor and took the steps up.

"Hello?"

Within moments Dupin was standing in a large room that served as living room and kitchen in one. Despite the sunny day outside, it was twilight in here.

Even so he could clearly see the man lying on the light-colored stone floor. In a massive pool of blood.

In one move, Dupin was on his knees next to him.

"Hello, hello! Monsieur! Can you hear me?"

No reaction.

He felt the man's throat for a pulse. Nothing. His body temperature too was below normal.

"Shit!"

The next moment Dupin was back on his feet with his cell phone back in his hand.

"Service d'Aide Médicale Urgente," a man's voice answered.

"Commissaire Dupin, Commissariat Concarneau. A man's been shot. Tréhorenteuc. In the manor belonging to Fabien Cadiou. If you're driving into the area, then—"

"We're from Ploërmel, we know our way around. What's the situation? Vital signs?"

"No pulse, no obvious sign of breath, temperature lowered. Probably dead."

"How many shots and where?"

"In the stomach area," Dupin said, and carefully lifted up the man's polo shirt, which was soaked with blood. "Two—two gunshots."

"We're on our way."

"Step on it." *why? The guy's dead.*

Dupin dialed the next number. Nolwenn, Riwal, and Kadeg would be sitting comfortably in the Maison des Sources.

"That was quick, Monsieur le Commissaire. Very good, we're—"

"A man's been shot, Nolwenn—Cadiou probably—in his own house. I've just found him. Dead, as far as I can tell."

Dupin was walking up and down the room, watching the man on the floor carefully.

"You're joking, Monsieur le Commissaire." It was easy to tell from the tone of her voice that Nolwenn didn't doubt Dupin's words one bit.

"I've called an ambulance."

"Have you called the police as well? You should . . ." She hesitated, then started again, "I think . . ." Another pause and then she continued in a low voice, "You are on an unofficial mission here. You're doing a favor for your Paris colleague, who did you a favor in a different case, one in which you were in no way officially involved."

That was true.

"I'll think of something."

"Such as?"

"Something will come to me."

She seemed to be thinking hard. "You're assuming it's Cadiou?"

"I . . . just a moment."

Cadiou was an Arthurian scholar and head of some institution here. Dupin tapped on his phone and found a photo straightaway.

"That's him—Dr. Fabien Cadiou—director of the Centre de l'Imaginaire Arthurien."

"We're coming, Monsieur le Commissaire. We're on our way." Nolwenn ended the conversation.

Through a door toward the main entrance Dupin could see a hallway. That was where the staircase to the upper floors was.

He headed for the door, with his phone back at his ear. It took Jean Odinot a long time to answer.

"So, how was the interv—"

"Cadiou's been shot. I've just found him, in his house. Almost certainly dead. The medics will be here imminently."

"What? Cadiou is dead?"

"What's the story here, Jean?"

Dupin had reached the first floor and entered a room, clearly a study, with shelves and books right up to the ceiling. At first glance there was nothing unusual to be seen. A normal untidiness. No obvious sign of third-party involvement.

"I . . . I've . . ." Dupin had never heard his friend stammer before. ". . . no idea what's going on. Georges, we . . ."

"The one thing we need is a good story, a good reason why I'm here in the first place. In a few minutes the gendarmerie and a commissaire from Rennes are due to arrive, Thierry Quéméner probably. And then the préfecture from Rennes will be involved in the case."

Dupin didn't have the slightest interest in getting entangled in all of this, not the slightest compunction to get involved in a game of question and answer with someone. But that was exactly what he was going to have to do. His last case had been complicated enough with the relevant commissaire from Trégastel; it had taken a lot of effort to avoid a scandal back then. And the scandal wasn't the worst thing that could have happened; it could have come to a complaint to the service monitoring authorities, a court case most probably.

"I'll deal with it, Georges," Odinot said. He seemed to have pulled himself together again.

"Meaning what?"

The second large room, a bedroom with a double bed, appeared unremarkable at first glance. Nor was there anything unusual to be seen in the bathroom.

Dupin was already on the stairs up to the second floor.

"Leave it to me to deal with."

Another study. Three desks, one opposite the door, the others against the walls on the left and right. Carefully tidied. There was another bedroom and another bathroom, exactly the same layout of rooms as there had been on the first floor.

"Did you speak again to Cadiou, Georges?"

"After you and I spoke? No. Just that one time, last week—what about you?"

"No. Have you found anything suspicious inside the house?"

"Still looking around. No."

Dupin had reached the third floor, where everything was different. The whole floor was a single room. Two sofas, brightly colored carpets on the naked stone walls, an old commode. All very cozy but it looked as if nobody had used the room in recent times. Thick layers of dust lay everywhere, including the rough hallways.

"That's not good at all." A typical comment from Jean. "Odette Laurent is going to ask for the exhumation of her husband again. And the judge will have to allow it."

Dupin was already on his way back downstairs.

In their two brief telephone calls, Jean had only briefly sketched out what his meeting with Cadiou was to be about.

Early in the summer a Parisian historian called Gustave Laurent had died from a heart attack during a research trip to England. Unfortunately, the late Laurent happened to be the brother of the minister of the interior. To make things worse, Laurent was the husband of an obsessively suspicious wife, who just happened also to be a busybody who didn't believe it was a natural death, despite the fact there was no indication of anything but a heart attack. Laurent had suffered from high blood pressure for a while, and his regular doctor was really not surprised by the news of his death. Nonetheless his wife had put pressure on her brother-in-law, who had in turn put pressure on Jean Odinot. Gustave Laurent hadn't been on his own. He had been traveling with a group of scholars, amongst them, at least temporarily, Cadiou, who'd been a friend of the deceased. Obviously the police had spoken to everyone on the spot. But it hadn't become an actual case. And his widow was insisting on that now too. A certain degree of pressure had built up, and that resulted in Jean, and as a follow-on Dupin, being asked to question Cadiou again. But Cadiou had been traveling and the interview had only become possible now. Nobody—apart from Widow Laurent—was in a hurry.

"Tell me again everything you know. Everything, that is, I—" Dupin interrupted himself. What was he saying? "Never mind! Forget it, Jean! It's not my investigation. I'm out of it before it even starts. Got it?"

Dupin was serious.

"I'll call you right back, Georges."

Dupin was determined to add something, but Jean had already hung up. He went back into the ground floor. In a minute he was next to Cadiou.

"Shit!" He ran his hands forcefully through his hair.

* * *

Things had gotten busy.

Nolwenn, Riwal, and Kadeg were the first to arrive, then the medics, the gendarmerie from Ploërmel, the gendarmerie from Paimpont. Any moment now the pathologist and the crime scene squad would arrive, both from Rennes, as well as Thierry Queméner, the presiding commissaire. Dupin knew him, if only slightly. He was a pleasant fellow—the jovial type, much loved—almost of retirement age. One way or the other, things could have been worse. Even so, his good-natured attitude had limits, and this was his beat.

"Dead. And not just a few minutes ago" was the speedy conclusion of the young medic, who declined to give any estimates about the exact time of death. "It would appear we are no longer needed," he added, and they were gone.

Dupin had murmured something to the gendarmes about "office excursion" and "curious coincidence." At the moment, they had other things to worry about and didn't ask him any more questions.

The gendarmes' chief, Colonel Aballain from Paimpont, set the tone. He had separated his team into groups and given them tasks, so most of the gendarmes in the yard and on the gravel path leading to the manor were looking for tire tracks and footprints. The gendarmes had been careful enough to park on the road; only the medics had driven into the yard.

Riwal and Kadeg had offered to help. Dupin wasn't keen but he hadn't wanted to intervene.

Colonel Roland Aballain had got hold of Cadiou's wife, the worst of all moments for all police. She was in Paimpont. Two gendarmes were on their way to see her.

Nolwenn and Dupin had gone into the courtyard and were standing a bit to one side.

"Given that we have no convincing tale, Monsieur le Commissaire, I advise you to tell the truth. At least partly. Make no mention of your illegal investigations in Trégastel, but tell them truthfully that your Parisian friend, Inspecteur Général Jean Odinot, had asked you for a favor. It's too bad," Nolwenn said, "that there always have to be corpses everywhere you show up."

"I think—" Dupin interrupted himself. Thierry Quéméner had turned the corner of the house and was coming toward them.

Dupin walked up to him. There was nothing wrong in being as friendly as possible. And then to get out of here as fast as possible. He would take Nolwenn's advice. Which, in any case, was usually the best idea. Maybe he might just get out of this lightly.

"Commissaire Quéméner." Dupin reached out his hand to greet him with a jovial tone of voice. "I—"

Dupin's phone rang. He glanced quickly at the number. Jean Odinot.

Answering the phone was inappropriate, but Dupin did so nonetheless. Maybe Jean was going to tell him what he ought to tell the commissaire from Rennes.

"Just a second, Commissaire Quéméner." Dupin had almost touched the hand of the man opposite, but turned away. He took a few quick steps toward the forest, in the direction of the wall. Behind him he could hear Nolwenn trying to save the situation. "How are you, Commissaire Quéméner? And your wife? I . . ."

"Yes?" Dupin said in a low voice.

"I've spoken to my boss, and he in turn with the minister of the interior in person. *You* are going to investigate the case. Totally officially. On the order of the Paris police and the Police Nationale. A particular order on our behalf.

"You will lead the task force as a special investigator. All the regional prefectures and commissariats will report to you in this situation."

It wasn't easy at the best of times to knock Dupin off-balance, but Jean Odinot had just done it.

"Say that again!"

"Just like I said, this is *your* case."

"But I don't want it."

Dupin really didn't.

"It all seems to be a particularly . . . interesting story, Georges, don't you think? And we'll be working together again, at least part of the time. Officially even. Just like in the old days. Now that's something!"

Dupin had gone silent. Jean seemed to be joking. Even though there was nothing remotely amusing.

Dupin could hear another phone ringing just a few meters behind him.

"Are you still there, Georges?"

"You're kidding, right?"

"I'm not kidding. In for a penny, in for a pound. It's your case. And I'm your point person in Paris."

"I'm . . ." Dupin fell quiet. "I—"

"I'll be in touch, Georges. I have another call." He hung up.

Dupin stood there a moment, motionless. Then he shook himself and looked at Nolwenn, who had stopped next to Commissaire Queméner, giving Dupin a questioning, even accusing look. Queméner made a phone call but then immediately hung up.

There was a smile of sorts on his face. He walked over to Dupin, Nolwenn following.

"Excuse me, Commissaire Queméner, it was a very important call. I had to take it, I—"

"I've just heard from my prefect that you are now the boss here. All the better. It's my mother-in-law's seventy-fifth birthday tomorrow. In Nice." By the look on his face, he was happy about it. "My wife was worried that I wouldn't be able to come. Because of the corpse."

It was like an absurd piece of theater.

"But now it's turned out for the best—the case is yours, Dupin, my dear colleague!"

The commissaire from Rennes didn't make the slightest attempt to conceal his happiness.

Dupin was about to protest, but Queméner got in before him.

"To be quite honest," he said, "I'm happy as a pig in clover not to have anything to do with it. A famous, well-respected television celebrity shot dead. Here in Tréhorenteuc." He waved good-bye. "All right, I'm out of here. Good luck!"

Nolwenn gave Dupin another look, but didn't say a word.

"But," Dupin said, "I need you. I mean, I need someone who knows their way around here. A local. Someone who knows the people here."

Each sentence sounded more helpless than the last. "Someone who might have an idea what it's all about."

"Almost certainly the Holy Grail." Queméner had wanted to appear jovial but in fact sounded very serious. "And when we say the Grail, we mean something significantly more than the object itself. So you are now a knight of the Holy Grail. Oh, and before I forget, the pathologist will be late, unfortunately. And stick with Colonel Aballain, he's a local and an excellent gendarme, you wait and see. Oh, and another thing: my boss said your special status means you can call on any local unit you want."

"Forensics, specialists, IT, et cetera?"

"Exactly. It will be coordinated from Rennes. But in practical terms, you already have your team with you."

Dupin wanted to contradict him, but let it go.

The commissaire from Rennes loped off.

Yet again, Dupin had to restrain himself, and this time he found it a lot harder.

"Madness, this is pure—"

"*Our* case? Why is it *our* case?" Nolwenn interrupted Dupin. There were deep furrows on her forehead.

"The minister of the interior and the president of the Paris police handed the case over to me on Odinot's recommendation. A special agent of . . ." He paused angrily. "The Parisian police."

Nolwenn began, "I . . ." but then she trailed off as a dark car drove up at high speed, causing two policemen to leap to one side. The stylish Volvo raced up the manor entrance and came to an abrupt halt, spraying gravel.

The driver's door flew open. A woman in a dark gray suit leapt out of the car and headed straight for the front door. Dupin quickly headed toward her.

"Madame Cadiou?"

The woman finally noticed him. She looked at him with a blank face. The next moment she had disappeared into the house without saying a word.

When Dupin entered the room, Blanche Cadiou was on her knees next to the body of her dead husband. She was looking down at his face, blankly, with no reaction. Dupin remained standing in the doorway, glad that the crime scene team hadn't arrived yet and they were alone.

Blanche Cadiou stayed there, unmoving.

Two, three long minutes passed by.

"I'm going to . . . find his killer."

The words were almost inaudible. Blanche Cadiou had not so much spoken them as hissed them; harsh, trembling, cold.

She stood up slowly. Dupin approached her carefully. Only now could he see tears on her cheeks: pain and shock, but at the same time a sort of repressed anger.

"Commissaire Georges Dupin," he said, halting a little to one side of her. "Can I do anything for you? Would you like me to call a doctor for you, Madame Cadiou?"

"No."

Her response was prompt, and decisive, without looking at Dupin. She kept her eyes on her husband. It was as if she had regained her composure right away. There was silence again, then she asked in a monotone, almost ghostly voice: "What have you found out so far, Commissaire?"

"Nothing at all. How about you, Madame Cadiou, do you have any idea what might have happened here?"

She glanced at Dupin for the first time and looked him up and down.

"Are you in charge of the investigation?"

What was he to say? The way things looked at the moment, unfortunately it seemed that he was. And even if he tried—as he intended—to change something, this would not be the moment to say so.

Dupin tried to put a touch of decision into his voice: "I am."

She nodded silently.

"Terrible as it is, Madame Cadiou, do you have any thoughts about this horrible crime? Who might have done this? And why?"

"No," she said, shaking her head slightly.

"Have you noticed anything unusual about your husband recently? In the last few days? Anything about his behavior? His mood?"

"He was the same as always." She brushed her dark brown hair back from her forehead.

"Any fights? Arguments? With anybody at all?"

Yet again the most minimal shake of the head, as if she wasn't really there. Her look was once again focused on her husband. She was in a state of shock.

Nonetheless, Dupin knew that one principle always held true in any investigation: anybody, no matter who, could be guilty.

"Right at the outset of an investigation we are after every hint, Madame Cadiou. Every little thing that occurs to you could be of relevance, no matter how unimportant it might seem to you."

"Everything was completely normal, as always."

"Your husband knew Gustave Laurent. In the early summer, they—"

"Boss!" Riwal burst into the room. Something had to have happened; Dupin knew the expression on his face.

"Another murder! We have another body."

Blanche Cadiou turned abruptly toward Riwal.

"What?"

This was complete madness, Dupin thought.

"There's a second—"

In an instant Dupin was alongside his inspector. Kadeg, Nolwenn, and the colonel from Paimpont had turned up behind Riwal.

"Who is it, Riwal?"

"Paul Picard. A professor from Paris. An archeologist and specialist on the Middle Ages. He was found in the wood," Riwal went ever paler as he spoke, "near the Fontaine de Barenton. They're waiting for you there, boss."

"How did he die?"

"A stab wound, he bled out." Riwal took a deep breath. "This isn't a coincidence, boss. There's something going on here. They've—"

"That's nonsense." Dupin had spoken quietly, but everyone had heard him.

"A colleague," Madame Cadiou said in a monotone, mechanical whisper. "Paul Picard is a colleague of my husband's. A friend. He had come for the conference."

"Conference?" Dupin asked.

Apparently Riwal was already informed. "A conference on the latest developments in Arthurian research. It takes place every year. This year it was about notable finds."

Dupin paced back and forth.

A terrible incident had recently taken place here. And he wanted to have nothing—absolutely nothing—to do with the investigation. He needed to talk to Jean urgently.

"Where does this conference take place?"

"In the Centre de l'Imaginaire Arthurien," Riwal replied. "In Castle Comper, where Monsieur Cadiou is the director—*was* the director. The conference was supposed to begin now and last until Friday afternoon. Seven scholars. The crème de la crème of Arthurian researchers. The five others had been waiting for this pair, they thought they were just late."

"Are they still there?"

"You mean in the Centre? As far as I know, yes."

"They should all remain there. No one is to leave the Centre. I—"

"Here I am," said a short, lean, bald man who had appeared behind Riwal. "Where is the body?"

The pathologist nodded to them jovially. As a matter of principle Dupin was at war with people of his profession, and this representative, he could already tell, would be no different.

"We'll meet outside in a half minute," he said to Riwal. "I'll be right with you." He went back to Madame Cadiou, who was still standing next to the body.

"Has anything yet come to your mind relating to the events, Madame Cadiou?"

Dupin was aware he was putting a lot of pressure on her, but there was nothing else for him to do. "I mean relating to the second deceased, the professor from Paris?" He hadn't caught the name. "What's going on here, Madame Cadiou?"

Dupin looked her directly in the eyes. They were an intense deep brown, astonishingly the same color as her shoulder-length hair. She shook her head.

"I really can't tell you anything." She paused. "I wish I could."

"Your husband and the second victim were friends, you said?"

"Yes."

"Good friends?"

"They didn't see each other often, but yes, friends."

"And their research was in the same area, if I've understood correctly."

"You have indeed."

Dupin would have liked to ask a lot more questions, but it wasn't possible; he had to go.

"Thank you, Madame Cadiou. Once again, my most sincere condolences." He suddenly realized he hadn't actually said that yet. "This is a dreadful tragedy. My colleague from Paimpont"—he really had to memorize his name too; one of Dupin's great shortcomings—"is on-site. He is team leader here. You can get in touch with him at any time. And should anything occur to you, then please call me at any time. My colleagues will give you my number."

Madame Cadiou had turned back to her dead husband without a word. The pathologist was already examining the body.

It occurred to Dupin that the crime scene team hadn't turned up yet.

"First and foremost, I need to know the time of death," Dupin said to the man as he was turning to leave. "Please let me know as soon as possible."

By the time the pathologist had looked up from the body and was preparing an answer, Dupin was already outside.

* * *

The narrow road they were on ran in a straight line like a railway track cut through the great wood. It seemed as if the forest was forever trying to heal this wound by spreading back over the swath as fast as it could. Bushes and shrubs grew over the path and in places the treetops grew together to form a green canopy. Nature was making it clear that the track here was no more than a fleeting phenomenon.

After trying in vain to get hold of Jean Odinot, Dupin had had a brief chat with Nolwenn, Riwal, Kadeg, and the colonel. Aballain, his name was, Dupin had finally recalled. Nolwenn would drive to the hotel to do some research there. Kadeg would stay with Aballain at the manor. Riwal was driving with Dupin to the spring where the other body had been found.

While they were talking, the crime scene team arrived—four of them as usual, including a ballistic specialist. They went through all the routines, computers, phones, landlines, the bank accounts of the two deceased.

Dupin called Jean Odinot again from the car.

"Georges? I just tried to reach—"

"Two!" Dupin almost yelled. "There are two murders now, Jean! That's weird. A professor from Paris has been found dead by some spring in the forest. That's—"

"I know. The commissaire from Rennes has already been informed. He was eager to make certain with me that everything remained exclusively your case. Given that the two incidents are connected, of which there can be no doubt, he wanted to have nothing to do with them."

"Me neither! There's no way I want to take over this investigation."

"Even if we tried, Georges, there's no longer any way out of this. Not a chance. We're stuck with it; both of us."

The volume in the ancient car speaker hadn't been working for weeks now and was turned to maximum. Their voices were terribly distorted.

"Why doesn't Paris send somebody else from Rennes, for God's sake? Or send someone themselves?"

"Because you're the best! And I'm in charge. I need you, Georges. I've no idea how we ended up in this. We just seem to have slid into it."

"I . . . " Dupin began, and then stopped.

He was stuck with it. That was how it was. Unfortunately, Jean was right. And it wasn't Dupin's thing to wriggle his way out of something.

But he was aware of a strong emotional response. Not just because now he had something to do with the Paris police again—having been appointed their "special representative"—but he felt somehow uneasy about this case. Apart from that, it had also suddenly occurred to him that he couldn't leave Claire alone at the moment to deal with innumerable cardboard boxes on her own.

"Do this for me," Jean pleaded. His friend couldn't be handling it more cleverly.

What was Dupin to say?

There was a long pause. Dupin gave Riwal a quick glance. Riwal tried in vain to act as if it had nothing to do with him.

Dupin gave a long sigh and put his foot down on the gas, sending them flying up the summit of a hill. "Tell me once again about this heart attack, the Laurent guy and his business trip. And his wife."

"I've spoken to Madame Laurent on the phone." Odinot sounded greatly relieved, despite trying to conceal it. He obviously hadn't been sure he could keep Dupin on the team. "Laurent was taking part in a dig, the whole of May: a team of four researchers, some green hill in the southwest of England. Cadiou had been to see him for two days. They knew each other well, were the same age, shared a position as junior fellow at the Sorbonne in Paris and at one point published a few pieces together, but later became competitors. That was how she put it."

Dupin hadn't missed the fact that Riwal was squirming around awkwardly in his seat.

"Did this Laurent die while Cadiou was there?"

"Two weeks after he left. We need to have Laurent exhumed as soon as possible; we've already applied to a judge for it to go through urgently." Jean had the same difficult, but highly useful, practical attitude as Dupin: he expected everything to happen immediately. It was one of the reasons they understood each other so well, and also why they had a reputation for being manic. "I also spoke to Madame Laurent again about her husband's high blood pressure. He took three different pills each morning. Beta blockers, ACE inhibitors, anti-calcium tablets. Even so, the blood pressure was still too high in stressful situations, the individual readings reaching critical levels. Obviously"—there was a certain tension in Jean's voice—"somebody could have switched his medicines for placebos or even drugs that did the exact opposite to his. It's possible to get hold of things like that."

"Did Madame Laurent say anything about Cadiou?"

"She had excluded him in particular from any suspicion. Which in her case meant something. She definitely wanted us to talk with him."

"Did she give any more exact reason why?"

"No, just repeated that she didn't believe her husband had died naturally."

"But without the vaguest idea on why it should have been murder?"

"Indeed. We need to find out more. That was why I wanted to have Cadiou questioned again. She insisted on it, hoped that he knew something."

"But Cadiou hadn't noticed anything suspicious."

"Exactly."

"And Madame Laurent had no particular suspicion against anyone in particular?"

"No, she doesn't even know the names of the others on the dig."

"So what was it that launched her suspicion?"

"She had the feeling that in recent months before his death her husband had somehow changed. She couldn't say any more. He had been working more than usual, but unlike his usual way, he didn't tell her anything about his work, not even if she asked. He was always lost in his thoughts. Absent."

"Anything else?"

"He seemed very tense, but she didn't have the impression that he felt threatened. Nor did she know anything about any conflict."

"Do you have the names of the other researchers on the dig?"

"Yes. We're rattling their doors continuously. I've also sent two police officers to Picard's apartment, in the sixth arrondissement."

While Jean was talking, Dupin had been rustling around in the glove compartment in a risky maneuver, looking for a pen and something to write on, Riwal having turned his legs awkwardly to the side. The only thing Dupin had found was the yellowed, tattered car instruction manual. He had pushed it into Riwal's hand, who had immediately understood and opened a page at random to take notes.

"What do we know about the state of the Laurents' marriage?"

The word jogged his memory; he needed to call Claire and give her a heads-up.

"Very happy, according to Madame Laurent."

"Believable?"

"Hard to say at the moment. I've got a meeting with her at half past five."

Jean was right. It was always important to have these conversations in person.

"Which doesn't—"

"Turn right here," Riwal called out.

The high speaker volume meant people had to speak very loudly.

Dupin took the turn sharply, the tires squealing. They had left the forest and were now driving along its fringe, the road ahead gently hilly.

"What else? What was the purpose of this dig?" Yet again, from the corner of his eye, Dupin noticed a certain disquiet in Riwal.

"A castle from Arthurian times or something of the sort."

Riwal couldn't restrain himself.

"Inspector Riwal here, Monsieur Inspecteur Général Odinot. I'm sitting next to Commissaire Dupin. Cadbury Castle is the name of the castle. The green hill you refer to is an archeological sensation. There have always been stories about Arthur in that area. Some fifty years ago, they discovered massive fortifications there belonging to a structure that fitted exactly with the time scale attributed to Arthur, between the years 500 and 550. Some people take it to be Camelot."

"I understand," said Odinot in a neutral tone of voice. "Thank you for informing me, Inspector."

Dupin found it not uninteresting. "Did Laurent's dig unearth something spectacular, Riwal?"

"Some other impressive building ruins."

"What were they looking for?"

"Objects related to the historic inhabitants of the castle. Inscriptions, stone tablets, writings."

"But they didn't find anything?"

"No. But they're still looking."

For the moment that was enough for Dupin. "I'll be in touch, Jean!"

"Okay."

"Do you have any other information about Fabien Cadiou?"

"None. No. Up until now there had been no reason to investigate him."

"What about the other deceased?"

"Nothing there either."

"We'll start researching immediately."

Nolwenn should arrive at La Gacilly soon. A gendarme was driving her.

"Good. And make the most of your status as special investigator with extended powers. You have your back completely covered . . ." Jean hesitated, probably recalling something or other from their shared past. ". . . for almost everything."

That sounded interesting. Dupin hadn't yet seen the situation from that point of view.

"Good. Okay, we're on it, Jean. Talk soon."

Dupin tapped on the little red key and ended the call.

The road curved but Dupin drove no less fast. He was thinking about the two deceased men. "What was the professor doing here in the forest? Have our colleagues found out anything?"

At the manor, Riwal had spoken with one of the two gendarmes who had already been at the scene where the corpse was found.

"They have no specifics yet."

"We should speak with the other researchers after this."

In fact, Dupin thought, he would have preferred to go to them directly. The man down by the spring was dead, in any case.

"By the way, Colonel Aballain has sent two of the crime scene team to the Centre, to have a look around Cadiou's office," Riwal said.

The start of the case had been a total mess. Dupin hadn't thought of a few obvious things. It would take a while before he felt back in the saddle.

They had reached a little village of no more than fifteen or twenty houses. He braked gently.

"La Folle-Pensée. Once upon a time the druids treated crazy people here, with the water from the fabled well, the Fontaine de Barenton," Riwal said.

Craziness hit the spot. It was an idea that had gone through Dupin's head already during the past hour and a half. He should take a gulp from the well just in case. A big gulp.

"We need the list of these researchers as soon as possible. And everything we can find out about them."

"Right, boss."

In next to no time they were through the village. Dupin put his foot down again with a vengeance.

"We need to turn right here," Riwal said worriedly. The landscape had gotten hillier and was hard to see across. "Watch out, here!"

Dupin had taken his foot off the gas pedal briefly, then just before the turn accelerated again. The road they were driving along now was more like a single track, not much wider than the car itself, and with tight bends. Riwal held on firmly to the door handle.

"I don't know if you've read about it in the newspapers, but there's a bitter fight going on in the wood here. Or rather, there's a bitter fight about the wood here. For the past year now."

Every morning Dupin read the papers, starting with the regionals, *Ouest-France* and *Le Télégramme*. As a rule he missed nothing, but this was new to him.

"So tell me . . ."

Suddenly something appeared on the road directly in front of them. Dupin stamped hard on the brakes and swung the steering wheel around. The car lurched to the left; Dupin counter-steered and regained control. Even if it was already too late.

There was a horrible noise. The Citroën sideswiped a huge tree. There was a single, loud, brutal blow as the side mirror ripped off.

A few meters farther on the car came to a groaning stop. A ghostly silence reigned. Riwal and Dupin had been pulled tight by their safety belts. The car didn't have airbags.

"Damn it." Dupin broke the silence. "What was that?"

It took a while for Riwal to answer: "Some animal." His voice was shaking. He tried to get a grip on himself, his face ash gray. "That was close."

Certainly had they come any closer they wouldn't have just grazed the tree.

It was only now that they looked at each other.

"Are you hurt, Riwal?"

He just shook his head.

They both climbed out carefully.

"It looks bad." Riwal stood stock-still next to the car.

Dupin had gone to the rear. He remained silent, his eyes glancing along the side of the car. Almost the entire length was bashed in, the paintwork scraped off. Deep scratches in the metalwork. It was a miracle that the damaged door had even opened at all.

"What sort of animal could it have been?" For some reason Dupin was almost more concerned by that than anything else.

"Nothing big. I only saw something fleetingly. Maybe a fox. Or a marten. Maybe even a hare."

"It . . ." Dupin faltered. ". . . was white."

Riwal didn't react.

"How far is it from here to Cadiou's manor? Directly through the wood?"

An absurd question, an absurd thought.

"As the crow flies, maybe—"

Dupin's cell phone went off with an ear-piercing ring in the front pocket of his pants.

"Yes?"

"Commissaire Dupin? Gendarmerie de Paimpont. I'm the fellow officer waiting for you at Fontaine de Barenton. Along with my colleague here—"

"What's up?"

"When will you get here?"

"I'll be there immediately. Do you have a pathologist already?"

"We need to wait until he's done with Monsieur Cadiou. He . . ."

"Get another one. No matter where from."

"But . . ."

"He needs to set out right away. This is a special investigation on behalf of the minister of the interior."

Yes, that felt really rather good and made him forget his trembling knees for a moment.

"I see."

"Like I said, I'll be there immediately."

Dupin hung up. At the same moment Riwal's phone rang.

"Ah, Nolwenn, excellent." Riwal sounded relatively relieved. Probably it just felt good to hear her voice after what had happened.

"Yes, go ahead."

Riwal was listening. He obviously had no intention of mentioning their accident.

"One moment."

The inspector walked round the car and got the car manual from the foot well.

"Okay, next?"

Riwal had his phone jammed between chin and shoulder as he listened and scribbled a few notes in the manual.

"Thanks, Nolwenn. And one more thing: we need a lineup of everybody who attended the conference; there were five of them. And all the information we can get about them."

A pause.

"Exactly. See you later."

The commissaire was about to get back into the car, and Riwal was doing the same. Dupin would have to get an appointment at the garage as soon as possible. Which would also mean that Nolwenn was going to ask him again if it wasn't high time to buy a new car, a question that for a long time now had been getting ever more urgent.

As Riwal opened the car door, Dupin gave him a questioning look.

"A few details about Paul Picard: privately educated, no university chair. Historian, specialist in the early Middle Ages. Also a trained archeologist, unlike Laurent, who was just a hobby archeologist. Fifty-eight years old. Does repeated teaching stints at the Sorbonne. Also in other countries. Three years' guest professor in London. Highly respected, apparently."

"And a friend of Cadiou's." Dupin turned on the engine and put his foot gently down on the accelerator. He didn't want to admit it, but he was still a bit in shock.

* * *

They had to leave the car where it was, as the only way to get to the Fontaine de Barenton was on foot. And it was more than just a few meters.

The nearby woodland path quickly turned into a narrow, bumpy track, which wove its way through ever thicker, wilder forest, gradually rising. "Yes, this is the official direct way," Riwal confirmed a few times. Dupin had assumed Riwal had chosen a particularly "interesting" route. It was a long time since they had seen anybody. In several spots the route rose sharply.

To their left there was a romantic little natural stream which the path clearly followed. Every now and then you could hear the gentle gurgling of the water. The route to the spring was very occasionally marked by loose indicators rather than actual signposts, and Dupin would undoubtedly have gotten lost. Even Riwal hesitated at two or three spots. On one occasion they took a turn and then a few minutes later retraced their steps.

The wood seemed impenetrable. Giant oaks, pines, chestnut trees, firs, beech, hawthorn hedges, various ferns and mosses, vines and ivy growing amidst the trees. Some of the vines were wound around the trees' highest branches as if the trees were being strangled. There were green tones of every shade from bright to dark, with mixtures of blue, brown, yellow, and red.

For some stretches the path lay almost in the dark since the rich rambling wilderness was swallowing the light. One had the feeling of being alien, an invader, not belonging to this world. The feeling that the wood wanted to be on its own. Wanted no people. That it would rapidly close over the paths that had made it possible for them to move around in it. There was no trace of the heat, the bright burning summer sunshine, not even in those few spots of the path touched by the rays, a stark contrast to the gloom. There was also a certain damp-ness, the unique, immutable scent of the forest in the air, a heavy, ethereal smell which the summer couldn't dissolve.

The length of their strenuous stroll, the inspector and the com-missaire spent most of their time on the phone: perfect reception here, five bars.

"Ah, I understand, Professor Guivorch. Many thanks." Riwal hung up.

Dupin had just finished his conversation with the pathologist in Cadiou's house at the same time. "Eleven in the morning, give or take an hour. The murderer was there quite a while before me."

Dupin took the Citroën manual from his rear pants pocket. He would have to make do with that until he found a newspaper shop. At least the manual was portrait shape, almost like a notebook, plain gray with black text, the front page more or less neutral with, in the background, the Citroën trademark clearly visible in red and white, 133 pages all in all. Dupin wrote down a few notes. Unlike Riwal, who had chosen a random page with lots of free space—the dividing page before the "Maintenance" section—Dupin began at the beginning in an orderly fashion, on the "Contents" page, with its tiny text and more than enough room around it.

"I've already spoken to the deputy director of the Centre, who is also here for the conference. Professor Auffrai Guivorch. The sole Breton." The name itself made the last sentence unnecessary. It also sounded like the only non-suspect. "He had an explanation for Picard being here in the forest. Four weeks ago, Picard asked for permission for a dig. The little chapel is referred to in the very first of the reports about the Fontaine de Barenton. Some people say there was even a castle here."

"And what was he doing there today?"

"Guivorch assumed that Picard wanted to see the location for himself. As I said, he only got the permit four weeks ago. Picard arrived from Paris last night and was staying in the Relais de Brocéliande in Paimpont. He hadn't bothered to check in at the Centre."

Once again they had to climb, this time over sharp-edged stones jutting up from the ground, before they came to a sort of plateau from which the wood looked more impenetrable than before.

"This Breton professor—is he still with the group of researchers in the castle?"

"Yes."

"Good."

Dupin stood still briefly, looking around him. Riwal walked on.

"We're almost there. This is one of the most famous wells in the world. Even back in prehistoric times this was a holy place, especially to the ancient Celts; it was a realm of the fairies. The place of druids.

As far back as human memory goes, the water from the well was con- 50°F
sidered magical. It has a constant temperature of ten degrees Celsius
exactly. Every now and then—impossible to say when—it bubbles."
Riwal's tone of voice became dramatic. "Because of that they used to
say in the old days 'the water boils even though it is cold as marble.'"

He hesitated, then added, "When you're at the well, if you make
a wish and immediately after the water bubbles, then your wish will
be fulfilled."

Dupin could think of a couple of wishes.

"At the same time there would be a red glow in the water. Like
fiery red eyes," Riwal went on in a matter-of-fact tone. "Next to the
well there's a stone slab known as either the Margalle de Barenton or
Perron de Merlin. If you sprinkle water from the well on it in a particular way, it will rain. In drought years whole processions take place
here. Anyone who knows this ritual particularly well can conjure up
real storms: mighty, cataclysmic storms that devastate the world—
apocalyptic." It sounded like a solemn finale.

"I—"

Dupin's cell phone rang. He still had it in his hand.

It was the prefect. Dupin was not interested in the ludicrous ag-
gravation of the butter crisis. Nonetheless, he had to answer the call.

"Yes? Are they storming the Bastille already?"

"I've heard about this special investigation business!" The prefect
was seriously agitated.

A pause. It was perfectly clear what was going to happen. There
was going to be one of the prefect's angry tirades. Where was lousy
reception just when you needed it? Instinctively, Dupin held his phone
away from his ear. Maybe he should just put it down.

"I am," the prefect paused again, "how should I put it, I am extremely proud, mon Commissaire. This is a great distinction for the

prefecture! The minister of the interior and the Police Nationale hand over a case of national importance to Finistère! There could hardly be a higher accolade. I would like you to be aware of that and to prove yourself worthy of it. You know you are investigating on my behalf! And I don't want to be blamed by the nation!"

"I will try to avoid that," Dupin said mechanically. It was too absurd.

"That won't be enough!" The prefect's tone of voice was now slipping toward raging fury. But once again he changed tack. "I mean that you will handle the task with bravado and style, mon Commissaire. I have not the slightest doubt of that.

"As always," the prefect continued with a sweet voice, "I expect to receive regular reports. Not least because of the press, which I myself have informed. And also the special status on a national level which the prefecture will receive."

The double murder on its own would be enough to attract major attention, and now the prefect had stoked up the press further.

"The ministry is depending on our most extreme discretion, Monsieur le Préfet. A serious order."

"Oh, really?" The prefect sounded deeply disappointed.

"The local and regional press are bound to have already got wind of it, but anything further is totally unwanted."

A long glum silence.

"All right, in that case I wish you a successful investigation," the prefect said. "Excuse me, but I have something urgent to deal with."

It wasn't hard to guess what. The prefect had almost certainly called a major press conference.

"Be in touch, Dupin! I should say, mon Commissaire! *Au revoir.*"

Dupin hung up. A deeply satisfied smile appeared on the commissaire's face. Unfortunately, there was no time to enjoy the moment, not least because Riwal resumed his sermon. He had been collecting stories for the office outing for weeks.

"In the Arthurian world many important events took place here; Merlin, the greatest wizard of all time, met the fairy Viviane here and began an immortal life. Morgan le Fay sang her sad stories here by the well . . . but the most important role it played was in the story of *Yvain: The Knight of the Lion,* by far the most important knight, the nephew of Arthur. He . . ." Riwal halted.

"Up ahead, boss." They could make out three people in the distance through the trees. It seemed to be the crime scene.

Over the last few hours Dupin had been busy with so many things at once, everything had been so confusing, that he had forgotten a series of basic obvious questions. Those that he normally asked before anyone could answer them.

"Who found Picard?"

"Just some man, a hiker probably. We're going to meet him now."

The path turned once again around a thick group of trees and suddenly they were there.

They saw a pool, surrounded by large, irregular stones. Maybe a meter and a half in length, in the shape of a droplet, at the widest point somewhat over a meter; bright green moss-covered stones above, on the ground leaves and branches; not much water was visible. An unremarkable little stream—a gully walled in by large stones— flowed from the pool. Near the pool was a huge stone plateau, of which half had already sunk into the forest floor.

Nothing, absolutely nothing hinted at the well's fame. No signposts, no boards. Dupin had expected rather more after all the stories.

Riwal's commentary was late in coming and seemed curiously subdued. "That's it." There was deep emotion in his expression. It seemed too solemn a moment for worldly remarks.

There were three people standing in the clearing, two gendarmes and—presumably—the man who had found Picard.

Dupin stared at him. There was nothing else he could do. Long, gray, wavy hair that fell far below his shoulders, steel-blue eyes with bushy eyebrows. He was wearing a sort of bright-colored jerkin under a sleeveless brown felt robe and a black cape. From a belt hung little bottles, talismans, and pieces of fur. He looked like a participant in a medieval festival, except that, curiously, he didn't seem to be wearing a costume.

"That's Inwynn, born Monsieur Philippe Goazou," said one of the two gendarmes who had come up to Dupin. The commissaire thought he recognized the voice from the phone. "He is a *conteur*, one of the professional storytellers of the wood. He found the body."

"There are twelve professional storytellers who, as in the ancient Celtic oral tradition, present the legends and stories of the forest. They are very highly respected," Riwal said eagerly. "Some of them wear historically accurate clothing and even use authentic names."

"I see." Dupin really wanted to get to the heart of the matter. "Where is the body?"

Dupin couldn't see it anywhere.

"Over there, toward the Hêtre de Ponthus." The storyteller, who had replied in recognition to Dupin's greeting nod, turned to the side. "Come along."

Yet again Riwal intervened. "A three-hundred-year-old beech. Not quite as old as the Guillotine Oak, which is at least one thousand five hundred years old, which goes to say it originates in Arthurian times—"

"The wood, monsieur, is much more than just King Arthur's Wood." The storyteller had raised his voice dramatically with a sort of fury that made unmistakably clear "I am the one who tells the stories of the wood here."

"Even thousands of years before," Inwynn continued, "it played a meaningful role in this world. To be more precise, in the spiritual other world. It embraces a much, much older realm."

Riwal seemed already to have an answer on the tip of his tongue, but let it drop.

The storyteller moved farther and farther into the undergrowth, walking as surely as a sleepwalker, even though he was looking up at the treetops. His feet were nimble, while all the others had difficulty not falling over.

"What you see here," he stopped for a moment, "isn't the real wood. Thousands come through it, but only a few see it. The real wood isn't to be found on any map, not to be detected with our poor senses. Only our deepest feelings might perceive it, *but* it is the wood itself which decides who might catch sight of it. Who can enter it. It is the wood, not us, that is the greater being. The wood lives, and lives as one being."

He hurried on melodramatically. Despite the extravagant and esoteric language used, Dupin understood it in a way. He himself had already felt the forest's resistance to their presence. For a while there was an impressive silence.

The storyteller ducked down under a provisional red-and-yellow tape the gendarmes had tied around the trees in a large radius. Beneath the tape Dupin saw an inconspicuous sign that read *TRAVAUX ARCHÉOLOGIQUES. INTERDIT DE PASSER.* Archeological dig. Do not enter.

"He's over there."

There was a large hole cut into the ground and on its edge a square block of stone, angular, obviously only recently and only partly unearthed; next to it piles of earth. The work must have only just begun. Just a little farther on they seemed to have progressed somewhat. There were a handful of exposed stones on the ground, which seemed to have come from a wall.

Professor Paul Picard lay there, apparently peacefully, in the middle of the hole. On his left side, his arms next to his body, his legs stretched out. There was no sign of any blood, nor any open wound.

"Three stab wounds as far as we can make out," said the same gendarme who had already spoken to him, "around his heart. He has to have been put into the ground straightaway."

Dupin knelt down next to the lifeless body.

"Do we know when he arrived at the hotel yesterday?" Dupin asked. The body didn't look as if it had lain there all night.

"Not quite. Probably around eight in the evening."

It was surprising how relaxed Picard's face looked: his eyes were closed, no sign of pain, nothing that hinted at a fight to the death.

"In this place, many have failed the test," the *conteur* said. "One day at King Arthur's Round Table the knights were told about the miraculous forest of Brocéliande, the hidden well with magical powers, a mighty Black Knight, and the wonderful adventures to be experienced there. The young knight Iwein, the king's nephew and alongside Lancelot unquestionably the most noble of all knights, decided to take a ride into the wood." Inwynn's objection to the reduction of the wood to just the King Arthur stories didn't stop him from presenting it effectively. "The mighty forest and the well were to be his fate. Almost immediately he came across a wild man willing and able to guide him along the route to the Fontaine de Barenton. Iwein wet the great stone plateau with water from the well because he knew about the legend."

The artful way in which he altered his voice was amplified by few but all the more effective gestures. "A fierce storm broke out, raging with the most extreme force. After it died down, the Black Knight, the guardian of the well, appeared. He challenged Iwein to a duel. Iwein defeated him but was grievously injured and barely made it to a castle where Laudine, the lady of the spring and wife of the Black Knight, nursed him back to health. They fell in love and got married. Shortly after their wedding Iwein was again struck by the lust for adventure. Vain adventure intended purely to increase his fame. He wanted to take part in a famed tournament. Laudine allowed him just one year, after which he had to be back."

There was a stringent silence for an instant, then: "It ends with the inevitable. Iwein misses the set time. Laudine ostracizes him. He becomes the 'wild man in the forest.' For months on end he wanders unhappily around the woodland. Deciding to win back his wife, he submits to the most difficult of challenges: giants, dragons, lethal tournaments, hunger, loneliness, misery. Finally, he faces the hardest challenge of all: insanity. Iwein loses his mind."

It seemed the wood was frequently plagued by insanity. Dupin got to his feet and walked once around the deceased.

"During his wandering, Iwein saved a wonderful lion locked in a fight with an overwhelmingly powerful dragon. From then on, the lion joined forces with him, and he became known as the Lion Knight. It was the lion that purified Iwein. He learned to fight selflessly on behalf of others, and no longer for his own fame. As a result—and thanks to a miraculous ointment—he regained his sanity and in the end, his wife too. As a result Iwein became the guardian of the well. And as such, the fisherman king, the last keeper of the Holy Grail, one of the greatest mysteries of humanity: a miraculous vessel that conveyed eternal youth and happiness."

The storyteller stopped. He seemed to be wholly spent. Dupin didn't wait a second:

"How did you find the body? What were you doing here?"

The body was well hidden. There wasn't a path or a track nearby.

"I had an appointment. For storytelling, next to the well, at three P.M. I always turn up a bit early. In order"—seamlessly Philippe Goazou was transformed back into Inwynn—"to get to know the forest again, quietly. Then I check out the area, avoiding the most popular routes, and that's how I came across him."

"By coincidence?"

It was a strange question, Dupin knew, but it had just burst out of him.

"Is there such a thing as coincidence? Do you think so?"

"Were you alone?"

"Oh yes."

"And the body lay where it is now?"

"I haven't touched it."

"What did you do after finding it?"

"I informed the gendarmerie." He reached into one of the hide purses on his belt and pulled out a wholly modern cell phone.

Dupin stared at the man in surprise. But of course, why shouldn't the man have a phone?

"The wood decided how to heed my call for help."

"Unreliable reception," Riwal translated.

It was nothing unusual in Brittany.

"What time was it exactly when you found him?"

Dupin had pulled the Citroën manual and pen from his rear pants pocket. Inwynn seemed to be amazed.

"I called the gendarmerie at 2:36."

Dupin took a note.

"Whom had you agreed to meet?"

"With a small tourist group from the Pyrénées, who had booked me. I never accept an audience of more than eight."

"We sent them away," the gendarme joined in.

"How can people book you?"

"Via the Centre de l'Imaginaire Arthurien."

"Did you know the dead man, Professor Picard?"

"No." The answer was clear and sharp.

"It's been suggested," Riwal had been looking around all through the whole conversation, "that he wanted to inspect the primary work on the dig."

"Archeological digs are sacrilege." All of a sudden Inwynn burst into a fury. "The events of the past are hidden from the people of today for good reason. They ought not to be touched. It can lead to unimaginable evil. Those who have second sight see everything anyway. Including the past. The others are not worthy of them. And can't cope with them!"

His words exuded a dark energy.

The gendarme said: "There are serious protests about the digs, including from the *conteurs*."

Inwynn nodded ferociously. "For how much longer are we going to abuse the wood? How much longer are we going to damage it, abuse it, exploit it? The quarries, the roads beaten into it? The fields gouged out of its land. A new archeological dig today. Disneyland tomorrow."

"That's just what I was trying to tell you in the car, boss, before . . ." Riwal faltered. He meant their minor accident, that Dupin in the meantime had strangely almost forgotten. "That's the fight over the forest that's been plaguing the region for a year now, even more so over the last months. There are plans to build an 'experience park,' a colossal project. Huge exhibits would be built on the sites of major Arthurian events, helped by modern technology and engineering. Such as holographs, for example. Here by the well, for example, there would be a 3-D projection of Iwein's battle with the Black Knight, observed from a stage. There would be eight of these things altogether."

"It would create hundreds of jobs in a region very short on structural attractions. We have no beach here." For the first time the second, short, and rather tubby gendarme opened his mouth; he sounded shy, and sad: "It's—"

"It's sacrilege!" the storyteller interrupted. "That's why there's a curse on the project. The wood gave the first sign many years ago"—his voice dropped to a somber whisper—"when it burnt nearly to the ground! To the ground! And it set itself on fire, believe me."

"Cadiou's wife," the first gendarme said, "is the chief executive of the company that wants to bring the project to life."

"Blanche Cadiou?"

This was going to be interesting.

"What is the company called?"

"Le Parc de l'Imagination Illimitée."

The sign on the door. Exactly. Dupin felt a strong need to talk to Madame Cadiou once again. Should he drive back to her first after this and then later to the scholars?

"Who's for and who's against the park?"

"Everybody to whom the wood means anything loathes the idea," Inwynn said excitedly. "There is even an organized resistance, a citizens' initiative."

"The politics are solidly in favor," the shy gendarme made clear. "The whole of the local economy too, not just the hospitality sector." The man risked a glance at Inwynn.

Dupin turned back to the storyteller and asked, "Do you belong to this initiative?"

"Of course."

It sounded as if he had nothing to hide, which, along the lines of "attack is the best defense," could also be a clever tactic. Or the sign of a strong character.

"What was Monsieur Cadiou's position on this?" Riwal asked the gendarme.

"No idea."

"What about the scholars, the participants in the conference? What do they think about the project?" Dupin asked.

"I can tell you even less about that. They aren't from here. Except for one."

"How advanced is the project?"

"We're due to vote on it at the local council meeting the week after next. After that, it will be Rennes's turn; part of the financing will have to be at the regional level."

He was well informed.

"But if the vote the week after next goes the wrong way, then it's all over before it starts."

It was clear on which side the gendarme and his shy colleague stood.

Dupin had expected an intervention by Inwynn, but he remained silent.

"Okay, anything else?"

The commissaire had taken no side in the discussion. He felt a deep restlessness, as he always did at the start of a case. He would have preferred to tackle everything at once.

"No." A prompt answer from the first gendarme.

"Have you had a good look round here?"

"We have. Nothing noticeable."

"Have you found Picard's cell phone?"

"Not so far. But he may have it in his rear pants pocket. On the side he's lying on."

"The crime scene team will have to check out whether he brought a laptop with him on the trip."

"Obviously."

"What about the pathologist?"

"The 'special investigation' business works well." The gendarme seemed impressed. "They're sending somebody else from Rennes. He should be here imminently, as should the crime scene team."

Out in the middle of nowhere everything took a little longer. Dupin would have to accept it. Right now he had nothing more to do here.

"Good. Keep me in the loop on everything. Our head office is the hotel La Grée des Landes in La Gacilly, ask for Nolwenn, my assistant."

"Thank you for your help, Monsieur Goazou," Dupin said to the storyteller. "If you think of anything else, just let me know." Dupin nodded to the gendarmes. "Messieurs, we're out of here."

"One more thing," the storyteller added solemnly on leaving. "Not only Iwein but also Lancelot, Tristan, and even Merlin himself found themselves challenged by madness. They saved themselves by being reborn, alone and naked, in the middle of the wood, near the well."

Dupin was pretty sure there were other ways of avoiding madness. He for one was not going to be holding his breath waiting for redemption naked in the wood.

He would get a grip much earlier, and not fall victim to insanity.

The words that reached him as he was already on his way were more disconcerting.

"But for now, and this is certain, your very soul will become singly disoriented. Lost in the woods."

To be honest, the storyteller was describing the heart of Dupin's profession. The heart of investigating. There was no way of putting it more precisely.

* * *

The commissaire had to admit it: it was exactly how he had imagined an enchanted medieval castle. Protected by high walls. The Château de Comper looked like a perfect fantasy. The kind attributed to that fabulous era.

The moat had become overgrown down the centuries, with the occasional puddle, thick ivy, and old oaks covered in mistletoe. A bridge over the moat led to a magnificent entrance leading to a white stone arch which must once have had a mighty door but had since been replaced by a finely worked construction of wrought-iron braces.

The water of the puddles reflected part of the mighty castle walls; seven, eight meters high. Large, reddish stones, some weathered, overgrown with bright lichen, some with green moss, grass growing out of the cracks. They looked so irregular that it was easy to fear some of them could fall out of the wall at any moment. The result was an ambiguous impression that the fortress was simultaneously massive and fragile.

Directly behind the entrance stood a little yellow wooden house, the ticket office. "Hello, are you looking for me?"

It sounded more like an order than a question. An assertive young woman in dark glasses and a blond ponytail had called over to them. Dupin and Riwal had walked right past her.

Her next questions were rather more stern: "Tickets for two? Adults?"

Riwal reacted first, babbling, "We're here . . . on business." He pulled himself together. "Police Nationale. We're expected."

The young woman gave him a straightforwardly critical look. Eventually she determined that it was possible.

"Very well. The deputy director and the scholars are in the main hall. Best if you go through the bookshop. The entrance," she pointed along the castle, "is on the side, facing the lake."

"Many thanks." Riwal did his best to be explicitly polite. "Very kind."

They now found themselves in the castle's lavish inner courtyard, which must just recently have been restored—with a lot of style and at great expense: large expanses of fine reddish gravel and a short, well-kept lawn. The castle itself was a long, rectangular building of architectural austerity and particular beauty, with a high pointed roof of dark gray tiles and tall, elegant bay windows. It was built from the same reddish stones that had been used for the rough fortifying wall, but here particularly well laid, with light-colored plaster recently applied. The wooden window frames and a door were painted in tasteful russet, matching with the color of the gravel and stone.

Opposite the castle sat a few little houses with flat roofs—the servants' quarters back in the day: maids, houseboys, cooks, riding masters. And beyond the ticket office on the other side, stables. It was a completely different world. Precisely arranged. One of the buildings now housed a coffee shop.

Dupin and Riwal walked the length of the castle speedily. When they turned the corner, they faced a breathtaking view.

"Viviane's lake," Riwal said, his voice trembling slightly.

From here it was obvious that the strong walls were only necessary to protect the castle from the sides and front, while for the rear the astonishingly vast lake did the trick. It began behind the castle and continued deep into the forest. The surface was flat, a perfect mirror. It was as if there were two skies—with a bit of earth embedded between them. Oddly distorted trees embellished the sky-blue reflection, and only at a few sharply bordered spots did the surface of the lake look curiously wrinkled, disturbed, even though there was no breeze.

"Unusually deep, boss. Full of crevices and underwater holes. Impossible to make out the bottom."

Dupin had unintentionally stopped, which Riwal took as an opportunity to carry on his tale; he seemed determined to prove there was a raconteur hidden in him too. "In fact, it isn't a lake, just an illusion of a lake. A trick. Because of his eternal love for Viviane, Merlin built a castle of pure crystal in the middle of a paradisiacal garden *here*, so magnificent that he wanted to hide it from the envious and greedy gaze of human beings. So he surrounded it with a spell that let people see nothing more than the lake. Only those whom Viviane wants to let into the castle can see more than the lake. She is the famed Lady of the Lake, dressed in brilliant white—"

Dupin interrupted him: "I need a *café*, Riwal."

It meant a short delay, but one that would have an immediate effect. Also, even though it wouldn't be simple, he was definitely going to have to call Claire.

"Of course, boss."

The inspector and Dupin had been working together for a long time. There was nothing about the commissaire that Riwal didn't know.

"You'll get one in the little café opposite."

Dupin nodded and headed back toward the inner courtyard.

"Something else has occurred to me, boss."

"Yes?"

"I've been wondering how the killer could have known that Picard was in the wood. Either he was with him. Or they spoke on the phone.

Or it was well known that Picard was going to be at the site of the dig today."

"Or," Dupin added to the possibilities, "he followed him, and waited until he was deep into the forest."

"Or," Riwal whispered rather than spoke, "Inwynn did it. It would have been easiest of all for him. He only had to get rid of the knife, and then call the police."

It was theoretically possible.

"What we definitely need is Picard's cell phone call list."

"That's going to take a bit of work, boss. Right now we don't even know that he had one."

"I'll be right back," Dupin said, walking off.

Riwal took out his cell phone. "I'll give Nolwenn a call in the meantime."

A good idea. Dupin stopped at the café.

On their way to the castle Riwal had familiarized him with the Centre de l'Imaginaire Arthurien. The inspector had first been there in May with his little son, on the Tournament Day with music, exhibitions, and sword fights. Riwal had shown his colleagues lots of photos. Riwal was an enthusiastic father. Dupin liked that, and a few weeks ago they had learned that the family was to have a new addition: another boy.

The Centre, founded in 1988, was a cultural center, a museum, and an important research institution all in one. It was dedicated to the legend of King Arthur and his Round Table, and the Forêt de Brocéliande as one of the important locations linked with Arthur. At a secondary level, the Centre was also concerned with the local sagas and myths the storyteller in the wood had spoken about so passionately. The Centre organized guided walks through the wood, exhibitions, displays, readings, lectures, multiday medieval exhibitions, as well as scientific conferences. The research work was carried out in close cooperation with the University of Rennes.

"Two *petits cafés*, please."

Only two tables were occupied. So far Dupin hadn't seen a single other visitor. On a fine day like today tourists were lying on the beach, and for the locals it was just an ordinary working day. Apart from that, Dupin had seen at the entrance that the Centre closed at 6 P.M. The few visitors who were in the café had already finished their visit.

There was a jovial atmosphere in the café. It had old, simple wooden chairs, rectangular wooden tables. The stone walls kept the place pleasantly cool.

The man behind the counter, in his early twenties, probably doing a vacation job, gave him a bored nod and then started fiddling around with the coffee machine. A proper espresso machine, nonetheless.

Dupin sat down by the window. He watched Riwal walking up and down while on the phone. The situation still seemed sort of crazy. Dupin hoped the *café* would get rid of that feeling too.

"Voilà." The young man set down the porcelain cups, damaged in several places, in front of Dupin and turned away again. He produced a little receipt from the old-fashioned cash register, and laid it on the bar.

Dupin drank the first *café*—good, if far too hot—in two careful slurps, followed by the second.

Dupin gathered his courage and pulled out his phone. Even if he didn't know how to do it, it had to be done.

"Claire . . . it's me," he said in a low voice.

"Georges! I'm just leaving the clinic now, ready to dive into the next cardboard boxes. You've got the day off, you lucky man. How's things?"

It didn't sound scathing.

"All's well." An unfortunate answer, given what he had to say.

"How's the office outing going? Have you met Merlin yet?"

"We've had . . . we've had a couple of incidents, Claire." He had to come to the point, nothing else would help, and it wasn't his fault. "We've had two murders here and somehow it's become my case. It's a complicated story."

There was a long silence. Dupin was ready for anything. Claire was going to want to know the details. Obviously she would know it wasn't his jurisdiction.

"Nothing to do about it. How long will you need?"

Before Dupin could reply, Claire did it herself.

"Be back here tomorrow evening. Tomorrow evening, got it? Up until then it's all fine by me."

He could hear a car door closing. Claire had climbed into her car.

"I'll hurry."

That in itself was a rather unfortunate reply. He understood Claire. They were at the beginning of a life together. The office outing in itself hadn't been well timed, even though Claire hadn't complained in the slightest.

"You don't have to check in regularly. Just tell me everything tomorrow evening. When you're back." She hadn't sounded angry but that didn't mean anything. Claire had hung up.

In general it hadn't been that bad, if he ignored the strict timetable for his return. Dupin had suddenly remembered being given the same ultimatum set by Iwein's wife for her husband. And the unpleasant consequences.

Dupin sighed and looked over at Riwal.

It was time to talk to the scholars. Two of their colleagues had been killed. Maybe even a third, back in May.

* * *

The lady in the dusty, old-fashioned bookstore, with the look of an accomplice on her face, had shown them the way. Through a narrow door, along a corridor—the wall covered with display boards—as far as a steep, narrow spiral staircase. "Third floor, right at the top."

Riwal had already got a first layer of information about the scholars from Nolwenn and had made notes on four pages, which he had handed to Dupin. Who in turn, at least in order to have everything gathered in one place, had put them into the Citroën's manual. Journalists had turned up not just at Cadiou's house but also at the well in the forest. *Ouest-France, Le Télégramme*—unfortunately Dupin didn't know the editorial staff from Rennes—as well as three from the radio and, as he had feared, TV Rennes 35, the local television channel. The news was out. There would be no stopping them now. On top of everything Riwal had been on the phone with Aballain. Apparently nothing unusual had been found in Monsieur Cadiou's office.

It was easy to get genuinely dizzy on the creaky, gnarled, narrow wooden staircase; Dupin was reminded of climbing the lighthouse on the Île de Sein. This had to be the staircase for service staff. The noble men and women of the castle wouldn't have deigned to use it.

A sign warned: *No access to the public.* When they got to the top they found themselves standing in a somber, musty anteroom right in front of a dark wooden door.

Dupin opened it, without knocking, and unleashed an insane noise: a loud groaning and cawing, as if from some animal being tortured.

The room on the other side took up half the length of the building, boarded in wooden panels, rising into an ill-defined darkness—the ceiling was barely visible—with a couple of chandeliers hanging down. To the left and right were tapering dormer windows which apparently, even on the brightest of summer days, let in only the dimmest light. Not even the chandeliers managed to have any effect upon the gloom.

Here too it smelled musty, dusty, like floor wax, which Dupin knew from his grandparents' magnificent Paris house. The floor was even more gnarled than the staircase. Suits of armor stood in front of the wood-tiled walls. Between the bays and the armor were large historical engravings, fantastical scenes: knights, woodland, ponds and streams, dragons, and giant wild boar. And also a knight with a lion.

"About time! It's outrageous to have kept us here so long!" came an indignant but at the same time distinguished female voice, which filled the entire room.

In the middle of the room was a round wooden table which, despite its imposing size, looked lost in the vast space. The scholars sat collected around it on huge chairs with tall cloth-covered backs. Each chair was decorated by endless carvings.

"Mesdames, messieurs, I am Commissaire Georges Dupin," he announced calmly as he approached the table. Now he could see whom the voice belonged to—an elegant elderly lady with a somewhat careworn face. "And this," he nodded with a flick of his head toward Riwal, "is Inspector Riwal. I am leading the investigation into the murders of Fabien Cadiou and Paul Picard. And possibly a third murder." Dupin paused and looked carefully around the group.

"The murder of your colleague"—he took out the Citroën manual with Riwal's list—"Professor Laurent, from Paris, with a chair in Poitiers at the Centre d'Études Supérieures de Civilisation Médiévale." Nolwenn's news was worth gold; it was always useful to be thoroughly informed. "Who seemed to have died a natural death in May, but will now have to be exhumed and reexamined in light of the new situation."

It was a great starting point. Dupin was pleased.

"Yes, what is it?"

A tall, broad-shouldered man with a noticeably pointed skull and bald head, dark woolen trousers, and a black shirt with its arms rolled, had stood up and was coming over to Dupin.

"My name is Auffrai Guivorch," he held out a well-tanned hand to the commissaire, "deputy director of the Centre de l'Imaginaire Arthurien, and by training archeologist and ancient historian, Prof—"

"Professor at Université Rennes 2," Dupin completed the sentence for him. "Département de l'Histoire de l'Art et de l'Archéologie as well as researcher on a project for the Maison des Sciences Humaines en Bretagne in Brest. Forty-seven years old. You live . . ." Dupin dithered, took a fresh glance at the information that Nolwenn had put together and Riwal had copied down. ". . . on a houseboat." An unusual detail. Nolwenn would have had her reasons for noting it. "A very pleasant life. Do come by for a long interview. You'd be very welcome."

Guivorch had seemed jovial at first, but now the lines on his face seemed suddenly serious. "Is it true? Was Gustave Laurent also murdered?" he asked.

"We don't know for sure, yet." Dupin's eyes glanced openly once again at the varying faces. There was nothing to suggest they felt any sympathy for the fate of their colleagues.

"It's horrible, what's happened here. Dreadful." The second woman at the table, clearly younger, around forty, had bright red medium-long hair with blond streaks, tousled and falling to one side in an artistic look, and shining pale blue eyes, in a remarkable contrast to the color of her hair. She had a thin, noble nose, and wore a black tailored jacket. She was very attractive and had a habit of overenunciating, stressing every single syllable.

"Professor Adeline Noiret, I assume." Nolwenn had noted down that the other female researcher, Professor Sébille Bothorel, was "seventy-one years old," which meant that name belonged to the other, older woman, who had complained earlier. "From Paris. Specialist in medieval literature. Also Présidente de la Societé de Mythologie Française. Married to . . ." Dupin glanced at the man standing next to her, small and lean, curly gray hair and almost circular spectacles. ". . . Professor Bastien Terrier." Dupin had never had to deal with so many professors and doctors at once. "Renowned," he added, consulting Nolwenn's list, "professor in Lyon for medieval archeology. Sixty years old."

Bastien Terrier smiled, arrogant and slightly ironic at the same time.

"Exactly. And lives in Paris," he said. The second sentence was clearly an important addition for him. He was wearing a shirt in ostentatious Bordeaux red.

"And you, Madame Bothorel," Dupin turned to the elderly woman, "hold a famous chair at the Sorbonne. For literature." Sébille Bothorel blinked skeptically, but didn't say a word.

"Only one missing then." Dupin glanced at the notably youngest member of the group. "Professor Marc Denvel, also from Paris. Already promoted at just twenty-two years old. A miracle kid." That's what it said on the list. "Already guest professor at Oxford for almost two years and before that at Yale. Also an expert in medieval history."

A good-looking young man with thick, short, dark blond hair, parted to one side, full lips, and green eyes with unusually long eyelashes nodded decisively. Unlike the usual cliché of a scholar, he didn't look at all slight but, on the contrary, athletic. He was wearing sporty dark blue cloth pants, and a pale blue polo shirt.

Deputy Director Guivorch had sat down again. Three chairs at the table had been left empty. Two of them stood next to each other, between the redheaded Adeline Noiret and Guivorch, the Breton. In front of the two seats there were orderly piles of paper; conference documents, Dupin surmised. In front of each seat, relatively far toward the middle of the table, sat a small, dim desk lamp. Directly in front of the third empty seat were neither papers nor lamp.

"All right," Dupin continued. "We'd like to know if you have any thoughts about the murders or anything that might be connected to the murders. No matter what it is."

Silence. Dupin waited a bit longer before pressing the issue further. "Does anyone have an idea why your two colleagues might have been murdered?"

When there was still no answer, Dupin sat down, making it clear that he had time on his hands. He glanced at Riwal, indicating that he should do likewise. He thought he detected a slight unease on Riwal's features. Something seemed to be disconcerting the inspector. While walking toward one of the other empty seats, the inspector passed very close to Dupin, and whispered to him in the lowest of voices, "Le Siège Périleux." The Perilous Seat.

Curious glances from the whole group turned toward them—even if they hadn't understood. "A professional message," he explained. "Well then, I'm listening. What went on here, tell me."

A long, embarrassed silence followed. Yet again, Dupin tried to read in their faces a feeling of some sort. They seemed genuinely apathetic. Whether it was faked or genuine, he couldn't tell.

He set the Citroën manual in front of him on the table. Noiret and Guivorch stared at it in irritation.

The deputy director was the first to break the silence.

"Naturally we've asked ourselves that. All of us together and each of us on their own. Hard as we tried, Commissaire, nothing occurred to us."

"You're in the company of the most renowned researchers in our field." The elderly lady, Madame Bothorel, spoke with the greatest arrogance. "The only thing we're interested in is our research."

"What specifically, at this moment, should your meeting be about?" Riwal's question was a good approach.

"About a whole spectrum of highly relevant subjects that the new digs have brought to light," said Bastien Terrier, the one with the curls and the round spectacles.

"Absurd questions, if you ask me." Madame Bothorel was worked up.

Adeline Noiret reacted promptly, friendly but in an icy tone: "You don't have to be here if you don't want to. There's no peer pressure. Your presence is voluntary."

Madame Bothorel only cast a dismissive glance at her young colleague.

It hardly seemed to Dupin to be a particularly friendly meeting.

"Putting it simply, it's like this." Guivorch, the deputy director with the houseboat, turned to Dupin. "Materials concerning Arthur were once thought to be true reports, then reconsidered as poetic, artistic fantasies. Now it would seem that there is more real history in them than was previously assumed."

"It's of no importance to literary studies," Sébille Bothorel said harshly.

Guivorch continued persistently. "As a result, a series of targeted digs has been started in connection with the Arthurian myth. At Cadbury in England, for example, or here in the forest. These projects involve all of our disciplines: archeology, medieval history, as well as medieval literature and language studies. However, back to your question: Bastien Terrier, Paul Picard, and I were planning to report on details from the digs today. Cadiou as well. Each of us in our own branch of study. We had planned discussions for tomorrow and the day after."

"All that matters is the texts," announced Madame Bothorel. "Archeology takes itself far too seriously."

Dupin got it. The different experts and their own fields of activity were in competition with one another, and each considered their own most important. Which made the situation here all the more interesting.

Up until now the young professor had remained silent.

"How about you, Monsieur Denvel." Dupin turned toward him. "Do you see a possible motive for the two murders?"

The young man inclined his head to one side, earnestly, measured, without being theatrical. He was genuinely good-looking, something downright classic about his face, like a young aristocrat, beaming but not arrogant.

"Much as I'd like to help, I too can't see why any of us should try to take the life of another."

Denvel had spoken with deep concern in his voice. And yet Dupin felt he was being almost ironic.

"No. I can't see a motive." He shook his head decisively to stress the brief conclusion.

"Which archeological discoveries are we talking about here?" asked Riwal. "And who made the find?"

Guivorch spoke first. "Primarily those at Cadbury Castle. For ages now this hill has been—"

Dupin interrupted him: "You mean the hill where Monsieur Laurent was occupied on the dig back in May? And where Monsieur Cadiou also spent a few days on the project?"

Bastien Terrier was continuously taking his glasses off and putting them back on again; all of a sudden something seemed to have made him nervous. "My department is also heavily involved with the project."

Guivorch smiled generously. "Along with a couple of others. A team from London started excavations there again three years ago. They—"

"We already had permission one year earlier." Terrier sounded angered. "But the British national research was given priority, and it was only later that we were allowed to start. Another thing about Gustave Laurent: he was a medieval historian, Monsieur le Commissaire. Not an archeologist! I only say that to get the investigation onto the right track. He had a position at the Centre d'Études Supérieures de Civilisation Médiévale in Poitiers. Although naturally he lived in Paris. And we all know that the project in Cadbury was the single archeological undertaking in which Laurent took part, as a hobby archeologist."

"At the very beginning of the dig, toward the end of the 1960s," Guivorch continued, "they came across substantial and widespread walls dating to the middle of the first millennium. It had to have been an important seat of an elevated person, that much was clear. And it's clear that it did not belong to a well-known historical figure."

That was a suggestive way of expressing it, Dupin thought with amusement.

"It was clearly all going to end exactly as the alleged discovery of Camelot in the twelfth century: laughable." The amount of mockery in Sébille Bothorel's voice was impressive. "They identified the Roman amphitheater in Caerleon, which was only a ruin, as Arthur's court. A grandiose false interpretation! A huge mass, in a round shape, brilliant architecture—unfortunately by the year 400 it was already a dilapidated ruin. Farcical."

"What we're supposed to be discussing here today is a genuine sensation," Terrier interrupted, as if he hadn't heard the poisonous comment just before. "Toward the end of last year, long before Laurent's group were even there, *we* had uncovered a stone slab with the inscription 'Pater Coliavi Ficit Artogonov.'" He took a deep breath. "Which means more or less: the father of Coliavus laid the gravestone here: *Artogonou!*"

Dupin wasn't sure where this was all going.

"Don't make too much of this stone slab," Madame Bothorel hissed.

"You have to understand," Guivorch said, and raised his index finger, "what the most historically plausible theory is: simply, that Arthur was a so-called little king who, after the collapse of the Roman Empire and the withdrawal, around 410, of the last troops, continued to rule over one or two of the Roman settlement centers in the south and west of England that remained until the middle of the sixth century. And he took up the struggle against the invading barbarous Angles and Saxons, organizing it and leading it. Over the course of the decades, however, he surrounded himself with a sworn society of knights who lived according to strict ideals: justice, equality, charity, gentility, humanity."

"In the *Historia Brittonum* from around 820," the young star historian took up the story, "the twelve battles of Arthur, last defender of the Britons, were described. The Warlord was his title there." For a moment Dupin thought he saw a strange smile on Denvel's lips as he repeated: "The Warlord!" Or was it just his imagination?

"What objects were found during your excavations? Objects of particular value?"

In reality he'd heard enough about excavations, but it seemed sensible to keep with the theme, if it absorbed the research group that much. And also, in his seven years in Brittany, the issue of "legendary treasures," which in a Breton case might be important, had become one of his go-to considerations.

"Who do you think we are?" Terrier's glasses almost fell off his nose. "We aren't some bunch of profane treasure hunters!"

"A few bronze and golden shields, plates and beakers," Guivorch intervened. "Not much. But even those added further hints toward a particular lord of the fortress."

"And where are they now?"

"All of them meticulously preserved in the Department of Conservation and Scientific Research of the British Museum."

"Perhaps some objects were embezzled? Somebody simply took them for himself?"

Once again Dupin calmly evaluated those present.

"We have a code of conduct!" Terrier protested, then added rather less irately: "And there is an official state overseer who is always on-site."

Obviously there had to be somebody of the sort. And Dupin knew one thing above all: greed made people inventive. And people would do certain things out of greed. Some people—and there were more than a few—might do anything.

The young Arthurian researcher had begun to busy himself with his smartphone, with focus, but not demonstratively. He started typing.

"Which of you had—"

Dupin's phone rang.

He looked at the display: NUMBER WITHHELD, it said. It had only rung once.

"Which of you," Dupin had put his phone back on the table, "was directly involved in these Cadbury excavations?"

"Apart from me," Terrier replied, "just Gustave Laurent. But his group didn't find anything else."

"Does everybody agree with that?" Dupin looked around.

Nobody looked ready to respond.

"And what about Monsieur Cadiou? Why was he there?"

Terrier again: "He had advised Gustave Laurent now and then. As a literary scholar."

"Can you be more precise?"

"I have no idea."

They got no further.

Dupin made a few notes. King Arthur's world was confusing.

"Was there anything of particular interest in Paul Picard's dig?"

"He's still in the early stages. As far as I know, nothing so far," the deputy director said.

"Monsieur Guivorch, you're the only one in this group here who is from Brittany. May I ask where specifically?"

"I'm a *Breton pur beurre*, the only Breton on the board of the International Arthurian Society. I'm from Saint-Péran, one of the tiniest hamlets in the forest. It was the wood that got me into a career in the subject."

"I understand. Back then were there other digs in the area? Here in the wood, I mean."

Guivorch replied, "Since January this year, my department has been excavating in the Val sans Retour. In the 'House of the Fée Viviane,' a megalith area."

The "fairy house" had been an obvious inclusion on the list for their commissariat office outing.

Terrier spoke up: "Last year I led an excavation at the edge of Merlin's Grave, originally a twelve-meter-long stone alley from Neolithic times. We were interested in how old the construction was."

Dupin interrupted Terrier before he could get into more details.

"So at the moment there are three archeological works going on," he summed up. "Picard's is still at the beginning while the other two have not yet turned up any significant discoveries."

Nobody objected.

"Have the Centre and Fabien Cadiou also got something to do with the digs?" Riwal asked.

"Generally," Guivorch explained, "in that the Centre deals with evaluations and recommendations. But that's all. Fabien Cadiou was already on the job when the application for Picard's project was made, although not for previous ones."

"When exactly did Cadiou become the director of the Centre?" Riwal asked further.

"On November first, last year."

"And," it was Riwal again, and Guivorch was looking at him carefully, "by then your project was already approved."

"Exactly."

"Have there been other international digs this year or the one before in which you," and here he was addressing all of them, "have been involved?"

"This summer, Picard was involved in a small excavation project in Glastonbury," Guivorch said.

"Infantile. Totally infantile, if you ask me." The elderly professor, Sébille Bothorel, had kept quiet for a while. "That tops it all, little boys going searching for the Grail. And they call themselves scholars! Laughable."

Guivorch, undisturbed, continued: "It was all about dating the enclosure of a well."

Wells seemed to have played a large role in the world of King Arthur.

Riwal cleared his throat. "According to a legend based on the Gospel of Matthew, the chalice used in Jesus's Last Supper ended up in England. Joseph Arimathaus himself, who caught Jesus's blood in it, brought it there, founded a monastery in Glastonbury, and hid the chalice under a well. The Chalice Well. And until this very day the red color of the water is attributed to being touched by the chalice used at the Last Supper." The inspector had done his very best to sound completely factual.

"And this expedition in which Picard had taken part, had something . . ." Dupin hesitated—all in all, even by Breton standards, this seemed too fantastical—"to do with this Holy Grail?"

Never, never in his life, had he imagined himself uttering a sentence of this sort in the middle of an investigation.

"Ridiculous," hissed Madame Bothorel.

There was a silence, until Guivorch spoke up.

"As I said, it had to do with looking for objects that would have permitted a potential dating for the enclosure of the well."

"And were any found?"

"No."

"Monsieur Denvel," Dupin turned once again to the youngster of the team, "have you never taken part in something similar?"

"Nothing that might be particularly useful, I fear."

"In various pieces of poetry"—Adeline Noiret, the redhead scholar, had now joined in, stressing heavily the word "poetry"—"references to the Grail refer to very different objects. In one it's a beaker, in the other a chalice made of several different materials, in another a carved stone. Green particularly frequently. Occasionally it has been said to be made from a meteorite. Or it was an anointment vessel, or a golden pot."

Riwal nodded eagerly. "And it's not just that people imagine the

Grail made from different materials, there are lots of them. Dozens of grails in dozens of castles. With dozens of histories. Each one more fantastic than the other. And each time it is naturally the genuine Grail. You'd be amused in how many churches it's supposed to sit. In England, Spain, Israel, France. Each of them claims it as their own. Recently there was a piece in the papers that it had been found in a private attic."

"And taken seriously." Madame Noiret stressed her words with the greatest seriousness. "It's just a thing. But it's precisely that which provokes the fantasy. The tricky thing is that some scholars believe themselves to have recognized parts of the ancient texts and base their research on them. As if a 'source' has been found from which all the Arthurian and Holy Grail stories stem, but was unfortunately lost."

"It's not easy to search for something and find it, when nobody actually knows what it is." One of Riwal's dark philosophical sayings.

"And the Church of the Holy Grail?" This was where Dupin had parked the car when they arrived. Only a few hours ago, when he had still thought he was on an office outing, with a single irritating chore to complete at the beginning which could be dealt with quickly. "What links the church to the forest, what meaning does it have?"

"None. The church is just the highly impressive work of a busy priest," Guivorch countered, "who only began at the end of the war to turn the old church here into a church of the Grail. The pictures on the walls inside tell the story of the Holy Grail. He devoted his entire life to it."

"But this church, if I understand it properly, and its history, have nothing in the slightest to do with the Grail."

"The story goes, the priest *knew something*. About the Grail and its hiding place. And that the wood here played a decisive role. It was also said that the priest hadn't come here by chance. That he belonged to a long line of carriers of the Grail." Now Guivorch smiled too. "No, there is no connection. Despite these local legends."

His words echoed in the expanse of the room. Nobody wanted to add anything.

"*La porte est en dedans,* said the strange sign over the door of the chapel," Riwal said. "And there's another one: *Be aware that all you see is not real, and you do not see what there really is.*"

Dupin drew his hand across his forehead and sighed audibly. Had the power of the *cafés* lessened already?

All this was leading nowhere.

Suddenly there was a horrendous, penetrating noise. It lasted for a long moment. It was the mighty wooden door from the other side of the room. A sort of multitoned scraping and scratching, as if the door were a sophisticated wind box, an instrument from hell.

Little by little, the door opened, revealing a dark hallway beyond.

A second later a dark figure appeared.

Dupin recognized the young man from the café. And behind him the girl from the ticket office.

"Apéritif!"

The word reverberated through the room like a trumpet.

The pair of them were carrying a great basket, heading toward a table to the right of the door, which Dupin had hardly noticed in the twilight. There were several bottles of red wine on it.

Guivorch felt obliged to give an explanation.

"Our meetings usually extend into the evening. We don't, however, take dinner together." A strange piece of information, which nonetheless took nothing from this bizarre situation.

"*Pâté de campagne, terrine forestière,* and *rillettes de cerf et sanglier,*" the young woman announced cheerfully. "Everything from Brocéli-ande, a cooperative for regional charcuterie. The rillettes were made exclusively from deer and wild boar from our region. The mushrooms and herbs in the terrine also come from our forest." She nodded her head—unnecessarily—to indicate where the forest was.

Dupin loved the tradition of the apéritif and the Breton pride of their regional products, but this was not the right moment, even for those.

"Thank you very much, mademoiselle," he remarked, "but we are in the middle of an important investigation."

"We'll just drop everything off," the girl said, clearly unimpressed. "The plates and cutlery too. Just help yourselves."

Nobody reacted.

Dupin rubbed his temples. Nonetheless, it would be over soon.

The table was getting fuller and fuller. It was a miracle how much they could fit into that basket. They kept producing more things.

"That's it," the girl announced. She still had a sort of platter in her hand, which she set down in a remaining empty place. Dupin had no idea what it was, above all what it was for.

"Who can give me concrete details about Picard's current dig?" Dupin finally said to put an end to the situation—even if nobody had made any indication toward getting up and starting in on the apéritif.

Guivorch felt he was being addressed.

"People assume there was a chapel described in reports and stories, they—"

"I've heard of that," Dupin said, to speed things up.

"This spring, Picard and his team used ground radar and the latest software to search the area around the well. In one place, where there have always been a few visibly worked stones, they were lucky. Picard was able to prove that there were many more objects. The data is never easy to interpret, but it could quite possibly be the outline of an extremely ancient chapel. That would be a sensation."

"And it was about the chapel, nothing else?"

A strange question, Dupin knew.

Even the young Denvel looked up from his phone at Dupin's question. Everyone glanced at the commissaire. Nobody answered. Madame Bothorel simply made a scornful gesture with her hand.

Dupin waited. For a long time. In vain.

There were a few other topics. He kept going. Everything was taking too long.

"And what about the park?" Dupin leafed through the Citroën manual, getting strange looks again: "Le Parc de l'Imagination Illimitée?"

A tangible subject, this side of the fantasy world.

"Has anybody—" Once again Dupin was interrupted by his phone. And once again it stopped ringing before he got it to his ear.

"Reception here in the wood is a bit of a problem," Guivorch said. "Often you can lose the signal during a conversation."

"I was warned about it," Dupin muttered, shoving his phone back into his jeans pocket, and resuming: "Was Monsieur Cadiou part of the 'experience project'?"

Guivorch's answer was prompt and deliberate: "No. That was his wife's business. Fabien Cadiou never mentioned it either in the Centre nor in our scientific circle."

"And Paul Picard, did he have anything to do with the project?"

Dupin looked around the circle.

Yet again it was Deputy Director Guivorch who answered.

"I don't think so."

"Does anyone else know anything about this project that might be relevant?"

Head shaking all round.

Dupin didn't let it go; for some reason he was particularly interested in the subject. "Is any one of you involved with the project?"

For a moment there was a trace of irritation on all their faces.

Surprisingly Marc Denvel felt himself moved to reply: "Personally I know very little about it. Nothing, really. Somebody mentioned it once. Madame Cadiou was involved, you'd best speak to her directly."

Dupin was going to do that anyway.

"Madame Bothorel?"

The old lady had uninhibitedly begun to go through some of the papers in the pile in front of her.

"It'll only bring more loads of tourists wandering through the wood. I haven't the slightest thing to do with it."

A clear answer.

"And you, Madame Noiret?"

"Every bit as little." The redheaded professor shrugged.

Terrier pursed his lips, as if he was thinking about it intensively. "The same goes for me."

Dupin looked at Guivorch.

"Nothing," he said curtly.

"When have you last met together in this group?" That was another interesting question, one Dupin had wanted to ask earlier.

"September last year," Guivorch told him.

"And where?"

"In Paris."

"Do you meet regularly?"

"Once a year."

"How did you come to get the group together?"

Maybe there would be a hint there. The three dead men belonged to this illustrious circle. That couldn't be a coincidence.

"We're the board of the French section of the International Arthurian Society, the Société Internationale Arthurienne," Terrier replied, and obviously thought it fitting to do so in an extremely formal manner. "A scientific body with three thousand members in France alone. And groupings in altogether forty-seven countries in the world. I am the deputy." Terrier paused; something seemed to be on his mind. "And now also the sitting chair of the society. Paul Picard was elected two years ago and was to hold the office for a further year. He had in any case received only a few more votes than I did." It was unbelievable just how little effort Terrier made to conceal his satisfaction at his new status.

While he was answering, Dupin had, for no obvious reason, stood up and walked over to a knightly suit of armor. All their eyes followed him curiously, only Terrier continuing undeterred to talk. Dupin stopped in front of the armor and fixed his eyes on the point of a lance. Close up it seemed to be rusty. As a small boy he had always seen rust on the blades of old knives as dried blood.

"Is there something in particular that interests you?" Guivorch interrupted the silence that had set in.

Dupin let the question evaporate. Then he turned around and went back to the table.

"This hotel, where Paul Picard was staying, were you all there?"

"Yes, it's the hotel where we traditionally stay when we're here. Everyone except me has a room there. It's a pretty, extremely pleasant hotel," Guivorch replied.

Dupin flickered through his Citroën manual. "The Relais de Brocéliande in Paimpont."

"I would—"

Dupin's phone rang.

"Yes?"

"Monsieur le Commissaire?"

"Yes, Kadeg, what is it?"

Dupin lowered his voice, walked to the door, and left the room.

"Several people have been trying to get hold of you. The pathologist examining Picard's body is estimating a time of death between midday and one o'clock. It . . ."

Dupin went into the tiny anteroom, which seemed stuffier than ever. And far too hot.

"Yes, it . . . ?"

Dupin was deep in thought. "If they are connected, the murders happened one after the other relatively quickly."

"There were three stab wounds, from a knife with a blade of nine centimeters, the pathologist says. The length of a normal pocketknife. A smooth blade. There are no indications of a struggle. He'll be in touch when he has more information."

"Good."

"The pathologist who examined Cadiou, on the contrary, sees clear signs of a struggle, he—"

"Where? What kind?"

"Hematomas on the left and right arms. In particular on the upper arms. Not so much widespread as localized."

"Any DNA traces?"

"He couldn't say yet."

"What about the weapon?"

"It's thirty-eight caliber, nine millimeter. Nothing special. Made by Ruag."

The most common caliber for pistols. A common ammunition. That led nowhere.

"Anything else?" The stuffy air in the anteroom was unbearable.

"We have provisional reports from the crime scene team. They've been over the area of the wood near where the body was, but found nothing unusual. No sign of a phone either. The killer probably took it with him. But we'll get the call log."

"What about Cadiou's mobile and landline?"

"His mobile was found in the kitchen. Protected with a code and fingerprint sensor. Here too they've been looking into his communication. They've checked the call records on the landline. So far they've found nothing interesting. It wasn't used much."

"Do we know if Picard had a computer with him?"

"Yes, the crime scene people took it from his hotel room. There was nothing obviously out of the ordinary there either. They're trying to get access to his laptop. The same goes for Cadiou. His wife doesn't know the password. They found nothing unusual in their manor. Nor in the courtyard. The side door was never locked."

"I see—no tracks on the gravel in the forecourt or on the road?"

"No tracks apart from those of the medics and from Madame Cadiou. And nothing conspicuous in Monsieur Cadiou's car. They went through it thoroughly."

That was unproductive.

"And who wanted to talk to me, Kadeg?"

"To talk to you?"

Sometimes, the man could be infuriating.

"You said various people had been trying to get hold of me."

"Oh yes: Nolwenn! And your friend from Paris."

"Anyone else?"

"No."

"Okay, I want"—Dupin faltered—"somebody to look into this professional storyteller called . . ." He clamped the phone between his shoulder and chin and flicked through the Citroën manual. "Philippe Goazou, stage name Inwynn. I want to check his alibi between nine o'clock and one o'clock."

He couldn't get him out of his mind.

"I'm on it."

"And I'd like you to come to Castle Comper, Kadeg. With a couple of colleagues."

Dupin had wondered if it was overdoing things, but then decided it was appropriate. For now at least, all of the academics were suspects.

"Got it."

Dupin hung up.

Lost in thought, he headed back into the Knights' Hall. The door screeched deafeningly.

They all looked at him, as if it were a play taking place on a spectacular stage.

"One more thing, which of you were in the British Isles in May? You for one, Monsieur Denvel."

"Indeed." Denvel reacted very calmly. "My current temporary home."

"This place, where the excavations are taking place, Cadbury Castle, how far is it from Oxford? By car."

"A hundred and fifty kilometers." Riwal knew his stuff. "Less than two hours."

Hardly a long way, then.

"I was also in England in May, purely by coincidence. In Cornwall and the English West Country." There was a hint of a smile on the deputy director's lips. "By coincidence" was a dubious expression to use in a murder case.

Celtic Cornwall and the adjoining counties of Devon and Somerset formed a peninsula jutting southwest into the sea, just as the similarly named Breton province of Cornuaille, also home to the Arthurian legends, jutted northwest toward them.

"I had to give a speech. In Exeter. And on the way back to London the following morning I stopped in Glastonbury. Purely out of private interest. Given that I happened to be there." Yet again the hint of a smile.

Dupin made a note for himself.

He knew what Glastonbury represented: the red well of the Grail.

"What exactly were you doing there, Monsieur Guivorch? Was the Grail calling you?"

Riwal, tapping on his phone, butted in before Guivorch could respond. "Glastonbury and Cadbury Castle, where Professor Laurent was, are about thirty minutes apart. Exeter is an hour's drive away to the south."

What a series of coincidences.

"Every year in mid-May there's a gathering of the regional Arthurian society, and I was invited," Guivorch answered matter-of-factly. Depending on what the exhumation turned up, Dupin would have to go into the topic thoroughly.

"Madame Bothorel, what about you?"

"If I was on the island in May?"

A purely rhetorical question.

"Precisely."

"No."

"In Paris?"

"Yes."

For a brief moment, Dupin had noticed, she let her eyes drop to the floor. "No trips?"

"No trips to the island. And everything else," she said with a feigned indignance, "is private."

"Madame Noiret, how about you?"

"The last weekend in May?" She glanced at Terrier. "I was in London for two days with my husband. There was an exhibition, 'Impressionists in London,' at the Tate Gallery that we didn't want to miss under any circumstances."

Impressive. All of them, with the exception of Madame Bothorel, had been in England in May, at the same time as Gustave Laurent had been there. More coincidences. On the other hand, if Dupin understood properly, they all necessarily had regular business in England. The island had been King Arthur's home, so it was no wonder that those researching him were drawn there.

"One last question: Who amongst you knew that Paul Picard wanted to visit the excavation site before the beginning of your symposium today?"

No reaction.

As usual, the deputy director answered: "I suspect we would all have taken it for granted if someone had asked us. He arrived last night, the preliminaries had just begun, so it's understandable that he went straight there."

From that point of view, Guivorch was right.

"Very good."

Dupin took another look at the knight's armor, with the red, shimmering lance. "In that case we have a first picture of the scene."

He had deliberately left the sentence vague.

"Obviously you are all suspects."

He glanced at Madame Bothorel, waiting for heavy protest. But inexplicably, it didn't come. The look on her face remained stony.

"So I'll take my leave. But I'll see you all again soon for sure. My two inspectors will in turn ask you for your alibis. And then with the help of a few of our competent colleagues, they will check these out. Point for point."

Dupin made not the slightest effort to minimalize the provoca-tive self-satisfaction in this announcement.

He turned away. There was nothing more to say.

Riwal wasn't surprised in the least; he knew Dupin too well.

"We'll do just that: I'll speak with each of you in turn, and we'll put together a list. Systematically. I'll begin with Madame Bothorel."

Dupin was already at the door when he suddenly stopped and took a couple of steps back into the Knights' Hall.

"One more thing," he said in a loud voice. "This experience park project of Blanche Cadiou's. What was your impression? What did Monsieur Cadiou think of it?"

He had directed these final words at the deputy director.

Guivorch was surprised, but replied without hesitation: "He was in favor of it, but kept his opinion to himself. I think that sums it up accurately. The Centre is a scientific institution only in second place; its primary role is to spread the Arthur fascination amongst as many people as possible. And in this respect, he welcomed the park without getting involved with it personally."

Guivorch made sure to show to what extent he respected Cadiou's attitude.

"So you did talk about it with him." That wasn't how it had sounded previously.

"Just casually. Twice at most, maybe. And only briefly."

"Has anybody else here anything to say about the subject?"

The usual shaking of heads.

"Very well."

Dupin turned around and hurried out of the twilight of the Knights' Hall back into the fresh air.

* * *

Not far from the castle Dupin had encountered two police cars coming toward him on the narrow road and had to brake sharply. In the first car he spotted Kadeg in the passenger seat. The inspector greeted him enthusiastically, and then stared in amazement at the battered side of Dupin's Citroën. Dupin had nodded vaguely, then driven slightly onto the green in order to be able to put his foot on the gas. As he was coming out of the bookshop he had been mobbed by a horde of reporters, eight at least, two with running video cameras, bombarding him with innumerable questions. Dupin had grumpily replied to them all with "No comment," repeating it several times as they followed him over the courtyard. He had had to hold himself back. But he knew that—just like him—they were only doing their job. For the rest of the way to his car, he had run rather than walked.

It was almost certainly a quarter of an hour to Cadiou's manor. He had urgent calls to make.

"Jean Odinot here." The voice rattled out of his hands-free device.

"Did she tell you anything more?" Dupin came directly to the point. Jean must have met Laurent's widow by now.

"The problem is that she had very little, more like nothing at all, to do with her husband's work. A very 'traditional' marriage, it seemed to me. With a large inheritance in the background, from Laurent's father, who had been in parliament for thirty years. They have three children and she volunteers for a dozen different charities. The sort of person who constantly worries, who sees wrong everywhere."

"In this case, she might be right," Dupin squeezed in. "But she had absolutely no idea what it might have been about?"

"We had a long chat. She showed me her late husband's office, there in their house. She had left everything in his room untouched. I set three of my men to go through it all as closely as possible. And to document it. We took his laptop with us. He hadn't kept a diary.

But he was a constant writer: newspaper articles, reports. During the excavation in May—this is common—he had kept a sort of journal on his laptop."

"I want to know about everything Laurent had been up to recently."

"His life—"

There was a loud, metallic crunch and the line went dead.

Dupin pressed the button to repeat the call.

"You were just going to—"

"Go on—"

"Laurent had dedicated his life entirely to science, according to his wife. Now and then he would get in touch with an old school friend. Cadiou as well, but not often."

"Yet he too is now dead."

Dupin was lost in thought again.

"Madame Laurent couldn't think of anyone else we should talk to," Odinot said.

"Where exactly was Cadiou at the end of July, beginning of August?"

"On Corsica."

"Why?"

"No idea. Vacation, I assume."

"I'll find out. I'm on my way to see Madame Cadiou now. What's up with the archeologists from the team he was part of in May?" Dupin asked.

"We've spoken to all of them and done a bit of research."

Dupin grinned. He hadn't previously asked what it meant when Jean "did a bit of research." But it almost invariably produced results.

"Unfortunately nothing worth mentioning, not a trace of suspicion."

"Anything else?"

"They're going to exhume Laurent's body tomorrow morning."

"Did Madame Laurent say anything concrete as to how her husband had changed in his last months?"

"Not really. He was 'more isolated than normal.' He had kept to himself in his study. All very vague."

"I've been talking with this team of researchers." Dupin gave a brief summary of what, if anything, there was to sum up.

"Did you get a feeling?"

A suspicion, Jean meant.

"No."

"Come on, Georges, what does your *gift* say?"

Jean Odinot had regularly driven Dupin mad in the past with his use of that word. Even back in his Paris days Dupin's "feeling" had been legendary, much to the chagrin of Dupin, who didn't want to hear anything about his "gift" or his supposed "special method," which didn't exist.

"Talk to you later, Jean."

"One more thing. There was nothing out of the ordinary in Picard's apartment. We found nothing suspicious. And no computer."

"He used a laptop. We have it."

"Good."

"Okay, talk soon. *Salut!*" Dupin hung up.

He was on one of the long, straight firebreaks through the wood. The sun was substantially lower than last time. The wood on both sides was beginning to yield to the shapeless dark. Much earlier than it ought to.

Dupin tapped in Nolwenn's number. She picked up straightaway, her voice reverberating in the car.

"I have a few bits of interesting information, Monsieur le Commissaire. Extremely interesting, I think."

Those were the sort of words he loved to hear from Nolwenn. And the sort he needed to hear now.

"This professor, Adeline Noiret, she was—"

A sudden high-pitched beeping sound, almost unearthly, three seconds long. Then Nolwenn was gone.

Dupin pressed the button to resume the call.

"That was weird, Monsieur le—"

"What about Noiret?"

"She used to be married to our second victim. Professor Picard, she—"

"What?" Dupin suddenly sat up straight.

"To put it more precisely, he was her ex-husband. Picard and she got married when she was twenty-three; in other words, twenty-one years ago. The marriage only lasted a couple of years. She married Bastien Terrier three years ago."

"Nobody said anything to us about that. Neither the one nor the other." Dupin shook his head.

This was unbelievable news.

"This morning somebody murdered her ex-husband and she made no reference to that, not a word."

"Maybe they'd had nothing to do with each other for ages. I'm afraid I know nothing about that. But consider that her current husband was there. Maybe he had some objection to emotional outbursts."

Dupin hadn't thought about that.

"But surely he would at least have understood some small reaction."

"Scholars! The emotional side of existence is normally not their strong point," Nolwenn said drily. "Nor is the social side."

"Her ex-husband was brutally murdered and she didn't say a word." Dupin was speechless—a rare occurrence. He was more than keen to turn around there and then and give Madame Noiret a serious talking-to.

"Where did you get the information from, Nolwenn?"

"I had a chat on the phone with the secretary for the Langue et Littérature Française du Moyen Age of the Université Paris. We got on very well." Nolwenn had the skill of immediately turning total strangers into collaborators.

"She's been working there for thirty years and knows all the stories. In the meantime I've also chatted with all the other secretaries, who were all eager to talk."

Nolwenn had her methods and she was relentless.

"Was Picard in a new relationship?"

"Apparently not. He was single. But there is more, Monsieur le Commissaire."

A dramatic pause. Dupin was entering a tight curve. He had noticed that he was driving more slowly. More slowly than before the accident.

"Sébille Bothorel is the stepmother of Marc Denvel, our young star."

"Stepmother?"

"She used to be married to Victor Denvel. One of the most famous French historians of recent decades. Director of the interdisciplinary institute at the Sorbonne, which in fact had been founded for him. Young Denvel is one of two children born to Victor before he married Sébille."

It was a confusing mesh of interconnections. But somehow it made sense with this unique group.

"Nobody mentioned any of that either."

"They all know it."

"Do you know anything about the relationship between the two?"

"They apparently have little to do with each other. The word is that they see each other only at occasions such as the meeting here."

"I see."

"This group have known one another for years, decades. There have been no new members of the committee for the last seven years. I've just been putting together what I've heard here and there. It's almost certainly not complete. There are friendships, rivalries, battles for power, injuries, disappointments, affairs, marriages, separations, a divorce, as I mentioned. Strong emotions are involved. It's about jobs, appropriations, third-party funds, and of course all about getting a good name. Respect."

Dupin believed every word.

"If you ask me," Nolwenn summed up, "it's all to do with simple narcissism, more or less elegantly concealed. Officially, as you know, everything is about research. Not about high office, power, or money."

Nolwenn knew people. She understood the reality of "human-kind," the depths. She hadn't been formulating any of this cynically. It was simply the truth.

"Particular animosities?"

"Maybe between the two women: Madame Noiret and Madame Bothorel. Madame Noiret at one stage accused Madame Bothorel of plagiarizing her stuff. Publicly. At lectures. With some interpretation of a medieval text."

"When was that?"

"Eight years ago."

"A long time," Dupin muttered.

"Some wounds don't heal. It depends on the people involved." Nolwenn was right, of course.

"And as a rule: *Tra mà vo daou zen war ar bed, ar jalousi a reno bepred*—even if there are just two people in the world, envy will win out."

That was true too.

"Anything else?"

It was only three kilometers farther to Tréhorenteuc. The deep forest gave the impression you could go on and on in it without coming to an end, that you could get lost in it.

"Terrier, Laurent, Cadiou, Picard, Guivorch—the five men had fought over the same positions again and again. There were disappointments and injuries. Most recently, Cadiou and Guivorch fought about the post of director at the Centre, which in the end went to Cadiou. Even Picard was rumored to have had ambitions to get elected."

"And three of the five are dead."

Dupin had said the words calmly, but nonetheless—seen like that—it seemed naturally dramatic. A battle for money, security—and above all, recognition and respect. The mainsprings of human ambition.

"Even Terrier and his current wife, Adeline Noiret, at one stage rivaled each other for a position in the middle ranks of the university, one that Noiret got in the end."

Everything Dupin had only just found out made the curious situation and atmosphere in the group a little bit more comprehensible. He wished he'd had Nolwenn's information earlier. They'd known one another for ages, and had endless emotional entanglements. All of which had to be multiplied by the "science" factor.

"Any more particularly tricky points?"

"For the mom . . ."

Nolwenn's voice faded away. Dupin heard a "that," followed by a long, monotonous, reverberating hammering on the line. As if from a long way off.

Then Nolwenn called him back.

"Connections here in the wood are pretty unstable." Dupin feared he was going to have to use that explanation frequently.

"It could be a lot worse, Monsieur le Commissaire. Some people get no reception at all in the wood. There's nothing more for the moment."

"Keep your ear to the ground, Nolwenn. Listen for recent conflicts, the sort that might have occurred this year. And see if you can find out anything about this professional *conteur*. Inwynn. Otherwise known as Philippe Goazou."

"Do you suspect him?"

"I don't know. You've also certainly heard about the park—"

"That Cadiou's wife wants to create."

"Exactly. The decision in the local council is due the week after next."

Dupin turned from the road onto the gravel path toward the manor.

"I know. One more thing. None of the persons known to us have permission to carry a weapon."

That would have been too easy.

"Incidentally," Nolwenn's voice sounded slightly mischievous, "about a dozen or more journalists have turned up. Three of them have already been here in the hotel. You—"

"I know." Dupin had no enthusiasm for the aggravating topic.

"There are crazy rumors going around, online as well. Among

others, that one of the researchers is not far from discovering the Holy Grail, and that on that account the Président de la République himself wants to be involved in the investigation."

Dupin sighed audibly.

"Speaking of wild"—Nolwenn suddenly changed topics with a particularly strong tone to her voice—"the new car is on the table. At last. There is no way around it. We're going to get you a chic car, with the most modern technology."

For a second Dupin asked himself if the reception here would suddenly turn really bad and the connection simply fail once again, but luckily Nolwenn didn't continue the topic; that would be for another time, he knew.

"Also, the prefect called, Monsieur le Commissaire, he sends his congratulations. I'm to reassure you that he'll support you with all his strength. He's 'at your side continuously—you can be happy to boast of that in Paris,' he said expressly. I quote: 'Finistère is ready for battle, if necessary.'"

Dupin had witnessed the prefect being subservient in the past, but that topped it all. If it hadn't been such a serious situation, Dupin would have taken pleasure from the moment, laid back and enjoyed it to the full.

"And you're not to worry about Concarneau, he's got everything under control. The butter crisis in particular."

Dupin had arrived at the tall laurel bush and steered the car to the right, onto the meadow.

"I think that in light of possible riots dangerous to the state, it would be appropriate if the prefect were to go on patrol through Concarneau himself. You never know what might happen. I would feel safer. Nolwenn, let him know that, next time he gets in touch."

There had to be a little fun. Dupin's mood improved immediately.

"Absolutely. That seems very appropriate to the situation," Nolwenn affirmed in all seriousness. "And two other little things: I'm going to send you a list of all the telephone numbers. Those of everybody involved. And for later I'll have something to eat sent up to your room. Unfortunately our dinner will have to be canceled."

It had been a long time now since the picnic in the car. All of a sudden Dupin realized he was hungry. And above all, he urgently needed more caffeine. In the last few days—above all because of the little sleep he'd had while they were moving—he had drunk more coffee than normal, and he was probably now used to a higher dose. Even if Claire found theories like that laughable. Ever since he had recently read an article about a new, groundbreaking scientific study by an international research team, Dupin had no longer seen any need to restrain himself. They had analyzed the death rates of more than half a million people from ten European countries over sixteen years. Dupin had committed the information to memory in order to pass it on correctly to Claire and his own overly strict general practitioner, Docteur Garreg. In "men with high coffee consumption"—that meant: "more than 580 ml per day" (and he drank more than that)—the likelihood of dying within the observation period was a remarkable 12 percent lower than in those who didn't drink coffee. And also clearly better than "in men who drank low or medium quantities of coffee." At the same time coffee had a substantial "positive effect," the study claimed: for example, a "significantly better liver profile" or a "higher immunity level." Sometimes, it seemed to Dupin, science could produce simply wonderful results.

"Thanks, Nolwenn, talk later."

Dupin pressed the red button on the phone and climbed out.

He walked across the gravel path toward the manor. A lot had happened since he was last there.

The wood was now throwing strange long shadows over the meadows and fields. No shadows of individual trees, just a huge strange great something. A dark mass. Involuntarily, Dupin looked up at the sky, as if to be sure that on this August evening there was still a lot of light in the sky. An enormous amount. It would be light for a long time yet. But with every step he took toward the wood the warmth of the summer day faded. Just like earlier that afternoon, a strange feeling came over him. A sort of shudder.

Two gendarmes were standing by the stone steps that led to the house entrance as Dupin came around the corner into the yard. He greeted them with a snappy, but friendly, gesture.

"*Bonsoir,* Monsieur le Commissaire."

"What are you looking for?" The second sounded as rude as the first had sounded respectful.

"I am here to see Madame Cadiou," Dupin growled grumpily.

He made his way between them and was about to ring the bell.

"Not there," the cheeky one said.

"What does that mean?"

"She left about half an hour ago."

"I'm sorry?"

"She—"

"Where was she headed?" Dupin stopped the senseless repetition. The tone of the question showed things were clearly getting unpleasant.

The other policeman mediated.

"To Paimpont . . . her office."

"Now? After all that's happened today? And you let her go?"

"Why not?"

"Because she . . ." Dupin thought it over. Of course there was no reason to prevent her from leaving. "Because she may have been in an unstable condition."

"She seemed very fit and able."

The conversation was meaningless. Dupin turned around on the spot.

After two or three meters he stopped and brusquely turned back to the two policemen.

"Where exactly is Madame Cadiou's office?"

* * *

The two policemen had recommended he leave the car at the parking lot by the end of Rue du Général de Gaulle, right next to the abbey, and continue from there on foot. Rather reluctantly he followed their advice. An old lady who had just parked in front of him gave him a deeply worried look as soon as she saw the battered side of his Citroën. The abbey and nearby buildings—surrounded by neatly laid out gardens and extensive lawns—were much grander and more imposing than Dupin had expected.

The effect was remarkable: you drove through a lonely wild forest, and then turned to the right along the bank of a peculiarly deep green lake and almost as quickly came across the artistically arranged parking lot with the imposing abbey at the end.

A large cross-shaped church was attached to the abbey on the long side, with a U-shaped, equally grand extension behind it. The building had unusually pointed slate roofs and was made of red stone, lighter and more firmly joined than any other Dupin had seen to date. Everything exuded a wholly different atmosphere, had a completely different charisma from that which radiated from Comper Castle, if no less extraordinary. A bright color scheme. Buildings and surroundings in top condition, nothing that gave the impression of a ruin. The effect was crazy: the size and splendor contrasted with the wildness of the wood and the minuteness of the village. If this was the effect on a modern visitor, what must it have been like a few hundred years ago for someone making their way arduously through the gloomy wood in a coach or on foot? It must have been a vision. A brilliant island of the highest civilization, obviously a fortress of God in the midst of the dark heathen forest.

Dupin wandered around at a loss. It turned out there were two Rues du Général de Gaulle running parallel, or, to put it another way: the Rue du Général de Gaulle ran in a large U shape. The building in which Madame Cadiou's office was located was not by the parking lot, but on the village main street. Here too everything had been lovingly restored, with a pretty row of terraced houses from the Middle Ages running through. And of course there was no lack of suitable stores. Au Pays de Merlin, La Maison du Graal, Boutique Féerique, Boutique Magique . . .

Not far from this end of the Rue du Général de Gaulle lay the Relais de Brocéliande, the hotel where the scholars were staying.

"The house directly next to Le Brécilien" was where Madame Cadiou's office was located. Dupin had already noticed Le Brécilien: it was a traditional café that looked wonderful. Dupin assumed it had to be the most important place in the village, the locals' café and not just that of the tourists, who would be here in large numbers in season. It was a café and bar all in one, the typical combination he loved so much and which existed only in France. Places to spend the whole day, from early morning to night. It had a simple, honest, classless charm with its red-and-white-striped awning and bright red geraniums in large boxes on the windowsills: everyone came to drink their wine here, from the painter to the lord mayor.

Madame Cadiou's sign was smaller and less conspicuous than that of the manor: *Le Parc de l'Imagination Illimitée.*"

Dupin rang the bell. There was a momentary pause.

"Hello?"

He recognized Madame Cadiou's voice despite the poor quality of the speaker.

"Commissaire Dupin here."

Silence.

"I'd like to ask you a few questions. It won't take long."

He heard the hum of the door being opened.

Dupin walked into a narrow, dark hallway, which led to a narrow, dimly lit staircase. The air was stuffy and stale.

"Up here."

A few seconds later Dupin was upstairs. He walked through an open white door and found himself unexpectedly in a sort of modern loft with a long, bright, high-ceilinged roof. The light was blinding. On the street side there were two small windows, and toward the rear a whole window front at least ten meters wide that gave a spectacular view over the abbey, the parking lot, and the lake.

"It's pretty, isn't it?"

Madame Cadiou had spoken softly, with a broken voice. Dupin found it hard to understand her. She was standing in front of the panoramic view, her gaze lost in some unknown. She was wearing the same suit as she had in the afternoon.

"Yes, very." Dupin had stopped just in front of the window, right next to Madame Cadiou. Soft, mild sunlight fell through the glass onto his face. Light that marked the end of summer. Evening light, falling on this whole atmospheric world. Almost forgiving, maybe a little melancholy.

Dupin looked around. The room was sparsely furnished: a large desk, a white tabletop on a stainless steel frame, with a smart, large computer sitting on it, and a chair behind it. Papers and several files lay on the desk. There was no shelf, no other equipment anywhere in the room. At the other end of the window front there was a little round white table with three chairs. A light-colored, elegant wooden floor. There was a small door to the right near the entrance door; a restroom, Dupin supposed. Maybe a small kitchen too.

The wall between the narrow windows on the street side and the wall at the end of the room were wide and covered with drawings and sketches. Dupin walked across to them. Madame Cadiou remained immobile.

The drawings and sketches, Dupin realized as he drew closer, were outlines for the planned attractions of the park, laid out with a clever graphic program. Their names were written at the top in large capital letters: SIÈGE DE MERLIN. FONTAINE DE BARENTON. LE CHEVA-LIER NOIR. LAC DE VIVIANE. Madame Cadiou didn't seem to pay attention to Dupin's brief inspection.

"How are you doing, Madame Cadiou?"

Madame Cadiou turned around slowly and looked at Dupin directly for the first time. Dupin noticed a few strands of gray amidst her dark hair.

"I'm getting over it, thanks."

Dupin found that hard to imagine.

"I'm okay, really." She seemed to have read Dupin's mind.

"It must be a nightmare." Dupin remained standing in front of her, staring her right in the eye.

"Yes, it is," she answered after a while. "That's exactly what it is: a nightmare. It's something I never remotely imagined." Just like that afternoon, everything she said was uttered without any visible emotion.

"Excuse me, Madame Cadiou, if I pester you with further questions in a situation like this. But you are . . ." Dupin hesitated. ". . . an extremely important source of information for me. Perhaps the most important."

"I think it'll be all right."

"Good." Dupin's tone of voice had changed seamlessly. "Why have you come here? To the office? Was there something urgent that needed seeing to?"

"I couldn't stand being in the house anymore. I kept thinking he was still there, upstairs in his office. Or he would shortly be on the way home from work."

Her voice was flat, but now he noticed an expression of horror in her demeanor.

"You shouldn't be alone at a time like this. Do you have family? Friends?"

"I want to be on my own."

"I understand." He moved away again, took a few steps along the bay window, then turned around and came back.

"This afternoon, you said"—he lowered his voice—"'I'm going to find his killer.' What did you mean by that? Do you have a serious suspicion?" He hadn't been able to get it out of his head.

For a fraction of a second there was a look of surprise on her face. She seemed completely amazed that Dupin had heard her say that. Either she had been too seriously shocked . . . or she was pretending to be surprised. In which case she was doing it well.

Almost immediately, however, she pulled herself together again.

"No . . . I wasn't being myself. I'm still not. I don't know what I said. I hardly remember the afternoon. Everything is a blur." She hadn't seemed that confused. But sometimes that meant nothing. A first impression could be totally misleading.

"You spent a lot of time here in this room recently, I assume."

Dupin was beginning to sketch out possibilities.

This time Madame Cadiou followed his lead.

"Hours and hours."

"So you haven't seen your husband often recently?"

She clearly found the answer difficult.

"No."

"The week after next is the date for the decisive vote on the project. What do you think, will you get agreement?"

She answered without hesitating. "Yes."

"I've heard there's large-scale opposition to the project."

"There's very little objection. And even Guivorch's initiative won't alter that. We have politics on our—"

"Guivorch? Auffrai Guivorch? The deputy director of the Centre?"

"Yes, last week he was elected head of the citizens' initiative against the park." Madame Cadiou announced this without any sign of getting worked up, but with an increasingly firm voice. "Tomorrow evening there's going to be a demonstration here in Paimpont, connected to a folk festival. He's going to make a speech."

"Your husband's deputy is leading the opposition to your park project? A project which your husband had spoken in favor of, however discreetly, if I understand correctly?"

Dupin was naturally used to the fact that, during a murder investigation, some people didn't tell him everything, that they kept certain things to themselves. But in this case, the situation was already extreme. Nobody told him anything. Even the most important things he only came across by chance, as an afterthought, if at all. And everybody was somehow connected to everybody else in some complicated way. A way that Dupin found disagreeable.

Madame Cadiou remained silent.

"What about the other scholars? Is there somebody else on the opposition side?"

Why had Guivorch not told him this? Of course, he hadn't asked specifically about it, but they had talked about the park and the question of whether anyone from the group was in any way involved.

"No."

"Did anyone actually involve themselves with the park project?"

"Paul Picard had put in an academic opinion, an evaluation from his point of view."

"What? Did the others know about this?"

"No."

That at least explained why she hadn't told him.

"Are you aware of who is taking part in the current meeting in the Centre?"

"The usual gang." It didn't sound contemptuous.

Dupin had taken out his temporary notebook.

"So Paul Picard submitted an academic opinion for you in which he was in favor of the park?"

"Precisely."

"Why him?"

"He's a very renowned scholar. And I've known him for several years. He is a friend of my husband's." Madame Cadiou had switched to a professional business tone.

"Was he also a friend of yours?"

"Up to a point, I think."

"Did Monsieur Picard receive a payment?"

"But of course."

"How much was it?"

"Ten thousand euros."

Quite a lot, Dupin thought.

"Will it be important for the result, do you think?"

"Obviously it'll play a role. Along with other important facts."

"Are there other opinions being submitted?"

"Just Picard's."

"What does it say?"

"It confirms the high level of professional content in the project, its closeness to the original material, the excellence of the teaching and instruction. At present we're thinking of eight stages."

"And Picard spoke out in favor of the park without reservations?"

"He confirmed how excellently the enterprise had been thought through and planned."

"When did he write it?"

"We received it from him at the beginning of January."

"Who is 'we'?"

"My two colleagues and I."

"And when did you submit it?"

"Along with all the other documents, at the beginning of February."

"Are the public aware of it? The fact that Professor Picard spoke out in favor of the project?"

"The document containing his opinion might have been mentioned in the local press, in the context of a bigger article. But I don't think his name would have been mentioned. People here don't know him. In any case it wasn't a matter of interest."

"It might well have been." Dupin made a note with an exclamation mark. "What is a fact," he added almost as an aside, "is that Paul Picard has been murdered."

There was a long silence. Dupin looked at the draft image of the white Lady of the Lake.

"I assume there's a business plan for your project. According to your vision, what would the extent of this enterprise ultimately be? What sort of return are you anticipating, in the best of cases?"

"Twenty million," she said, totally calmly, "with a profit of three million a year, of which the local community would get one million."

"And the other two million?"

"One point three million would go to the upkeep and protection of the forest, a lot more money than now."

"And the rest?"

"Around seven hundred thousand euros would go to my firm."

"Which belongs one hundred percent to you?"

"Yes. The community doesn't want to take the risk of becoming owner-operators."

"So at the end, how much money would you walk away with?"

Dupin did not make an effort to put it more elegantly.

"I would have to employ more staff." She remained businesslike; it didn't seem she had a problem talking about money. "So all in all, somewhere between three hundred and four hundred thousand."

That was a substantial sum.

Dupin had immersed himself in the plans for the project. If he had understood correctly, they intended to build a glass pathway from Lake Comper which would in part go over the water to lead into a small glass room anchored several meters deep in the lake, so that visitors would be in the midst of the water. Undoubtedly very impressive. Dupin found himself wondering what the fairy would say about that. And it was clear what opinion Inwynn the storyteller would have. Dupin realized that he was considering Inwynn and Philippe Goazou to be two different people. Strange.

Eventually Dupin moved away from the draft designs; not,

however, without reading the written piece of paper attached to the edge: *Attention: Arthur's sword Excalibur also came out of the lake!*

"What did your husband really think about the project?" The commissaire turned back toward Madame Cadiou and kept his eyes on her.

"The idea had pleased him from the beginning. He had spoken in favor of it, occasionally also in his role as director of the Centre, although seldom and with reservations. We had agreed on that."

"Was he in any way criticized by anyone for the fact that he had spoken out, however reservedly, in favor of the park?"

"Not openly. But a few people are sure to have done so. Guivorch initially demanded that my husband stay neutral."

Guivorch had said nothing about that either. Dupin was going to need to talk to him again urgently, on his own, in detail.

"Did the pair of them argue over that? Do you know of any quarrels?"

"No, they got on well."

This was a sentence murder case investigators heard frequently, and in the end it often turned out to be the opposite of the truth.

"Was there anything more than that?"

"They weren't friends as such, but they had a friendly professional relationship."

"What about the late Gustave Laurent, who died back in May? Did he have anything to do with the park project?"

"No."

It was still pure speculation that Laurent's death too had been murder. But if it were the case, and the park project were to turn up as a motive—in whatever aspect—then that would constitute a link to Gustave Laurent.

"No official opinion, no point of view. Nothing?"

"No."

"Think, Madame Cadiou. Was Paul Picard's name mentioned in the reports on the application?"

"I really can't say."

A job for Nolwenn.

"And none of the other scholars knew about his written opinion?"

Another question he had asked before.

"I don't think so. No."

"How . . ."

Gentle synthesizer music started up from the desk, where Dupin spotted a phone.

Madame Cadiou had moved off. "Excuse me." She looked at the display. "I thought as much. My sister. She lives in Montreal. I left a message for her. I'd like to take the call."

"Of course."

Dupin hadn't asked all his questions yet.

"I'll be back . . ." He would give her some time. ". . . in about twenty minutes."

He hadn't felt particularly sympathetic. Without doubt it was a disturbing conversation for Madame Cadiou, but it was also in Madame Cadiou's interest that the investigations proceeded at pace.

Madame Cadiou nodded, picked up the receiver, and turned to face the large window front.

Dupin left the office.

He knew immediately what to do with the time.

* * *

The commissaire had sat down at the outermost table with a view of the beautiful little square in front of the abbey. Le Brécilien was perfectly laid out. Three tables farther along sat a quietly amicable couple and next to them two girls whose jovial laughter set the atmosphere for the entire street. Right at the far end of the row of tables on the narrow sidewalk was an old man with disheveled white hair, just sitting there seemingly comfortably lost in his thoughts. There was also a pleasant-looking bar opposite: La Terrasse de l'Abbaye.

Between the bar and the far end of the abbey was a completely unexpected view across the lake which had turned into a glistening steely blue surface underneath an ethereal blue sky. Magic. The lake was perfectly still, but the sun still reached it. It looked more like an abstraction than a natural piece of water. Here and there were glimmers of pink, as if added by a painter. Thick forest hugged the shore, casting pitch-black shadows onto the surface. It seemed as if the wood around the edges of the lake came together into a dark, prepossessing fortress, its boundaries become walls.

Dupin turned his glance away. It really was a gentle, perfect late-summer evening. The light in the streets had turned milky; it nestled generously into the arms of the world, the houses, the red stone, like a plea for quiet and peace here in this unique village in the middle of the wood.

"*Voilà*, monsieur!"

A pleasant woman with short hair set a glass down on his table, with a friendly smile. "Your Sancerre!"

Dupin looked at the misting glass. "I didn't order any wine, I—"

"Oh," she laughed and took the glass back, "in that case it was for Yannbol. Excuse me, I must have got the order—"

Dupin couldn't bring himself to let it go. "Feel free to leave it. I'll be happy to have it!" The temptation was too great.

"Of course, monsieur!" For a moment she had seemed surprised but now the world was back in order again.

She put the glass down in front of him again. Sometimes things just turned out to be good luck by accident.

"And a small *café*, please."

Then he would be clearly above the minimum quota needed today, according to the study, for him to remain healthy.

"Straightaway. And maybe a sandwich *au beurre salé*? We still have locally produced butter. Delicious!"

"No, thanks."

The charming waitress turned around and vanished.

Dupin leaned back and took a first sip of the wine.

A delightfully cool white wine on a mild summer's evening was a thing of wonder. That typical, lightly mineral taste, with a note of apricot.

Unfortunately reality didn't match the wine. Dupin reached for his phone. Two bars. Even so.

It took a little while before the deputy director answered.

"Yes?"

"Commissaire Georges Dupin here. I need to have a meeting with you, Monsieur Guivorch."

He responded immediately. "The invitation is open. I already made the offer. Come and see me. Anytime you like."

"You kept some things from me."

"Such as?" Guivorch didn't seem particularly surprised, nor embarrassed; more mischievous, in fact.

"Where are you at the moment?"

"In the car. Your colleagues going through alibis took a long time. But I'm almost home and can meet you there. Do you have something to write with?"

He had to have a very quiet car; Dupin couldn't hear the engine.

"Yes."

"Best to put the village of Painfaut into your GPS, and when you get there Route de l'Île aux Pies. There are three jetties. The last one."

Dupin had written it all down. Once again he had forgotten about the houseboat. He didn't like boats. But he calmed himself down, telling himself it was just a river. A little river, probably. And the boat tethered firmly to the bank.

"See you shortly, Monsieur Guivorch."

Dupin hung up.

"Here you go."

Dupin started involuntarily. He hadn't seen the waitress coming. All of a sudden there she was standing next to him.

She carefully put the cup down next to the empty wineglass.

"One more?" She blinked seductively.

"Thanks, but no . . ." But he couldn't do it. "Oh well, yes, it *was* only a small glass."

It was all taxing enough.

"It is the end of the day, after all! Time to relax," she said cheerfully, and was off again.

Dupin downed the hot *café* in little sips.

It was time to be systematic.

He opened the manual at the penultimate page, where it said "Remarks" in tiny letters at the top of the empty page, took out Riwal's list of pertinent names, drew two triangles in the middle, and wrote down the names of the deceased. At the edge he drew a third triangle, but in brackets, then little ovals round the triangles. The suspects—to date—in groups. Noiret and Terrier, the married couple, she a long time ago having been married to one of the victims; Bothorel next to Denvel, stepmother and stepson; Guivorch on his own; Madame

Cadiou and Inwynn, the storyteller, equally so. Was the name of the killer already on the page?

Dupin made a second diagram of the excavations and who was involved with which; leaving a third, the park, to follow.

His phone interrupted him.

Riwal.

"Boss. It's taken a long time, but—"

"I've already heard. How are the alibis?"

"All of them woolly. Mostly unverifiable. Can't be ruled out that the person concerned couldn't have been at the scene of the crime at the moment in question. That's true for Inwynn too. I've just taken down the report from our two colleagues."

Dupin sighed deeply. Couldn't anything be simple?

"I'm going through it all quickly."

"Of course."

"I've had the list photographed. I'll send it to you and Nolwenn when I've finished."

An excellent idea; that meant Dupin wouldn't have to copy it all by hand.

"So: Bastien Terrier arrived yesterday evening. From Lyon, by TGV, to Rennes. Arrived here at 7:22 by taxi. Reserved table in the hotel with his wife, eight fifteen. After dinner Madame Noiret and he retired to bed. Worked on an 'important task' until one A.M., he maintains. Didn't see Picard or any of his other colleagues. Same goes for all the others we asked. They seemed to avoid one another when possible. This morning, breakfast at eight. From nine onward back in the room, working continuously until one thirty P.M. Lunch in the room to save time. Then drove to the castle with his wife."

"No little walk in the meantime, nothing at all?"

"Nothing. His wife, Madame Noiret, turned up around six P.M.

Came by car from Paris. A string of telephone calls before dinner. Breakfast this morning at quarter past nine until ten, or so she says. Then a walk, round the Étang de Paimpont. Exhausted after a lot of work in the past few weeks. She says she saw nobody."

"Wonderful: Terrier alone in the hotel. Noiret on a walk alone."

Even closer examination would at most give a vague reconstruction of events.

"Marc Denvel arrived in Rennes at ten forty-five, from Oxford. Taxi gets to hotel just before midnight. Bed. This morning seven thirty breakfast, then writing in his room until lunch at one, in the hotel restaurant."

Of course. Writing, publishing, for scholars the chief element in their lives. The thought of spending life glued to a keyboard horrified Dupin.

"Madame Bothorel at first refused to say anything. Only when we told her we would keep everyone there until we had her alibi, did she concede."

Dupin could imagine that easily enough.

"She has a driver who brought her from Paris. She got to the hotel about seven o'clock. Dinner in the hotel, she couldn't recall from when until when. This morning she went to Vannes. According to her statement, she went shopping, then had lunch in La Gourmandière, didn't come back until two. No receipts for anything. Not so far at least."

"Is the man who drove her here her regular driver?"

"Yes, has been for thirty years."

Madame Bothorel reminded Dupin of his mother: the Parisian *grande bourgeoisie.* With various domestic staff. And a driver. Above all, with that inborn arrogance and condescension toward everything and everyone—even in Paris—who didn't belong to "her circle." Sometimes clichés were just a poor copy of reality. Or to put it otherwise, reality was more of a cliché than the cliché itself.

As for the driver, he was a driver of the old school and would say whatever he had to in the service of his matriarchal employer.

"Guivorch spent this morning on his boat. Breakfasted, then worked until one P.M., then drove to the castle. He wanted to be there before the others, to prepare a few things, documents for the conference. Along with Cadiou, who didn't turn up.

"Philippe Goazou, alias Inwynn, was at home with his wife the whole morning, until around two P.M. He lives in Tréhorenteuc. According to him he was at the well or nearby from around two thirty P.M. To prepare himself."

"And Picard? What do we know to date about his whereabouts?"

"Colonel Aballain asked about him in the Relais. Picard was at the hotel from about eight in the evening. Came by train. Drank a *grand crème* this morning, about eight A.M. At precisely what time he turned up at the well, nobody can say."

Unfortunately none of that helped either.

"We're now checking what we can. Kadeg and I are going straight to the hotel in Paimpont. After taking a quick look in Monsieur Cadiou's office first."

"Do that. I'll talk with Guivorch now."

"One thing I forgot, boss. Cadiou had a computer in his office too. Connected to the Centre network. Our colleagues from the crime scene team took it away with them to give to the IT experts in Rennes. Apart from a few irrelevant documents, invitations, official letters and such, they found nothing. He apparently didn't use it much."

"No references to Cadiou's research material? What he was working on at present?"

"No. On the other hand, the laptops of Cadiou and Picard weren't so easy to crack. That might take a while."

"Get our colleagues to hurry up. Anything else, Riwal?"

Yet again Dupin had missed seeing the waitress coming. Almost immediately the second glass of Sancerre was sitting in front of him. The same size as the first. But fuller. Right to the brim.

"No, that's it."

Dupin put his phone down and lifted the glass to his mouth.

This Sancerre was really spectacular. Unfortunately he had to go back to Madame Cadiou. He would really have liked to stay here.

He pulled himself together and got to his feet.

In a few moments he was at the bar with his wallet in his hand.

"You're not from round about here."

It wasn't a question. But nor was it meant to be unfriendly. The waitress was busy at the beer taps. *Lancelot*, the tap read. Obviously. What other beer would they drink here?

"No." Dupin hesitated. "I'm here on an excursion." He hesitated again. "With a few friends."

"Don't be frightened, but there's police everywhere in the wood at the moment. There've been two murders."

Dupin raised his eyebrows. "What's it all about, do you know?"

"The two victims were scholars. It's all to do with King Arthur, it seems they all belong to a society. A sort of secret society, people say. Who knows . . ." She paused dramatically, tending to an artistic foam head on the next Lancelot. ". . . anything's possible. You can imagine anything here in the wood."

"Such as?"

"There are no boundaries to your imagination around here."

"What do you think about this King Arthur park project?"

"Awful, but it's going to happen."

"Why are you against it?"

"We have enough visitors as it is. The places in the wood ought to keep their original magic, not become some sort of amusement park."

A similar attitude as that of the storyteller, just put in a more worldly, down-to-earth way.

"Madame Cadiou has her office close by here."

All of a sudden the server looked at Dupin with a completely different look on her face.

"Then . . . then it is you! I was right. My husband said I was imagining things."

"Excuse me?"

"You're this special investigator! It's on the internet, that you're leading the investigation. But I wasn't certain. You look very different in your photo online."

Charming. But it was to be expected.

"A lot younger somehow." A cheeky smile; she hadn't meant it to be denigrating. "And you're from Paris, like all these scholars." That, on the other hand, sounded more accusing.

Dupin's eyes had moved to the postcards and brochures in a stand on the bar.

"Weren't you on TV?"

"What?"

"TV Rennes 35. We saw you fleeing from the journalists. At the Château de Comper. You swore at them loudly, one journalist said."

The whole of Brittany would have seen it.

"Do you have a suspect?"

"No," he said, as decisively as he could. "Please excuse me, Madame Cadiou is waiting for me." Dupin turned to leave.

The waitress raised her eyebrows meaningfully. "I understand.

The iron lady. She's going to push the project through. She gets everything through."

"Is she a customer of yours?"

"No, she always goes across the road." Dupin assumed she meant the bar he had seen earlier. "But that's got nothing to do with it."

"I understand. If I understand your words properly, she's very . . . self-confident."

"Exactly! Yes. She knows what she wants. And she gets it."

Her serious expression suddenly exploded into laughter.

"But that's not necessarily something bad. I don't want you to think I consider her the murderer."

"Don't worry there. And the new leader of the citizens' initiative against the park. Do you know him?"

"Guivorch. Of course. A professor but still one of us, a Breton through and through."

Dupin glanced at his watch. "I'm afraid I have to go! Many thanks for everything, madame."

"Glad to be of service. And take this with you. It might be of use to you!" She extracted two thin brochures from the stand: *Brocéliande: Little Stories from the Wood* and *The Grail: Myth or Reality.*

"There's a map in the brochure too. Of the whole wood."

"Thanks." That was definitely something he would need.

"If you need more information—or a Sancerre—please drop in."

"I will."

Dupin had put the brochures in his jeans pocket along with his provisional notebook and was on his way to the door when it occurred to him: this bar would be a perfect location for their headquarters. In every way.

* * *

Madame Cadiou had left the door open and was sitting at her desk. She raised her head only briefly when Dupin entered the room.

She seemed unchanged. The emotionally charged phone call she'd had to take had left no visible traces.

Dupin had to concentrate, be precise about the remaining points he had to address. He had had only two glasses of wine, but on an empty stomach.

"Tell me about the friendship between Picard and your husband. Did they know each other from student days, like Laurent and your husband?"

Too many questions at once, Dupin realized.

"No, as far as I know they got to know each other at a conference. A long time ago, maybe twenty years. In those days they occasionally went on trips together."

She put a strange emphasis on the word "trips."

"Was it a personal friendship, or a scholarly, business one?"

His formulation was clumsy. "I mean, did they chiefly share their scientific passion?" Probably a nonsensical question. Dupin walked up and down in front of the desk. He wasn't eager to sit down. And Madame Cadiou hadn't asked him to.

"Hard to say. Everything in my husband's life was tied to his work one way or the other. It was an obsession, always had been. His work was everything to him. He was never away from it." Her commentary on his life was free from judgment, she was just trying to describe it.

"I don't think he had any friendships outside his scholarly work. His work was the center of everything. Back then, Paul"—she had switched to first names—"would come to visit us from time to time."

"How did this friendship evolve? I've heard they weren't free from occasional rivalries."

The comment didn't seem to jar her.

"I know nothing about that."

"Do you know of a position both were vying for? Or a project that both of them wanted to be in charge of?"

"No. Fabien never mentioned any tension."

They probably wouldn't be able to check that out.

"When did Paul Picard last stop by your place?"

"In March, because of the excavation at the Fontaine de Barenton. Because of what they found in the x-ray. We spent the evening here together. I cooked. Prior to that it had been a long time since he was here."

"Did he spend the night here?"

"No. He stayed in the Relais de Brocéliande. As always."

"Were you with them for the conversation all evening?"

"No. After dinner I left the two of them on their own."

"And up until then, what did they talk about?"

"Everything. For example, we talked about the Côte d'Azur. Paul loved the south. He went down there often. It was a harmonious evening."

"Did you discuss private matters as well?"

"Paul didn't talk about himself a lot. But things were going well for him, I thought."

"Did you also see Paul Picard on his own? At that meeting back in March, or some other time?"

"No."

"Did you have any sort of contact with him? By email, letters? Telephone?"

"No. Just about his academic evaluation."

"Via email?"

"No, I called him on the phone. And explained everything to him."

Dupin took out the car manual and made notes.

"Very well. There was competition between your husband and Guivorch about the role of director of the Centre. Was Paul Picard also involved?"

"Paul briefly thought of trying for it, but let it go at the last minute. That's all I know."

So Nolwenn had a good tip here too.

"And how do you know that?"

"My husband told me. Paul and he had talked about it frequently."

"Did he not want to challenge your husband?"

"I don't know about that."

Who, if anyone, could still tell him anything about that?

"Do you know if Paul Picard had a girlfriend or any sort of relationship?"

"It was a long time after the divorce before he had any relationship. And that didn't last long. After that he was on his own, but as I said, he didn't mention it much."

"Do you know of other friends?"

"No. I think he was like my husband, a scholar through and through. That was what defined his life."

"Let's go back to the director job. When was the application deadline?"

"At the end of February last year. The process was very meticulous. The decision was made in August, and the winner took office on the first of November."

Dupin would have to draw up a calendar of the last two years and set out everything in chronological order.

"What about Laurent?" Another board member of the King Arthur society, another figure in the game, however he met his end. "Did he also apply for the position in the Centre? Or at least consider it?"

"I don't think so. He has an important professorship. In Poitiers."

Dupin opened another page in his "notebook." He had gotten through the comprehensive chapter entitled "Get to Know Your Vehicle," which was followed by "Driving," "Comfort Controls," "Maintenance," "Tips and Suggestions," "Technical Details," and "List of Keywords," but there was still sufficient space. Right now he was on "Dashboard Displays," featuring "control lights": symbols that Dupin had never noticed as well as those he had apparently permanently misunderstood. For example, a red cross strangely located between brackets and with an exclamation mark, which was apparently a warning about the "brake fluid level." Dupin had always thought it meant the hand brake wasn't on properly or hadn't been released fully.

"Would you also consider Laurent as having been a friend of your husband?"

"They might have been friends once upon a time. They were connected through the years they had spent together at college." Madame Cadiou suddenly appeared thoughtful. "But then at some stage things went wrong between them. Something happened, but I don't know what. My husband thought Laurent had become terribly arrogant. Overconfident. He used to curse when an academic magazine appeared and there was an article by Gustave in it."

"Over something in particular?"

"I don't think so."

"So the only real competition was between your husband and Guivorch. He had also applied officially for the job."

"Things like that happen. They were able to live with it, I believe. My husband never suggested it was the cause of any unpleasantness."

"Tell me about your husband's trip to see Gustave Laurent in

May." Dupin had found the place in the manual. "It had to do with further excavations around the stone with the supposed 'Arthur' name on it. Why did he attend that?"

"He told me they needed his expertise. That's all I know."

And, a seriously important point here: "And in the last few weeks, your husband had gone into retreat, to Corsica. Why?"

"We have a house there. Near Sartène. In the south. He was there for a little over three weeks. A writing retreat. That was something he used to—" She broke off, suddenly appearing unbelievably exhausted. She continued speaking haltingly: ". . . do regularly. He was working on an article. Or maybe it was his book. I . . ." another pause, ". . . really can't say."

"And what was the subject of the article?"

"I think it was about the stone you mentioned. I don't know more than that."

Dupin leafed through his Citroën manual again.

"In Cadbury Castle?"

"Yes. Your colleagues took Fabien's laptop this afternoon. I assume they'll find something in that."

A good lead. He would ask Riwal or Nolwenn again. It couldn't be that complicated.

"I assume you don't know your husband's passwords. Is that correct?"

"No, I don't. He was always changing them," Madame Cadiou said. For a moment, she seemed irritated.

"And the book he was supposedly working on in Corsica. What was that about?"

"He's been struggling with it for two years, and still hasn't got very far. It's to do with a supposed prequel to *Arthur*." Madame Cadiou seemed to have pulled herself together again.

"Did his colleagues know about these, the book and the article?"

"Definitely not. Up until publication my husband kept all his research as secret as possible. He was always like that. As long as I've known him. They're all like that. Every one of them. Afraid that someone else would steal one of their ideas."

"What about Picard? Did he know of the book?"

"I can't say. Probably not."

"Were there any arguments between your husband and the rest of the board?"

"No, not that I know of."

"How about allegations of plagiarism? Did he ever raise them against anyone of the group?"

"Terrier!" she replied straightaway. "It's a few years back, and I have no idea precisely what it was about. He eventually let it go."

"You don't know anything concrete?"

She reflected on the matter, took her time.

"No. I'm afraid not."

"Do you think your husband might have been rightfully upset?"

"I really shouldn't say anything about that. I really can't judge."

Madame Cadiou looked Dupin in the eye. "They all clearly felt the same, not just my husband. Academia is a peculiar world. It's hard to describe."

That was Dupin's view too.

"Was he himself ever accused of plagiarism? In particular by somebody in the group?"

"No. At least he never mentioned it to me. But Picard was the only one of the group I was in touch with, who could have said something to me."

"You never spoke to Monsieur Guivorch? Your husband's deputy?"

"As I said, my husband's relationship to him was rather distant." It sounded somewhat different from how it had earlier, Dupin thought.

"My husband only had the job since November. Prior to that I had never knowingly seen Monsieur Guivorch before, and after that only two or three times at an exhibition organized by the Centre. We said hello politely."

"To return to possible problems with other members of the board—how about Monsieur Denvel? Or the two ladies, Madame Bothorel or Madame Noiret?"

"Nothing that I know of."

"Do you think your husband would have told you of anything like that?"

She brushed her hair behind her ears. "He . . ." She hesitated. ". . . never spoke much of anything personal, never revealed anything. He was a rather reclusive type. Always had been."

Dupin wondered if it was true.

"Did you love him?"

Dupin hadn't intended to be so direct. But at that moment, the question was somehow hanging in the air.

Madame Cadiou opened her eyes wide. "Yes. I did. I loved him."

"How long had you known each other?"

"Nine years." She stopped abruptly. But her voice remained firm: "I was thirty-two. We were married for eight years."

"How did you meet?"

She paused for a moment again. "My husband was born in Paris. His family, on his mother's side, came from Rennes, which is where I am from too. Our families knew one another. We got to know each other when his mother was still alive. Over dinner, to which the Cadious were invited."

That was life. Chance and circumstance.

"You were living in Rennes?"

"Yes. But Fabien was in Paris. Initially we came and went between Rennes and Paris. The house here has belonged to my family for almost two hundred years. Fabien loved it. He was the one who at some stage decided we should move here. Long before he worked at the Centre."

"What was your husband's profession?"

"He didn't have a steady job. Every now and then he got teaching jobs, guest professorships, most recently—until the end of the year before last—in Poitiers."

"Where Gustave Laurent was the chair."

It all went together seamlessly. One way or another they were all connected. Everyone with everyone else, everything with everything.

"My husband was a student of literature. A different faculty. That had nothing to do with him."

"But they would have seen each other."

"Not often, I imagine. My husband was only there for a year, and only two days a week. He lived in a hotel."

"And prior to being a guest professor in Poitiers?"

"He was working on a book. Which he continued during his time in Poitiers."

"What was that about?"

"It was published at the beginning of last year. *King Arthur—Myth and Reality.*"

"An academic book?"

"For the public at large. It actually became a minor bestseller."

Dupin made more notes.

"Who made the decision as to who would get the directorship of the Centre?"

"A committee. A professor from Rennes, another from Brest. A representative of local politics, and someone from the Conseil Régional culture department. Plus the tourism chief from the *département* Ille-et-Vilaine. The Centre is much more than a research institution."

"But nobody from the board?"

"No."

"How did you get involved with the park project?"

"I studied tourism in Brest. And worked at the Bureau du Tourisme in Rennes. When I was there I got occupied with the Forêt de Brocéliande. And I realized how attractive development in the wood could be. And also that the community itself couldn't take it on, even if they were interested in the idea from the outset. So three years ago I set up the firm."

"This tourism representative from the committee, I assume you know him."

"Of course, Patrick Lombard. I know him well."

"Does he also have something to do with your park project?"

"Of course. He's my point person at the *département*."

Yet again, there were incidental overlaps. The man from the tourism branch, who was apparently a keen advocate of the park project, was one and the same as the man in charge of deciding who got the position that went to the husband of the woman driving the project. Blanche Cadiou nonetheless felt herself in no way obliged to add that the two things were in any way connected.

"And the other two? The politician and the culture representative. Did they also play such a direct role in bringing the project to life?"

"Not as decisive, but yes, of course."

"Don't you think . . ." It was almost hilarious that he had to pose the question. ". . . that these amalgamations of roles were decisive when it came to appointing the director?"

"To tell you the truth, no. Often in a situation like that, things can be disadvantageous for the candidate. The committee could have gone against Fabien out of fear of being considered biased in his favor."

It was true that it could be considered the other way around.

"I think," she concluded, "they had simply decided only to take the best qualifications into account. The best candidate. Nobody else had had such influence in the scholarly circle. My husband's book had moved tens of thousands."

"Why did Monsieur Guivorch not come into consideration?"

"You'll have to ask the committee that." She turned away and exhaled audibly.

That was enough. He couldn't put any more strain on her.

Dupin walked over to the window again. "I apologize again for having pestered you with so many questions after the murder of your husband. Including very personal questions." He gave her a probing look. "You've been a great help to the police."

Madame Cadiou said nothing.

"Just one more little thing. Where were you today between nine o'clock and one?"

"I was here in the office. Working on my presentation for next week. From around nine to . . ." She closed her eyes, lost her composure for a long moment. ". . . until I received the phone call."

"And you didn't leave this room even once?"

"I went for a coffee. Just before eleven. In the Terrasse de l'Abbaye. Opposite."

"For how long?"

"Maybe a quarter of an hour."

"And then you came straight back to the office?"

"Correct."

"Can your fellow workers bear witness to that?"

"They're in Le Mans at the moment. Looking at the firm that we've hired to build the attractions and install them. They're working on the final specifications, in preparation for next week's session."

"How was your morning at home? What time did you and your husband get up?"

"I got up around eight, I think . . ." She stumbled a bit. ". . . my husband got up earlier."

"Did you see each other?"

"Yes, briefly. In the kitchen. He had a *café*. I had made myself one too, and was in the bathroom. He went into his study," she took a deep breath, "and I called out 'See you this evening' as I left."

"Everything seemed perfectly normal to you?"

"That's our everyday life, always a bit hectic."

Dupin paused for a moment.

"In that case I'll finally take my leave of you for today, Madame Cadiou. Is there anything we can do for you? Should I send one of my colleagues to drive you home?"

Madame Cadiou closed her eyes briefly. Her answer was crisp and clear. "Thank you, but no. As I said, for the moment I'd simply like to be alone."

Dupin understood.

"You can call me at any time. You have my number. Don't think twice."

"Thank you, Monsieur le Commissaire."

One thing was noticeable. At no stage had Madame Cadiou inquired about how the investigation was going. She hadn't asked him a single question. He had never come across that before.

* * *

Dupin closed the car door.

He had driven down to the river. Guivorch had referred to three jetties and he was already at the first. Dupin stopped automatically. The landscape took his breath away.

In the last few years he'd seen a lot of Britannies; it was Nolwenn's favorite phrase: "There isn't *one* Brittany, there are many Britannies." And Dupin knew it was the truth. He had stood on the summits of the legendary Monts d'Arrée, one of the oldest mountain ranges in the world; roamed the roughest, wildest beaches, where waves that had traveled thousands of kilometers broke; mighty, rugged cliffs; the soft Mediterranean atmosphere of dreamy bays; idyllic Caribbean beaches in bright colors—coral sand from the days when Brittany lay on the equator—fantastic stone formations as if on Mars; enchanted valleys; fields and meadows devoid of people. The "inland Brittany," the "Argoat." And now the deep, dark, magic forest of la Brocéliande. But no landscape was like this: a complete river landscape in the *campagne*. A hauntingly beautiful river landscape for the summer. Scenery so perfect that it seemed to have been conjured up by a painter, one of the great impressionists of the late nineteenth century.

A thickly forested fairy-tale valley, with hills on both sides stretching down to the water. The Oust river, ample and wide, almost a long, extended lake. Meadows and luscious, burgeoning bushes along the riverbank with, opposite, a spectacular steep gray crag that broke through the softness, reminiscent of real mountains, topped by a solitary, wind-blasted pine tree.

The landscape exuded a deep harmony, a deep peace. The constant, ethereal chirping of the crickets was the only sound. Dupin loved this quintessence of a balmy summer evening, with the carefree song of birds and the occasional splash of water, probably a fish that had just snapped up a fly.

Not just the air but the entire scene was well tempered. The entire tempo of the world here was determined by the gently flowing river. The water gave out wonderful freshness, which Dupin knew from his childhood, seemingly endless holidays in the Jura, his father's home, the picture-book landscapes of the Doubs. A green aroma of plants and earth, not heavy and muddy but clear and light. You could smell the freshness of the water. River landscapes were a world of their own. There were many famous ones in France: the Loire, the Seine, the Marne—Dupin knew those well—but he hadn't expected to find any in Brittany. The river landscapes that he had since seen in Brittany were those in which river and sea came together—the Aven, the Belon, harmonies of land and sea which with the tide reached far inland.

The sun had just gone down. The heavens were awash with gentle, airy colors, like gossamer strips of fabric, pink, orange, violet, sometimes clear-edged, sometimes intertwining with one another. On the surface of the river they seemed almost ethereal, just a light shimmer, in pastel colors.

Dupin decided to drive here with Claire sometime, when this case was over. She would like it.

He jerked himself free from the spell.

The last jetty, Guivorch had said. Dupin walked along the path by the riverbank. Each jetty was home to a boat in perfect condition.

On the drive here he had spoken on the phone with Nolwenn. She had just reserved another suite in the hotel, suitable for a "special investigation on behalf of the minister of the interior"—and had brought in a computer. It was now the headquarters for the case; there had been more unconventional places used in the past. "A pretty view out over peaceful farming countryside, Monsieur le Commissaire," Nolwenn had informed him jovially. And indeed, Dupin had twice heard a rooster crow in the background. The question as to whether

Paul Picard's "written opinion" had been mentioned in any official report on the park project wouldn't leave Dupin's mind. Nolwenn's research into the matter had revealed nothing. But she would keep at it. Nolwenn herself had had some news: she said the call log between Cadiou and Picard was available. In general—with one exception—they were relatively nondescript. Picard had called Cadiou twice that morning. At 8:20 and at 10:00. One call lasted three minutes, the other for twelve. Maybe they had wanted to meet up? Apart from that Picard had also briefly called Cadiou the previous evening, at 9:32 P.M., just after he'd arrived. As he had in the weeks before, four times altogether. Perhaps it was about something scholarly. And they had exchanged text messages. Picard had had no other telephone contact to the members of the Arthurian committee, at least not from his cell phone, or his landline in Paris. In May, Fabien Cadiou had had several phone conversations with Gustave Laurent. Just prior to his excursion, three while he was there, and afterward—before Laurent's death—four. Cadiou had also called Guivorch a few times—all very briefly. That might have had to do with the Centre and its functions. Beyond that there had been no calls to anyone from the group, neither yesterday nor today.

Dupin had subsequently tried to get hold of Riwal, then Kadeg. In vain in both cases.

However, he did get through to Jean Odinot, who, unfortunately, had nothing new to report. Dupin had brought his friend up to date with a few short reports. Then he spotted the final boat at the jetties: thick greenery had barred his view of the river for a while. Right in front of him lay a modern cabin boat, on the deck of which a group of men was eating dinner. One had white hair, a captain's cap on his head and a glass of rosé in his hand. The scene looked extremely pleasant.

Right at the end of the jetty, there was one more boat—a broad white stern and an elegant cabin in light brown wood, old but well maintained. A proper *salon* with dominating panoramic windows all around. A wooden door, almost like in a Paris bistro. A sundeck in front of the cabin with, beneath it, just above the waterline, two port-holes. The boat seemed well kept, but not too perfect.

Guivorch was sitting on the sundeck, at a little bistro table, with a laptop and a bottle of red wine on it. He had arranged his seat so that he could look at the imposing cliff. He seemed absorbed.

Dupin, a few meters away, already had "*bonsoir*" on the tip of his tongue. He suppressed it. A broad wooden dock led to the boat.

A few moments later he was on the boat.

It appeared Guivorch hadn't noticed him yet. He was moving a finger on his mouse pad.

"*Bonsoir*, Monsieur Guivorch," Dupin greeted him at last, standing by his side to the rear. While greeting him Dupin had blatantly glanced past him at his screen. Guivorch sprang up and suddenly turned toward him.

If Dupin had correctly interpreted what it was he had seen—just a sketch and for a fraction of a second—the deputy director was occupied with an architectural drawing, possibly a floor plan.

"There you are! You creep up like a cat!"

If Guivorch had seemed confused for a moment, he was now in control of things again. Just like when Dupin met him in the castle, with an ironic smile playing on his lips.

"The—"

"What's that you're studying?" Dupin raised the subject, as if he hadn't heard Guivorch say anything. "Plans for an apartment, Monsieur Guivorch? Are you thinking of moving?" Guivorch stood still, between him and the table with the laptop, the smile still on his lips. He turned around calmly, closed the laptop, and sat down again. Then he nodded toward one of the two chairs that stood next to each other.

"I live on the boat between May and October. The rest of the time I live in my house in the wood. My parental home. But believe me," he laughed, "nowhere is as fine as here. Take a look, out there to the front . . ." Guivorch pointed along the river. "The river widens out again substantially. The Îles aux Pies, a real natural paradise, sea pine, gorse, and ferns. This is where the entire landscape is dominated by rivers: the Aff, the Vilaine, and the Nantes-Brest canal all meet here.

"They flow into one another, turn into lakes, meander, then flow apart again. There's a great tangle of waterways, and mechanical sluices as there were a hundred years ago. Almost nobody knows this, but the interior of Brittany is to a large degree a water landscape." As if to prove the fact, a handsome fish jumped out of the water right in front of them.

"Over a hundred rivers and canals flow through Brittany, Monsieur le Commissaire." Guivorch was a typical proud Breton, but also had a mischievous side to him. "Some thirty thousand kilometers in total, nearly all navigable. You can get to nearly every part of Brittany on the waterways, not forgetting the many lakes."

Dupin nodded at the empty seats. "Do you often have visitors, Monsieur Guivorch?"

"There were friends here last night. An evening as magical as tonight."

Nobody mentioned that during the questioning by Riwal and Kadeg. But that meant nothing.

Dupin decided to sit down. He moved one of the two chairs so he was able to observe Guivorch from the side.

"Coming back to the floor plan sketch on your laptop."

"I'm using the summer months to remodel my house."

Dupin pulled out the Citroën manual and made a couple of notes as if he had all the time in the world.

"What in particular are you remodeling?"

"I'm planning to knock through two walls." The answer was prompt. "Between the kitchen and living room."

"You're starting late, summer's nearly over."

"Don't worry about that, it'll all be fine."

"By the way, is there a Madame Guivorch?"

A broad grin spread across the face of the deputy director. "Not at the moment, Commissaire, but now and then."

"You weren't by chance at one point married to Madame Noiret? Or had family relations with any other members of the group?"

Dupin's tone of voice made it clear that the question wasn't intended as a joke.

"Everyone has ties to everyone else. Except for me."

Dupin let his gaze drift in a wide semicircle, then fixed it on Guivorch. "Why have you kept quiet about your activities as leader of the protests against the park?"

Guivorch raised his eyebrows dramatically. "Ah, that's the way the wind blows. That's what got you so acutely interested in me."

"In both murder cases there are connections to the park project. Both of the victims were in favor of it." Dupin was still looking him directly in the eye.

Guivorch's gaze wandered away from him and down the river.

"The fact that you wanted to hinder the project and kept quiet about your activities makes you a major suspect, Monsieur Guivorch. Also in conjunction with the fact you have no alibi for this morning."

Guivorch went quiet for a while.

"Did Paul Picard speak up for the park?" he finally asked.

The follow-up question was smart. If Guivorch had found out the written opinion from the paperwork—yet acted as if he hadn't—and even if he really hadn't known about it. And wanted to make that clear.

"Once again, Monsieur Guivorch: Why did you not tell me anything about your involvement with the park?"

The deputy director remained silent.

"Why are you so energetically opposed to it?"

"The wood doesn't need a Disneyland."

"What in particular are you worried about?"

"More people means more damage. The wood is burdened by large numbers of people. That's already the case. And that's without long lines at ticket offices in the midst of the thicket in order to watch Iwein fight the Black Knight! People sitting in an arena with popcorn and sodas? Ridiculous and undignified."

"Were you against the project from the start?"

"From the first moment I heard about it."

"Have you seen Madame Cadiou often in recent months?"

"No. Only occasionally. At one or two events."

"Where?"

"In the Centre."

That was in tune with what Madame Cadiou had said.

"Did you speak with her for long?"

Two seagulls had come and sat on the railing.

"No. Just to say hello."

"What sort of protest actions are there, apart from the demonstration tomorrow evening?"

"List of signatures in all the districts that will be affected by the park. We want to show that the politicians and tourist agents do not speak for everybody here."

"What else?"

"We've been talking to politicians. And the press."

"Will that stop the park from being built, do you think?"

"I don't think so. No." He sighed. "We're fighting a losing battle."

"How would you describe your relations with Monsieur Cadiou?"

"Cordial. Respectful. Professional."

That could mean anything and everything.

"Did you know each other well? Were your relations friendly?"

"Not particularly, no. A good working relationship, but not personal."

Others in the same situation would almost certainly have said "very good relations," or something similar. It seemed guarded.

"Did you see each other every day?"

"No. Just Tuesdays and Thursdays. Always in the morning."

"But you had known him before in your scholastic circle?"

"For around twenty years."

"Without getting to know each other better."

Guivorch glanced upward, then turned to look at Dupin.

"You think we're strange, don't you, Commissaire, am I right? We academic types, our whole group."

"I think everybody's strange, Monsieur Guivorch. Including myself. Everyone in their own way. But that is no bad thing, it's just how it is. It's just bad when someone thinks that his own individuality is worth more than others' and that gives him the right to take things from them. Their life, for example."

"You misunderstand the way things are between us in the group," Guivorch said, once more looking at the breathtaking landscape.

Dupin kept quiet. Waiting.

All that was left of the various colors was the soft pink. But now it was the shade of the whole sky. Touching the entire world, as far as the shores, the stones, the trees and the grass. As if somebody had colored in the entire world. The misty streaks from earlier had now literally dissolved into nothing.

"It's only a game," Guivorch continued. "Everything, just silly jockeying."

"That doesn't interest me in the slightest, Monsieur Guivorch. Only when it results in a deadly outcome."

A silence once again.

If anyone on the riverbanks had seen Dupin and Guivorch sitting there like that, they would have thought they were two friends enjoying the unique atmosphere of the place.

"Do you know Inwynn?"

"Of course. Everybody knows him. The best *conteur* of all."

"How well do you know him?"

"Apart from everything else, I'm responsible for the Centre's storyteller program. I hired him."

That was new. And very interesting.

"And before you ask," Guivorch said in a typically ironic tone of voice, "we occasionally drink a beer together, Philippe and I. Not regularly, but we also have a private side."

"Inwynn not only considers the project to be a mistake but a disgrace, sacrilege. Do you feel the same, Monsieur Guivorch?"

"To a certain extent, yes."

Dupin switched topics abruptly. A sort of "method," a direct parallel to his own shift of thoughts in an investigation: "How frustrated were you when Cadiou got the job of director and you didn't?"

"Very, but . . ." Guivorch laughed so loudly that the two seagulls on the railing flew off. "But not enough to kill him there and then."

"I think you now have a good chance of being the next director."

"That's true enough."

"I've heard that Paul Picard might also have been interested in the job."

"I know nothing about that."

"That's remarkable."

Guivorch didn't react.

"What do you think of the fact Madame Cadiou knew at least one of the people who belonged to the committee that decided who got the director's job, knew them very well: I mean this guy in charge of tourism, who's also her chief liaison with the *département*! And there's more: both of them are on the same side regarding the park."

Guivorch shrugged and said: "That's the way the world goes, Monsieur le Commissaire, on all levels."

"How big is the difference in salary between the director and the acting director?"

"I get approximately half as much."

"Would you have had to give up your professorship in Rennes to take the director's job?"

"No."

"Is there no time limit to the professorship?"

Guivorch's face turned stony for a fraction of a second, Dupin noticed. Guivorch tried to speak casually, not to let his sudden irritation be noticed, but in vain.

"It ends at the beginning of next year."

"Which must have made your motivation to get the director's job all the more imperative?"

Guivorch had pulled himself together again. "I have no worries about my future."

"What plans do you have for the future?"

"I don't know yet. Perhaps the post will be extended. A decision like that is often made late."

It didn't sound very convincing.

Dupin made a note, and finished it off with an exclamation mark.

Yet again they heard a loud splash. A fish must have jumped out of the water near them. And as if it were a sign, the two seagulls came back. This time they dared to come a bit closer.

Dupin watched them for a second, then he stood up and headed deliberately toward the cabin. He looked carefully through the window.

"Fabulous, isn't it." Guivorch had followed immediately and was now standing close to the commissaire. "Everything you need there. And what there isn't, you don't need."

On the right was a little galley kitchen, and opposite: a square table, four chairs. A narrow sofa. On the table lay books and a heap of papers. The door from the deck into the cabin was wide open.

"Take a look inside."

Dupin ducked inside and went over to the table, but before he got there Guivorch popped up next to him.

"Are you interested in anything particular, Commissaire?" He sounded less relaxed now.

Dupin calmly inspected the table. His eyes fell on a large book with lots of handwritten notes. *Historic Weapons and Armor in the Early Middle Ages.* There were several Spanish books next to it. English ones too. A few in French. Most of the titles meant nothing to Dupin. But one did: *Cadbury Castle. The First Excavation Stage. 1966–1970.*

Ever since the investigation began, he kept coming across Cadbury Castle.

"What is it in particular that you're interested in?" Dupin nodded toward the pile of books.

"Different subjects." Seemingly deliberately at random, Guivorch lifted a book in one hand. "For example, this is an anthology covering a conference on new technology in archeological work."

"What about this?"

Dupin picked up a large book full of Post-it notes.

"*The Chronicle of San Juan de la Peña,*" Dupin read aloud, "*A Fourteenth-Century History of the Crown of Aragon.*"

"You go very far, Commissaire."

All of a sudden Guivorch's voice had changed. A tone lacking in irony, still self-controlled, but openly aggressive.

"What do you mean?"

Dupin looked Guivorch straight in the eye. The unexpected sentence had opened a new dimension to the conversation. And not just the conversation, but in hindsight everything about the person standing in front of him.

"The English translation of an important Middle Ages book from Spain." Guivorch was clearly trying to keep himself together and stay calm. "A chronicle of the Kingdom of Aragon, written about 1342, when it ruled over the whole western Mediterranean and was at the highest cultural level, which brought forth the most famous poets, painters, scholars, and musicians of the period. For a long time the book was considered to be a pure chronicle, but in the meantime it has become clear that it's a colorful mixture of facts and, let's say, cleverly cobbled-together fantasies, to enhance the power and glory of the rulers. Nonetheless, despite all the propaganda, it still tells more of the real history of Aragon than any other work does." The mischievous smile was back now, the ironically sparkling eyes. "Should I be more detailed, or will this superficial introduction suffice for now?"

Dupin didn't react. Instead he walked calmly around the table. Then he pulled out his phone and took photos of everything.

He didn't say a word while he was doing so. Only when he had finished did he say: "I assume that was okay with you?"

Without waiting for an answer, he picked up one of the piles of paper. It was a printout entitled *PdlC Paimpont/P27/Val sans Retour—Viviane House/Journal 1.*

"The excavation you began at the beginning of the year, isn't that right? A sort of diary. In—"

"In which," Guivorch took the papers out of Dupin's hand, "we unfortunately found nothing special."

"As you know, I have recently discovered a huge interest in archeological projects. May I have this printout?"

"I think not." Guivorch didn't let himself get rattled. "We scholars have the peculiarity of keeping things to ourselves initially."

"So this journal does contain particular findings?"

"Moderate and specific to the subject. They'll be there to read in my next publications."

"What in particular did you find during the excavation?"

"Nothing relevant, as I just said. There's already a preliminary report, with the commune and in Rennes too. You can read through it there."

Probably genuinely uninteresting. But he would let Nolwenn go through the report all the same. And perhaps later on they might be in the position to ask for a search warrant for the boat. Factually based and regardless of his opinions on Guivorch.

Dupin picked up another pile of papers, as if the previous conversation hadn't occurred. *List of the stock of medieval books in Cornwall and Wales* it said on the cover sheet, which was also a printout.

"What's this?"

"I think we should go back on deck now."

Guivorch took a few steps toward the door and made a point of waiting. Dupin turned away from the table very slowly. When they got out onto the deck he took his seat again without being asked, turning his chair so that he could now see the river. The pink glow, on the water and the whole world, had lost its strength. These were the moments of late-summer evenings when the contrasts were astonishing. They only lasted a few minutes. The sky in the west was still bright as day; to the east it was already night. The day drew on, you could literally see it moving with the revolution of the Earth. Here, in this watery landscape, the trees on the riverbank became lost in a black mass.

Guivorch had sat down next to Dupin, clearly against his will.

"That was very revealing, Monsieur Guivorch."

Dupin had looked away from the river. He heard a theatrically deep inhalation next to him.

"I think it's extremely possible that you murdered both of your colleagues." Dupin waited a moment, then continued calmly: "It's important to me that you know that. And now I'll be going."

With those words Dupin got to his feet.

Guivorch remained sitting.

"Let me reassure you, Commissaire, I'm well aware of that. I—"

Dupin's telephone interrupted him.

Nolwenn.

"Good evening, Monsieur Guivorch."

Dupin left the boat hastily and took the call on the riverbank. "I'll call you back in a minute, I—"

"Adeline Noiret. She's been attacked. In the hotel. She was found unconscious. Stabbed by a knife. Just like Paul Picard," Nolwenn said in her usual staccato style. "Serious loss of blood."

"Unbelievable."

What had Guivorch called the situation? A game? It was a seriously murderous game. And it seemed to have moved into the next round.

Dupin had begun to walk at a trot.

"Where has she been taken?"

"She's on the way to the hospital in Ploërmel."

"Is Riwal in the hotel?"

"I can't get hold of him. Nor Kadeg."

"Kadeg and Riwal had planned to go to the Relais in Paimpont together."

"I know." Nolwenn sounded angry.

"What happened?"

"She was attacked in the hallway in front of her room."

"Are there others of the researchers in the hotel?"

"All of them except Guivorch."

"Ask Aballain to gather them all. I will go and see them, the whole group. Damn it, where are Riwal and Kadeg? I need them. Find them, Nolwenn. I'll drive to the hotel as fast as I can."

There had almost been another murder. The third within twelve hours.

Dupin remembered the ultimatum Claire had given him. It was a catastrophe.

* * *

The parking lot lay on the left side of the hotel, which was made up of four picturesque old houses, close together, with a modern extension behind them in the right corner. It was built from bright reddish stone, with a gray slate–tiled roof, and tall bay windows. The window and door frames were in a dark red. The whole building was illuminated on the outside with warm light. As in the wood, here also in Paimpont—the little civilized island—it was already dark.

Dupin reoriented himself—as the crow flies it was no more than five hundred meters from Madame Cadiou's office and the café where he had sat to the hotel's main building. On the street right outside the entrance there were three police cars. He had already seen two in the parking lot.

Dupin had spoken to the hospital in Ploërmel while he was still in the car. The doctor had said Noiret's injuries were not life-threatening, but also stressed that she had been lucky. Three knife blows—the doctor had suggested a kitchen knife—two on the outer side of her upper arms, one on the inner side which could have nicked her major artery. Madame Noiret had lost a lot of blood, but was over-all in stable condition. She hadn't seen the perpetrator, and couldn't even say if it had been a woman or a man. Her attacker had clearly crept up from behind. She had fallen to the ground, unconscious. It had all happened very quickly. Bastien Terrier had driven to the hospital with his wife.

After speaking to the doctor on the phone, Dupin had had a quick chat with Nolwenn. He had new tasks to give her, amongst them to find out what the state of Guivorch's position at the University of Rennes was and if there were any chance of an extension. Apart from that he asked her to read through Guivorch's interim report on the excavation at the Maison de Viviane and check on the remodeling of his kitchen. The other person who had called her was the prefect. Brilliant as usual, Nolwenn had told him that the commissaire was not only unfortunately unavailable to speak at present, but had been forbidden by Paris in the upcoming "highly virulent" phase from any communications except for those directly relevant to the case.

Top-secret level. All of it made up, but effective all the same. Even though Locmariaquer wasn't happy, he had still swallowed it.

Dupin had reached the two gendarmes outside the entrance to the hotel.

"No access for the press, monsieur. Strict orders from Paris. The minister of the interior."

An extremely strict way of turning him away. With a strange justification.

"That goes for the whole hotel, monsieur. This is under the control of the special investigation by Paris police."

"I—" Dupin began.

"I'm sorry. No exceptions. You're the eighth already."

Dupin had no idea why he gave the impression of being a reporter. But he was pleased to see that the press were actually being kept away. The news of the attack would undoubtedly have made the rounds and the journalists would have been based nearby anyway.

"Monsieur," the strict gendarme continued, "you are welcome to—"

His explanation was interrupted by his colleague clearing his throat noisily.

"Em, Pierre. This is—I think—the commissaire, the one from Paris. The boss here."

Dupin wanted to argue. He wasn't from Paris. But there were more important things right now.

"Oh, is that you, monsieur?" The gendarme went red.

"Yes, that's me. Where are the scholars at the moment?"

"We've gathered them together in a seminar room. There are just two of them left: Marc Denvel and Sébille Bothorel."

True, the group had been rather diminished.

"And where is Colonel Aballain?"

"Also in the seminar room."

"Where did the attack take place?"

"I'll show you. The buildings are linked together internally, and each one has its own entrance. Either to the street, the parking lot, or the garden, all of them built against one another. A little labyrinth."

The now rather friendly, if somewhat obese, employee with his hair shorn unfavorably short took the lead.

"Straight through here."

They were in the reception. A sturdy wooden staircase at the end of the room led upstairs. Next to it was a door with a dark red sign above it, announcing "Restaurant Bistro."

"The researchers have rooms in different houses. Madame Noiret was here in the main building." The gendarme took the stairs surprisingly briskly. "There are exactly five entrances to the first floor, where her room is. And where it happened. Her husband Bastien Terrier's room is in the annex. It—"

"They don't share a room?"

Dupin stood still. Obviously he had assumed that they shared a room. The fact that this had escaped him so far fitted in perfectly with this case. With the behavior of everyone involved in the case, to their "communication pattern." What somebody said—more to the point, what they didn't say. Only the most precise and emphatically posed question got an answer. Reluctantly.

"No."

"Why?"

"I'm afraid I don't know." The gendarme blushed again.

"How is it that all the King Arthur scholars have rooms in different buildings?"

"I can't tell you that either."

They had reached the first floor. The staircase led on to the second.

The gendarme opened a heavy door and stopped abruptly. Dupin nearly ran into him.

"Here we are."

The gendarme nodded to the left, into a narrow, poorly lit corridor, with a small square window opening onto the street.

Four rooms on each floor, two to the rear, two to the front, with the corridor between them, almost symmetrically, with a Bordeaux red carpet.

"This is where it happened, Commissaire." The policeman had gone into the corridor. "Almost exactly outside her room."

A policewoman who looked to be eighteen at most greeted them shyly. The place where the injured woman had lain was marked in chalk.

"It's hard to distinguish the blood on the carpet." The gendarme was pointing to a spot diagonally opposite the door.

Dupin had already got down on his haunches. It really was hard to make out. Only by looking closely. There were just a few tiny spots and one larger one some forty centimeters across.

"The perpetrator grabbed her here. Madame Noiret was coming out of the restaurant. Her attacker could have come from anywhere, above, below, from the side."

Dupin got up.

"And Madame Noiret's husband was in *his* room?"

"Yes, he said he had to work on an important article. He had turned down the cheese course and went up early. Around half past nine. Madame Noiret remained sitting in the restaurant on her own."

"And nobody in the hotel noticed anything unusual? No suspicious person?"

Dupin had taken out his provisional notebook. The gendarme's attention was taken by the Citroën logo. He hesitated with his answer.

"No. We've spoken to nearly everybody in the meantime, staff and guests currently in the hotel. And so far nobody has reported anything."

"How busy is the hotel?"

Dupin walked up and down, stopping every now and then to crouch down to look at the floor and the walls before getting up again. The young policewoman found it hard not to stare at him.

"Apart from the academics' rooms there are only seven others occupied. None of them on this floor. The high season is over."

"What about the restaurant you mentioned, the bistro? You can get from there to the rooms too."

The gendarme looked at the Citroën manual again. "We've asked all the dinner guests to remain."

"Who found Adeline Noiret?"

Up until moments ago Dupin had assumed it was her husband, while he had thought that the pair shared a double room.

"A hotel employee from the reception. She heard screams and immediately ran upstairs. When she saw Madame Noiret lying here, she immediately sent for help."

"I'm assuming she saw nobody else here. Just the victim?"

Dupin had walked over to the little window, then turned around. The doors to the other buildings had been left open. The perpetrator had had it easy.

"Indeed," the gendarme said.

"What time precisely was it when you were notified?"

"We were called at two minutes past ten. That means that the employee, who doesn't recall the time exactly, had found her some two or three minutes earlier. It must have happened about a minute to ten."

Dupin wrote everything down. One thing above all was certain: it couldn't have been Guivorch. At that time Dupin had been sitting with him on his houseboat.

"Were all the scholars in the hotel at that time?"

"Aballain says yes."

"What about the crime scene squad?"

"They should get here any minute. It is a special investigation."

It sounded as if otherwise they wouldn't be here until the morning.

"I assume there's no trace of the weapon?"

A superfluous question.

"No."

"And Madame Noiret was unconscious when the hotel employee found her?"

"Yes, but she came to right away."

"How do I get to the seminar room?"

There was nothing more to do here. If there were any traces, the forensic team would find them.

"I'll take you there."

The gendarme turned toward the door that led into the stairwell.

"Have you heard from my colleagues, Inspectors Riwal and Kadeg?"

"No."

What was going on? Where were they?

"I want nobody to be allowed into the hotel."

"What about hotel guests who went out for dinner?"

"Take their names and room numbers when they get back, and ask them to go directly to their rooms."

The gendarme held the door open for Dupin.

"Up the stairs."

"One more thing: make sure that two officers keep watch in a car overnight on the road to Cadiou's manor."

The gendarme nodded. "As protection or surveillance?"

"I don't know. They just have to keep an eye out. For everything."

Upstairs the layout was identical to that on the floor below.

The tubby gendarme seemed uncomfortable. "There was one point I wasn't clear on: Professor Denvel's room is also in the main building, on the second floor, however."

"Where?"

"Also toward the front." The gendarme nodded toward the door of a room. "The room exactly above Madame Noiret's."

He walked through one of the connecting doors.

"The seminar rooms are on the top floor of the extension. Mind your head."

Dupin ducked and walked along the narrow corridor that led to a door.

The gendarme opened it.

They walked into a white-painted room with sharply sloping roof on both sides and open wooden construction in the room itself: the roof beams, old wooden tables of varying heights, arranged into a rectangle, modern white wooden chairs with high arms. No pictures on the walls. Spotlights set into the ceiling made the whole room almost as bright as day. Functional. A flip chart at the end of the table—one of the obligatory items in all seminar rooms.

Aballain came up to him and Dupin greeted him amicably. Sébille Bothorel and Marc Denvel were sitting at one corner of the table. Two of the current serious suspects. There was a large distance between them that seemed almost demonstrative.

Dupin nodded in greeting.

"It's outrageous for you to—"

Dupin wasn't in the mood. He interrupted Sébille Bothorel angrily and came straight to the subject:

"Where were you at ten P.M.?"

He stood directly facing her.

She answered straightaway. "I ate, shall we say, a 'modest' meal—there's nothing more to be had here—and then I went to my room. Suite Merlin. To read. As I do every night."

"Which part of the building is the suite in?"

Dupin took out the car manual and opened it at the chapter entitled "Comfort Controls." It wasn't impractical: at the same time he was getting to know his car in a new way, a car which might soon end up in the junkyard. Dupin was going to make a sketch of the hotel. The sub-chapters "Glove Compartment," "Ashtray," "Cigarette Lighter" left him enough room to write.

"On the side, but my window looks out onto the garden rather than the parking lot." The phrase "parking lot" was spoken with extreme disdain.

Marc Denvel looked indifferently around the room. His hair was a little more disheveled than in the afternoon.

"When were you in the restaurant?"

"I think"—Madame Bothorel still sounded outraged—"from eight forty-five to nine forty-five. I just had the crayfish in lambic."

"When did you leave the castle? Your driver brought you here, I assume."

"It took forever, it was quite ridiculous."

"When?"

"After eight. I went straight to dinner. I sleep badly if I eat too late."

"You were in your room when Madame Noiret was attacked?"

"I've already told you that."

"And you heard nothing, no screams?"

"Please! No."

Dupin was going to inspect the hotel himself, look over the position of all the rooms.

"How is Madame Noiret? What do the doctors say?" Denvel asked, albeit without much emotion. He showed a minimum of sympathy; whether real or faked was hard to say.

"She'll make it." Dupin's eyes wandered back and forth between the two. "But it was a close call. To come back to you, Madame Bothorel, did you see Madame Noiret or any other of your colleagues here in the hotel this evening?"

"No."

"Maybe later in the restaurant?"

"Madame Noiret and Bastien Terrier. But Monsieur Terrier left first, early. And Madame Noiret was still sitting at the table when I left."

That was what the gendarme had said too.

"Did Madame Noiret seem in any way different? Nervous maybe?"

"I hardly know her. But I didn't have that impression."

"You've known her for many years."

"Please, the years mean nothing that suggests we *really* know each other."

"Did she speak to anybody else? When she was sitting there on her own? Or previously, when her husband was still there?"

"No."

"What about you?" Dupin turned to the young star scholar. "Where did you eat? Not here in the hotel?"

Denvel looked serious. He was wearing a button-down shirt this evening, not a polo shirt anymore. Yet again it was bright blue; it seemed to be his favorite color. The sleeves were rolled up casually.

"I went for a bit of a walk. I strolled through the village and took a seat in the La Terrasse de l'Abbaye, where I ate a good *tête de veau*, hard to find these days." He folded his hands slowly, a gesture that didn't fit his youthful age, any more than the dish did. Dupin didn't know anybody who still ate calf's head. "You're going to ask me what time this was."

"Correct."

"I need to think . . . After our meeting I was in my room for a brief time. Then I went out. I think I sat there about one and a half hours. I—" He interrupted himself and got briskly to his feet.

"Something just occurred to me. It will make things easier for you. And for me." He reached into his rear pants pocket and pulled out his wallet. "Here you go, the receipt from the bistro."

He handed it to Dupin and sat down again. Dupin was impressed; he almost always lost his own receipts, usually immediately. Including those for large amounts which he could claim as expenses.

Dupin looked for the time on the slip of paper.

"Nine thirty-seven," he read aloud. "That's the time on the check. And from the bistro to the hotel is five minutes. Early enough, therefore."

"Which rather makes the check something of a burden," Denvel said with a feigned hangdog smile.

Dupin had the strong desire to phrase what he was going to say in a way that made his meaning unmistakable: "You have no alibi for either this evening nor this morning."

"I'm seriously sorry. I'm telling you the truth as to where I was and when. I think that's what you want from me." Denvel shrugged lightly.

Dupin was only too familiar with statements like that, and he ignored it. "When you were leaving the castle did you see any of your colleagues in the hotel? Or later, when you were coming back from dinner?"

"Neither, I went straight to my room."

"Which is right above that of Madame Noiret."

"Indeed."

"Have you come across anything unusual? Anything at all?"

"I can assure you I would already have told you. We are all mainly concerned with the solution to this crime."

The young scholar's sentences often came across as arrogant, even though it wasn't because of his tone of speech or their content. Maybe it was his aristocratic attitude.

Dupin walked around the table, so that he could have both Denvel and Madame Bothorel in his sight. "Why have you basically told me nothing about your, let's say, close family connections?"

"Because it's none of your business," Madame Bothorel hissed.

"In a murder case, everything is my business, madame."

Dupin had spoken casually.

"How does the personal relationship between you work? How often do you see each other?"

"As I said, it is not in the least your business." While she was talking, Sébille Bothorel looked straight past the commissaire.

Suddenly there was an unusually loud knock.

A tall gendarme walked in. Dupin didn't recognize him. The "special investigation" mission was equipped with an impressive number of staff.

"Excuse me." The gendarme turned to Aballain, standing next to the flip chart. "We now have the names of all the guests and have spoken briefly to all of them. Nobody has seen anything unusual. Some of the guests were impatient and wanted to go. We . . ."

"They're to stay where they are," Dupin declared decisively. "I'll be downstairs straightaway. They're all going to have to be patient that long."

The policeman shot Aballain a querying look, which got a minimalist nod as an answer.

"I'll pass it on." The policeman disappeared.

"My stepmother and I . . ." Marc Denvel had lowered his head. He seemed suddenly rather unsure of himself. ". . . have no private contact. But we see each other now and then at academic occasions." There was a completely neutral tone to every word he said.

"This is true." For some reason Madame Bothorel felt the need to confirm it.

"Never outside academic events?"

Denvel once again took on the task of answering. Madame Bothorel's features seemed relaxed; it didn't seem to matter to her that he was speaking about the relations between them. "That's been the case for several years. Four, maybe."

"Five," she corrected him gently. It was hard to say what dynamic between them was at play in the background here.

"And I imagine I'm not going to hear anything about the reason?"

"Quite right," Madame Bothorel confirmed.

"And when you see each other at conferences, then it's only in the group. Not outside it? Not even for a coffee or to eat?"

This time it was Madame Bothorel who answered with an expressionless face.

"No."

Dupin held her eyes, then abruptly changed the subject. "Madame Noiret had made serious allegations against you, putting your academic reputation in question."

The expression on Sébille Bothorel's face froze, if only for a second. Dupin had surprised her.

"Her accusations were so absurd. I had expounded my thesis years before her. In public. Everybody knew that. If there's anyone here who stole anything, it was her!"

"Did Madame Noiret repeat her accusations? Recently, for example?"

"She's a second-class scholar. The truth remains the truth. In any case, she didn't get her professorial position for scholastic merit."

"For what then? Can you be a bit more specific, Madame Bothorel?"

"She is an extremely ambitious, attractive young woman in the midst of a lot of successful elderly men, who decide on positions. What can I say? That's the way it goes."

Things were brutal in the group. Dupin recalled Guivorch's words: "It's just a game." But it wasn't a game, everything was deadly serious.

"You're suggesting she has affairs. With whom?"

"I'm not suggesting anything. Interpret it as you will. I won't say another word."

Dupin made a note.

"Did she repeat the allegations?"

"I haven't heard her do so, but I wouldn't put it past her."

"Monsieur Denvel." Yet again Dupin changed his questioning strategy. "What is your personal relationship to Madame Noiret?"

"I see her at meetings of the board of the King Arthur society. That's all."

"Have you ever had an argument with her?"

"Now and again we have very different positions, but no personal differences. No."

Dupin had seen enough of the academic world to know that the former could be more decisive.

"You're a historian, your stepmother is a student of literature."

Dupin had taken a piece of paper with the details of all the people from his notebook. "Neither of you are archeologists. Just like Madame Noiret." Dupin knew exactly what he wanted to get out of them. "But all three of you took part in excavations as experts. That's so, isn't it?"

"We know the historic and cultural background. That's useful."

"Were you consulted about one of the excavation projects in which Monsieur Picard, Monsieur Guivorch, or Monsieur Terrier were involved? Or even Monsieur Laurent, the—I quote—'hobby archeologist.'"

"No." Denvel was first to answer. "Not directly. Not in the sense that I was involved with them and their project at the time. But I was at places they were also at, in other circumstances and with other groups."

That sounded complicated. And vague.

"In Cadbury Castle, for example?"

"Exactly. A good example. I belong to a group made up of two specialists in ancient history and two philologists. We examined the inscriptions in late antique Latin capital letters, the ones we referred to this morning in the castle."

Everything had to be dragged out of them. It was enough to drive you mad.

"You're referring to the inscriptions that Monsieur Terrier and his team discovered."

"Which had nothing to do with our activity. As was true the other way around too."

"But it was all in the same place."

"Yes."

"And you all were dealing with the same object."

"Yes."

"Was there another project in which you and the others were involved? In this indirect manner?"

"I can't say that for sure. Probably; we were all visiting the same relevant places."

"But not, for example, at the excavations here in the wood, at the well?"

"Haven't you already asked that question?"

"I mean in the *indirect sense*."

"No."

"And what about you, Madame Bothorel?"

She shook her head.

"Monsieur Guivorch, the acting director of the Centre"—yet another calculated change of topic on Dupin's part—"was interested today in a certain floor plan, a building blueprint. Does anything occur to you in that respect?"

"I don't quite follow," Denvel said, clearly condescendingly.

"Why would he be interested in it? What building might it be? And why?"

Dupin couldn't get it out of his head. "Is there some reason for Guivorch to be interested in a particular building here in the wood? Or in something in a particular building? The question is for you too, Madame Bothorel," the commissaire added loudly and clearly.

"It sounds far-fetched. Why should I know what Professor Guivorch would be interested in?"

Dupin took two steps backward and ran his hands through his hair.

"For me things are like this: this story isn't over, wherever it's leading. Any one of you could be the next victim. And either of you could be the perpetrator. Perhaps . . ." Dupin gave a crooked smile.

". . . maybe both of you. There aren't too many left of you. Whichever. We'll soon find out."

He turned away briskly and headed for the door in a leisurely fashion. "You aren't to leave the hotel until tomorrow morning. Not for a minute, not a single step. Until I say you can."

A moment later he had left the seminar room.

* * *

"This is Monsieur Herbé, the owner of the hotel," Colonel Aballain said by way of introduction.

A very friendly-looking, totally bald, middle-aged man with a deeply disturbed expression on his face stood behind the bar in the reception. Despite Aballain's suggestion that he deal with the impatient guests in the bistro, Dupin had insisted that he undertake this conversation first.

"*Bonsoir*, monsieur." Dupin nodded politely.

"This is terrible." The man appeared totally distracted. Dupin understood completely. This was the last thing that a hotel owner wanted. But he had no time to lose. "How is it that the scholars all have rooms in different buildings?"

"It was a specific request."

"Whose?"

"Monsieur Guivorch. He made the reservations for all of them. At least two or three months ago."

"How, precisely, did he phrase his wish? Do you know that?"

"I spoke with him personally at the time. He said they all liked having personal space. Or something like that. Academic types!"

Unusual as it was, it seemed suitable. Fitting for such an odd group.

"And who got which room, did Monsieur Guivorch have influence over that?"

"No. That was up to us. And that naturally depended on late availability."

"You mean who slept in which room, in which part of the building, wasn't something anyone could know in advance?"

"Impossible. In the case of important guests, I look after that myself. I decided it the day before."

"Did you tell anyone about it?"

"It was on the room chart from that evening."

"And I assume your staff could see that."

"Yes, they have to."

"And the Noiret/Terrier couple, the fact they wanted different rooms, that was part of the arrangements that Monsieur Guivorch had organized?"

The hotelier raised his eyes. The question seemed unwelcome.

"No, that wasn't Professor Guivorch."

"Who, then?"

"That was Madame Noiret herself. Monsieur Guivorch had booked a double room. But a week before, Madame Noiret called and asked for two rooms. She said they both had a lot of work to do and needed their rest. They needed two working rooms, was how she put it. Literally."

With any other couple, one might have assumed that betrayed something about the state of their marriage. But insofar as Dupin had gotten to know the scholars, it would fit. And in their eyes it would have been a "sensible" decision.

"I understand. Did you or any other member of your staff notice anything unusual in the hotel? Were there any unusual events?"

"No."

"Did you speak to Monsieur Picard yesterday or this morning?"

The hotel owner seemed totally intimidated.

"Your colleagues already asked me that. I happened to be here at the reception desk as the guests checked in one after the other. We exchanged a few friendly words, but no conversation in depth. Monsieur Picard seemed quite normal."

"Like all the others?"

"Indeed. Do you think the attacker is a guest here in the hotel?"

He was clearly afraid.

"I don't know."

"Do you think it might be because of an argument between the women and the gentlemen professors?"

"I don't know that either. Thank you very much, monsieur."

Dupin felt himself drawn into a calming appeasement. "We're going to solve the case, you can rely on it. And nothing will be attributed to your fine hotel." It was a highly unusual statement for the commissaire.

He set off immediately.

"This way!" Aballain went ahead of him. "Just through this door."

Dupin had almost left the reception area when he suddenly turned once again.

"Monsieur Herbé, do you think I might have a *café*? Or two?"

"But of course," said the hotelier, clearly confused, sending a speedy "Right away" after him.

Dupin disappeared with a loud "Wonderful!" that echoed through the restaurant where he unexpectedly found himself in the next moment. It was a bright, generously proportioned room, tastefully decorated, with large, airy lampshades that gave out a warm light. Oval, round, and rectangular tables, red tablecloths, wooden chairs with high armrests, a single ancient cupboard. Above all, lots of people, who sat there quiet as mice, staring at Dupin and Aballain. Dupin had stopped still; he hadn't expected to be the center of events. Nonetheless, this way he had gotten everybody's attention.

"*Bonsoir,* mesdames, messieurs. I'm Commissaire Georges Dupin," he said, and took a few steps into the room, taking a look around. "Commissaire de Police, Concarneau. A serious crime has been committed in this hotel, an attempted murder. While you've been sitting here. I need to know if anybody left the restaurant around ten o'clock. No matter how briefly. Maybe only to smoke a cigarette. Or to fetch something from their room—if they were a hotel guest."

The tall policeman came up to Dupin with several pieces of paper in his hand.

"Here you are, sir, we've already collected these from everyone." He handed the list over to Dupin, somewhat unintentionally formally. His words could be heard throughout the room. "We identified four people who left the room during the time in question, briefly in each case. Two to smoke, two to the restroom."

That was the answer to Dupin's question. Maybe he should have had a word with the gendarmes first.

The restaurant was full to the brim. Most of the guests were probably locals; the high season was over.

He turned to face the whole room. "Who are the four who left?"

A few hands were raised hesitantly. Those of two young people near the door. The smokers, Dupin guessed. Then one embarrassed-looking elderly lady at one of the larger tables and a red-haired woman at the end of the room.

The gendarme came over closer to Dupin and lowered his voice, which didn't really help as it had gone so quiet you could hear a pin drop.

"We've talked at length with the four people. They were right at the top of the list." He indicated the pieces of paper. "We have not the slightest reason to suspect them in any way."

Dupin had a response on the tip of his tongue but held it back. The gendarme would be right.

"I would like to—" Dupin turned to face the room again, and stopped short.

His glance had halted on one face. That of a man at a table directly near the door.

It took just a moment for Dupin to recognize him, even if he had tied his hair back into a ponytail and now looked completely "normal," in a black T-shirt and black jeans. Inwynn. Philippe Goazou. The storyteller.

Everybody was waiting tensely for Dupin to continue what he was going to say.

"I . . . I thank you all for your attention."

Without further comment, Dupin went directly toward the storyteller's table. As if the scene just now hadn't happened. Nobody dared to speak, as if it were a theater performance. The faces of Aballain and his tall colleague reflected puzzlement.

"You may all resume your conversations," said Dupin, turning around again.

The room remained totally silent.

He moved closer to the table. Everybody's eyes remained fixed on him. He no longer noticed the curiousness of the situation.

"A remarkable coincidence, Monsieur Goazou. You being here this evening." Dupin stood no more than half a meter from the storyteller.

He brought out his Citroën manual, also under the curious—now astonished—glances of the collected public.

Dupin flicked through it.

Philippe stared at the commissaire uncomprehendingly.

"So, Monsieur Goazou?"

"So . . . what?" The storyteller sounded genuinely mystified.

The conversations at the other tables hadn't resumed yet.

"I'll tell you what, let's you and me go outside for a minute," Dupin said, and glanced over at Goazou's companion. "And your friend here."

The next second Dupin was already headed for the exit. He opened the door and waited for the two men to follow him.

A moment later they were standing outside on the terrace in the balmy night air.

"What do you want of me?"

It was strange. Philippe Goazou was nothing like Inwynn this evening. He seemed sober, humorless. Introverted. And pale somehow. Unimaginable that he had still recited colorful fantasies that afternoon.

"That's the second time in one day that you've been at the scene of a crime, Monsieur Goazou."

"And yet again it's pure coincidence, Monsieur le Commissaire."

"A remarkable coincidence."

"I was hungry. My friend Didier Boyard and I come here now and again. The food is very good."

"Which of you had the idea today?"

"Of coming here?"

"Yes."

"I did."

"And when did you ask your friend if he'd come with you?"

"Sometime this afternoon?"

"Spontaneously?"

"Quite. It's a thing we do sometimes."

Dupin turned to the other man. "Are you also a storyteller?"

"Yes. And a forestry worker in my main job."

Dupin had just been guessing about the storyteller. Now he noticed the man's broad, athletic shoulders.

"Then you must know Monsieur Guivorch?"

"Yes."

He was even more taciturn than Goazou.

Dupin turned to the pair of them. "When did you get here this evening?"

"Close to eight thirty," Philippe Goazou replied.

"A smoker?"

Both hesitated briefly.

"Yes."

"Yes."

"Then you almost certainly left the restaurant at some stage?"

"No." Philippe Goazou again. "We didn't."

"When did you last speak to Monsieur Guivorch?"

"Hm." Goazou ran his hand over his head. "I saw him yesterday in the Centre. In the afternoon. I took a group from the forest there."

"Where precisely?"

"Mostly along the lake."

"And did you talk to him on the phone after?"

"We speak seldom on the phone."

"What about you?" Dupin turned to the second storyteller.

"Might have been last week."

"What? That you spoke to him on the phone?"

"Precisely."

"And saw him?"

"Beginning of last week. It's past the high season, so there isn't much going on for us storytellers."

"Are you also opposed to the park project?"

"I should think so."

"And involved in Monsieur Guivorch's protest actions?"

The forestry worker made a perplexed face. "What's that supposed to mean?"

"Whether you've been involved in collecting signatures, for example? Maybe you are involved in organizing them? If you're going to the demonstrations tomorrow? Or are involved in some other protest action?"

"No."

It was a waste of time.

Dupin had to do things differently. He stepped back into the restaurant. The puzzled storytellers followed shortly after him.

"I have to ask for your attention yet again." Dupin spoke with a loud, demanding voice; the conversations at the tables had gradually resumed. "To do with a matter of extreme importance to the police. Has anyone noticed if either of these men"—he nodded at the two storytellers, standing by their table with an incredulous look on their faces—"left their place here this evening? Either one of them on their own or both together? Please, think it over."

Dupin glanced around.

Nothing. He looked at everyone at every table, one after the other, almost imploring them to come forward.

Dupin went up to a four-person table, closest to that of the two storytellers. "Nothing occurs to you?" he addressed the group. Two women and two men.

"No," replied one of the two women in a nervous voice.

"Surely you would have noticed if your neighbors left their table?"

"I don't know," the same woman said. "We were engrossed in our conversation."

"You see!" Dupin turned once again to the whole room, aware that it sounded somewhat desperate. "Maybe you just missed it."

Silence. Even more oppressive than before.

"I—" Dupin cut himself short. He ran his fingers through his hair.

"Excuse me, Monsieur le Commissaire?" It was the hotelier.

"There's a Madame Nolwenn wanting to speak to you. She says she can't get through on your cell phone."

"I'm coming."

Saved at the right moment. He hurried out of the restaurant.

The hotelier nodded toward the counter in the reception where a cordless telephone lay.

"Yes?"

"I'm beginning to get worried, Monsieur le Commissaire. Really worried."

It was a sentence that in all their years working together Dupin had never heard Nolwenn say even once.

"And why?"

"What do you think? Our inspectors! Riwal and Kadeg. I can't get hold of either of them. Either they've been in a communications black hole all this time, or there's something wrong."

He could tell from her voice which option she favored. "They were still in the castle at 8:35. Riwal spoke to you, then me. Kadeg and he wanted to set off for the Relais de Brocéliande. But they never arrived."

The hotel owner had disappeared back into the restaurant. Dupin was on his own. But even so, he spoke quietly.

"Have you asked the gendarmes who were last in the castle?"

"I have. There were still four of them there. With two cars. The gendarme who saw them last was up in the Knights' Hall, but couldn't say what time he himself left it."

"They wanted to go take a look around Cadiou's office."

"None of the four gendarmes were able to say anything about that. They finished up in the castle around eight twenty, there was nothing more to do."

"Then they left the castle without the inspectors?"

"Yes. The gendarme who had spoken to them upstairs in the hall had offered to leave Kadeg one of the cars. Kadeg turned him down. The gendarme had no reason to ask him again. He assumed you would pick up the pair of them. I had suggested to Riwal and Kadeg in the afternoon that they commandeer two cars from Rennes. Or to just rent one here. The hotel, by the way, has offered to lend me a car if I need one."

"There has to be a logical explanation."

Dupin said so without being wholly convinced. It was truly strange. On the other hand: maybe they were just following up a hunch; they both had more than enough of them. Crazy ideas, quirks, whimsies. Maybe for some reason they were acting secretly, which was Kadeg's favorite modus operandi: watching someone. Or maybe they had discovered something they would later reveal triumphantly.

Nolwenn continued: "I've sent a car to the castle. They're to take a look around. And asked Guivorch which of his staff was last to leave the castle. He thinks it would be the two young people who worked in the café and ticket office."

"Do we have their telephone numbers?"

"I do."

"Maybe Riwal and Kadeg were given a lift by one of the scholars?"

"Extremely improbable. Out of the question, I would say."

Nolwenn was right.

"In which case they should have got to the Relais and someone should have seen them."

Dupin himself didn't think that was a possibility.

"Did Riwal mention anything? Was there somewhere in particular he wanted to go? Someone he wanted to speak to?" Dupin knew it sounded helpless.

"Not to me. But he might have had a spontaneous idea."

"That's probably it," Dupin replied, unconvinced.

But it certainly wasn't out of the question. Riwal was stubborn. Something like that actually was quite possible.

"I have a few important bits of news, Monsieur le Commissaire."

It sounded as if Nolwenn was happy to change the topic.

"Fire away."

"First of all, the clinic in Ploërmel called. The doctor has given the green light for a few questions, and Madame Noiret has agreed. Just ten minutes, the doctor said."

"Very good!" He had been waiting for that. It now had priority. "I'll head there straightaway."

"And there's a strange thing. The experts . . ." It was clear Nolwenn was only half concentrating. ". . . have searched through Cadiou's laptop." She paused.

"And?"

"And found nothing, or next to nothing. I mean . . ." Nolwenn tried to pull herself together. ". . . no data: no emails, no documents, no photos. In Picard's case, however, everything is encrypted by a highly professional program. So far, they've got nowhere."

"What does that mean? He must have also written his articles and books on the laptop."

"It probably means that he didn't save his data on the computer. And almost certainly not in a 'cloud,' the IT specialists say, but rather on external USB sticks, external hard drives, that sort of thing."

"Why?"

"Maybe he was afraid of his data being stolen."

"That would require someone," Dupin was thinking aloud, "to be very worried about their data. Or else: the data would have to be incredibly important for him to be that worried about it."

"I take every care to look after my data, Monsieur le Commissaire. We should all do so."

She was referring to discussions that were held almost perpetually in the commissariat, for example about Dupin's strenuous refusal to obey the strictly recommended regulation to change his password every four weeks. Data security was one of Nolwenn's things. And in the end Dupin had to admit that he was criminally negligent.

"And Picard had used a professional app to encrypt his data?"

"Yes. An extremely efficient app. Specialist software. The experts are still working on both computers."

"I see. I have a few things myself." Dupin pulled out his notes. "Find out if Madame Noiret has had—or is still having—affairs. Sébille Bothorel insinuates she has. She suggests it wasn't academic achievements that got her her chair, and that it's widely known."

"An extremely serious accusation. And like everything else only to be dealt with in the morning—it's already late."

"And finally," Dupin concluded, "see what you can find out about a Didier Boyard, a woodman from round about here who's also a professional *conteur*."

"Okay, I haven't found out much about Inwynn. So far at least. He's very popular, more booked up than any of the rest. He's even asked for interviews occasionally. I'll keep on the case."

"Good. And let me know at once if you hear anything about Kadeg and Riwal. I'm off to see Madame Noiret in the clinic."

* * *

The journey through the wood at night was a journey through the deepest darkness. A featureless black. The trees were impossible to make out, even when they were right in front of him, only the dance of the Citroën's headlights suddenly showed them up now and then, a part of the trunk, a branch, leaves.

It was extraordinary; there was the wood, right there, all around Dupin, and yet he couldn't see it. For some fifteen minutes Dupin had felt himself as if in a spaceship, hurtling through the universe. Also because directly above him the stars were dazzling; they seemed amazingly near at night, particularly when he came over a hill. It was just a strip of sky revealed by the invisible treetops to his left and right, but revealing a real sea of stars, blinking and flickering nervously. It amplified the impression that down here on Earth he was driving down a creepy, narrow, lightless alleyway. Dupin had a strange feeling of loneliness, an unfamiliar trepidation that was new to him.

The Centre Hospitalier lay to the north of the town center and was easy to find.

He left the car directly outside the door and within a minute was in the rooms used by the emergency ambulance. The merciless fluorescent light was as insufferable as it always was in hospitals, as was the smell of cleaning and disinfection materials. Dupin hated it.

Madame Noiret was sitting on a stretcher in a little treatment room without windows. The room was totally dominated by medical apparatus. Next to the stretcher was a huge piece of equipment on wheels.

She looked miserable. The fact that she could sit up at all was thanks to her considerable self-control. There was a large bandage on her left lower and upper arm. Her face was pale. Haggard.

"*Bonsoir*, Madame Noiret," Dupin greeted her with a quiet voice.

The doctor on duty, a young man who was busy with one piece of apparatus, came over to him purposefully, while the nurse who was taking Madame Noiret's blood pressure on her right arm looked up at Dupin in alarm.

"You can't just—"

"Commissaire Dupin, I'm leading the investigations."

The young doctor had stopped right in front of him; he looked tired.

"You have a maximum of ten minutes, I told your boss."

Dupin didn't correct him. In reality, Nolwenn actually was his boss.

"It's all okay," Madame Noiret insisted. "I've already told you I'm fine. And in any case, I have no intention of spending the night here in the clinic."

She was speaking more slowly than she had that afternoon, and her voice was weaker.

"You've just been through a severe trauma, lost a significant amount of blood, and are under the influence of various drugs. Have a brief chat with the commissaire, but I cannot discharge you this evening."

Dupin flinched. Bastien Terrier was standing right behind him, this evening wearing a green shirt and khaki pants.

The doctor left the room, without paying any attention to Terrier. The nurse watched him go, helplessly, concentrating on the instruments before removing the support on Madame Noiret's upper arm and then leaving the room herself.

"Thank you, Madame Noiret, for seeing me under such circumstances." Dupin had greeted Monsieur Terrier with no more than a brief nod before turning his attention to Madame Noiret. He stayed at the foot of the bed and looked at the academic. Her husband leaned against the wall.

Dupin had no time to waste. "Who was it? Who attacked you?"

Madame Noiret's eyes opened wide. "I already told your colleagues. I couldn't see the attacker."

"Not at all?"

Dupin stared at her.

She didn't yield to his stare.

"It was very dark in the hallway outside my room. I came up the well-lit stairwell and was looking for the room key in my handbag. I was knocked over and somebody stabbed me. Or stabbed me first and that knocked me to the ground. There's nothing more I can say." A pause. "They came from behind. I screamed as loud as I could, and fought tooth and nail."

That was presumably what saved her life.

"It all happened so fast. The attacker was wearing a cap."

That was new. Nobody had mentioned it up until now.

"He had pulled it far down over his eyes, I couldn't recognize anything."

"A man?"

"I don't know, I already told you."

"What's your gut feeling?"

She raised her voice. "It happened so suddenly. I was lying on the ground, and lost consciousness."

"How often were you stabbed?"

Dupin already knew the answer.

"Three times. The doctor said he was clearly targeting my upper body, going for the heart." Madame Noiret spoke calmly.

"He?"

"The attacker—he or she."

"You were very lucky, Madame Noiret."

Unlike Picard. But on that occasion, the attacker had more time. In the hotel, he would have assumed that somebody would soon come across him. That he hadn't finished his task clearly indicated they weren't dealing with a cold-blooded killer, but that vague assumption didn't exclude any of the persons in question.

"How tall was this person approximately?"

"I couldn't tell you. Normal height, I think."

"Try to remember. Is there nothing that comes back to you? The slightest little detail could be important."

"I think the person was in dark clothing . . . And . . ."

"Yes?"

"I don't think he or she *was* wearing a cap, but a hood pulled over the face. I . . ."

She fell silent. For the first time she really appeared to be in shock.

Dupin realized that he was no longer concentrating. His thoughts kept returning to Riwal and Kadeg. Nolwenn wasn't the only one worried.

"I think that'll do, my wife has been through enough, Monsieur le Commissaire."

Terrier had prized himself away from the wall. "You have to put yourself in her place: she's just left dinner, is standing outside her door, looking for the room key in her handbag, and all of a sudden someone knocks her to the ground and she has a knife in her upper arm."

"We want to get hold as soon as possible of the person who intended to kill your wife, monsieur. And to do so, we need all the information we can get our hands on."

"It's all right, Bastien." Madame Noiret had regained her composure again. "This is important."

"Did you notice anything else unusual beforehand? Did you feel anyone was watching you? In the restaurant, for example?"

It occurred to Dupin that he had forgotten to ask where precisely Madame Noiret and Monsieur Terrier had sat. Quite possibly near the two storytellers.

"No, not in the slightest, I've been racking my brain over that myself."

"What about you, Monsieur Terrier?"

"No, it was a perfectly normal evening. I had gone up to my room earlier. My wife remained sitting downstairs on her own."

"Where were you sitting? Coming from the terrace, outside."

Madame Noiret seemed to be reflecting. "On the right to the rear, in the corner."

So at some distance from the two storytellers. But of course they could easily have seen when Monsieur Terrier and Madame Noiret left the room. As far as Dupin was concerned, the whole thing seemed to be a miraculous coincidence. That Inwynn had been sitting in this restaurant that evening. But then of course, things like that happened.

"Did you notice two men sitting directly next to the door? One of them with a ponytail?"

"Not me." Madame Noiret shook her head. "But then I was very much taken up with my thoughts. The gruesome incidents of the day were on my mind," she said, then hesitated uncertainly.

It was incredible, the way she formulated it. And the perfect opportunity to come to an important point that Dupin had wanted to discuss before she was attacked.

"I can understand that only too well, but nonetheless your ex-husband was one of the victims."

All of a sudden Madame Noiret's eyes went blank and she breathed deeply in and out. "Indeed." She uttered the word with no obvious emotion. As if all her strength had faded away.

"Were you still close? You and your ex-husband?"

"No."

"Were you still in contact?"

"Not publicly. We still saw each other at the committee meetings and occasionally at conferences. But rarely."

It was unfortunately impossible to get confirmation of this from Picard.

"Monsieur le Commissaire, what has this all got to do with the business in hand? What has it got to do with the attack on my wife?" Terrier asked, thin-lipped.

"Why did you tell me nothing earlier, in the castle, about your personal relationships?"

Dupin was angry with himself over the question as soon as he had begun to formulate it. He wasn't on point. The expected answer came straight back.

"Because we didn't feel obliged to involve you in the details of our private lives. That has *nothing* to do with *your* murder case."

"In which your wife was very close to being the next victim. You think that's *my* case?"

This discussion was useless.

"So, back to this evening." Dupin had become pleasant again. "Were you aware of the two men near the door?"

"Not in the slightest."

"Did you hear the screams of your wife outside her door?"

"No, I was deep in my thoughts."

A brief pause followed.

"Madame Noiret, Monsieur Terrier, I'd like to ask you a personal question." Dupin spoke as if their little argument simply hadn't happened. He wasn't expecting an answer. "What is your relationship like? What is the state of your marriage?"

Dupin switched his eyes between the one and the other. And noticed that they exchanged glances. Madame Noiret spoke first.

"I simply don't understand why this question has any relevance to the situation in which we find ourselves here, but if you really have to know, we have a very happy marriage, Monsieur le Commissaire."

Terrier nodded in agreement. Long enough for him to be certain that Dupin had definitely seen it.

"Do you always reserve two rooms when you're traveling together?"

"We both happen to be in an intense writing phase," Terrier said, outraged. "We both have important articles to complete, and need to focus all our concentration. Above anything else, we both have our own writing rhythm."

Dupin had been here often enough. Much of what the academics said was hard to understand and sounded strange if not downright curious. But naturally that could just be how things were. It didn't have to mean anything. Maybe Madame Noiret and Monsieur Terrier simply ran their marriage the way that was best for them and their jobs. Maybe they really were happy. Dupin had to be careful not to judge them preemptively. He knew only too well how different relationships could work differently. Everything was possible. There were no rules on how to make things work for the best.

"Wouldn't two rooms with a door joining them be a good solution?"

Dupin hadn't learned when to stop. Both of them put on indignant faces.

"Not for us," Terrier answered sharply. "And I think that's enough of this ridiculous topic."

Dupin glanced at the clock. It was almost midnight. Where were Riwal and Kadeg? The subject tormented him.

"Well then, thank you very much, madame. Thank you very much, monsieur. Do let me know if anything else should occur to you. Get well soon, Madame Noiret. Look after yourself."

"Many thanks. Good night, Monsieur le Commissaire."

Dupin turned around, then stopped for a second and turned back to them.

"Just one question, Monsieur Terrier. After leaving the restaurant, did you leave your room again? Before the attack on your wife? Between those two times, I mean."

"Me?"

Terrier looked as if he'd been struck in the face. Somewhat exaggerated, Dupin thought.

"Yes, you."

"No. Of course not. I spent the whole time working."

"And that was easy enough? After a day like this? With two colleagues you had known so long brutally murdered?"

Dupin had asked the question perfectly calmly.

"It's my deadline for submission at the end of next week. As I said earlier without wanting to seem vain, it's an important publication for the *International Journal of Historic Archeology,* the international version of the leading magazine on the topic."

"I see."

He wasn't going to get any more.

Dupin turned around again to depart. "Good night. Look after yourselves."

Before long he was standing outside, in front of the clinic's big automatic sliding door. He walked back to his car.

The warm, yellowish lights of the little town lit up the sky like a lighthouse beacon. He called Nolwenn. "Anything new?"

She knew immediately what Dupin meant.

"There are two gendarmes in the castle. Everything dark. No sign of Riwal and Kadeg. I've spoken to the student from Rennes. She really was the very last to leave the castle. Shortly after nine P.M., according to her, about forty minutes after the gendarmes. She went out through the bookshop and locked up. Beforehand she and her colleague had taken the things from the Knights' Hall back to the café and cleared up. She didn't see anyone else, either in the castle or down below."

"And in Cadiou's office?"

"The gendarmes haven't been able to get into the castle yet. There are three master keys—Cadiou had one, Guivorch had one, and the last is kept in the castle. Guivorch had given that one to Riwal because he wanted to look at Cadiou's office. A colleague from Paimpont is picking up Guivorch's master key and taking it to the two policemen."

Nolwenn had obviously decided to devote all her energy to the issue, not a good sign.

"Where could the pair of them still be?" Dupin ran his left hand through his hair.

"Without a car?"

A good question.

"Maybe somebody gave them a lift."

"And who might that be?"

Obviously Nolwenn was right.

"What about the young man, the other student? When did he leave?"

"About eight forty-five P.M.," she said.

"In his own car?"

"Yes."

"In terms of timing, that was perfect. Maybe they asked him to take them with him? Give them a lift somewhere?"

"Unlikely." Nolwenn hesitated, and then conceded, "But not out of the question. Unfortunately I can't get hold of him. I have his cell phone number, but he's not answering."

"Where does he live?"

"Near Rennes."

"Do we have his address?"

"I'll get it and send someone there."

Judging from her voice, however, Nolwenn didn't seem very convinced of this idea.

Dupin's brain was going in circles. "Which areas are important to us? Where could the pair of them have wanted to go?"

By now Dupin had walked around his car ten times. After the second time going past the left-hand side, he raised his glance significantly, to avoid seeing the damage.

"Paimpont, the hotel, Madame Cadiou's office. The Cadious' manor house. Tréhorenteuc. The Fontaine de Barenton. But they'd hardly have gotten lost in the wood and tried to get back to the well. And even if they had, they'd have been back long ago."

"Which other buildings are of interest?"

"Buildings? In what way?"

"Which buildings play a role in the history of King Arthur?"

"Not really buildings. Places. Apart from those you already know by now, there's the Maison de Viviane at the top of the Val sans Retour, a megalithic monument, a grave, stones like menhirs, arranged in elliptical form, then . . ."

"That's the place where Guivorch has been digging, isn't it?"

"Indeed. And then there's the Grave of Merlin, where . . ."

". . . Terrier is digging."

"Precisely. Where all that's left today is two large slate rocks. It's not a grave, but rather the place where Viviane locked Merlin into a castle in the air so that he would live forever by her side in the Brocéliande."

"That's everything?"

"Yes. I've also spoken to the director of the university in Rennes."

"At midnight?"

"We have to get somewhere. I had to call on a few contacts to get there. Guivorch's dig has a time limit, but it's really a pure formality. It will be extended. Probably they'll drop the time limit altogether."

"And why didn't Guivorch tell us that?" Dupin sighed.

"And another thing, at full moon—and it's a full moon today—Merlin comes out of his castle in the air, and fulfills the wishes of those sitting on his stones," Nolwenn added casually.

"I see." Dupin was deep in thought. "Does the abbey in Paimpont have anything to do with Arthur?"

He'd already asked himself that question.

"No."

"In no way at all?"

"No."

Dupin fell silent. He couldn't think of anything else.

"I'm going to drive to the castle myself, Nolwenn." It was a spontaneous decision. "Tell the gendarmes to watch out for me."

* * *

The moon was indeed full. Nolwenn and Riwal had talked a lot about it on the drive here, and considered it a portentous coincidence that

Dupin and Cadiou had agreed on a meeting precisely on this date. Obviously the full moon played an important role in the Brittany of legends and myths, where it made spectacular entrances in innumerable stories. Nolwenn and Riwal agreed that the full moon was also the best time to "get close to" the wood. And it wasn't just any full moon, as Riwal had discussed in detail during yesterday's lunch break in the commissariat, while Dupin joyfully cracked open the langoustines he had bought for everyone in the nearby market hall. The full moon tonight was 22 percent brighter than other full moons: it had to do with the Earth's elliptic orbit and its "Earth-nearest point," if Dupin had understood correctly. There were nights when the moon appeared fuller, rounder, brighter. And not just nearer but much nearer. Without doubt this was one of those nights.

This unique moonlight was that of the "other world." It was the light that turned things upside down. You could see by moonlight and that only made the world darker yet. It left only the surfaces visible and swallowed everything else. A light beyond colors. The light itself had no color, and more than that: it sucked all the color out of everything. The world was pale, wan. The "otherly light" was how they referred to it in the fantasy stories. The world was no longer recognizable, more confusing. It was a different world. "Anyone who hasn't seen Brittany by full moon," Nolwenn liked to say, "hasn't seen it at all." Dupin found it a challenging statement.

He looked up at the fairy-tale castle, which no longer had anything in common with the castle in daylight. It was as if a spell had been cast upon it. The outline of the whole structure tonight seemed almost to look like something curiously organic. It was no longer a building but a living creature, ready to defend itself.

The twinkling of the stars in this clear night had grown brighter to become a highly nervous blinking. A regular pulsing. Enough to induce dizziness trying to look at a particular star or a strip of the sky. Normally a hint that the weather was about to change, usually a heavy one. But the weather forecast hadn't foretold it; quite the contrary: a continuation of the perfect late summer.

The commissaire headed up the path to the cast-iron door, behind which stood the ticket desk. The moon was now right above the pointed roof of the castle. Beyond it lay the lake.

Dupin recalled the scouting adventures of his youth. His mother had enrolled him without asking him, and eventually he had enjoyed it. Tents, campfires, fishing, building shelters out of branches and twigs. Dupin felt as if this was one of the tests of courage, the scouts' rituals back then. Walking at night through a ghostly wood to a spooky castle, where there was something to find, a flag perhaps that had to be brought back. The advanced version was where the others in addition thought up "surprises" to scare you. It had been terrifying but the absolute determination not to show fear in front of the others helped Dupin to come through it. Ever since, he had merrily wandered through every dark forest—the others didn't have the fire that he had in his stomach—which brought him a reputation for boldness. But this was no ordinary dark wood. This afternoon he had noticed how loud the gravel beneath his feet crunched. An eerie noise. The same went for the clicking of the cicadas, which sounded completely different from those in the gentle river landscape. It was strangely dissonant, chaotic. There was no trace of celestial harmony. Every now and then he heard an owl.

Dupin had reached the bridge over the castle moat when he suddenly stood still. The gate, it occurred to him, would normally be closed. He hadn't thought of that. He was surprised to have been so deep in thought. He couldn't get into the castle from here tonight. But there had to be another entrance. An entrance for the staff.

That's where he had to go.

Dupin walked back to the car along the road he had come, until he saw an unpaved path that he hadn't noticed before and which led off to the right side of the castle. There were tire marks on it. It crossed a roughly mown field: bushes, shrubs, the odd tree that looked like a bizarre figure. To the left a high stone wall, more protection for the defensive walls.

After a while he suddenly came across a parking lot with a police car standing in it. Dupin felt relieved.

He walked across the parking lot, then followed the path leading away from the other side.

Before long, behind a couple of trees, he could make out the castle moat in the moonlight, and to the right the magnificent lake. It had an unimaginable shimmer, a color that Dupin had never seen before, a sort of silvery blue-gray, lying there like an immaculate metallic surface stretched taut. Dupin involuntarily thought of the crazy story Riwal had told them: that the lake was only an illusion. Which tonight seemed obvious.

There had to be a second bridge across the moat here. And indeed, before long, there it was. He was almost there when he heard a noise. He flinched. There was something in the bushes directly by the moat, to the left. Automatically he tensed his muscles, and as a reflex reached to his right side. In vain. He wasn't carrying a weapon. He clenched his fists. He was standing still, staring at the undergrowth. There was nothing to see. And nothing more to hear. Then there was a sudden movement, and for a moment he glimpsed something white. It stopped, then shot at lightning speed toward the moat, and vanished without noise, not even a splash of the water.

What had it been?

Yet another animal? It had been white, there was no doubt of that. His senses wouldn't play the same trick on him twice. The question was: What sort of animal? Was it the same one, in two different, relatively distant places? Were there more of them?

Dupin forced himself back into the real world. He crossed the bridge and saw the entrance at the side of the castle.

The door was locked. And there was no light to be seen anywhere. Everything looked abandoned. No sign of the two policemen.

Dupin got his phone out. Hit Nolwenn's number. In vain. Not a single bar showing.

"Damn it," he cursed angrily.

And where the hell were his two inspectors. It appeared he had—rather they all had—something better to do right now, rather than look for them and wander around a magic castle in the middle of a magic forest.

But he was getting more and more worried.

Grumpily, Dupin tramped farther around the building. There had to be yet another entrance. He tried the rear side.

Finally, right at the end of the long side of the building, there was a lit window. And soon after that a door that stood wide open. Dupin went in and, at the end of a gloomy hallway, saw a weak glow. A narrow spiral staircase—exactly as on the other side—led upward, feebly illuminated.

A stuffy corridor, with closed doorways left and right, presumably the administration floor. The wooden floorboards squeaked deafeningly.

There was a light on in the last room. They had left the door ajar.

Dupin walked into an unexpectedly large room. Opposite the door was a window, and in front of it to the right, a large, modern wooden desk; on the other side of the room was a seating area with a sofa and two armchairs, black leather, with a flat table in the middle.

Left of the door there were shelves reaching to the ceiling, filled to bursting with books. The walls were roughly whitewashed. Minimalist elegance, no administration office atmosphere here.

"We deliberately left the light on and the door downstairs open so you would find your way to us more easily. But at full moon it's virtually daylight anyway." One of the gendarmes, who had already been here at the castle this afternoon, greeted Dupin. He was pale, had a daring haircut, and bushy, protruding eyebrows. He was standing against the window. His colleague, tanned, athletic, and with a neat haircut, was sitting on Cadiou's seat at his desk. Dupin didn't remember him. It seemed they had been chatting.

"Our colleague Bruno brought us the key. Your boss said we should meet up here, directly in the office of the director," the pale gendarme said.

Nolwenn seemed to have put herself across as boss again.

"You've got reception here?" Dupin asked, amazed.

"Absolutely."

They must have special models made for the forest. Fantasy phones.

"We used the flashlights"—the pale one pointed to two enormous examples sitting on Cadiou's desk—"once to go around the whole castle, and then once again to take a quick look inside the building. Right up to the big Knights' Hall. Nothing unusual anywhere." He stopped briefly before moving to the obvious conclusion: "We haven't found your inspectors."

"Nothing? Nothing at all unusual?"

"A light had been left on in the cafeteria. A stack of books in the library had fallen over. There was a car sitting up front in the visitors' parking lot. When we arrived we saw a fox."

A résumé of the ordinary.

"Do you get white ones here too?"

"Foxes?"

"Precisely. Or . . ." Dupin hesitated. "Or other white animals about the same size?"

"Arctic foxes?"

"I know"—Dupin wondered how to phrase it—"that there are no arctic foxes here . . ." In fact, it was just such a curiosity he had been hoping for. "But animals about that size with white fur?"

"Hmm." The policeman scratched his chin. "Have you seen a white animal?"

It was too much for Dupin. It sounded as if he had said he had seen white mice.

"And what about this car in the visitors' parking lot?"

"A brand-new Citroën," said the tanned officer, with admiration in his voice.

"What's it doing there?"

"We don't know. Somebody left it there. We took a look at it. Pretty cool. But nothing unusual about it."

"Why would someone leave their car here just like that?"

"Maybe because he had had a glass too much. It happens."

"You mean here in the café, that closes at six?"

Both shrugged their shoulders.

"What do you want to do now, Monsieur le Commissaire?" The pale gendarme by the window sounded serious for the first time. "It's nearly one in the morning."

To tell the truth, Dupin didn't have a plan, or even the beginning of a plan. It had just been a vague intuition to come to the castle on his own.

Instead of answering, Dupin began to walk slowly up and down the room. He looked around. Apart from the flashlights, the desk was almost empty. Just a few books. It didn't look as if Cadiou had done much work here. At least not at his desk.

"Did Monsieur Cadiou have a secretary? An assistant?" It was a question he should have asked earlier, like many others in this madcap case.

The tanned gendarme understood.

"Only in the mornings. For items related to the Centre. She's on holiday at present."

"Has anyone spoken to her?"

"Nobody has got hold of her yet." As if in explanation he added: "She's been away for two weeks and will be for another one. Thailand. A multi-destination tour."

Dupin took out his provisional notebook. Not without drawing surprised looks, which he ignored. He wrote something down. Perhaps he ought to talk to the secretary himself, whenever she was available. The list of pressing points was getting ever longer.

"And upstairs in the Knights' Hall?"

The pale policeman took over again.

"As we said, everything's normal. And unfortunately no hints as to where your colleagues might be."

Dupin made another circle around the office. He stopped by the desk. Took one book after the other in his hand. Three volumes of Chrétien de Troyes. *Tales of King Arthur.* Those were also on his desk in Concarneau. He thought for a bit.

"Well, that's how it is." With these words Dupin turned—almost cheerfully—to the two gendarmes. It was time to do something major. His inspectors had been gone for far too long.

"I want a car to go to every one of the sites linked to King Arthur around here. At least two men in each. Immediately. Tell them that both my inspectors should be officially declared missing. The gendarmes are to look around as thoroughly as they can. At every Arthurian site, I mean . . ." He flicked through the book. ". . . the Church of the Holy Grail, the Val sans Retour, the miracle well, and the spot where Picard's body was found, where the excavation was due to start." Dupin turned another page. ". . . then the Maison de Viviane and Merlin's Grave. And . . ." he hesitated briefly, ". . . Madame Cadiou's office in Paimpont. There's already someone at the manor. I want it to be quick. We have special investigation status."

It was nothing less than a major police action that he was ordering. In the middle of the night, no fewer than a dozen police cars hurtling through the forest. They would be from every commune possible. But, in the end it was about Riwal and Kadeg, and right now, Dupin was thoroughly alarmed.

Nobody moved.

"Come on, what are you waiting for? Call Colonel Aballain. He should get everything going. I am heading to the Cadious' manor. I need to talk to Madame Cadiou."

He would kill two birds with one stone and move the investigation forward at the same time.

"Can you remember all of this?"

Both gendarmes nodded decisively.

"Good, then I'm on my way."

Dupin hurried toward the door.

Still on the staircase he pulled his mobile out of the pocket of his jeans. Five bars. Maximum reception.

He dialed Nolwenn's number.

With as few words as possible, he put her in the picture. She was in agreement with his action; he even believed there was a trace of relief audible in her voice. She still hadn't been able to get hold of the student from Rennes.

Two police officers had gone to his apartment, but hadn't found him. And his mobile was still unreachable.

On the bridge over the moat the connection failed in the middle of a sentence. But they had already dealt with most things.

Dupin walked on for a few meters, then he noticed the abandoned Citroën. It looked strange there, as if lost. But then everything looked strange tonight. The car really was brand new, a "sport" model, like the ones that for ages Nolwenn had promised to "acquire" for him.

Dupin walked once around the car, then turned on his mobile's flashlight app and took a look inside. A few bits of clothes were on the rear seat, a jacket, a pullover, nothing else visible. All of it inconspicuous. Just like the gendarmes had said.

Shortly after, Dupin sat in his car and started the engine. He felt immediately how tired he was. Worn out. It was late, but more than anything, he had been running this way and that breathlessly, without even taking a moment to sit and think about this extraordinary, brutal case. An extraordinary day, as extraordinary as the world in which all this was happening. He just hoped now that Kadeg and Riwal would soon be found safe and well.

Bravely he put his foot down on the pedal.

* * *

Without noticing it, Dupin had turned off at the entrance of the village of Tréhorenteuc down a road that took him past the Church of the Holy Grail.

He slowed down, thought for a moment, and then stopped. Almost exactly where he had parked that morning, when everything was still a harmless, cheerful office excursion. Now the morning seemed like it was days ago. He would take a quick look around, seeing as he was there.

A few bright red slate stones shone in the moonlight, glowed in fact, as if they contained a unique crystalline light. The others remained pale. It was as if they made signs—mysterious, indecipherable signs. The church was a plain, long building with a short transept. The remarkably little church tower stuck up from the shining dark silver roof, as if it were missing a part. On the right side was an extension, like a little house that had grown out of the church, with a single round window.

"Hello, is anybody there?" Dupin shouted.

He walked up to the entrance, which was presumably locked.

"Hello!" Dupin knew how curious the scene would seem to a passerby. "This is Commissaire Dupin. Commissariat de Police . . ." He stopped.

Nothing moved.

Dupin hadn't the remotest idea what it was he wanted to say. Other than that he hoped to find Riwal and Kadeg. Even though he hadn't a clue why they might be here, of all places.

He would walk once around the church and then drive on to Madame Cadiou.

His eyes automatically swung over the buildings and the surrounding area. The only noticeable thing was that in the meantime lights had gone on and windows had been opened. Two sleepy-eyed people stuck their heads out. Dupin half expected that somebody would call the police.

In response to an undefined impulse, after completing his tour around the church, he walked back up to the entrance again. Above the door was the phrase that somebody had quoted earlier in the day. Had it been Riwal? *La porte est en dedans.* The door is only accessible from inside. As extraordinary as everything else here. It meant something like: only when you're already inside can you get in. It was more or less what the storyteller had said about the wood. And that was exactly what this case seemed like to him. Only when he was already inside would he find the entrance. And Dupin was undoubtedly outside.

The door was made of wood and painted red, a pale red in the moonlight, with a plain red metal handle. Dupin pushed it. The door swung open and in the next moment the commissaire found himself unexpectedly inside the church.

"Hello, anybody here?"

How come the church wasn't locked?

Dupin looked for a light switch. He couldn't see any near the door.

"Police!"

A surprising flood of moonlight fell through the windows on either side of the main door and one at the far end of the church.

Dupin stood there as if rooted to the ground. He was spellbound by two dramatic displays. On the left-hand side, the entire side wall of the church right up to the rounded ceiling was dominated by an almost blinding golden glow, despite the minimal light. Against a golden background was a crazy scene: a sublime, gigantic white deer with a golden band and golden cross around its neck, ringed by four flaming red monsters apparently hunting it. Wolves, maybe. The moonlight on the golden background lent the whole thing an almost supernatural appearance. Like a sort of hologram.

At the other end of the church was a giant stained-glass window overflowing with figures: plants, birds, knightly coats of arms. The walls behind the window receded so that the picture seemed to be a vision. From here the multiple individual depictions were not easily made out—but one was perfectly clear. The center of the picture, the one that the entire composition revolved around: a bright emerald green cup.

That was it. No doubt about it. The Holy Grail.

Dupin pulled himself together. He wasn't here to stand in admiration. He walked down the church pews. On the side walls were large paintings in heavy frames. He let his gaze skim over them: scenes of King Arthur, the Round Table. There were various large statues around the church—Mary and the infant Jesus, the local saints, Onenne and Judicaël—which looked particularly huge in the moonlight, some standing on stone pedestals against the walls, some on wooden cabinets. The door of the one behind the statue of Saint Onenne was slightly ajar. Dupin opened it wide. Books, lots and lots of books, apparently prayer books.

Almost directly under the stained-glass window, there was a little door set into the wall. It would lead to the extension that Dupin had noticed yesterday from the outside. Dupin tried to open it. But unlike the main entrance, it was locked.

The gendarmes, who would arrive soon, would have to get a key and take a look inside the room. He would make a point of that to Aballain.

"Hello?" He knocked and waited.

He gave a loud, deep sigh.

What was he doing here anyhow? Wasn't he just wasting valuable time with this silly business? There wasn't the slightest indication that Riwal and Kadeg might be here.

Dupin walked back to the main door. On the way his glance fell again on the imposing white stag. He caught himself—another sign that things weren't going well for him—wondering if it might have been a very tiny white deer he had seen earlier. A bizarre thought. One that got him thinking about all the stories about madness linked to the wood. The story about Iwein on his confused mission—and what else was this case?—wandering through the wood and gradually losing his mind.

Dupin was glad to be back in his very real car hearing the engine start up with its usual noise.

* * *

The commissaire drove into the manor yard. Up front where the path joined the road stood a police car on watch.

Dupin stopped briefly to chat with his two colleagues. They had arrived at about ten thirty. Madame Cadiou was already there by then. Since when they didn't know. They rang her doorbell when they arrived. Just to let her know they were there. Madame Cadiou hadn't left since. They had seen the light on until around midnight. Dupin had tried to call Madame Cadiou on his way there. He had let it ring several times but she didn't answer. Perhaps she had taken a sleeping pill. It was late.

She had parked her Volvo directly behind her husband's car, the bumpers touching. Monsieur Cadiou had parked it here yesterday, not knowing that it would be the last time. He had crossed the yard into the house—also for the last time; he would never leave it alive. The two cars together made a sad picture.

Dupin deliberately let his car door slam. It was now one thirty in the morning.

All the windows on the first floor were open. He made a quick but thorough tour of the yard, throwing a glance into the wooden shed. Then he walked across the gravel to the entrance to the house.

"Madame Cadiou, it's Commissaire Dupin here."

He stood still, looking up.

Everything remained in darkness. There was no reaction. He rang the bell. Just like that afternoon, the bell made no sound outside.

He rang a second time, then a third. For a long time. Nothing. He went back into the yard.

"Madame Cadiou?"

He called more loudly, clearly.

"Madame Cadiou, forgive me disturbing you so late at night, but I have to talk to you again."

Not a sound.

Dupin felt he was being overcome by serious nerves, an uncanny déjà vu: he'd already stood here in vain once today. And had rung the bell in vain.

"Madame Cadiou?"

This time he called so loud it echoed around the yard.

Walking fast, Dupin headed for the side door to the house, which once again was unlocked. The narrow hallway. The kitchen. The part of it where Fabien Cadiou had lain was closed off.

"Hello!"

He climbed the spiral staircase to the first floor. There was no one there.

"Madame Cadiou? Please don't be afraid."

Both doors on the second floor were closed. The bedroom was on the right, Dupin remembered.

Even though he found it difficult to not just storm in, he knocked. Waited for a while. Then charged in after all.

"Madame Cadiou?"

His eyes swept the room, lit only by the moonlight. He turned on a light switch next to the door. Within a second it was blindingly bright.

He saw Madame Cadiou in her bed, her right arm stretched out in front of her. The bedsheet had slid to the floor. She was wearing shorts and a black sleeveless top.

She wasn't moving.

Dupin rushed to her side.

"Madame Cadiou?"

He grabbed her by the shoulder. And in that moment, she moved. Slowly, but she moved.

Dupin stopped. Madame Cadiou turned toward him, confusion on her face.

"What . . . what are you doing here?"

There was no fear in her voice, just total amazement.

Dupin had dragged her back from the deepest sleep. That was all it had been. Not another crime.

"I . . ." Dupin had speedily retreated. "Please excuse me, I thought, you were . . ." He stopped himself.

"I was briefly worried . . . " He tried again. ". . . about you, I mean. I was just here in order to . . ." Yet again he fell silent, for longer this time.

Madame Cadiou swiftly pulled the bedsheet up.

He turned away discreetly.

"I assume you want to get dressed. I'll wait for you in the kitchen." No, the kitchen wasn't a good idea. "Or next door. That's better. Next door. In the office."

Madame Cadiou's look became more and more confused with every word Dupin said.

"I think . . ." Her voice changed; she seemed at last to have come to her senses. ". . . that would be a good idea."

Dupin hurried out of the room.

It took a while for Madame Cadiou to appear. She was wearing black linen pants, a thin anthracite-gray blouse, buttoned high. Over her shoulders was a dark green pullover, the sleeves pulled together like a scarf. Her hair, which had been wildly tousled, was now tied back into a tight ponytail. She had quickly put on some makeup, subtle but visible. She had black leather slippers on her feet.

With a deliberately and audibly controlled voice she began: "I would like to know why you suddenly appeared in my bedroom in the middle of the night."

Somehow Dupin had hoped she might pass over that embarrassing moment.

"There's been another incident, Madame Cadiou, a brutal attempted murder." That was a good strategy: to talk seriously, which, in any case, fitted the facts of the situation. "This evening there was an attack on a colleague of your husband, Madame Noiret. With a knife, as was the case with Paul Picard. She wasn't fatally wounded, but it was a close call."

He stopped. The information did its work.

Madame Cadiou's eyes opened wide. There was shock on her face.

"That's . . . that's terrible." But just like that afternoon, she didn't ask any follow-up questions.

"There are also a few more points I need to ask you about. Urgently, I'm afraid. But there's one more thing first. Have my inspectors been to see you this evening? Either one or both of them? Inspector Riwal or Inspector Kadeg? Either in your office, or here later?"

"No." She wrinkled her forehead.

"Did they call you on the phone?"

"No."

"And you've heard nothing from either of them?"

"No. Why should I have?" She seemed suspicious.

He would say nothing more about it. There was no sign in either the house or the yard to hint in any way that they might have been here. Or, when it got to this point they maybe had to take every-thing, truly everything, into consideration, no matter how improbable it might seem, that they had been held prisoner here.

"When did you leave your office this evening?"

"I think around ten o'clock."

"Where was your car parked?"

"In the parking lot by the abbey, not far from the office."

From there it was just a few hundred meters to Relais de Brocéli-ande. The scene of the crime.

"And you went from your office directly to the parking lot and from there directly home?"

"Exactly."

She would have given the same answer if it had been different and she had taken a slight detour via the hotel.

"Did you see anybody as you were leaving the office? Or at the parking lot?"

The gendarmes had said Madame Cadiou was already home by ten thirty. Theoretically the timing was all very tight.

"I don't know. I don't recall seeing any movement. In any case, I wasn't paying attention."

Dupin took out his notebook.

"Right, moving on. This professional storyteller. Inwynn—Philippe Goazou, to give him his civilian name—do you know him?"

"Of course, yes."

"Do you know about his connections to Guivorch?"

"Naturally. Auffrai Guivorch is responsible in the Centre for the storytellers, the routes they take, the whole organization."

"Are the two of you friends?"

"That's not for me to say."

Guivorch's own comments had gone a lot further.

"Your husband"—this was another reason why he had definitely wanted to speak to Madame Cadiou again—"telephoned Monsieur Laurent often before his trip to Cadbury Castle. Afterward too. Do you know what they were talking about?"

"The trip, I imagine. The project."

"You don't recall anything else?"

"No."

Dupin flicked a few more pages. "Do you know Didier Boyard, a friend of Goazou, and also a *conteur*?"

"Not personally. But the *conteurs* obviously play a role in our concept for the park. We want them to play a part. The idea is that we actually play up the storytelling role. It will be good for them."

"You're thinking of employing more storytellers?"

"That too. And give them more things to do."

"New storytellers means more competition between them."

"Primarily it means more jobs for more people."

"Didier Boyard is against the park, as are Philippe Goazou and Monsieur Guivorch."

"Indeed."

She remained in control. "I wanted—" She interrupted herself. Up until now she had remained standing; now she sat down on the desk chair. "I took a sleeping pill before going to bed, it's still having an effect."

It was intended to be an explanation of why she had sat down. For Dupin it was also an explanation why she hadn't responded to the bell, his shouts, or his knocking.

"I wanted," Madame Cadiou resumed, "to get in touch with you anyhow. Something occurred to me this evening. A colleague of yours asked me this afternoon if I owned a weapon. Which I don't. But my husband has a pistol, that—"

"Your husband carried a weapon?"

"I had completely forgotten, yes, he had it before we got to know each other. I only saw it once. Then never again. When we moved here, he said he would leave it in his grandmother's dresser. He never mentioned the weapon again, but I think it still exists."

That was unbelievable. Why the devil hadn't she mentioned it earlier? Because she had forgotten? Despite the fact that her husband had been shot?

"I—"

"Don't believe a word you say" is what Dupin wanted to reply, but he restrained himself.

Madame Cadiou was a puzzle to him. As were, unfortunately, all the other characters he had to do with in this case. He couldn't give a definitive assessment of any of them.

"I'd like to take a look at the pistol," Dupin said as a follow-up.

She stood up. "Of course."

"Is it registered?"

She walked ahead, Dupin following.

"I couldn't tell you, but I assume so."

"Why did your husband have a weapon?"

He could maybe understand an archeologist having one—they camped in the loneliest, most adventurous sites, and the things they were interested in were necessarily—given their enormous value—objects of interest to criminals. But a scholar of literature?

"He inherited it from his father. I don't think he was interested in it."

That would explain why, when they were checking for gun licenses all around, they didn't come up with Cadiou. Probably he just hadn't registered it in his own name.

"Did anyone else know about the weapon?"

"I would be amazed."

"Not even Paul Picard? His friend?"

"I don't think so."

They had come up to the third floor. Madame Cadiou headed directly for a rather battered-looking antique wooden dresser in the corner of the room.

"I don't know which drawer it is in."

She reached for the handle of one.

"Wait a minute! No!" called Dupin. Madame Cadiou flinched.

"There might be relevant fingerprints on the handles." Dupin looked around.

"May I?" He nodded toward a little tablecloth covering the sofa table.

"Of course."

She didn't seem to wholly agree. Dupin grasped the edge of the handle with the tablecloth and pulled open the first drawer, which was full of photo albums. Same in the second drawer: photo albums. In the largest: boxes of slides. Dupin took them out briefly to see if there was anything behind them.

Nothing.

In the lower drawer: flat cardboard boxes for slide negatives. All clearly neatly arranged and captioned.

In the very bottom drawer was an old cigar box. Dupin pulled it out carefully. The size was about right.

"Do you think it's in there?" Madame Cadiou seemed curious.

Instead of answering, Dupin opened it.

It was empty.

He left the cigar box where it was, and looked through the remaining contents of the drawer. Folders of papers. Dupin took one out. Notes, apparently from his studies. ORAL AND WRITTEN TEXTS FROM THE EARLY MIDDLE AGES.

Dupin put them back.

He raised his eyebrows and nodded at the box. "I think it was in here. Very interesting."

"What do you mean by that?"

"You never saw the gun?"

"No."

"Did your husband mention what sort of gun it was? Did he mention a make?"

"If he did, I'm afraid I no longer remember it."

"Beretta, Glock, SIG Sauer, Walther, Smith and Wesson, Heckler and Koch, do any of those ring a bell?"

"I don't know for sure. But it could be, Glock maybe."

"A make made for nine-millimeter bullets." Dupin spoke slowly. "The caliber of the bullet that killed your husband."

"What do you mean by that?" she asked nervously.

"I mean it's possible your husband was shot with his own gun. By someone who knew he had it. And more to the point, where it was."

A heavy silence fell. Madame Cadiou's gaze dropped and the expression on her face reflected an emptiness.

"I understand," she said in a monotone.

She was a very clever woman. She had almost excluded the possibility that a third party knew about the gun. In any case, if it had been her, why would she have told Dupin about it? If the gun wasn't registered in Cadiou's name, and there really was nobody apart from her husband and herself who knew about it, Dupin alone would never have found it. She would never have handed it over on her own. In combination with her lack of alibis at all the times when crimes took place, it would have made her a serious suspect. But would she have been that stupid as to place the burden on herself? Dupin didn't seriously think she'd have made that mistake. Perhaps she did it deliberately, as a particularly clever trick. An extremely refined tactical maneuver.

"We'll leave everything here as it is. I'll call the crime scene squad. There's no alternative, I'm afraid."

There was still nothing but emptiness on Madame Cadiou's face.

"I'll ask one of the gendarmes here to wait. I myself have to be elsewhere."

"Of course. I—"

Dupin's phone rang.

Nolwenn.

"I've an important call, Madame Cadiou. If I may . . ."

"But of course." She understood, and left the room.

Dupin took the call.

"It's as I thought." Nolwenn sounded reproachful. "The student from Rennes didn't give Kadeg and Riwal a lift. And he hasn't a glimmer of an idea where they might be."

"Goddamn!"

"He had gone on to a friend's birthday party after work, and only just got home."

Dupin had always known that he was clutching at straws. But then he had seen cases where straws had held firm. It had been the last possible logical explanation as to where Riwal and Kadeg might have gone after leaving the castle.

"The police cars should get to their destinations soon. I think we should hear from our colleagues any minute now." There was a brief pause. Nolwenn had read Dupin's mind. "Don't worry, they'll call from one of the landlines. I've kept our mobile numbers for the four of us."

Perfectly organized, as always.

"Damn, all this can't be happening."

He really had the feeling now that something was amiss. Even so, he had to keep a cool head. Dupin took deep breaths.

"Nolwenn, I need a crime scene team. Here in the Cadiou manor."

"I'll set that up straightaway."

Dupin told her about his conversation with Madame Cadiou.

"Unbelievable. There's something wrong with that woman," Nolwenn said with clear anger. "But then there's nothing right with any of them. Every single one of them. It's as if they're all in cahoots."

There was an infernal screeching sound.

"One moment, Monsieur le Commissaire! Hello, yes?" Nolwenn was speaking to someone else. Dupin could hear every word.

"Go ahead, tell me." It was an order.

It was silent for a while. Nolwenn was listening.

"I see. There's nothing suspicious to be found at Merlin's Grave. I'd still like you to search the neighboring area in depth. Over and out."

A brief silence, then:

"Exactly. Yes. Everything. A whole section of wood around the spot. No matter if it seems quite normal at first glance. Then come back to me."

Nolwenn had hung up. A second later she was on with Dupin again.

"I—"

The same screeching again. This time Nolwenn went off without saying anything. All Dupin heard was the familiar "Hello—yes?"

It took a while, then:

"I see. A local says there was someone suspicious in the Church of the Holy Grail. In the middle of the night. Really? First he walked around the church, then went in. He was driving a—" Nolwenn broke off.

Dupin knew which car the suspect had been driving. He knew what the troubled local had told the gendarmes who had driven to the church. And Nolwenn had realized it too. Dupin had forgotten to tell her about it. It suddenly occurred to him that there was something else he had forgotten. Something important.

"Nolwenn!" Dupin shouted into the phone.

"One moment," he heard her say. "I need to speak briefly on another line. Monsieur le Commissaire?"

"The gendarmes need to get the key to the tiny extension, to the priest's office."

"Can I go back to the other phone?"

Without waiting for an answer, she was immediately back on the other phone.

"The suspect was Commissaire Dupin himself, I've just been told. He hadn't told me either. He asks you to look at the extension, which is locked up."

An answer on the other line.

"I know how late it is. And yes, you'll have to haul somebody out of bed. We're not sleeping either."

Then she was back to Dupin.

"It's going to go on like that, Monsieur le Commissaire." It was as if to say: I need to be left alone to work now. "I'll let you know if interesting news crops up."

"Just one more thing. On the approach to the manor there's a police car with two gendarmes in it. One of them needs to come into the manor to me."

"Of course."

"And send the crime scene team."

"I've already made a note of that."

Nolwenn hung up.

Dupin sat down—something he rarely did—for a few moments, on the edge of one of the two well-worn gray cloth sofas. Dupin felt deep exhaustion. A few minutes later, he came back to his senses again, and went in search of Madame Cadiou.

He knocked on the door to her study.

"Just a moment," he heard her say.

It took a while for her to come out into the hallway.

"I just wanted to say good-bye, Madame Cadiou. For now, I think we have nothing more to speak about." It sounded harsh and he added, "One of my colleagues will be here imminently, and the crime scene team won't be far behind."

"I assume I won't be needed for this. I'd like to lie down again."

"As you like, Madame Cadiou. Don't you think you should lock the side door on the ground floor? After everything that's happened?"

This was almost certainly the door the murderer had come through.

The question seemed genuinely to confuse her: "I . . . we never locked it. I've never thought of it. But you're right, we—"

There was a gentle, deep buzz.

No wonder Dupin hadn't heard the bell.

Dupin saw Madame Cadiou's curious look.

"That'll be the gendarme. I'll just give him a few directions." Dupin turned to go. "Just one more thing. Your husband never mentioned ammunition for the gun?"

She fiddled with the green pullover that hung over her shoulders. "No, he always . . ."

"Of course!" Dupin suddenly cried out, then winced violently. Madame Cadiou almost did the same.

That was it! He was certain. It had just occurred to him.

The green jacket! He recognized the jacket that had been lying on the back seat of the Citroën in the castle parking lot.

"I'll be in touch later, Madame Cadiou," he said, already on the steps, storming down them, reaching for his phone with his right hand.

Damn! Why hadn't he thought of it earlier?

Never in his life had the commissaire run down steps so fast.

"All operational vehicles to the castle. Immediately. No detours!"

"What?"

Dupin was closing the car door the instant Nolwenn took his call.

"I want all cars to come to Castle Comper immediately."

"I hear you."

She was wide awake.

"Riwal and Kadeg have to be there somewhere. I'm absolutely certain of it."

Dupin had already started the engine and put his foot down.

"Why do you think that?"

"Kadeg's jacket!"

"Kadeg's jacket?"

Dupin's mind was racing, playing through different scenarios.

"Kadeg's jacket is lying on the back seat of a brand-new Citroën by the castle."

That was it. Dupin had glanced into the car and seen the jacket. Stupidly, without putting the two things together. A military green jacket. He had no doubt. It was only Madame Cadiou's sweater that had reminded him.

"What was it doing in . . ." She stopped dead. "Brand new, you said?"

"Yes."

"A rental car. They took a rental car. Kadeg—I advised him to do so but he never came back to me. And that was because . . . You can have a rental car delivered. Of course, that's it!"

"We need to check the license plate right away." Dupin had reached the tarmac road, which meant he pressed the gas pedal harder. The tires screeched.

It was a plausible scenario. And if it had been Kadeg who had called for the rental car, it would be even better. Dupin could imagine the call to the car rental agency:

"The fastest car you have, with the most powerful engine." And above all: "This is a special investigation for the Paris police on orders from the minister of the interior! Please bring the car to Château de Comper."

It was Nolwenn though who asked the crucial question: "But where are they? The two gendarmes have searched the castle."

"Then they missed something."

Dupin took an extremely tight corner and had trouble bringing the car back under control.

"Call Guivorch! He needs to come there now!"

Dupin had thought of the building blueprint he had briefly seen on Guivorch's laptop. Which had remained on his mind, even though he couldn't think precisely why. And there was another wholly practical reason.

"Guivorch will have access to a floor plan of the castle. Or at least will know where there is one. Including maps of the entire castle grounds. Maybe even the whole neighborhood. There might even be buildings in the wood that belong to the castle: hunting lodges, shacks, whatever."

"I'll call him right now and make sure he opens the door immediately. Should I come too?"

"Stay where you are, Nolwenn. We need an HQ."

She wasn't keen but she agreed with a heavy heart. "You're right. I'll call the two gendarmes with the master key straightaway."

"Excellent. See you soon, Nolwenn."

"Good luck." She hung up.

It was less than ten minutes before Dupin's car yet again roared into the Centre castle parking lot and this time came to a halt right next to the smart new Citroën. Within a few minutes Nolwenn was back on the phone to tell him that Guivorch was on his way.

Dupin leapt out of the car, phone already in his hand. "Yes?"

Dupin knelt down in front of the car. The license plate was just legible in the moonlight. The moon was even higher than before, but for some reason the light was weaker.

"The license plate is EJ-364-AS."

"Hang on a minute. I have everything ready. They're waiting for my call in Rennes."

Even at night Nolwenn could make the impossible possible.

Dupin waited. Already he could hear Nolwenn say on another line: "Yes, that's me. With the license plate. Put in EJ-364-AS."

Dupin ran nervously round the Citroën. The jacket and pullover were still lying on the back seat.

After a while, she said, "Yes, I understand." He could hear her writing something down. "I repeat, owned by Europcar Ploërmel, 22 Avenue du Maréchal de Lattre de Tassigny. A DS5 Performance Line, in metallic platinum gray, first registered May this year. Great, thank you very much."

That was the end of the call, but already the dynamic description "Performance Line" sounded like Kadeg.

"So, everything just as we thought." Nolwenn was back on the line to Dupin. "They had a car. They could have driven to the Relais de Brocéliande, like Riwal had said. But they didn't. That makes every-thing more urgent."

"Perhaps they were threatened. Forced to go somewhere. With weapons maybe. Without doubt there was a gun involved. Then some-body locked them up somewhere." Nolwenn was saying aloud what had already gone through Dupin's head. And obviously there was also a worse scenario.

Silence fell. Dupin walked back to the rental vehicle with the flashlight in his hand.

Two cars approached on the rural track. Their high beams had re-markable reach. There were also sirens in the distance, coming closer.

Nolwenn had heard them too.

"At last! They took their time. I told them they—"

"I can see the jacket," Dupin interrupted her. "Military green."

"Can you see a brand name?"

"Yes. A bit hard to make out, but there's a capital *S*—Salomon."

"That's it."

The two police cars reached the parking lot.

"Good, Nolwenn. We'll search everything here down to the last corner."

"Do that, and keep me in the loop. Aballain is in one of the cars."

"Good!" One more question had struck him. "Do you know if the King Arthur society often meet here in the castle?"

"Five times in ten years, every second meeting. I don't know any-thing about meetings before then. But they would all know the build-ings and the surrounding area well."

Nolwenn had understood what he was getting at. And both In-wynn and Madame Cadiou would also know their way around.

"Talk to you later."

* * *

In the meantime the rest of the police cars that had been in the wood had arrived. Nine of them.

It was a spectacular sight, all of them circled around Dupin's car with blinding headlights and flashing lights. All of this in front of the backdrop of a fairy-tale castle by a magical lake, beneath tonight's pale, particularly full moon.

And Guivorch now rolled onto the parking lot in a dark blue SUV.

Dupin had gathered the gendarmes—eighteen of them, all with heavy flashlights, guns, and radios—in a semicircle around his car.

Amongst them were the two colleagues he had met up with in Cadiou's room and who had Guivorch's master key. Leaning on the car door he'd outlined everything in a brief summary: their task, their mission. Dupin was staring into serious faces. Something like this didn't happen every day here.

"One moment, I'll be right back."

Dupin walked briskly over to Guivorch, who had just gotten out of his car.

He wasn't in the mood for any banter, not even a hello. "Do you have any idea where my two inspectors could be held?"

He had stopped maybe a meter away and was looking at Guivorch with narrowed eyes.

Naturally it wasn't without problems for the deputy director to take part in the search. Apart from anything else, he could be the brutal killer, even if he was not Madame Noiret's attacker. And he could have had accomplices; the storyteller, for example. And he might also be responsible for the disappearance of Riwal and Kadeg. It was the most ludicrous of situations. But for one thing they needed the plans of the building and the surrounding area. For another Dupin lacked any way to push things forward. He could watch Guivorch from close up and lie in wait for a mistake, if he were involved. Dupin would miss nothing.

"If I did know where they were, would I have voluntarily got up in the middle of the night in order to help you search for them, Monsieur le Commissaire?" A masterfully confident answer.

"Where are the maps of the castle and the neighborhood?"

"In my office. It's best if we talk there." Guivorch sounded particularly cooperative.

Dupin thought about it. It was a brief hesitation, but there was no easy way around it. They would have to take a pragmatic approach.

He turned around.

"We're going up to Monsieur Guivorch's office. All of us together."

Three minutes later they had gone through the visitors' entrance next to the bookshop and into Guivorch's room, where they all gathered around a large table. His office was on the same floor as Monsieur Cadiou's. But unlike Cadiou's, all the walls here were covered in shelves. And instead of lounge-style seating, here there was a large table with eight seats, while to the right was a desk, the same model as Cadiou's.

The plans were large, old-fashioned: two of them. One of the castle—which showed the ground floor and the three above—and one of the surroundings. Indeed, there was a row of buildings in a circle around the castle. And in the castle itself were rooms, nooks, and corners that the gendarmes had not yet taken into account in their inspections.

"What might have been of interest to your inspectors? Where could they have gone? That's what we have to ask ourselves. Strictly from their perspective." Colonel Aballain was approaching the issue from a strategic point of view. "And/or," his expression grew dark, "somebody threatened them and locked them up somewhere. Or took them somewhere, where they are now sitting. In which case we need to think from the perspective of that person. What would have been least conspicuous?"

Dupin kept a steady eye on Guivorch during the briefing.

"In the second scenario," the pale gendarme took over, "we need to start from their last known location. That means the Knights' Hall upstairs. If somebody grabbed them there that would strongly indicate they are somewhere in the castle."

"Professor Guivorch," one of the other gendarmes spoke up in a lively voice, "which rooms would you think of first? Which would be the best if one had two people to hold captive?"

Guivorch looked as if he was concentrating. "I think the attic. Those of us here in the Centre increasingly forget it ourselves. Just above the Knights' Hall."

Dupin bent low over the ground plan. "There seem to be proper rooms to the left and right of the hall. What's with that?" He nodded toward the plan.

"You can get there via inconspicuous doors from both stairwells."

Without hesitating, Dupin ordered, "Two of you take each one of the stairwells, then the other. Come back here when you're done with your tasks."

The two pairs left hurriedly.

"On the ground floor it's only on the eastern side that there are rooms which don't lead to the exhibition spaces. They're used more or less as spare rooms. Here," Guivorch indicated on the plan. "Oh yes." Something had just occurred to him. "There are two more rooms behind the bookshop. One of them is a sort of office. The other a storage room."

Dupin reacted at once.

"Two officers, check out these ground-floor rooms. Off you go. And then the whole of the ground floor."

In anticipation of their tasks, groups of two had formed up. Everything was going remarkably easily and simply. Dupin was impressed.

"On the first floor," Guivorch continued, "we have the west side and the middle with exhibition space. On the east side are the administration and interview rooms."

"We'll search everywhere!" Dupin glanced around and another pair set off.

"What about other secret rooms? And passageways?"

Guivorch gave him an inquisitive look.

"Like upstairs in the attic?"

"That's the only place there are any."

That couldn't be true. Dupin bent down over the floor plan again and went through the floors one by one.

It did seem that, in fact, each space was clearly devoted to a single room. But wasn't it the very point of hidden rooms that they did not show up on floor plans?

"Really? This is all there is?"

"Yes."

"Let's look at the other buildings in the area around the castle," Aballain said, and took the second map and laid it next to the first. He didn't seem to quite trust Guivorch either. "There are the buildings inside the walls, here," he pointed to the map, "the former stables, the former servants' quarters." Dupin had looked at them that afternoon. "And then there are those outside the walls. Here, the former forestry workers' house, on the road that leads toward the visitors' parking lot, and a smaller building near the staff parking lot."

"That's a general warehouse," Guivorch added, anticipating Dupin's question.

"Apart from those," Guivorch said, "there's also a toolshed, close to the visitor entrance. It's not easy to see." He pointed to the map, the gendarmes looking closely.

"Then outside the wall there are two huts and a little house in the wood by the lake. Here," he tapped on the map for each, "here, and here." All the gendarmes remained gathered closely around Aballain and Guivorch.

"What sort of little house?" Dupin didn't like things to be left vague.

"There's an exhibition about the various flora and fauna of the wood," Guivorch added willingly.

"Are those all the buildings?" Dupin wanted a definitive list. "No other huts, shacks, or anything similar?"

"No." Guivorch looked as if he was hesitating.

Dupin leapt in. "What are you hiding from us, Monsieur Guivorch?"

All of a sudden the air was tense.

"There's another hut by the lake. With a shelter. We use it on tours, if it rains."

"Two men there." Dupin gave the order almost infuriatingly calmly. "And one team," he added, "to the toolshed near the public entrance, and then to the two huts and the 'flora and fauna house.'"

"And then," Guivorch added enthusiastically, "there's the cellar here in the castle. Quite labyrinthine. You should certainly look in there."

"There's a cellar? Why didn't you say that in the first place?"

"I was going to, but the colonel," Guivorch nodded at Aballain, "went straight to the buildings in the surrounding area, that suddenly sounded more important."

"Does the area of the cellar cover all that of the building?" Dupin asked sharply. "Are there plans of the cellar rooms?"

"No. They're actually more vaults than proper rooms. We use some of them as archives, and some as storage areas. Warehouses. The area of the cellar is substantially larger than that of the castle itself. There's just one entrance, behind the bookshop."

"The castle is bigger under the ground than it is above it?"

"Precisely."

"And there's no ground plan?"

Guivorch hurried over to his computer. "Just for the front part. It just occurred to me."

Dupin frowned.

"An intern here made this."

They had gathered to the left and right of the computer.

"Here!"

Guivorch opened a file, on which they could see an outline of the castle—a sort of blueprint—and on top of that, in black pencil, sketches which indeed went out a long way beyond the outline of the castle and were clearly intended to show the extent of the cellar. In several places there were gaps, and several question marks.

"The bit up front is the area we actually use."

"What's in the 'warehouse'?"

"All sorts of items collected from the excavations. When they're identified, they go to the archive."

"Items from the excavations in the forest or round about? You're storing items from the excavations here?"

"It's one of the scientific tasks of the Centre."

A prosaic explanation.

"I need to take a look at these rooms, Monsieur Guivorch. And you're coming with me."

Guivorch nodded, and was almost immediately ready to go.

"What about the rest of the cellar?" Dupin nodded at the screen, at two areas, one behind the other, with pale-drawn lines, indicating an extension of the cellar to the east and the lake. In two of these places it looked as if they might even continue out under the lake. But there was no indication where they ended. "And what's with all these areas with question marks?"

"To be honest, I don't know precisely. The cellar was Cadiou's business. I don't like cellars."

It was the first time that Dupin had felt any sympathy for Guivorch. He didn't like cellars either.

"The former owners had also used the rear part as a wine cellar. Cadiou had once come across a few old bottles."

"The cellar was Cadiou's territory?"

"Yes."

"Did the inspectors know about the cellar?" Aballain asked the commissaire.

"I don't know. But—"

Guivorch interrupted Dupin. "We discussed the cellar briefly up in the Knights' Hall. About the rooms and the excavation finds."

"When?"

"After your inspectors took down all our alibis, they posed a few extra questions."

"Such as?"

Dupin was beside himself, about to lose his composure. Guivorch had to have known that this information was of burning interest to him.

"It was all about the excavation projects here in the wood. The more congenial of the pair was very interested in this point. And about the wood in general too. He seemed extraordinarily well informed."

Dupin smiled. Riwal would have been proud: a renowned professor of archeology praising his knowledge . . . "What do you mean by 'about the wood in general'?"

"He wanted to know precisely which of us had been involved in excavations over the past few years, and to what extent. The questions you had already asked."

"Was Inspector Riwal interested in anything in particular?"

"Like I said. We came back to the projects you already know about: Cadbury Castle, Glastonbury. And the three current projects in the wood."

"Colonel Aballain." Dupin spoke calmly, but determinedly. "I'd like you to go back to the other scholars, find out what Riwal and Kadeg spoke to them about."

He might have been deceiving himself but Dupin thought Guivorch had the suggestion of a smile on his face.

"Now?" Aballain looked at his watch.

"Now."

The colonel took out his phone and walked out into the hallway.

Dupin turned brusquely to Guivorch. "Do the others know about the cellar?"

"Yes. The last time the symposium took place here, the program included a tour. Led by the former chairman of the archeology faculty of the Université de Rennes, who in the early days had once been the administrator of the then rather modest Centre. He's dead now, but had put a lot of energy into the excavations, throughout his life. It was his hobby. The archive goes back to him."

"Is it possible the first finds from Picard's dig are there?"

"Like I said, as far as I know, the excavation still hadn't properly begun. They were still on the preliminary work."

"The two remaining teams," Dupin ordered decisively, "into the cellar. One team to take the front part, the other to the rear where the question marks are on the plan."

The four remaining men headed off without hesitation. Dupin stayed behind with Guivorch. Aballain was still on the phone in the hallway.

"If this is a game," Dupin spoke softly, but sharply articulated—he was scarcely in control of himself and couldn't care less—"and if it turns out you're the one we're after, there'll be nothing left when I'm done with you."

Guivorch turned his glance toward Dupin. The commissaire stared him straight in the eyes.

After a second Dupin turned abruptly away, went over to the window, and looked out at the lake in the moonlight. The lake that wasn't a lake, just the illusion of a lake, beneath which lay the truth. In the mystery which Dupin was to solve here—and that he would, his anger told him—they would find no glorious crystal-clear truth. The dark words of the priest in the Church of the Holy Grail came to him: be aware that not everything you see is there, and that you don't see everything that is.

"I . . ." Guivorch began, "have nothing—"

"I know you're keeping something from me, you and all the others," Dupin interrupted him, still looking at the lake. "That you all know much more than you tell us. All of you."

There was no longer any doubt about that. An uncomfortable silence followed.

Dupin stepped back to Guivorch.

"This undefined area here . . ." He was standing just a few centimeters from Guivorch, pointing at the faint lines on the sketch of the cellar toward the lake. ". . . have you ever been there?"

"No, as I told you, the cellar was Cadiou's territory. He had always talked of expanding it."

"And?"

"I think we would have—"

Colonel Aballain entered Guivorch's office, walking briskly, and interrupted the deputy director.

"I've just spoken to Denvel. I can't get hold of either Bothorel or Terrier at the moment."

"Go ahead," Dupin said as if Guivorch wasn't there.

"After the two inspectors were finished taking down the alibis of all of them, they had a few extra questions. Professor Denvel remembered some of the topics. Inspector Kadeg had wanted to know who had campaigned to get Cadiou's job. That had seemed an important point for him. And he announced he was going to check out all the alibis thoroughly. Inspector Riwal was primarily interested in the excavations, particularly the three here in the wood, and another in Spain." Aballain too was speaking as if Guivorch wasn't there. "Then about the cellar, the archive, the warehouse. He focused his questions about these on Monsieur Guivorch. Amongst other things he was interested in tunnels, underground passageways." Aballain paused briefly before resuming. "Denvel remembered that Riwal wanted to know how well they all knew the castle and the area, and when they were last here. He asked in particular about the last three months. And that was that," Aballain concluded.

It all sounded consistent. And very revealing. Everything made sense.

"Very interesting, Monsieur Guivorch," Dupin said coldly. "These are very interesting deviations from what you have told us here."

"You know, Commissaire, that everybody's story will have deviations. I think that's normal. Nobody was taking notes, as far as I know."

"And everybody probably had a good reason not to tell something or other." Dupin followed on from Riwal's line of questioning. "What was the excavation in Spain?"

"Your inspector began to discuss it all of a sudden. He asked if any of us had been present on this project, which we all denied. None of us had been there."

"What is this project about?"

"Today at my place you saw the Spanish priest's book. The monastery in—"

"The story about the Grail," Dupin interjected. He remembered it.

"Exactly."

"What are these underground tunnels the two of you talked about?"

"Way back in the Middle Ages," Guivorch said, "they were digging tunnels under the lake. A few of them led from the castle, but not all of them. They were also dug from the other side. There are supposed to be dozens. But we only know a few and they don't go very far. In the meantime, some of them have collapsed, their entrances caved in or crumbled. A few of them are alleged to go all the way underneath the lake, forming a complete system. People wanted to get to the heart of the legend, literally." Guivorch smiled his supercilious smile that Dupin already knew. "Over the centuries more and more adventurers claimed to have found the castle of Viviane, but wouldn't explain how to get there. An eternal secret.

"Madame Cadiou," Guivorch continued, "intended to turn one of these tunnels into an attraction for the park. The Fairy Castle of Viviane"—there was the utmost irony in his voice—"on the lake bed."

"For the park?"

"Yes."

Dupin remembered the drawing board in Madame Cadiou's office: Station Lac de Viviane. It represented just the gangway and underwater panorama.

"Which tunnel is it supposed to be?"

"No idea."

"And which of your members was here in the last three months?" Dupin had no intention of forgetting Riwal's other question.

"I made a note of what Denvel said," Aballain informed them. "Picard and Terrier on account of their digs, Terrier yet again to give a lecture, and Denvel himself, also for a lecture."

"Denvel too? When?"

"Six weeks ago," Guivorch answered. "I invited him to Rennes. We were having a little conference, he came to the Centre too. We drank a *café* together."

"You invited him? Are you and Monsieur Denvel more closely connected?"

"No, but I know which of us is currently working on more financially lucrative academic themes."

"Is Denvel's answer complete in respect of the past three months?"

"He forgot his stepmother's lecture in Nantes a few weeks ago. That's not all that far away."

Dupin had walked over to the window again and looked out over the lake.

"Where are the known entrances to the tunnels? Those that start outside the castle."

What was it that had made Riwal so interested?

"There are a few maps on the internet showing the officially recognized ones, and the presumed ones. I'll show you."

Guivorch pulled up the maps.

"There. These three entrances." Guivorch pointed them out on the screen. "And then another two entrances, here in the cellar."

There was a loud cracking noise over the radio: "Dubois here."

"Aballain, receiving you."

"We're finished with the attic and the hidden rooms. Negative. Nobody's been here in years."

"Okay, come back."

"Monsieur Guivorch, what do you know about these entrances from the cellar?"

"Nothing. Other than that they've been closed down for safety's sake."

"And what about the three entrances outside the castle?"

"Two of them collapsed. The third is the biggest and is on the northeasterly bank of the lake."

Without saying another word, Dupin walked back over to the window.

For a while he stood there motionless, then he turned to Aballain.

"Tell the gendarmes to go and look at both tunnel entrances in the cellar. Straightaway. And the team from the attic need to go and see to the other one by the lake. You—"

Dupin interrupted himself and ran his hands through his hair.

"No, we'll do it another way. I want to take a look at that entrance myself."

Didn't Inwynn say in the Relais de Brocéliande he himself had taken a group along the lakeside for the first time yesterday?

"You want to go to that tunnel?" Aballain seemed surprised.

Guivorch, on the contrary, was hard to read.

"I do."

"But . . ." Guivorch spoke up now. "Even by the lakeside you won't get into the tunnel. The entrance is blocked. I know it."

"Here we are again." The two gendarmes from the attic. "We—"

"You're coming with me," Dupin interrupted them. "You too, Guivorch." Dupin stared him straight in the eye again. "Inspector Riwal is single-minded, if he wants to get somewhere, he gets there."

Dupin stood briefly in the door frame. "Colonel Aballain, just to be sure, send the next free teams to both the collapsed tunnel entrances outside the castle. You're mission central here."

"Okay, here, take this." He handed Dupin one of the walkie-talkies. "It won't work deep underground. Nonetheless. For before and after."

Dupin headed off, with Guivorch and the two gendarmes trailing behind him.

There wasn't a single star to be seen in the sky. Nor were there any clouds gathered, just a sort of blurry mist.

In the thick wood through which they were walking—already some distance from the castle—neither the moon nor the stars would have been visible. The darkness that reigned here was deep black. A black that was no longer a color but a substance. A black you had to wade through. Heavier than air.

The spheres of light thrown by their flashlights let visions of the world here and there pop up before being devoured by the darkness again. The sharply focused light didn't reach very far. The mist had changed the balmy summer night. It had cooled down noticeably. That happened: as a Breton you knew that the temperature could fall rapidly within a quarter of an hour. There was a scent of earth and wood.

They couldn't be that far off the bank of the lake, maybe twenty or thirty meters, but the lake wasn't visible. Dupin had seen it in the bright daylight of the afternoon. The thick woodland reached right to the lakeside, as if to say "The lake belongs to me."

"It's not far now," Guivorch said.

Gradually one after another the teams had checked in with Aballain or Dupin after finishing their searches. So far none of them had discovered anything suspicious. Aballain had given the teams new tasks as appropriate.

Dupin was extremely worked up. His concern wasn't just pushing him onward, into action, but also into doubt. Was he really doing the right thing? Deep down he knew that what they were doing here was highly speculative. In reality it might all be quite different. Maybe Kadeg and Riwal had unknowingly found something.

Dupin felt guilty. He should have gotten actively involved earlier. But it had been plausible to assume that the two inspectors had followed a trail of their own. Dupin remembered a few such excursions Riwal and Kadeg had made during previous investigations.

For some reason the four of them—Dupin, Guivorch, and the two gendarmes—had all fallen into a stubborn silence. Perhaps it was the growing tension to which they were all subject.

"Turn right here. Be careful, this is a narrow, uneven forest path with roots and stones. It's very easy to trip and fall even in daylight."

The path led slightly downhill.

After a minute of walking quickly and silently, continuously encountering shrubs and branches, Guivorch stopped dead.

"This is it."

One of the gendarmes shone his flashlight on a low shack.

Dupin quickly began to walk around the shack, which stood in a little clearing. It was built of crude, moss-covered wood that seemed rotted in various places. Dupin found a door, which was in the same dubious condition, but was sealed with a sturdy padlock. He shone his flashlight at it.

It seemed in good condition. He rattled it, as hard as he could. The hinges were sound.

"Nobody's got in through this door," one of the gendarmes concluded. Dupin had moved away again.

"Maybe they climbed over the roof?"

"We should—"

Dupin was interrupted by the ear-shattering screeching of the walkie-talkie: "Mandon calling. Anyone hear me? Over."

"We hear you, loud and clear."

"I'm just coming out of the cellar." Mandon sounded completely out of breath. "We think there's been an accident down here." He was trying hard to keep his voice under control. "It seems to have caved in, and there's water coming from the roof. It's possible the inspectors may be trapped in one of the tunnels."

"Have you had any sign of them?" Dupin asked in alarm.

Background noise.

"I can't make you out."

"Have you been in contact with the pair of them?"

"No. Not so far. It's just a suspicion. But there are tracks here of at least two people." The gendarme seemed even more distraught now.

"Maybe more than two people?"

"Can't say at the moment." Once again he was hardly audible.

"We're on our way." With those words, Dupin had already stormed off.

* * *

The first part of the cellar had seemed quite normal. Then they passed through a room that had walls built up out of rough stones, but no more concrete flooring. They were walking on beaten-down soil, to reach a dilapidated door that led into a remarkably large room of just plain earth.

There were damp patches in some places, on the floor too. But the most conspicuous thing was the U-shaped wooden beams, held together by cross struts which seemed to be supporting the walls and ceiling. Their primitive condition suggested the beams dated from a previous century.

The whole construction looked like the skeleton of some huge animal. As if they were inside a whale.

Dupin guessed it was some thirty meters to the other end of the vault.

It downright stank, bitterly, of old earth, moss, mold, fungi of some sort. Putrefaction.

To be accurate they were no longer in a cellar, nor a vault, but in a provisionally dug out hollow space under the ground. An artificial, obviously fragile cave. Dupin didn't like underground spaces. Cellars made him feel unwell, anxious, uneasy.

The fire service and two ambulances were due to arrive from Ploërmel any moment. A specialist team from Rennes was due to follow them. Aballain had updated Nolwenn with the latest state of events. Dupin had briefly considered sending Guivorch back to his office, but then changed his mind and took him underground with him.

"The tunnels in question start from over there." Aballain pointed his flashlight at the opposite side of the room. "But I have to tell you, Commissaire," he clearly found this hard to say out loud, "It doesn't look good."

Dupin headed for it.

There was a hole in the earthen wall, as high as the room itself.

Behind it, a similar structure supported by beams, except that here they were not so much professionally constructed pillars as medium-sized tree trunks roughly hewn out of necessity. A meter in, they came across a primitive door pushed open, with two large faded warning signs: *NO ENTRY, DANGER OF DEATH.*

Dupin ran straight past them. Aballain and two gendarmes followed him.

Then they saw it.

"There used to be a second door up in front, it's . . ."

"I see it."

The construction had completely collapsed. To the right above them a huge hole in the ceiling gaped, and the earth had fallen through it.

"Riwal? Kadeg?"

"The earth swallows up the sound." Aballain lowered his voice. "Even if they could hear us, any noise they make probably wouldn't get through. Knocking on stone we would hear, but not knocking on loose earth."

Dupin stared ferociously at the earth as if he could bore a hole in it with his eyes.

"This happened recently. There's the smell of fresh earth."

Dupin himself had noticed it. He was feeling faint.

"We really shouldn't stay here. The specialists advised us over the phone to clear all the surrounding area. The gendarmes with us are here as volunteers. A task undertaken at their own risk."

It was only now that Dupin properly paid attention to the gendarmes. It was the same couple who had been in Cadiou's office with him: the pale one and the suntanned one.

"You need to get out of here!" he shouted to them.

They both shook their heads decisively.

"We need—"

Dupin interrupted Aballain. "Where are we? I mean, where exactly?"

"Probably under the lake," Aballain said, and nodded toward the side wall. Behind one of the tree trunks, water was running down the wall, creating a puddle all the way along the wall.

Dupin turned to Guivorch: "How old is this construction here?"

"Nobody knows."

"How long is this tunnel and where does it lead to?"

"I have no idea, and I imagine there's nobody still alive around here who does."

"Given what you know of the situation here, and given your specialist knowledge—could this collapse have been caused deliberately?" He had lent a sharp tone to his voice.

"You mean . . ." There was shock in Guivorch's expression. "This could have been attempted murder?"

"That's exactly what I mean."

Guivorch stared for a while uncertainly at the pile of earth.

"It certainly can't be excluded. But you'll need to ask the experts."

Dupin fell into a despondent silence. The dizziness in his head was growing.

On his way down through the vault-like rooms Dupin had spotted something. "Did Cadiou store archeological finds in the vaults before this room? Stones, for example?"

"It would appear so."

"Which?"

"It's beyond my knowledge. Whether you believe me or not, I can only repeat: the cellar was Monsieur Cadiou's terrain. His predecessor stored lots of things here too. These could be his."

"I would like—"

"Hello?" a deep voice called. "Are you here?"

A fireman appeared, roughly Dupin's height, with a full head of gray hair, combed backward, a bushy white mustache, leathery skin.

Behind him were two other firemen in full gear and two clearly worried paramedics.

"Fire brigade, Chief Bouvet." He gave a formal nod, and looked carefully around. "So this is where it happened." He indicated the large pile of earth.

His colleagues came over. The paramedics stayed at a comfortable distance.

The fire chief carefully examined the location of the collapse.

"We're going to keep as far away as possible from that while we wait for the experts. I'm going to call them and give them my initial thoughts. I'll be back in a minute."

He signaled to his colleagues: "You stay here. And should anything happen . . ." He held up his walkie-talkie.

The firemen gathered around Aballain and the brave gendarmes.

Guivorch had moved off to one side. Dupin went over to him.

"Don't you think it's time we had a talk?"

Yet again Dupin felt a monstrous rage rising, not just against Guivorch, but the whole group of scholars.

"Even if you don't have Cadiou and Picard on your conscience—and for now I still think it perfectly possible—you know something. I even think you know what all this grim business is about. You know the motive."

It was still as it always had been in Dupin's mind: they all knew something and denied it.

All of a sudden Guivorch looked exhausted, almost nervous; his eyes had shrunk, his forehead wrinkled deeply. Dupin shot a quick glance at his watch. It was five past four.

"You were looking at building plans when I was with you on the boat. Were they plans for the cellar here?"

"You have a vivid imagination, Monsieur le Commissaire."

"Do you know what I'm going to do?" Dupin was losing patience. "I'm going to tell two of my colleagues to go with you right now to your house in Saint-Péran. I want to know if there really is an extension being built. Then you're going to show the two of them the computer on your houseboat, including the file you had open when I arrived."

Dupin ought to have done this earlier. Been more direct. More forceful.

"You know you need a search warrant to do that."

Dupin was about to lose his composure.

"But if you promise me, Commissaire"—all of a sudden all his weariness had vanished and the wily old Guivorch was back—"that this will let me go to bed, then I'll take your whole gang with me, if you want!"

Dupin ignored Guivorch's final sentence and gave the plucky gendarmes orders to go with him to Saint-Péran, to search his computer, not letting him out of their sight.

Then Dupin went back to the scene of the collapse. The little stream that ran down the wall had gotten noticeably bigger. The puddles on the ground had spread wider. What must it look like on the other side? Dupin's nerves were frayed. He had worried the whole time about Riwal and Kadeg. He had had a bad feeling. And it seemed to be coming true.

* * *

Dupin couldn't have said how long he'd stayed at the entrance to the scene of the collapse. At times his mind was playing tricks on him: the entrance to the tunnel seemed to suddenly expand to become a

gigantic cave, then shrink back down again, the walls coming noticeably together. Once Dupin found himself going dizzy and thought it
was the ground moving.

Dupin tried to go through all the developments in the case over
the day systematically, one by one. He failed miserably. He wasn't
capable of thinking logically.

"Move to one side, please. There are too many people here." A
man in dark blue overalls, wearing several belts and carrying a helmet
with a light on the front under his arm, pushed his way through. He
had short dark hair, a high forehead, dark eyes, a trim, sinewy stature.
"I ordered a complete evacuation of the cellar."

Dupin made space for him. He was clearly dealing with the rescue team leader of the SDIS, the Service Départemental d'Incendie
et de Secours.

"Commissaire Georges Dupin, I'm in charge of—"

"That may be so," the man interrupted him, "but we're going to do
our work here first."

The man had taken up a position right in the middle of the entrance to the collapsed tunnel.

"It's my inspectors in there, I'm staying here."

The team leader hesitated. He shot Dupin a curious glance and
muttered: "It's your own responsibility."

"Fine." Dupin nodded.

The man took his gloves off and knelt down. He took a handful
of soil and felt through it, then repeated the same in various places.

"But at least can you leave the entrance to the tunnel?"

He was still hunched down. He rubbed some of the earth between thumb and index finger. Smelled it. Deep in concentration.

Dupin saw another three men, with the same gear and sizable alu-
minum cases, pushing their way into the entrance. Aballain and the

two firemen had retreated to the vault, making space for them. Two of the men came to the front with a long, thin, telescopic pipe, which they extended. Dupin guessed it measured seven or eight meters. The third man was carrying a lantern in his left hand, and in his right an impressive piece of technical equipment that resembled an outsize radio. He set up the lantern, turned a knob on the piece of equipment. And waited.

"No fresh air," he said dryly. "But not poisonous either."

His boss gave a measured nod. "Then let's go."

Dupin retired to the rear part of the tunnel entrance.

Everything seemed to be going ahead professionally.

The pipe—which looked to be made of a special type of fiberglass—was set up about twenty centimeters above the floor. The two men, equipped with special yellow gloves, began to turn it so as to bore into the soil. Their boss had stayed up front near where the piping entered the earth, watching it closely. The lantern illuminated the whole scene without blinding them.

A couple of times Dupin wanted to say something like "How is it going?" But in reality he had a whole row of panicky questions on his tongue, all of which would have wasted time and which nobody could have answered.

Time went by. It was obvious that the men were doing everything extremely carefully.

The seconds turned into minutes. To an eternity. The air was filled with the utmost tension. Dupin's eyes were glued to the pipe where it was boring into the earth. Now and again he looked to see how much remained. Hopefully there would be enough.

All of a sudden there was a jolt.

"Yes!" Dupin exclaimed. That had to mean they had broken through, didn't it?

None of the men gave a reaction. All three of them looked to their boss, who put on yellow work gloves without saying a word and picked up the pipe. He moved it very carefully back and forth a couple of times.

"Probably just some loose soil. Keep going."

The heavy silence resumed. But this time not for long.

The boss gave the order. "Now." He moved the pipe back and forth. "We're through."

Dupin had seen nothing. No jolt. Nothing at all.

"I'm going to open the lock."

He turned a mechanism on the side of the pipe.

"Now."

One of the two men lay down on the ground, supporting himself on his elbows.

He looked up at the team leader. "Okay."

"This is the SDIS rescue team," he said slowly. "Can you hear me?"

He held his ear to the pipe.

Nothing.

Once again.

Still nothing.

"We'll put the sensor in." The team leader was still calm itself. "Then we can see something and find out what the air on the other side is like."

"The oxygen level here in the entranceway," the man with the air-quality measurement equipment said, "has dropped."

The rescue team leader remained calm. Unlike Dupin.

"Insert the sensor, we need to—"

"Hello?"

A curiously echoing voice. Not very loud. "Hello, hello, boss?"

A pause. "Boss, is that you?"

"Riwal! That's Inspector Riwal."

Dupin dashed up to the pipe and threw himself down to the ground.

"Riwal?"

The answer came immediately. "I knew it! You're there."

"Are you hurt? Is Kadeg with you?"

"Yes, he lost consciousness when the earth collapsed." Riwal hesitated a moment. "But he's okay now."

"How are things on your side?" Dupin wanted to know.

"Stable so far. There's a lot of water coming in. But it's spreading across the ground. The tunnel seems to be very long."

"We'll get you out, Riwal."

The rescue team leader knelt down on the ground next to Dupin.

"I'll take over," he said.

Dupin moved to the side. He felt extraordinarily relieved. Riwal and Kadeg were alive.

"This is the rescue team leader. I want you to do exactly as I say." The man waited for a second. "Move far away from the area of fallen earth. Look and see if there are any other stone passageways. Then wait and stay calm. We're pushing a pipe through the earth that will be big enough for you to crawl through. Do you think you are able to do that yourselves, or do you need help?"

"Not necessary. We'll manage."

The statement sounded decisive.

Dupin stood up.

The other men in the team were preparing the big pipe constructed of several thin elements which they linked together, each about a meter long.

"I'll be right back, messieurs. I have something I urgently need to take care of." There was no alternative for him but to get in touch with Nolwenn, to offer her some relief.

The team leader nodded, and turned back to his colleagues.

Dupin said a few brisk words to the little group in the vault, without slowing his pace. He ran up the tunnels, through the bookshop, and into the open air, his phone already in his hand.

Nolwenn picked up immediately, as if she had been holding her phone in her hand all the time.

"We have them. They're unharmed."

Those were the most important two sentences.

"Where were they?" Nolwenn sounded endlessly relieved.

"In an ancient tunnel under the lake. A pillar collapsed, and tons of soil fell down. They were cut off, but we're in contact with them and the rescue is under way."

"In that case we've been lucky once again," Nolwenn sighed. The vast relief was followed up by the typical Breton black humor reaction to such challenging moments: "But there you are, like they say: *N'eus nemet un dra a bouez: Chom bev a-hed e vuhez*—the most important thing in life is to stay alive, as long as you live!"

It was true enough! Dupin smiled.

"I'm going back down." He wanted to be the one to greet his inspectors.

"Yes, do that."

* * *

"Leave me alone, I'm fine."

Kadeg had insisted on being the last to crawl through the pipe. The whole business had gone smoothly. The rescue team boss couldn't know it, but Kadeg's grumbly tone was the best proof of that. Nonetheless, Kadeg was pale. Dupin noticed a bleeding wound on his right cheek. Kadeg swayed a bit, and it was easy to see from his face how shaken he'd been. His clothes were wet and covered in soil. The back of his hair and his temples were muddy, as were his arms and throat. He looked wild.

"All I need is a shower and clean clothes."

A paramedic came over to the inspector. Another was already with Riwal.

"Come on, move," the rescue team leader said in an impatient and unmistakably authoritarian tone of voice. "Everybody out of the cellar. And I mean now."

The whole tribe set off immediately, with Colonel Aballain in the lead. After a bit of initial resistance, Kadeg let himself use the support of the paramedic while walking.

Astonishingly, Riwal seemed to be doing just fine.

"What happened? What were you doing here? Were you forced down here by somebody?" Dupin could wait no longer to fire off the most important questions.

"It was all my fault. We—I, rather . . ." The inspector hesitated. "I wanted to take another look at something, boss."

"Another look?"

"I wanted to take another look at the archeological finds in the cellar. They were stored in various parts. Always had been, but Cadiou spread them out further. He . . ." Riwal was almost stammering. "We came down here of our own accord. It was my idea. . . ."

Dupin understood.

"You were just pursuing a lead. Just as expected from any policeman. You were doing your job. Nothing more." Dupin tried to calm him down.

They had gotten out of the vault, which cheered Dupin up immensely. "It was my stupidity," Riwal muttered. "I thought that maybe there was . . . something hidden here. We had talked with the scholars and looked through the catalog in Cadiou's study describing all the archived items. They included several items from this year, including Terrier's and Guivorch's excavations. And I thought to myself . . ." He paused and looked crestfallen but continued: "We discovered there were finds everywhere. In every area, not just the ones that were marked as stores or archives. That's how we got here, to the entrance to the tunnels, which made a classic hiding place, if . . ." He trailed off.

"And then? Was it an accident? Or was there someone else down here?"

"We came through the first wooden door, then the second, which was a bit harder to open." Just the memory caused fear to be written on Riwal's face. "As soon as we came through, we heard funny noises. Really loud. Everything happened so quickly, and that's when we ran."

"So no attack?"

"No."

"And Kadeg? How did he get hurt?"

"He bumped into one of the beams. Hard."

"How long was he unconscious?"

"Just a few seconds. He was lucky just to be caught on the cheek."

They reached the steps.

"Riwal, was there anything in particular on your mind that you were looking for down there?"

The inspector wrinkled his brow. "I thought that they . . . might have . . . found something . . . during the preliminary phase of Picard's dig." He stopped on one of the steps. "Something valuable, maybe. Which Picard and his friend Cadiou might have brought down here. Because they didn't want the others to see it, they might not have taken it to a spot where they usually stored things and instead took it to a place nobody would have guessed and where nobody would have gone."

Riwal had lowered his voice for the last couple of sentences. They were above ground now. They went through the bookshop and into the open air.

Where there was an impressive welcome party waiting for them: lots of police who had been on duty all night, and more paramedics.

There was a barrage of relieved applause. For those who had been saved and also for those who had saved them. Normally Dupin objected to reactions like this, but he had to admit he felt the same way. A little pathos was justified.

"The ambulances are waiting," said one of the paramedics.

They were standing just a few meters away, with their sliding doors open. Behind them were two fire trucks and one for the SDIS. They were equipped with massive searchlights that illuminated both the front and side walls of the castle, presenting a dramatic view of a dramatic backdrop.

"So," the rescue team leader said, "that's it. The show's over. We'll be off."

He reached out a hand to Dupin, who shook it long and hard.

"Thank you." Two words summed up everything.

"It's only a scratch," Dupin heard Kadeg protesting in the background. "I don't need an ambulance."

Riwal, on the other hand, had already climbed into the second vehicle and sat down on the stretcher, where a second paramedic welcomed him, ready to take his blood pressure. Aballain, who already had his phone out as they left the bookshop, came up to Dupin. He seemed somewhat excited.

"The ambulances are to go directly to the hotel in La Gacilly."

"To a hotel?"

"Nolwenn's orders. She has everything organized. On the way there they're to be examined and treated." Aballain saw Dupin's curious glance. "If there's anything medical to be done, then naturally they'll be taken to the clinic. I was to inform you in case you got worried. Like I said, Nolwenn has organized everything."

Dupin ran his fingers through his hair, then shrugged.

If both of them were fine from a medical point of view, it was better not to take them to a depressing clinic, but to a comfortable bed in a comfortable hotel, where Nolwenn herself could look after them.

"I'm also to tell you that the chef is already . . ." Aballain hesitated. ". . . preparing something for them."

Dupin looked at Aballain incredulously.

"Nolwenn said . . ." She had already obviously anticipated Dupin's reaction. "I was to tell you that the pair of them haven't eaten anything since lunchtime, and need to be given something to eat as soon as possible. And that the best therapy after serious shock is a particularly good meal. A . . ." He looked under stress but glad to remember correctly. ". . . 'particularly medicinal as well as psychological recommendation.' Those were her exact words."

Dupin's phone rang. He glanced at the screen. Nolwenn.

Dupin didn't even have the strength to move a few steps to one side.

"Yes?"

"I'm expecting you, Commissaire. Everything's been arranged."

"So I hear."

"This way's the best. For everyone. Believe me."

"I know." Dupin heaved a deep sigh. "We're on our way."

He pressed the red button.

Aballain looked considerably relieved. "It'll do you all good," he said in confirmation.

"A couple more things: I would like to have the entrance to the cellar under constant, twenty-four-hour guard. Nobody enters without my permission." Dupin had decided to take up Riwal's idea.

"I'll see to it."

"And send a few fresh colleagues here. Those already here have more than earned their sleep. You have a damn strong team."

Aballain couldn't suppress a beam of a smile.

"And in the morning . . ." Dupin corrected himself, ". . . I mean, soon, when the staff at the Centre arrive, I want a full list of all the archeological finds kept in the castle. Recent ones in particular. Over the last two years. Particularly important is the question as to whether anything has been added over recent weeks. And if so, what? According to Riwal there's a file in Cadiou's office with a list."

"Will do. And by the way, the press has already got wind that there's been something going on here at the castle. I've declared the castle and surrounding area out of bounds."

"Well done. And finally: the order to go to bed applies to you too. Delegate these tasks to somebody you trust, and tell him to get in touch with me."

Aballain didn't protest. Quite the contrary. There was a happy smile on his face.

"Good night, then."

Dupin walked over to the ambulance. He had good news to give his inspectors.

* * *

Fifteen minutes later they walked into the restaurant Les Jardins Sauvages.

The paramedics had tended to Kadeg's flesh wound during the journey, cleaned it up and put in a few staples. Apart from that there appeared to be nothing wrong with him or Riwal.

All three of them went up to their rooms briefly only to shower and change clothes. Dupin had driven his car, and arrived a few minutes before the ambulances. There were already two hotel employees standing ready to take them and the bags that had been in the trunk all day long up to their rooms. One of the police officers had driven Riwal and Kadeg's rental car to the hotel. Nolwenn had already posted a police patrol outside the hotel early in the evening to keep the press out. But it was a tactic that wasn't going to last much longer; sooner or later they had to announce the state of the investigation.

It was the latest—or the earliest—dinner of his life. Dawn had already set in to the east. In the early light he could see through the window the herb beds that gave the restaurant its name: at least a dozen raised beds surrounded by wooden planks, with large shrubs of rosemary, thyme, lemon balm, and mint. Dupin also recognized zucchini, tomatoes, carrots, and little lettuce plants.

They were sitting at one of the light wooden tables in a corner of the restaurant. The entire hotel was made of natural wood, a modern, light building on a hill directly above the picturesque La Gacilly. All the other tables were already set up for breakfast. On their table were laid out four large plates, bread, water, wine—and whisky.

A jovial, wide-awake man with a white apron came over to the table—the chef. "I've got three fine entrecôtes ready for you, okay?" That proud announcement was followed rather sadly by "And one plate of steamed vegetables."

"Entrecôte, no question," Riwal burst out. "I'm dying of hunger. By the way, I've given orders for the entrance to the cellar to be guarded. And everything that has been stored down there over the past two years, and particularly over the last two weeks, will be checked out." He gave a smile that was both satisfied and proud at once. That was his trademark.

"I feel certain," Kadeg said proudly, "that we were on the right track." That in itself was remarkable. Kadeg, agreeing with Riwal. That didn't happen often.

"When you told us earlier what you spoke about to the scholars, upstairs in the Knights' Hall, you referred to the themes discussed in the previous committee meetings. What exactly did you mean by that?" asked Dupin.

"I'd—"

"That's enough for today," Nolwenn intervened. "The case can take a break for the moment. And you, too. I want to know what happened to you down there in the tunnels, while we're eating. Then we all need some sleep. Then we can get on with things." She leaned back in her chair.

She was right, enough was enough for today.

Nolwenn had raised her whisky glass. "But before anything else, *Yec'hed mad.* Let's drink to life!"

That was how it went, what the Bretons always toasted. Life, in all their written stories.

"And of course: *Yec'hed deomp tout! Hemañ zo'vont en e roud!* To good health for us all. Drink up!"

They raised their glasses, and took a big swallow. And another.

"It's good for the nerves." Nolwenn turned to Riwal and Kadeg. "So, tell me everything." Nolwenn's actions were straight from a psychology volume on managing shock: get the patients to tell all the worst, getting it off their minds. Paired with an entrecôte, it was the best medicine after a stressful day. Nolwenn was unique.

"The tunnel ceiling," Kadeg began enthusiastically, "collapsed right on our heads. Dozens of cubic meters of earth came tumbling down. It's almost a miracle that we survived. Just the . . ."

By now it was clear that the episode would from now until eternity be one of the legendary stories of the Commissariat de Police Concarneau. Riwal's and Kadeg's grandchildren would still be telling it. And not just them, the whole town.

Dupin didn't say anything. He was overcome with a warm feeling that brought a smile to his face.

The Second Day

At one minute to seven the telephone in Dupin's room screeched mercilessly. More loudly than any telephone on earth had ever rung, of that the commissaire was certain.

He had been in bed for only a half hour. More precisely, had fallen on the bed like a stone, only to collapse into a deep unconsciousness. The entrecôte had been excellent. The red Bordeaux they had drunk for their nerves, in any case, had done them good. But they'd had a little difficulty putting an end to Riwal and Kadeg's adrenaline-packed tales.

"Yes?" Dupin growled into the receiver.

"Salut, Georges, good night's sleep? How was your night?"

Jean Odinot was bursting with energy. He had always been like that; even in the early morning he was ready for a joke or two.

"What night?"

Dupin found it difficult coming round to reality. Not just because he had had hardly any sleep—the half hour from which he had been rudely dragged had felt as if he had been drugged—but also from the penetrating headache he was suffering. However therapeutically the alcohol had worked—both bodily as well as spiritually—it hadn't been sensible, not least because it was already morning. A new day. In which he was going to need all his strength. The main reason for his difficulty with reality was, however, that the whole case felt completely surreal.

"All our scholar friends still alive?"

Dupin sat up.

"There are only five now," Odinot continued. "Three months ago there were eight. Striking how quickly a committee dealing with King Arthur can lose its members."

"You've heard about everything, I assume, including the great rescue mission?"

"I've just been speaking on the phone to the astonishing Nolwenn, who was in a great mood. She's a phenomenon, that woman. I'm slowly coming to see why people call her the Breton Tiger."

Unbelievable! Had Nolwenn not gone to bed?

"Meanwhile we've got the same problem here with Laurent's computer as your specialists. All the data except for programs have been uploaded to a cloud, then highly professionally coded and double and triple encrypted."

Dupin looked around for the coffee machine which he had discovered in his room the previous night.

"That seems to be typical. We made enquiries among a few people at the university here. They all have a panicky fear of losing data, either through simple loss, or theft. Things are hard in this world."

Unusually for him, Jean hadn't meant it as a joke.

"Laurent had a special program just for erasing data, one that not even our experts can get into. They can detect deletion procedures, but not what lies beneath them. He's already been out of the ground for a half hour."

"What?" Dupin was still feeling dazed.

"Laurent's body is already in the lab. Special investigation status is fantastic, isn't it? At long last things go at the speed we've always wished they would."

"Is it possible to detect anything after a body's been buried so long?" It was a question that—like dozens of others—had run through Dupin's brain yesterday without him having the opportunity to bring them to the fore.

"Not in the blood anymore, but in the tissue. We've had everything that was sent to Madame Laurent from England handed over to us; that is, the stuff from the archeological expedition. Everything her husband had with him during his stay there as well as everything she brought with her when she flew over after hearing the terrible news. We've also been through her call logs and everything else: her bank details, et cetera."

"And?"

Dupin had gotten out of bed, quickly filled the coffee machine with water, got the capsule ready next to it, and two cups.

"Nothing unusual about any of it. No suspicious transfers between accounts." One thing Jean Odinot often repeated during an investigation was that a crime was almost always to be found in some way or another in some bank account or another, and he was frequently right. But his knowledge went beyond that: Jean could read someone's entire life through movements in bank accounts—including credit card charges. Even when all he had was a few key pieces of data—purchases, standing orders—he bound these together so skillfully that line by line not just the silhouette but the whole person would eventually appear.

Already back in the olden days, for all their weaknesses, Dupin and he had belonged to the "old school," with their "old-fashioned ideas and methods." They followed leads like tracker dogs, tried to get inside their opponent, to understand the man in his entirety, his idiosyncrasies, motives, fears. Things that at some stage had seemed outmoded or even antiquated. Nevertheless, to recognize things that had *meaning* was the sharpest weapon they had—at least that was Dupin's deep conviction.

"The last weeks of his life—" A heavy droning broke up Odinot's sentence. Dupin had turned on the coffee machine.

"I just need a *café* immediately, go on."

"The last weeks of his life would appear to have passed completely normally. Including his sojourn in Cadbury. He stayed in a hotel called the Camelot in South Cadbury, ate almost every evening in the same restaurant. He made train trips occasionally, a few times to Aberystwyth, no idea why, that's the one thing we haven't managed to fit in. Maybe he knew somebody there, a male or female colleague. Ah yes, back in Cadbury he bought an expensive new telescope. We—" The droning started up again. More coffee poured into the cup. Dupin had put a new capsule in.

"Phone calls. What about his phone calls?"

"The calls we know about with Fabien Cadiou. Apart from that, nothing remarkable, no last-minute calls to other members of the Arthurian committee. If they did communicate, it must have been by email."

The first cup was about to spill over. Dupin swapped it for the second and, after putting in yet another capsule, pressed the button for the third time.

"A third?"

Instead of an answer, Odinot heard the machine set off again.

Even the second cup was getting another capsule. Dupin had the first cup with a double espresso already at his mouth. Even the very first sip did him a world of good.

"Very good," Jean said merrily. "Go for a fourth. Whatever you need. This is a special investigation, after all. That's it for the moment from my end. Do you have—"

Yet again the pair of them were interrupted, this time not by the coffee machine but by a loud knock on the door. And Riwal's excited voice.

"Boss! Boss!"

"I'm on the phone, Riwal, what is it?"

"Professor Terrier! The scholar, boss—dead!"

Within a second Dupin had ripped open the door.

"What?"

"Bastien Terrier. Stabbed."

Riwal was standing there in front of him, seriously distraught. He had probably been dragged from his sleep by the call.

The door of the adjacent room opened and Kadeg stormed in, confusion on his face.

"What's up?"

Riwal started over yet again. Dupin was pleased to see that he was capable of whole sentences again: "Bastien Terrier was out jogging this morning, in the wood behind the hotel. He does that regularly. His body was found by another jogger. He's been stabbed. Police and ambulance are already there."

Dupin was suddenly wide awake.

"He was out jogging? Only last night his wife escaped being murdered by a hair's breadth."

"Maybe"—Riwal didn't seem to think it all too strange—"he just wanted to distract himself from it. Or to calm himself down—there's proof that exercise can be effective in reducing stress. Either that or it's a ritual. Rituals also reduce stress."

Dupin went quiet. He was trying to get himself together. Riwal and Kadeg waited. He held his phone back to his ear. "Jean, did you get all that?"

"Yes, I can't believe it."

"I'll be in touch." Dupin pressed the OFF key.

Then he turned around and charged back into his room.

"See you downstairs in three minutes," he called back over his shoulder.

The door slammed shut with a bang. Exactly ninety seconds later it burst open again. And in another fifteen seconds, Dupin was at the restaurant.

He saw Nolwenn looking fresh and wide awake, as if she were on vacation. She was just finishing a phone call. "Yes, very good. You'll be at the scene of the crime in fifteen minutes."

She set the phone to one side. "Aballain. He's already on his way."

Nolwenn was already in the know—an unnecessary statement, as she was always in the know. It was just natural, but if you asked Dupin, it was also supernatural.

"Well, we're off to a great start. More chaos." There was pure anger in her voice: "And apart from anything else: our wonderful office outing! We're going to have to attempt it again, for sure."

Dupin was standing by the chair where he had been sitting previously. By each of the four seats was a steaming *café*, and in the middle of the table was a bowl with croissants. It looked extremely inviting.

Nolwenn was still furious. "This is getting ridiculous. Three murders. Four maybe. One attempted murder. Nearly five murders, then. When is it going to end? Before long all our scholars will be gone."

Even that sounded not so much macabre as angry. And Nolwenn

was always right. What had begun yesterday afternoon in such an strange but harmless way—an interview on behalf of his Parisian police friend with an Arthurian scholar—had become one of the most violent cases that Dupin had ever had to deal with in his career.

"I should have had them all watched," Dupin snorted furiously.

"Have someone go jogging with him? To his room with him? To bed with him? Absurd. This killer knows all the tricks, and is always on guard," Nolwenn said soberly. "But . . ." She leaned back and took a sip of her *café*. ". . . that isn't going to help him. He will lose. That much is clear."

"I think it's not all over yet, that the whole story has still to play out," Dupin said grimly.

The killer was making fools of them. There were two dozen police officers present. They could be everywhere all at once. And still he was continuing. He was taunting them.

"It doesn't matter, Monsieur le Commissaire," Nolwenn said pragmatically. "One more thing, before you set off. The forensic teams finished with the dresser in the Cadious' manor about four thirty A.M. All they found were the fingerprints of Monsieur and Madame Cadiou. Fresh, clean ones. On the handle of the lower drawer where the cigar box was, on the middle of the handle, as if it had been opened carelessly. There were no prints or partial prints from anyone. And nothing is smudged. They exclude the possibility that someone tried to avoid the prints. But of course somebody could have used gloves and only touched the handle at the edges."

"They couldn't say how old the prints were?"

Dupin knew that was hard.

"Naturally they couldn't date them precisely, but they think that they were from the last two or three weeks."

That meant one thing at least: Fabien Cadiou himself had been at the dresser. Had he taken the gun out himself? The same gun with which he had then been shot? What the devil did it all mean?

"What about Terrier's wife? Has she already been informed?"

"We've tried to reach her, but no luck so far."

"She shouldn't be that hard to find in the hospital. . . ."

"We're ready. Let's go." Kadeg and Riwal had already arrived in the restaurant. Both of them looked remarkably fit. Kadeg, who had been knocked around most, and whose cheek was visibly, although not dramatically, swollen, seemed full of energy.

"Drink a quick *café*," said Nolwenn, "and take a croissant too."

The inspectors glanced at Dupin.

"Terrier's dead anyway," Nolwenn reassured them.

They quickly slurped down the coffee.

Nolwenn nodded at the window bench, on which three guns lay. SIG Sauers.

"You need to carry those under all conditions," she said, and got to her feet. "I'll get back into the research then. Some questions are still open from last night."

There were a few outstanding things, if Dupin remembered correctly. Without Nolwenn and his Citroën manual he'd be lost.

* * *

The mist that had swallowed the stars the night before revealed itself this morning to be a thick fog with heavy swathes of varying density.

It seemed as if the wood itself was generating them. They looked as if they were streaming out of a gigantic sea of leaves. It smelled damp; not of the ground and earth, but more fresh. Refreshing. And it was deadly silent. It seemed as if the fog was swallowing all noise.

The spot where Bastien Terrier had been found was in the middle of the wood. And although there wasn't much to see, it felt as if the

wood went on forever. A strange feeling, which overwhelmed anyone who ventured within its spell even if they raced through it in a
car. Dupin had found it strangely difficult to go back into the wood.
Something within him resisted it. It was absurd, he knew. Laughable.
But he couldn't just shake it off.

They left the car at the D38 regional road, and set off on foot at
a rapid pace along a gravel path winding between the trees. There
was no reception. Naturally. They really needed it urgently. Dupin
wanted to know whether Madame Noiret had been found yet. By now
in this case he became instantly nervous when someone couldn't be
contacted immediately. And for good reason.

"He's over there." Aballain greeted them, also looking remarkably
fresh, surrounded by a mist of après shave. He made a vague movement of his head.

Terrier's body lay at the edge of the path, amidst the grass, and
looked horrible, which was clearly attributable to the white T-shirt.
The color white offered blood the most dramatic stage. Bastien Terrier had been left lying on his right side, his face, like his whole body,
clenched, in witness to a ferocious fight to the death. The killer had
stabbed him in the upper stomach, and there was one wound near the
heart. Just like in Picard's case. The T-shirt was soaked through with
blood. The most gruesome sight was his open eyes, which seemed to
stare uncomprehendingly into the world around him, as if looking for
help, for support.

Whatever it was that was happening here, it was inexorable, merciless. And Dupin—all of them—merely chased breathlessly after the
events. Now the media would begin to talk of a serial murder. And
the way things were going, they were right.

"Shit!" Dupin said, and turned his head away.

They weren't going to find any tracks here.

The killer had on several occasions already proved how clever he was, and that he was very careful. On top of that in the dry weather of the last few weeks the fine gravel had gone hard as concrete. There wouldn't even be traces of footprints.

A fair way away stood a group of police and paramedics. Near them was a solitary, frightened, serious, elderly man with sparse hair and scrawny arms and legs, wearing multicolored sportswear. Probably the jogger who had found Terrier.

Riwal, Kadeg, and Aballain had joined Dupin, a look of shock on their faces. Dupin turned to Aballain. "I want every one of the scholars kept under observation from now on." He made the instruction more precise: "Denvel, Bothorel, Noiret, Guivorch too, as well as Madame Cadiou, and the storyteller." He thought a moment and added, "His forest worker friend too."

The order had a double motive: each and every one of these people had to be seen not just as another potential victim, but also the killer.

"I'll see to it right away." Aballain stood to one side and reached for his phone.

At that minute Dupin's phone rang too. An unknown number.

"Yes?"

"We've found Madame Noiret."

Dupin started violently. "What?"

"She was in a deep, sound sleep. In the hotel."

Dupin was completely confused. "What are you saying?"

"Madame Noiret, Professor Terrier's wife." There was an element of self-doubt in the voice of the gendarme on the other end of the line. "She checked herself out of the clinic last night. And . . ." He was speaking slowly, with pauses, as if he was having to convey the content of his sentences to someone who didn't understand his language very well. ". . . and then went to the hotel. With her husband. Then she took a sleeping pill and fell fast asleep. She didn't reply to calls on her cell phone, nor the room telephone. It was only when I knocked hard on the door that—"

"I understand. Have you already told her?"

"I had to. There was no alternative. Even though the colonel said, he himself—"

"You did everything correctly, don't worry about it."

"She . . . she's completely distraught. She thought at first I was making some sort of macabre joke. It took a while before she—" The gendarme broke off. His voice had already got weaker. Now it broke down altogether.

Dupin understood all too well. It was one of the worst moments the job could bring with it. Different every time. But always equally horrible.

"Does Madame Noiret want to come to the scene of the crime?"

"Yes, definitely. She asked if I could accompany her."

"Do that. Where is she now?"

"In the bathroom."

"I'll wait here for you. See you shortly." The telephone call had sent Dupin walking up and down. He walked back over to Aballain, Riwal, and Kadeg.

"She's alive, everything's okay."

Three bemused men glanced at him. Dupin was still relieved.

"I mean she left the clinic last night and slept in the hotel, a gendarme is bringing her here now.

"She knows about what happened," Dupin continued. "She . . ."

Dupin trailed off. He had seen something white out of the corner of his eye. Yet again. That couldn't be possible. In the fog. And not ten meters away, behind the first trees, but still close to the path. He would have liked to ask one of his inspectors to pinch him. Was he hallucinating? Was it last night's drinks? Or was it the madness that had been almost prophesied to him? Was he already wandering lost through the forest like the Lion Knight?

Dupin shook himself. He looked into clueless faces.

He cleared his throat and spoke with particular emphasis. "Do we know at what time Terrier went out for his run? When did he leave the hotel?"

"I asked in the hotel," Aballain said. "Just before six thirty A.M."

Dupin shivered. The air had gotten markedly cooler. He could have used a jacket.

"The man who found him," Dupin nodded at the larger group, "was it the jogger over there?"

Aballain nodded.

"Precisely when did he find Terrier?"

"At 6:57. He knows because he immediately took out his mobile to call the emergency number."

"In that case, we don't need a forensic expert, we know the cause of death and the approximate time of death."

Aballain shot Riwal and Kadeg a dubious glance.

"You don't have to call him off," Riwal calmed him.

"When precisely did Noiret and Terrier come back from the clinic?"

Dupin still found it strange that Terrier had gone jogging early today. But of course, Riwal was right: some people ran to relieve themselves, as a form of meditation in difficult moments.

"The clinic said the pair of them left about one twenty-five. At their own risk and against the specific advice of the doctor. They had to sign the relevant forms," Aballain informed him.

"All of this is outrageously brazen," Kadeg said in outrage. "The killer must feel uncommonly safe."

Dupin had once again begun to walk up and down. He felt thin-skinned, irritated. Lacking concentration.

Kadeg wasn't going to be calmed down. "It's outrageous. We have to get tougher."

"What are you thinking about?" Aballain was looking at Kadeg expectantly. He hadn't known the inspector long.

"We should take them all into custody. It has to be one of them."

Crazy as the suggestion was, Dupin shared Kadeg's feeling; there was nothing he would rather do.

"There's one thing above all that we need to do, and that is to figure out what the killer is after," Riwal threw in. "That's the only way we'll get him."

"Yes, but what does he want?" Kadeg seemed to be talking to himself.

They genuinely didn't know. They had a whole row of places to start from, but nothing more than that. Dupin this morning had wanted to start off following up Riwal's hypothesis that it might be all about an archeological find. But once again they never managed to get very far, not even when they tried to start following up an idea systematically. They barely started on something when a new dramatic event happened and they were carried away by the stream of events.

Aballain's mobile rang.

"Yes?" Aballain listened conscientiously. "Very interesting. And what was he doing there?"

Once again he listened intensely.

"How long was that roughly?"

A long, detailed explanation on the other end of the line.

"That is important information, yes. Thank you."

Aballain ended the conversation.

"That was one of my gendarmes. Very interesting . . ." He raised his eyebrows meditatively. ". . . or then again, maybe not. It seems a pair who ate dinner last night in the Relais de Brocéliande have now remembered that Philippe Goazou did leave the table on one occasion after all. They reported the fact at the police station in Plélan-le-Grand."

"For how long did he leave the table? Where did he go?"

"They saw him at the bar. They couldn't say how long he was standing there. They didn't particularly pay attention, they say."

"What was he doing there?"

Dupin had meanwhile walked round the little group, which had to move with him.

"They don't really know. The gendarme rang the hotel and got the number of one of the waitstaff who had been working at the bistro yesterday evening. She didn't remember having seen Philippe Goazou at the bar, even though she knows him. She's going to ask around among the other staff."

Goazou and his friend had loudly denied having left the table, even once and briefly. Why, given that it was harmless, had they not admitted it?

"Kadeg." This was just the right job for the inspector, not least because of the mood he was currently in. "Give the pair of them a going-over about last night. And find out if they have alibis for this morning. No excuses."

A lopsided smile spread across Kadeg's face. "With pleasure. Right now?"

"Yes. And take two of our colleagues with you."

Going forward, Dupin had sworn that he was not sending his inspectors out to investigate without support.

A happy Kadeg took off.

"Riwal, what was up with these topics that came up at the last committee meeting, the one that last night, I mean just now, you wanted to tell us about?"

"Well, last year it was about the 'well,' one of the most gripping topics in the Arthurian world. I mean the question of the possible original texts. Wolfram von Eschenbach, the greatest Arthurian author, after Chrétien obviously, always mentions in his books an author called Kyot, from whose stories he had drawn. Chrétien too spoke explicitly about a very old book about the Grail, which had been given to him by Count Philippe of Alsace. One thing that is certain is Chrétien primarily relied on the material from the Celtic sagas that had been passed down orally over the centuries, rather than the English ones. . . ."

"We've got that, Riwal, but what was its relevance to the meeting?"

"It's about the 'grails,' in literature, history, archeology. About the well, the Chalice Well in England, a manor in Wales, a church in Genoa and one in Valencia, the monastery of San Juan de la Peña, the Château de Montségur in southern France. The question was what connections there might be."

If the first topic had been abstract enough for Dupin, the second was completely fantastical.

Riwal had read Dupin's mind. "Don't imagine it like Indiana Jones. It's the topic of a serious interdisciplinary scholastic discourse."

Riwal's words didn't make Dupin's imaginings any more concrete.

"Is there . . ."

Dupin stopped. He swiftly pulled out the Citroën manual and looked through it, and realized that he had already made a whole lot of notes. Riwal and Aballain watched with curiosity as he flicked through the whole manual.

Hadn't he made a note about this?

"Damn, I . . ."

There it was. "I've got it. Juan de la Peña. The monastery in Spain. It's considered one of the most promising potential sites for the Grail."

Riwal nodded emphatically.

"Guivorch," Dupin lowered his voice, "has a book on the topic lying on his desk in his houseboat."

Riwal's eyes sparkled.

"Do you think," Aballain said with an anxious look on his face, "that we really are looking for the Holy Grail here? I mean . . . does that mean you think the scholars here are looking for the Holy Grail? That they might have found it? Or at least one of them has?"

His words rang out with no immediate answer. Amidst the fog his words had taken on something unusual. It was a while before any of the three reacted.

"Absurd. Totally absurd," Dupin said.

What crazy ideas had he let himself be led into considering? He needed more caffeine. A clear head.

"Picard and Guivorch"—Riwal was trying to be as factually objective as possible—"were both involved in excavation projects in Spain."

"Really?"

"They weren't their own projects. And in Picard's case it was seven years ago; six in Guivorch's."

For a long time there was an uncertain silence.

"Right, let's go on." Dupin wanted them finally to come to another topic. "What else is there?"

"I would suggest I wait here until the crime scene team and the forensic expert get here. I'll coordinate the troops," Aballain said.

"We . . ." Riwal glanced at Dupin, ". . . should deal with three urgent matters right now: wait for Madame Noiret to arrive, deal with the cellar and the catalogued finds, and talk to the suspects again."

"I want . . ." Dupin didn't finish the sentence.

The second thing he wanted to ask Riwal about had just occurred to him again. Something from the conversation he'd had with Jean Odinot. When Jean had just dragged him from his sleep and Dupin's brain cells still weren't active.

"Riwal, does a place called Averwitch, or something, ring a bell? In England. In the southwest probably. Most likely not very far from South Cadbury, the place where Gustave Laurent stayed. *Avery-wi-*something."

"Aberystwyth?"

"Exactly. We know that Laurent went there a few times during his stay at Cadbury."

"It's a Welsh seaside resort. And the cultural center of the Welsh, one of the largest Celtic societies of today."

The six Celtic nations at the rugged northwestern edge of Europe to which—Dupin knew it by heart—the once mighty Celtic culture which had ruled almost the entire continent had been pushed back, was yet another specialty of Riwal's.

"Aberystwyth is home to the most important university in Wales. Prince Charles went there. Maybe Laurent had a contact at the university. They had to have a large archeology faculty. Wait a minute. I'll have a look."

Riwal already had his phone in his hand. He tapped deftly on the tiny screen.

"Here it is: History, Genealogy, and Archeology. Aberystwyth University."

That was a good explanation. But it was one less clue.

"Should I try to find out if he had any contacts there?"

A task that had something to do with a Celtic country was exactly to Riwal's taste. He had already been to Scotland on one of their cases, one of his favorite stories even today.

"Do that. But I don't think a trip there will be necessary. Meanwhile, back to the task at hand. I want to see everyone together. Not just the scholars, but Madame Cadiou and the storyteller too. And his friend."

And this time, at this meeting, things would be different from the previous day. Dupin had just gotten the idea but it was one that he liked. He was just following a feeling, but he thought it was promising. He liked occasionally letting his temper run free. In front of a whole group.

"Including . . ." Aballain hesitated. ". . . both the widows? Do you really want to bring them together in such a situation?"

"Both of them, yes."

It was important. At last they needed concrete clues. Results.

Riwal wasn't the slightest bit surprised by Dupin's idea. He knew his boss. "And where should we get them all together?"

The closest spot was the hotel. But for some reason, Dupin didn't like the idea.

"We could do it in our police station here in Paimpont." Aballain meant well. He knew nothing of Dupin's fierce objection to official buildings.

"Maybe in that café on the high street?" Dupin suggested, not without thinking that it would ensure his supply of coffee. "Le Brécilien."

Aballain looked confused. He regained his composure quickly. "It's busy at this time of the morning."

A serious objection. Dupin looked at his watch.

"In that case, let's go to Madame Cadiou's office. Where all the King Arthur theme park drawings are hanging on the walls." Yes, that would be interesting.

"I'll inform—"

Aballain was interrupted by an inappropriately jovial "Good morning, gentlemen." The forensics man came toward them out of the fog, and behind him the crime scene team, looking like they'd been up all night.

Which meant to Dupin that it was time to go.

He had already set off instinctively when he saw two more figures appear out of the fog. Madame Noiret, and a gendarme.

"Aballain," he turned toward the colonel, "tell them all to be there at nine fifteen."

He was keeping the schedule tight, but they had to make headway at whatever price.

Dupin turned away from the rest and went over to Madame Noiret.

* * *

"You got to the hotel about one forty-five, after leaving the clinic at one twenty-five?"

The first ten minutes had been dreadful. Madame Noiret broke down totally on her first sight of the corpse. Riwal had to keep her upright for a while. Even then, it was quite clear, she was doing her utmost to avoid needing him. She had used almost superhuman strength to stay strong. It had been a terrible sight. Tears kept streaming down her face. Madame Noiret was wearing a loose, short-sleeved T-shirt that really didn't seem to be her style, but the bandage that went around her shoulder was underneath it. She had a cardigan around her shoulders.

Dupin and she moved a bit away from the scene of death. A light wind had arisen, blowing impenetrable showers of fog over the ground, right toward them. Riwal and Aballain had already gone about their tasks.

"Yes, about a quarter to two." She spoke with a low, broken voice. More a whisper, really.

"And then you went straight to bed? With a sleeping pill?"

"Valium. I went to sleep right away."

"And did you see anybody when you came into the hotel?"

"The night porter on the reception. He was very friendly and guided us upstairs."

"Nobody else?"

"No."

"And your husband went to his room?"

A question that, in light of the circumstances, was a very painful question for Madame Noiret. But it was one Dupin had to ask.

"I . . ." She clearly wanted to say more, but reduced it to a simple "Yes."

"Where did you part from each other?"

"He brought me to my room. Then the night porter left, and we . . ." She needed a lengthy pause. ". . . said goodnight to each other."

"And your husband didn't want to stay with you, in your state?"

For Dupin, this was completely incomprehensible.

"I needed to sleep. I was so exhausted. It wouldn't have helped me if he had stayed. There was nothing he could do, other than have slept badly himself."

Except that maybe then he wouldn't have gone jogging, and might not have been killed, Dupin would have liked to add.

"He waited until I was in bed, and turned out the light as he left the room."

"Did he tell you that he intended to go running this morning?"

"No. But he did that as often as he could. At least three times a week. His doctor had suggested it to him. It helped his concentration. He . . ." All the strength in her voice faded and her eyes too. Dupin was afraid she might break down again. He supported her carefully.

"Keep calm."

She pulled herself together again.

"And the others, I mean the members of the committee, did they know your husband went jogging?"

"Yes." She thought for a second. "Yes, for sure."

"Did he run every morning, at the same time?"

"Not always, but usually."

"Then you would assume that others would be able to work out that he was out this morning?"

As it was, the question had already been answered. But nonetheless Madame Noiret seemed somewhat in doubt.

"I think so, yes."

"Do you know if anyone else from the group goes jogging?"

Madame Noiret looked at him somewhat uncertainly. Then she replied, "Cadiou and my husband often went running together at a meeting like this."

"And you, do you jog?"

"Once or twice a week."

"Madame Noiret." Dupin suddenly stopped and glanced at her with a steady eye. "Why were you attacked and your husband killed? What was the reason?"

"Excuse me?" Madame Noiret had stopped as well.

"All of this is an endless dreadful tragedy. Why won't you just tell me at last what is going on here?"

Dupin was certain that she too was hiding something, that she too knew or at least had an idea what the story was deep down.

Madame Noiret didn't seem either surprised or shocked.

There was only a growing, deep, sad despair. It took all of her strength to avoid collapsing again, like for a brief moment she seemed about to do. She took a deep breath.

"I don't know. I really don't know."

Dupin tried his utmost to keep himself under control, but only half succeeded. "What is it that's preventing you from telling me the story? Why are you doing that?" Maybe he needed to bring it to a head. "You yourself only narrowly escaped an attempted murder; the killer might try it a second time. I hope you realize that. You are in extreme danger of being killed! I mean that seriously, Madame Noiret. Very seriously."

Madame Noiret swallowed hard. Dupin noticed it, even though she tried to conceal the fact. Yet again Dupin had the impression that she was about to talk. To admit what she knew. She seemed to be wrestling with herself. But maybe it was just his misinterpretation.

Dupin let her take her time. They were both still standing in the same place. Wreathed in swathes of fog, in which Madame Noiret's fixed gaze was lost indefinitely. Dupin had the impression that the fog was lightening. It had gotten a little bit brighter, the swathes of mist whiter.

All of a sudden Madame Noiret turned around and began to head back. Still silent. Dupin followed, against his will.

Maybe she needed just a bit more time. She was still in shock. If his guess was even correct that she knew something, that they all knew something, the whole group, not just the perpetrator. Dupin would have sworn to it, but he had been wrong before.

"I . . ." she began after a while.

She fell silent again.

"I can't take any more," was all she followed up with.

Dupin had hardly understood the sentence, she had barely whispered it.

"I want to be alone," she said finally.

Dupin looked at her from the side, studied the expression on her face as closely as he could. He didn't want to leave her alone; he had the feeling he was on the verge of a breakthrough.

His phone rang. At the most unfortunate of times.

It was Aballain. He couldn't be far away.

"Excuse me, Madam Noiret, I have to take this."

Madame Noiret nodded and walked on. Dupin turned around: "Yes?"

"It's just occurred to the girl student who works in the castle that last night around ten to nine she saw Monsieur Denvel come out of the room behind the bookshop. From the room where—"

"—where the entrance to the cellar is? And it's only now that that occurs to her?"

"Yes."

"At what time did Riwal and Kadeg give up their questioning upstairs in the Knights' Hall?"

He reached for his book; he had made a precise note of it.

"Half past eight," Aballain anticipated him.

"That means that Denvel went straight down into the cellar directly after their conversation."

"Exactly. And wasn't seen by Riwal and Kadeg, because they were still in Cadiou's office."

"Tell the student she's a star. A bit late coming out, but a star."

At last. That was the sort of thing they had been missing.

Denvel had kept quiet about this decisive fact. They could prove it now. And it was clearly highly suspicious. Whatever his explanation might be, this put a significant weight on his shoulders.

"Do you think Denvel might have tinkered with something? Between the second door and the beam?"

Dupin felt a little shudder run down his spine.

It could not be ruled out. Denvel was no archeologist, but he could certainly know how to tinker with a construction like that. And on top of that they did have an archeologist in the group: Guivorch!

"I need to see him." Dupin rubbed his temples. "I need to talk to Denvel. On his own first. Just him and me."

Dupin wandered through the fog, lost in thought.

"And we'll put off the grand meeting?"

"Yes. By half an hour. Make it a quarter to ten."

"Fine. And there's other interesting news, by the way. Guivorch's car was seen at the entry to Paimpont this morning at about half past six."

"Excuse me?"

That was another piece of news of significant importance.

"Who saw him?"

"One of our two colleagues who stayed on duty overnight by the entrance to Cadiou's manor. His shift was over and he was driving home. He knows Guivorch. And he reported the fact when he heard about Terrier's murder."

Amazing! One of those lucky chances that even the best investigator needed.

"What was Guivorch up to in Paimpont at that time of the morning? He can't have gotten to bed before five."

"If at all."

"What is the business with his kitchen and the building plans on his laptop?"

He had completely forgotten. He had heard nothing at all about the gendarmes' excursion to Guivorch's house and houseboat.

"Oh yes. They reported in early this morning. Guivorch really is extending the kitchen and ground floor of his house. He showed our colleagues the plans for the extension. The blueprints. On the boat too he was happy to show them his laptop to check out your . . ."

Aballain hesitated, ". . . your theory. We couldn't find any floor plans on it. Not that that means anything," he added hurriedly. "Only an expert might possibly find something that Guivorch had erased. And even then, not if Guivorch knows what he's doing."

Dupin had been hoping for other news. For more incriminating facts.

"I need to speak with Guivorch."

"Before or after the big meeting?"

"Before."

"The big meeting," Aballain took it bravely, "so a quarter past ten, then. Just to be careful, I would suggest half past ten."

"Fine."

"Where do you want to see the pair of them? Denvel and Guivorch?"

"Somewhere that will annoy them."

"Sorry?"

It was one of Dupin's specialties: to choose places that were unusual for serious conversations and interrogations. Preferably in combination with interests of his own.

"We're bound to find a quiet corner in the café Le Brécilien, I imagine, for two people at least."

"Really?"

"In a quarter of an hour. Denvel first. Then, thirty minutes later, Guivorch."

"Okay. Maybe Madame Bothorel, too."

"Why . . ." Dupin had just felt a heavy drop of water strike him in the middle of his face. Had the fog turned to rain?

"Commissaire? Has something happened?"

"It's just starting to rain," Dupin said. "What's up with Madame Bothorel? Why should I talk to her one-on-one?"

"We know that she was already up extremely early this morning. One of the hotel staff who was preparing breakfast noticed that the curtains in her room were open by six fifteen."

That was the type of observation that always came to light after dramatic events. And which normally meant nothing. But of course in this case it could be different.

"Nonetheless, it's enough for me to see her with the others. Anything else, Aballain?"

Dupin had a lot to do. He had to get a move on.

"That's it for the moment. I'll get back to you soon."

Dupin said his farewell and hurried off to the crime scene. A second heavy raindrop landed on him. Then a third.

Dupin had hoped that the retreating fog would make way for a bright blue sky. He hastened his steps once again. And looked out for Madame Noiret. Maybe he would catch up with her.

A little later he made out the silhouettes of several figures emerging from the fog. The forensic expert and the pathologist were already at work.

But where was Madame Noiret?

He went over to one of the gendarmes. "Has Madame Noiret come by?"

"No. At least not in the last few minutes. The last I saw of her was when she came by with you, maybe ten minutes ago."

That was no help. Dupin turned around and walked on in the direction of the street where the cars were parked.

"By the way, there were four people from the press here," he heard someone say behind him. "We sent them away and have declared all pedestrian pathways off-limits."

"Well done!" Dupin shouted over his shoulder to the gendarme. Where was everyone, he asked himself. "Riwal? Colonel Aballain?"

"Here! I'm here, Monsieur le Commissaire." Aballain appeared from around a bend. "I'm organizing a—"

"Madame Noiret. Has she come past you, have you seen her?"

"No, but then I haven't noticed anyone."

It was dreadful. Dupin was nervous all of a sudden. He had sworn he wouldn't lose anyone. And by now he believed the killer could do anything, even here, close by to where he committed his last murder, at present surrounded by police.

"Madame Noiret?" shouted Dupin several times, at the top of his voice. "Can you hear me?"

No answer.

"Come with me." Dupin stormed along the path, Aballain trailing behind him.

"Madame Noiret!"

Dupin's phone rang. He stared at the number.

Jean Odinot. Right at the wrong moment.

"Yes?"

Dupin walked on, Aballain behind him.

"It doesn't look like a murder. They've done the first examinations and routine tests."

Gustave Laurent. The exhumation.

"The usual substances and poisons that can lead to a heart attack have been excluded. Obviously it could be exotic substances that he was injected with, but that requires special access and methods. Nobody among the persons in question at present had particular pharmaceutical or toxicological knowledge, as far as I know."

"Not as far as we know either."

"That suggests that in all probability," Jean sounded almost disappointed, "it was a normal death."

"Will any more examinations be carried out?"

Dupin had also intuitively assumed they were dealing with a murder. But as far as their investigations here went for the moment, it made no difference how Laurent had died.

"Definitely. I have put everyone under enormous pressure. I want to exclude everything one thousand percent. I'll call you as soon as I hear anything new."

"Do that."

Dupin shoved his mobile quickly back into the pocket of his jeans and shouted once more at full volume:

"Hello, Madame Noiret?"

* * *

They hadn't found her. On top of that the wind was rising further, and it had begun to rain heavily. They were standing by Dupin's car now.

"Where can she have gone?" Dupin was finding it difficult to maintain his composure. "This just can't be happening."

Aballain seemed to be just as nervous. "I'll put a couple of gendarmes on it." He already had his phone to his ear. A second later he was tersely barking out orders.

They were probably overdoing things. In the fog Madame Noiret had possibly just walked past the scene of the crime. Maybe she had decided to walk back to the hotel. Nonetheless, realistic as such a scenario might be, Dupin wasn't about to relax. Even so, they ought not to get hysterical.

"I'll go to the café, and speak to Denvel."

"It might be a while before he gets there, Commissaire."

That was okay too; Dupin urgently needed to speak to Nolwenn.

"Let me know as soon as anything turns up, Aballain."

Dupin opened the car door, and sat down on the comfortable car seat. That on its own was a reason not to give up on the old car—

modern cars, no matter how chic they looked, had nothing that comfortable. Dupin turned the key to start up the engine.

Barely five minutes later he turned the key in the other direction and parked.

He was in the parking lot, right next to the grand abbey. He only had to go around the corner to get to the café. Madame Cadiou's office was just nearby. By now she would have heard of her luck that the big meeting would be held almost on her doorstep.

The rain had turned into a cloudburst. An absolute downpour. One of the many types of rain they had in Brittany. The type that suggested that a deluge was imminent. Dupin would be soaked to the skin in just a few meters.

He climbed out quickly and was poking around with the key in the little lock when his phone rang. It was Aballain.

"Yes?"

"We've found Madame Noiret! She's in the hotel."

"Where had she been?"

"She walked back to the hotel. It seems she just passed everything by in the fog."

Just what Dupin had hoped.

"See you later then." He dashed off.

By the time he opened the door of Le Brécilien even his socks were soaked through. Inside the café it was warm and there was a cozy atmosphere. Dupin was breathless as he closed the door behind himself.

The morning rush hour was coming to an end. Most of the guests were standing at the bar drinking their coffee. Near the back all the tables were open.

That left him time for a *café* in advance. And for the phone call to Nolwenn.

"*Bonjour,* monsieur, here you are again. It seems you like it here."

It was the friendly woman he had chatted with yesterday, the one who had brought him the wine by mistake.

"Well, what a spectacle! There probably hasn't been so much blood spilled in the wood since the Revolution," she added. "A third murder, and a half murder before that. Just a few meters from us here."

She too knew all the news.

"Did you hear it on the radio?"

It was a rhetorical question.

"On the television!" She nodded toward the screen over the bar. TV Rennes 35. Blurred pictures from the foggy forest, accompanied by a poor commentary in a high, excited voice. Filmed by hand. It was like a horror film. Now it switched to the footpath with Terrier's body lying on it.

"We've already seen pictures of his wife. And the other scholars, professors from all over France."

Dupin wasn't up to further conversation. There was no time for it anyway.

"Two *petits cafés*, please."

"Gladly."

"I'll sit down over there—"

His phone rang again.

This time it was Nolwenn.

"Yes?"

"I've got something, Monsieur le Commissaire." A brief pause, then: "They've all applied for the recently advertised position as head of the internationally highly renowned Institute for Arthurian Research in Paris. All of them, save Madame Bothorel. The legendary chair of the legendary professor, Victor Denvel, the Arthurian luminary, Madame Bothorel's late husband. To hold this professorship is something on a par with the Holy Grail of Arthurian scholarship."

Dupin didn't believe his ears. He tried to gather his thoughts.

"Victor Denvel was Marc Denvel's father. He's been dead for more than two years, and it's been almost that long before they put the position up for tender. For the university that's a normal term, the mills grind slowly." Nolwenn couldn't stand slowness. Neither could Dupin.

"The job opening was only placed in April, and the application deadline is at the end of September, the first 'auditions' will be held in November. A selection of applicants will be invited to give a speech. Obviously, the candidates' submissions were handled with the utmost secrecy. That's why it took me a little longer."

"And how did you . . ." It didn't matter. Nolwenn had her methods. And usually it was better if Dupin knew nothing about them.

"The university director naturally can't say if there are leaks amid the committee making the decision." It appeared Nolwenn had already predicted Dupin's next question. "Whether each of them knew that the others had also applied."

"Including Picard and Monsieur Cadiou? Had they both applied?"

"Yes, them too."

"And Gustave Laurent?"

"No, but then he was already dead just after the position was posted."

"Anyway, it seems in his case to have been a natural death." Dupin had almost forgotten to report that, and it was important. "There are still certain tests to be done, but it was extremely likely to have been a heart attack."

"All the better, we have enough murders."

There was a brief silence. The television was loud enough to be heard. "I think . . ." some reporter declared, ". . . we're quite right when we talk about a serial killer."

"All of them," Dupin said, "our illustrious academics, they all applied for one and the same position. They are competing for the most important position in their area of expertise."

"Exactly. For the highest reputation. And a very fine remuneration. We're talking about some fifteen thousand euros a month. And several assistants. Two junior professors as well. On top of that, the head of the institute has considerable means of research which he can employ and share out as he wishes. It's a dream; not for me, but certainly for others."

"I understand."

This was getting better and better. And yet again not one of them had wasted a word on it.

"A goal to kill for."

"You think so?"

Obviously it was an important factor, a very important one, but was it also a motive?

"We've arrested people before with lesser motives. It depends on the most powerful of all motives: professional recognition. Or the lack thereof, which signifies a deadly disparagement, humiliation and injury." That was true.

"They're massacring each other. One of them began yesterday morning and unleashed a cascade of blood." Nolwenn was obviously in a dramatic mood. "Or maybe one of them had planned to get rid of all the competitors. That may be the more plausible alternative."

Dupin stayed quiet for a bit.

Was that the answer? It seemed quite possible. But that left open the crucial question: Who was responsible for the murders? Several of them, or just one? And in that case, who?

"That provides me with an extra wonderful topic for the big meeting we're about to have. I'm going to talk to all of them. First Denvel and Guivorch on their own, then all of them together."

The *cafés* arrived. Dupin tackled the first right away.

"I can deal with most of the tasks immediately. In this intermediary report on his excavations which Guivorch presented to the local council and to Rennes, there was unfortunately nothing of interest. And as the excavations have so far revealed nothing, the same is true for his report."

"Does he mention any finds, historic stones, stone slabs or anything like that?"

The *café* had been as wonderful as yesterday. Dupin drank the second cup. That made seven already and it was still early in the morning—he was well on his way to a record.

"Just a seventy-centimeter-long stone, which he himself wasn't certain had been worked on and belonged there. He described it as 'irrelevant.' Nothing more. But he had it brought into the castle, and it must be down there in the cellar."

"It's lying in the castle cellar?"

"Yes. You can go ahead and take a look at it. I'll continue here." Nolwenn was clearly not impressed by this stone. Dupin, however, leaned the other way. For one thing, Guivorch hadn't mentioned it.

"What about the forest worker, the other storyteller. It would appear he has other jobs. He works as a beekeeper, and as a mechanic. Every now and then something expensive goes missing from the workshop, a motorbike on one occasion. I spoke to the police station in Plélan-le-Grand. Everybody knows him there. But so far he does not have a record for having committed any crimes. A half criminal, I would say."

"A perfect henchman, in any case," Dupin concluded. "And perhaps capable of other crimes."

"I don't have much more on Goazou. Only that he hasn't been charged by the police, so far. A superfluous comment, but I mention it nonetheless: last night the gendarmes searched the little extension to the Grail church, and obviously didn't find the inspectors, but nothing unusual either."

As ever Nolwenn was thorough. "The forensic team found nothing worth mentioning in the whole of the Relais de Brocéliande."

"Thanks, Nolwenn."

"The press, on the other hand, are going crazy. There must be nearly two dozen journalists in town, all posted carefully at the various scenes. By tonight the case is going to have made it to the national evening papers. I . . ."

"Denvel's coming. I have to hang up."

Dupin had kept one eye on the door, and seen the young star scholar come in.

"That's a shame, I had more thorough reports on the endless calls by the prefect to offer you. He's been asking whether there'll be an appropriate press conference in Paris 'at the end.' And whether anyone apart from him should speak." She laughed.

"See you later, Nolwenn."

Marc Denvel had spotted Dupin. He had an authoritative look on his face. Courteous, stylish, friendly, all of those, but never genial. Nor warm. Aristocratic, that was the word that repeatedly occurred to Dupin when he looked at him. Masterful, totally self-confident, and obviously superior, a patriarch who didn't need to be unfriendly.

"Good morning." Denvel flashed an inquisitive smile, and then was suddenly serious. He sat down opposite Dupin. "I know this is not an adequate greeting for this morning, after everything that's happened. It is mind-blowing."

Dupin came directly to the point: "Last night after the conversation with both my inspectors you went off to the castle cellar and stayed there about a quarter of an hour. In the cellar"—he said the word in a particularly suggestive tone—"where my two inspectors found themselves the victims of an almost fatal accident."

Denvel made no effort to avoid Dupin's penetrating look; he faced it calmly.

"I'd been in the cellar once before, the year before last, when there was a tour. And after the conversations yesterday, I felt it was a good moment to go and have a fresh look at some of the finds. Obviously there wasn't much to do in a quarter of an hour. I would like to take more time, but just the fifteen minutes were fascinating."

"If I understand you properly, you wanted to take a more thorough look at the finds, calmly and in your own time, and decided to take a look in fifteen minutes, in order to come back sometime when you have time and peace."

Denvel didn't let Dupin's provocative summary bother him in the slightest.

"The discussion with your inspectors inspired me. I had almost forgotten about the collection in the cellar. And it's interesting. For example, there's a row of inscriptions from the seventh to ninth centuries."

"Such as?"

"They refer to the first kings of Brittany. Powerful, proud kings."

Since he spoke so openly, it would be of no importance to the case.

"Anything for you, monsieur?"

The waitress looked long and hard at the new guest. All of a sudden her previously skeptic features lit up. "You're one of the scholars!"

It sounded as if Denvel were a rock star.

He smiled politely. "A *café* for me too, please."

"Straightaway." She disappeared again.

"What . . ." What was the expression that Denvel had just used? "What *fascinates* you down there in the castle cellar?"

"Nothing in particular. But as a historian, and a historian interested in archeology, it's obviously a dream to come across original objects from the time one is studying. Just the aura. As it happens, the time I'm studying is for me by and large completely abstract. It's all so long ago. We only know the stories that are mostly based on other stories. Then, all of a sudden, you have the world from back then in front of you. Maybe in little pieces, but it only takes a little imagination to see the whole thing." Even his enthusiasm was moderate, never unbridled.

"Monsieur Denvel." Dupin pushed his chair forward and sat for a moment on the edge, speaking particularly calmly. "Tell me what's going on here! What the killer is after. What you all are after. You know, you all know."

Now it was Dupin's turn to sit back suddenly.

"Is that your hypothesis, Monsieur le Commissaire? That we all know the story that the murders here are based on?"

Denvel continued: "I can only speak for myself. I know nothing about the story. I'm seeing everything here as a crazy, dark nightmare." It was a concise description of the case. But coming from his mouth it sounded totally incredible. Denvel was a hard nut. There was nothing that might be called objectively controversial in anything he said, yet Dupin found nearly every sentence to be a cynical provocation.

"There's one possible motive"—Dupin kept his eyes on Denvel; he wasn't going to miss any reaction—"that I'm sure of. A motive you share: you want to become the leader of the institute where your father was a professor. The most important in the whole Arthurian world."

Dupin hesitated. "And that's what all the others want too. They've all applied for the post."

Dupin had done it. The expression on Denvel's face had shifted. For a moment he was perplexed. For the blink of an eye, it was Dupin, not Denvel, who was in charge.

It wasn't long before Denvel had the situation under control again.

"You see me looking worried, I admit it. It's normal that university job applications are kept under total secrecy."

"Normally job applications," Dupin was speaking in a challengingly relaxed tone, "aren't linked to multiple murders. That makes the situation rather unusual."

"You're right, of course. Don't misunderstand me, I was just surprised that there might be a connection between the appointment to this position and the murders here. Do you really think that's possible? That someone has murdered—that somebody has killed three people, almost four, colleagues that we've all known for a long time—just to eliminate a competitor? It seems an extreme assumption."

"If I understand this correctly, this position is a confirmation of one's own superiority"—yet again Dupin fixed his eyes on Denvel—"or an extreme humiliation in front of all the world. It's all about who's declared a knight and who isn't. If you ask me if that's enough for several murders, I would say definitely."

Denvel pretended to be pondering the issue. Dupin didn't buy it.

"And for you there must be a particular dimension to the issue. You would be moving into your father's job, carrying on his life's work, and in so doing maybe overtaking him."

Denvel was totally unimpressed.

"And *voilà*, the *café* for our scholar." The waitress had set the cup down on her way past.

Dupin kept at it. "Are you saying you knew nothing about the fact that the others had also applied for the position, Monsieur Denvel?"

Dupin had already withheld Denvel's stepmother. It was more interesting like that.

"Including my stepmother?"

Denvel had asked the question in a loud, forceful voice, which unfortunately couldn't be interpreted.

"Did you know about the applications or not?"

"Of course not. In situations like that I make a point of not getting involved with who else might have applied. There's always something incalculable and arbitrary in the choice, that's just how it is. You're badly advised if you pin salvation on it."

Dupin didn't believe a word he said. He was sure Denvel saw the position as his by right.

"So, everyone knew everything about everybody who applied."

Denvel raised his eyebrows. "It would appear you doubt the truth of my statements. I won't hold it against you."

"That's very kind. But believe me, it wouldn't matter to me either way."

Dupin smiled. Denvel looked bored.

"Of course. I'm one of your suspects. Taking people on trust isn't part of your job."

"Quite right, Monsieur Denvel. My job is to find out whom one can trust and whom one can't." Dupin had had enough of the nonsense, even if it was at a high level and important to get a better sense of Denvel's personality. "So, where were you this morning between six thirty and seven?"

"I was . . ." Dupin heard "still asleep" in his mind, but Denvel's answer was quite different, ". . . out walking."

"*What* were you doing?"

"I don't need much sleep. I'm an early riser. Ever since childhood, I get up at a quarter to six. Every day. Then I either get straight to work, or I go for a walk. It makes no difference whether I stay indoors or go out for a walk, it's always the same rhythm. Today I went for a walk, between six and seven, I think. I had a *café* in my room, and then set out."

"Where did you go for your walk?"

Was he having a laugh at Dupin's expense? He freely admitted that right at the crucial time he was already on his feet and had left the hotel. Was it a double bluff?

"By the lake."

"Where Madame Noiret was walking yesterday?"

"I guess so. Obviously I don't know her usual route."

"Did you see anyone?"

"No."

"Some people take their dog out for a walk at an early hour like that, while early risers go jogging, for example. You didn't run into anybody?"

"When I heard about the latest murder, it was quite clear to me that I would have to explain myself. You would suspect me because of this walk, with no witnesses. I thought about it thoroughly, Monsieur le Commissaire. There was no alternative."

Dupin was used to hearing a lot of things from suspects in the years of his police work. But this was really something new.

"I was, in any case, intending to tell you directly. I've already spoken to your colleague, Aballain."

"What did you tell him?"

"That I wanted to speak with you. That's what I told him when he—"

"You made no attempt to call me yourself."

"I didn't want to appear too self-important. It was clear to me that after this incident you would have more important things to do. That's when your colleague rang me."

Dupin stood up without warning and said, "Thank you, thank you very much, Monsieur Denvel. That's all. I'm waiting for another . . . guest."

Denvel got to his feet himself, without appearing in the least disconcerted by the abrupt end of their conversation.

"Your time," he said in an understanding tone, "is valuable. And it's in the interest—totally personal, I admit—of all of us, that you catch the murderer as soon as possible. And if I've got things right, we'll be seeing each other again soon enough. In a larger group."

Dupin had almost forgotten that. He reckoned it was the first time he'd heard such open contempt.

Denvel turned on his heels and walked over to the bar.

Dupin saw the young scholar pay. He hadn't even touched his *café*.

* * *

"Of course it's me, Kadeg! Fire ahead."

Dupin had just been looking for a note in the Citroën manual when the phone rang again. It was Inspector Kadeg, who, as always, asked a stupid question: "Is that you, Commissaire?" But Dupin could only grin to himself—he was just so happy that nothing had happened to the pair of them.

"So, we didn't get much out of the storytellers. I spoke to Philippe Goazou first, then with Didier Boyard. Goazou insisted he had been at the bar with the newspaper. He wanted to see if they had mentioned the upcoming protest against the park."

"That only occurred to him late in the evening over dinner? It's of such burning interest to him?"

"I asked him that too. He replied that he hadn't had a chance all day to get around to it. Not least because of the 'events,' was the way he put it. I also talked with two of the waitresses who were on duty yesterday evening. They couldn't remember if Goazou had gotten up and come over to the bar. So there was just the couple who had seen him."

"Why didn't he tell us that yesterday? That he had left the table, I mean? If it was completely harmless?"

"He said he didn't interpret it as 'leaving the room,' and afterward, you asked—"

"And the other guy?"

"He continued to insist that not only did he not get up from the table even briefly, but remained sitting there the whole evening."

Dupin gave a deep sigh.

"Forget about it, Kadeg. Go and see Riwal."

"On my way," Kadeg said in his usual snappy way.

Dupin set his phone down on the table and picked up the car manual.

Almost immediately the waitress arrived.

"Another *café*?"

"I'll have . . ." Dupin now began to think a minute or two about his level of coffee consumption. "I'll have . . ." he resumed, "a *café au lait*, with lots of hot milk."

"Of course."

She disappeared again.

The next moment there was Guivorch standing by his table. Dupin hadn't the faintest idea how he had managed to slip into the café without being noticed.

His typical gently mischievous smile was playing on his lips. But there were dark rings beneath his eyes that showed his lack of sleep. Even his tan looked paler than yesterday.

Guivorch was about to say hello, but Dupin spoke first. "That's what you get when you only get to bed about five in the morning and are up and about again at half past six. You end up looking seriously exhausted."

The smile increased. He wasn't getting past Guivorch that easily.

"It would appear someone was either watching me or watching over me. Either way, I feel rather flattered."

Guivorch sat down without being asked. On the seat where Denvel had just sat. It had to be still warm.

"Enough of the niceties. What were you doing near the entrance to Paimpont this morning around the time when your colleague Bastien Terrier was murdered?"

"I'd driven in to the office. I go via Plélan-le-Grand and Paimpont. Every time I—"

"You went to the castle? To your office? You set off," Dupin calculated, "around six o'clock. That means you got up around half past five, in order to—what? To get to your office around a quarter to seven in the morning?"

"Precisely."

It was clearly derisory.

"Why did you need to be in your office so early in the morning, after a night like that? You're playing me for a fool, Monsieur Guivorch!"

Dupin had spoken more loudly than he intended. He could feel the other guests' eyes turning toward him. He didn't care.

"I didn't even bother to lie down. That only makes things worse. I get by with little sleep, even none at all, if necessary. In any case the sleepless night was because of you and—"

"Why did you go into the office at that time?"

Dupin was angry with himself: he should have had the entire castle blocked off. Not just the cellar. He just hadn't thought of it. But the night had been total chaos.

"In the confusion of last night I left the keys to the boat on my desk."

He couldn't have thought up a more transparent lie.

"The weather's supposed to be fine again this afternoon. I thought I'd have a change of scenery. The advantage of a—"

"Why do you have the keys to your boat with you when you go to the office?"

"They were in the pocket of my pants. I took something out of the pocket—I can't remember what—and laid them on the desk. And forgot them."

The most obvious question had already come into Dupin's head: "Didn't you need them when you went to your boat with the gendarmes?"

Now he had him.

"I'm talking about the engine key. You need it to start up the engine. Just for that."

It was utterly frustrating, but Guivorch knew that Dupin couldn't touch him. Indeed, unfortunately for the commissaire, despite all the incriminating facts, they couldn't take him into investigative custody.

"You aren't," Dupin said harshly, "going anywhere with the boat. It's remaining where it is for the foreseeable future."

"I wasn't thinking about escape. I was thinking of the Île aux Pies, it's only a few hundred meters and it's a better place for fishing."

"Didn't you see any of the gendarmes when you came to the castle this morning?"

The other question, far more important for Dupin, was whether any of the gendarmes had seen Guivorch. That at least would have confirmed that Guivorch really was at the castle about seven.

"I saw two police cars in the visitors' parking lot, from a distance.

Nothing more. I parked, as always, in the staff parking lot and went in through the rear door. You know where that is."

"Terrier is dead." Dupin was no longer trying to contain his anger. "Surely you've heard—"

His mobile rang.

Nolwenn.

Dupin leapt up. "Stay here!"

He was outside in a second.

"Yes?"

"I've got something interesting."

Things were moving rapidly. Nolwenn sounded full of energy.

"Paul Picard and the assessment—his name has turned up in one of the articles about the park. Directly after Madame Cadiou had handed over the assessment to the town council. There's a note, admittedly only in the regional pages of *Ouest-France*. There's not much to it, but it's there. And if you ask me, it's impossible that Madame Cadiou couldn't have known about it. Or that she could have missed it."

Nolwenn was right. It was highly improbable. That meant Madame Cadiou had deliberately kept quiet about it, with some particular motive. Which clearly meant that in theory everybody could have known that Picard was working in favor of the park.

"Monsieur le Commissaire?"

Dupin was lost in thought.

"That's extremely interesting."

But it still wasn't clear to him how the park was linked to his case. What could the story be that linked everything that had happened in recent hours? Lots of things fitted almost perfectly, but others not at all. Then again, perhaps there was just one piece of the jigsaw puzzle missing.

"I don't have anything more than that, Monsieur le Commissaire."

Nolwenn ended the conversation.

Dupin still had his phone to his ear when it rang again. He looked out at the picturesque square in front of the abbey. He was standing under the overhang of one of the café's windows where, despite the downpour, it was still relatively dry. The wind had dropped.

"Yes?"

"Aballain here. I've got some explosive news." His voice was shaking. "Are you ready?"

"Fire away!"

Dupin had to keep his phone pressed against his ear, as he had done with Nolwenn, and almost had to shout over the rain.

"There are already a few stones stored down there, from Picard's dig, I imagine. Not much in the last two weeks. Five, it looks like."

"What?"

"As you wished, we went through the catalog of archeological items. Particularly stressing the most recent. The Centre secretary, the director's actually, who is currently on vacation, looks after them normally. She documents them in the file that Riwal and Kadeg also saw last night. But that's simply a printout from a data file she maintains in the computer. Our colleagues initially managed to speak to the secretary, who said that a few large stones came in last week but she hadn't been able to catalog them. But it was said that they weren't very important."

"Who said that, Picard?"

"His two assistants on the dig, who had done all the preliminary work. They brought them in."

Without thinking Dupin had taken a step forward into the rain. He quickly jumped back.

"And, one more thing, Commissaire. A little thing but one that would fit in perfectly."

"Yes?"

Aballain was keeping him on tenterhooks.

"Professor Picard himself came here at the beginning, for what they call the 'preparations' for the dig. Two weeks ago."

Was that the key at last? Was it all to do with the excavations?

"I suspect they found something. During the preparations." Aballain was accentuating Dupin's own thoughts. "By chance. Something of great worth." He was spelling it out wholly factually. "Maybe something of purely scholastic worth. But so important that it's worth killing for."

"And so important"—Dupin was merely spelling out what was already in the air, the two coincidences chiming together wonderfully—"that the discovery would ensure someone the most famed chair on the world of Arthurian research."

"Enough to make it doubly worth killing for."

That was the truth.

"Madness." Dupin took a deep breath in and out again. "Madness."

It would be simply too crazy. Which made the scenario all the more likely.

"It would also explain what it was that Denvel was looking for in the cellar," Dupin said.

"And what the building plans Guivorch was looking at really were. And above everything: all the researchers, every one of them, were after the discovery—it would reinforce the impression that they all knew the story, but nobody wanted to say anything."

"Exactly."

It occurred to Dupin that Guivorch was sitting in the café waiting for him.

"Well done, Aballain! Well done! Tell Nolwenn, Riwal, and Kadeg. Perhaps something more will occur to them."

"Consider it done."

"Where are these five stones?"

"Still in the cellar. I've sent the crime scene team to take a good look around. They're already there."

"What sort of stones are they?"

"Different sizes, clearly worked on, I haven't seen them myself."

"We need to go and look at them ourselves as soon as possible. And the long stone from Guivorch's excavation too. Okay, see you in a minute in Madame Cadiou's office."

"Just one more thing. I spoke to the leader of the rescue team from last night to ask him if he could imagine someone tampering with the tunnel."

The colonel was good. Dupin had a lot of admiration for him.

"And?"

"He said it would be quite possible, if whoever did it was an experienced expert. And he thought that a competent archeologist under the right conditions might be able to manage it. But it would be an extremely challenging and very dangerous task. Nobody could accurately estimate the actual condition of this ancient construction. There was a chance it could take out somebody tampering with it at any time."

Just one more factor in this ridiculous case: everything that at one stage seemed to have been sorted out came back again. All the more urgently.

"Might there be any way now to prove it?"

"Only if a freshly hewn wooden beam or something similar were to be found while digging further into the ground. Otherwise, no."

The rain seemed to have gotten heavier. Another thing you learned in Brittany: the rain could always get heavier, even when that no longer seemed possible. This was rain that fell like a torrential shower, or as if it were being poured out of a gigantic bucket.

Dupin put his phone in his pocket and went back into the café.

* * *

Guivorch did his very best to give the impression that he hadn't minded waiting. He had ordered himself a *grand crème* and a *pain au chocolat*, a delicious combination, of which there was only a little vestige remaining. He almost smirked when Dupin returned to the table.

The commissaire was just about to sit down, when he suddenly shot up again. Even Guivorch glanced up at him with irritation.

"I'll be right back."

With no further explanation Dupin headed for the door and pulled out his phone again.

"Aballain, a little change of plan." The idea had only just come to the commissaire, and he liked it. "Have the stones from the cellar fetched, as soon as the crime scene team have finished. We'll have the big assembly in their presence. I want to look at them with all the others."

There was a bit of a pause.

"Got it. Very well. But where should we bring them? Upstairs to the Knights' Hall?"

"Too dark."

Dupin thought hard. If the weather had been dry and sunny then he would have said outside in the courtyard.

"Where is there the best light?"

He wanted to see them first, before the others. Along with Riwal, Kadeg, and Aballain.

"Clearly downstairs in the exhibition rooms."

"Okay, there then." It would be the perfect stage.

"They were just opened to the public a few minutes ago."

"I want everything closed down until further notice."

"I'll see to that. I think three murders and a near-fatal attack will be justification enough."

"I think so too."

"What time should I move the meeting to?"

Dupin glanced at his watch.

"Eleven." That left him time enough for his conversation with Guivorch, and moving the stones.

"Fine."

"Are all our friends kept inconspicuously under surveillance until then?"

"As inconspicuously as possible."

"See you later then."

Dupin was already on his way back to Guivorch, and a few seconds later he was leaning back in his seat.

"We know the story now, Monsieur Guivorch," Dupin pronounced with pleasure, omitting all doubts and complications that objectively still existed. "We know what it's all about."

In fact, he had anticipated confronting Guivorch directly with the issue of the stones. But his feeling now was that it would be better to save this point for the conversation with everyone; to announce the grand finale. Also there was the possibility that Guivorch might warn the others if several or all of them were going to be under one roof.

Guivorch's eyes opened wide, even though he was trying hard to appear unmoved. "I'm incredibly pleased to hear that." His comment sounded surprisingly convincing.

"But we'll get to that when we're all together in the big grouping. Not now."

"So what are we going to talk about now?"

"Why you neglected to mention that you had applied for the renowned Arthurian professorship at the Sorbonne. That's what we're going to talk about now."

He had his eyes glued to Guivorch. The man's face reflected a mix between laughter and a deep sigh.

"It's quite simple: it would be seriously bad news for me if the university in Rennes found out. As you know, I would also be tied up with the option of a possible extension of my current position. At the same time I consider such an application essentially to be a strictly private matter. I think that is a more than adequate justification. And even if you know about it, you are required to keep it to yourself."

The last sentence revealed a specific hardness, even aggression, for the first time in their conversation. Guivorch hadn't tried to conceal it.

"In a special investigation of a triple murder, there is no such thing as privacy."

"The law says otherwise." The openly aggressive tone had vanished from Guivorch's voice, even if his voice was still hard. "You are obliged to handle all private information with absolute discretion, even in a murder investigation."

Dupin didn't take him on. "I've been told that the extension of your current position is a pure formality."

"Well, if that's what you've heard, then I've nothing more to worry about," he replied sarcastically.

"The university director says you don't need to get worked up about it."

"In a university continuously forced to make cuts, the only thing that is certain is what is already fact."

A good response.

"Did you know," Dupin let himself seem relaxed and bent over toward Guivorch, "that all your other colleagues from the committee here have also applied?"

Guivorch seemed to have every muscle in his face under control, which was quite an achievement. There wasn't the slightest sign of him stirring.

"I'm basically not interested in that."

"No?" There was a provocative tone in Dupin's voice.

"No."

"In that case we see things similarly, Monsieur Guivorch. Perhaps you'll tell us a bit more if the opportunity arises."

With that, Dupin got to his feet, took a coin from his pants pocket, and set it on the table.

"See you later then."

Before Guivorch could say anything Dupin turned around and stopped. He didn't even know why it had suddenly occurred to him again: the timetable Claire had set for him, that he had to be back by this evening, which meant that he had no more than about eight hours remaining to close the case. He thought of the devastating story of the Lion Knight and imagined a horror story, that he would miss the deadline and wander crazily through the magic forest until, like Iwein, he would lose his sanity, and would end up living as a chastened hermit guarding a mad treasure forever. This white animal—or thing— that it seemed he alone saw was clearly a prophecy of some sort. A warning. Dupin ran his fingers through his hair in a rare panic attack.

"Damn it." He shook himself.

The rain had stopped. There were occasional gaps in the dark, fat-bellied clouds, and through them fell dramatic rays of sunshine that let the soaked world shine silvery bright. Particularly the cobbles on the road. Dupin felt that his clothes were still unpleasantly damp, sticking to his body.

It didn't take him long to get to the car.

"Boss! Boss!"

Dupin turned around sharply.

Riwal and Kadeg were running up to him.

"Boss! We were looking for you in Le Brécilien. But you had already left, we . . ." Kadeg was always at his most tortuous when it was of least importance.

"What's up?"

"We have the answer." Riwal had come to a halt right in front of the commissaire, taking a deep breath after such a spectacular pronouncement.

"I've been researching Aberystwyth," he continued at last.

"Yes?"

Riwal took another deep breath.

"This Welsh seaside resort," Kadeg added enthusiastically.

"It's like this." Riwal seemed ready to launch into one of his lengthy explanations. "Aberystwyth has a library. Not just any library, oh no, the National Library of Wales, one of the most important of all in Great Britain, the home—" Another pause, but this time not to take air, but to amplify the theatrical effect. "—to an immense store of handwritten medieval documents."

"And?"

"The Llyfrgell Genedlaethol Cymru, the National Library of Wales, contains a store of more than four million books, including several extremely rare works, such as the first book to be printed in Welsh in 1546, or the first complete translation of the Bible into Welsh from the year 1588. But also medieval and early medieval manuscripts. They—"

"Riwal!"

Dupin had moved off. On the other side of the street, just a few meters farther along, the abbey park's lawns began, away from the hubbub, and a suitable spot for this apparently not unimportant conversation. The meticulously manicured lawns stretched the length of the lake, with its bushy trees along the bank.

"There are so many manuscripts that some of them have lain dormant for hundreds, even thousands of years in the archives, many of them given only provisional or even misleading descriptions, some mistaken or none at all. Some with false names of the authors or also none at all, just labeled 'Anonymous.'"

"Really?"

Dupin still didn't understand what this was about. They walked out onto the grass. "Monsieur Laurent," Kadeg took over, "went from South Cadbury to Aberystwyth several times, when he was on the island."

It seemed as if the two of them had agreed to play a sort of guessing game with Dupin.

"You're saying that Laurent went to the library?"

"All in all," Riwal was extremely worked up, "he was there eight times between the beginning of his stay there and his death. Sometimes even two days in a row."

"How do we know that?"

Dupin changed the way he was facing. The sun was blinding him. The little gaps in the clouds had grown larger, so large in fact, that the relation between the open sky and cloud covering was beginning to reverse. The battle between sun and clouds for the conquest of the heavens created phenomenal games with the light.

"I called up the library and spoke to the administration and the reading room. Laurent had gotten himself a reader's card, and every visit is marked on it. He was usually there for at least two hours, and twice for a half day each."

"Why? What was he after?"

Riwal breathed in deeply and then out again.

"Here it comes. He only ever wanted one thing in particular." Another dramatic pause. "To see one particular manuscript."

"What was the manuscript? Go on. Tell me." Dupin wasn't going to have them drag this out.

"A manuscript from the ninth century, by a certain Graddilis. A hundred and forty pages, in parchment, within wooden covers, twenty-seven by eighteen and a half centimeters, according to the details in the registry. The fact that it's on parchment shows how important it is."

"And what's the manuscript about?"

"*Allegedly* it's the 'Annals of the Lords of Homnia.' However, nobody has ever heard of this dynasty."

"Why do you say 'allegedly'?"

"Because," this was where Kadeg's voice piped up, "something different would have made a lot more sense. Something very different!" It seemed as if he was about to reveal the solution, but then left it to Riwal.

"I think . . ." Riwal settled to the task, and breathed in and out as deep as he could. "It's the Source."

"The source?"

"*The* text above all others in Arthurian legend. The very base, that can reveal more about the real Arthur than anything we know today, and above all," he raised his eyebrows, "about the Grail. A text that many of the early stories of King Arthur refer to, but which researchers later took to be a fantasy."

Even Kadeg sounded excited now. "A text that reveals the secret surrounding the Grail. What it is. Who had it in their possession. Where it was to be found. And maybe even where it is today."

Dupin had begun to walk in circles around the two inspectors, brushing his hands through his hair repeatedly. He was trying to stay calm. But he had caught Riwal's fever. He could feel himself getting goose bumps.

This new scenario, the "Source Scenario," wasn't unlike the "Stones Scenario." Something spectacular had been found. All the scholars in the group knew about it and wanted it. And it would definitely win one of them the much-sought-after professorship. As opposed to the stones, the sensational importance, if Dupin really understood properly, was above and beyond all imaginable discoveries in the Arthurian world.

"The discovery," Riwal seemed to have gone beyond his own thoughts, "would be considered one of the most sensational academic discoveries of recent centuries."

That sounded a rather lofty claim. Even something less startling would be enough. It certainly counted as a motive for murder.

"You suspect"—Dupin was trying to put it all together with a clear head, to concentrate on the purely factual—"that this manuscript in this Welsh library is not written by the author it is ascribed to, and does not contain what is listed on the library register, but is actually the famed Source itself; that Laurent somehow got wind of this, and actually found the book?" This part of the story they hadn't known. "And that all the events here are linked to that? Everything has somehow or other been an organized hunt for this book or manuscript?"

"Yes, I think that—"

Riwal was interrupted by his own phone. He glanced at the number and picked it up immediately.

"Hello?"

Riwal stayed next to Dupin and Kadeg, with his phone pressed against his ear. For a long time he just listened, then said in English: "I understand. Yes." Something had happened. They could hear it clearly in Riwal's voice. "Terrible. This is a huge loss."

A further comment on the other end of the line.

Then the inspector, again in English: "Yes, please, call me if you have any news."

There was an answer, then Riwal again.

"I have another question. A certain Mister Fabien Cadiou, was he also visiting in May? Yes, sir. C-A-D-I-O-U. Yes."

Then a little later: "Really? Are you sure?"

Another answer.

"Thank you very much. Bye."

Riwal ended the conversation.

"What did . . ."

"The manuscript," Riwal started to say. He had gone pale and was shaking. "It's vanished. The manuscript is no longer there. I asked one of the library staff to keep it safe. It must have been stolen, they say. They believe that it's impossible for it to have gotten lost there."

For a moment all three of them went silent. They set off walking, almost mechanically, lost in their thoughts, toward the lakeshore.

"Oh—yes—there's something else." Riwal found his voice again: "Cadiou! He was also there. Twice. On the two days when he was staying with Laurent. Together with Laurent." Riwal was trying to calm himself down, but not succeeding. "It means Cadiou's visit to Cadbury was only about the manuscript. According to the visitors' list he was there again on July 26, to look at the manuscript. Since then nobody else has asked about the manuscript. Until me."

"Madness," Dupin said.

"It brings our story perfectly together!" Kadeg concluded. "Every detail fits! Cadiou took the manuscript with him after Laurent died. He went back for it specially. So simple. So effective."

"At the end of July Cadiou was in Corsica," Dupin said.

"No problem. In summer there are direct flights from Bastia to London. From there, it's two or three hours to Aberystwyth. He might possibly have got there and back in a day."

Kadeg was in form. Of course, it could have happened just like that.

"And Cadiou had used the opportunity! The manuscript would have made him a legend. And given that it was a totally different manuscript to that described in the library register, it would be very hard to accuse him of theft. Maybe he intended to bring it back here. One thing is certain: he would have been known forever and eternally as the man who had found the legendary Source!" Riwal's eyes lit up. His enthusiasm was driving him on, even when they were dealing with a triple murder. "It would have been almost like discovering the Grail itself."

They had reached the lakeshore and stopped there, each of them next to the other, their gaze lost in the deep green water.

Dupin tried reimagining the new theory in a different context. "That would mean Madame Cadiou must have known about the manuscript too."

"It could certainly be sold, and bring in immense sums," Kadeg brought a supremely prosaic thought to the fore, "from some crazy collector. You can find them all over the world. There's always one to be found. There's no worry about legality. It would go for many, many millions."

"Maybe Cadiou had told Picard? Or Picard was part of the team, as Cadiou's friend and fellow traveler," Riwal mused.

"This is still all pure speculation." Dupin had moved on again, trying to bring himself—and all of them—down to earth. He walked along the lakeshore slowly, the inspectors behind him. Just ten minutes ago they had been working on quite a different hypothesis that sounded equally plausible.

Riwal protected his own concept: "Isn't it much more than that? That Laurent and Cadiou went to Aberystwyth together is fact. That they studied a particular manuscript is fact. That the manuscript suddenly disappeared is fact. That Cadiou was the last to ask to see the manuscript is fact. And what is also a fact, and one we mustn't forget, is that the Source, the legendary manuscript, was the theme of last year's symposium."

"Not bad, is it?" Kadeg was almost grinning.

It was true. The story was already more than just speculation. There were too many facts, and they fitted together too closely. Riwal had gotten the right scent.

For a while there was a deep silence. Dupin's brain was working overtime. He was playing the whole scenario over and over, trying to add some jigsaw puzzle piece from the events of the last few days just to complete the story.

"That also means," Riwal still couldn't contain his excitement, "that the manuscript is most probably here. Cadiou had it with him. Maybe even at home. Then he was killed, and the murderer took it with him."

"If it's here somewhere, then they all know about it. All of them *with no exception.*"

"Maybe they just don't know who has it now and where it is. Maybe those who did have it briefly were subsequently murdered? Or they at the very least knew where it was." Dupin was convinced of that.

"Or," Kadeg cut in again, "Monsieur Cadiou had hidden it away. And they're all speculating as to where it might be. Think about it: they all have clues and each one of them is watching the others. They're all just looking for it."

That would explain things. Dupin couldn't stop thinking—that was why they all seemed to be out and about the whole time since yesterday afternoon. Why Denvel had been in the cellar, Guivorch in the castle at the crack of dawn without having slept, Terrier already out walking at six thirty, Madame Bothorel already awake . . .

"Picard could then have killed Cadiou, which made it clear why he was the next to be killed," Riwal said.

They had, of course, been friends, but who knew what had happened? What might such a find have done to their friendship?

As it happened, the team consensus wasn't exactly to Dupin's taste. But in this case it was looking particularly fruitful. Following last night, he was especially happy to have his inspectors with him again.

"Or Picard," Riwal began, going down another chain of events, "knew about the discovery, maybe even where the manuscript was to be found. One way or the other he was a friend of Cadiou's, and the murderer had taken the manuscript when he killed Cadiou and would have to do away with him as well."

All the variants sounded plausible.

Dupin rubbed his temples. "What about Noiret and Terrier?

Where do they come into the game? Guivorch? The storytellers? How could they have known about the manuscript?"

Did they actually know, or did they just have an inkling of knowledge about it?

"Maybe Terrier found out somehow and killed Picard?" Kadeg tried stretching things further.

The problem was: the more probable it seemed one minute, the more it got lost in endless combinations. There were still too many possibilities. There was still too much that could conceivably be imagined.

"If the manuscript is the object at the heart of the whole story and that's what we're working on at the moment, should we not first of all maybe consider two main issues separately: Where is the manuscript? And who is the killer? Anyhow," he glanced at his watch, "we really need to get going."

Dupin turned around there and then and walked briskly down one of the stately pathways toward the abbey. Just before reaching it they would turn left to the parking lot.

It was a magnificent view, due primarily to the fierce light of the sun and a sky that was now almost totally deep blue. It fitted in with his mood. They had made real progress. Maybe he would make it to see Claire this evening as promised, after all.

* * *

They spent the whole time going down the little roads behind a tractor which, despite having been honked at repeatedly, wouldn't let them pass. Stubbornness was one of the proudest Breton qualities, to be displayed whenever possible. Dupin was sympathetic toward the principle, which he considered proof of steadfastness, but at times it was difficult to maintain such sympathy. Nonetheless it let Dupin and his two inspectors inform Nolwenn, Jean Odinot, and Colonel Aballain of the latest developments. Aballain couldn't suppress his disappointment that the stones had suddenly turned out to be a dead end.

In the meantime they had set up the stones in the exhibition hall. There were six of them altogether. They had brought them all up. Seven people—yesterday morning they were still ten—now sat down at the meeting. Seven people, amongst whom, it was highly likely, was the murderer. There might even be more than one involved in the killings. At least it could not be excluded.

Each of them was absorbed in his own feverish thoughts, following one idea or the other. In Dupin's head the thoughts were rushing back and forth ever faster, as new ones emerged. Nothing, not the slightest detail, contradicted the manuscript theory.

Except: Where could it be, and who was hunting for it so urgently?

The car swung into the castle's staff parking lot. The lake glistened emerald green in the strong August light. By now the sky was totally clear, a flawless summer blue. There was nothing more typically Breton than such a dramatic change in the weather. As much as Dupin was amazed by it, he still struggled to come to terms with it, as he had honestly to admit—Nolwenn would tut at him for still not being a proper Breton. It was a hard test, but true.

The commissaire and both inspectors jumped out of their cars.

Instinctively, laughably, as they crossed the bridge over the moat, Dupin stared into the bushes where he had seen the white animal—the white "thing." Naturally he didn't see it.

Aballain was waiting for them at the entry to the bookshop. Dupin nodded to him.

"Everything's here. The stones too. They're very heavy, and two of them are quite large. This way." Aballain had overtaken Dupin as they entered the bookstore and was now leading them down a narrow corridor. Dupin couldn't help himself, and took a glance through the open door into the room behind. The room which led down into the cellar. It was a funny feeling.

They entered the exhibition space.

There they lay, the six stones, watched over by two gendarmes. The two largest measured nearly a meter in length. Placed at random in the middle of the room. As if they were pieces in an exhibition. In fact, they really were, more or less. Two of the ceiling spotlights had been focused on the middle of the room, which only accentuated the effect.

Equally scattered around the room at random were the protagonists in the case. Marc Denvel, Sébille Bothorel, and Adeline Noiret—the latter had initially apologized for not coming, then changed her mind—stood leaning against the wall. Auffrai Guivorch was talking to Goazou and his colleague, and, isolated at the end of the room, was Blanche Cadiou. The whole scene was extremely theatrical.

The real main attraction in the room, the scene with life-size wax figures—young Arthur pulling Excalibur from the stone, thereby giving him the right to be the new king of England—was little more than a backdrop.

"*Bonjour.*"

Dupin was speaking like a teacher to his class. He had positioned himself directly next to the Excalibur scene. It was the best position—he had them all in his sight. Riwal, Kadeg, and Aballain, the tension visible on all their faces, had remained standing by the entrance.

"I will come straight to the point."

He really was going to. He was going to put all his cards on the table. He could see the extreme curiosity on all their faces; there was a silence bristling with impatience.

"We know," Dupin took his time, spoke calmly, enunciated each syllable clearly, "why we have seen three murders and an attempted murder. We know the motive. What the whole story is about."

He let his words have their effect, looked around, studied their faces, one by one. There was utter silence.

"We are missing a few details for the moment, but we'll know everything soon."

Another long silence.

"Gustave Laurent and Fabien Cadiou discovered the Source, the deep well from which the greatest Arthurian legends have their origins: the legendary manuscript that you discussed at your last meeting a year ago." He let his words sink in. Every one of those present had a poker face. "It may be that Paul Picard was involved. In any case, we assume that he knew about it. Just as we assume *that you all know about it.*" He repeated the decisive factor: "You all know about the discovery of the manuscript."

He was certain of what he had said to varying degrees, but in the moment there was only one thing to do: escalate. To provoke them further and further. He began.

"And also that the manuscript is to be found somewhere here—in the wood."

In Arthur's Wood, it had just now occurred to him, what a crazy turn that would be. Almost certainly, as he understood, the wood here featured in the manuscript.

"And potentially some of you either know or presume to know where exactly it is."

An extended pause. He looked each of them point blank in the face. One after another.

"And we know even more than that: that all of you are desperate to own it."

Now it came, the first resistance:

"It's preposterous! This manuscript doesn't exist. Any more than the Grail does!" Madame Bothorel was indignant. "It's absurd to put us . . ."

Dupin couldn't take it anymore. He'd had it up to here with this stuff. This was how it had been going all along.

"It exists, Madame Bothorel. And Laurent and Cadiou found it."

Dupin himself was impressed at how forcefully he presented a hypothesis as fact.

All the others remained stationary, rooted to the floor like trees.

"Have you seen it, and held it in your hands? Yes?" The tough old lady wasn't going to give up that easily.

"Going back to your serious wish to get hold of the manuscript. We are aware of your applications to become director of the Arthurian institute in the Sorbonne. Every single member of the King Arthur committee, with the exceptions of Gustave Laurent and Madame Bothorel, applied. I assume that the discoverer of the Source would win it. Not that an additional motive would be necessary." Dupin tried not to exaggerate this point.

"Do you know, then"—it was Guivorch, trying to put on a relaxed, unmoved tone of voice—"what a sensation that would be? You really have no idea."

Dupin looked him hard in the face. "I'm not going to have conversations like this anymore. I'm done." His voice was cutting. "We've had enough of all this show."

Dupin began to walk around the room, all eyes following him.

Suddenly he stopped in front of Marc Denvel. And stared aggressively at him.

"Tell me, Professor Denvel, tell me the story."

"What am I to tell you, Commissaire?" Denvel replied. "I still have no idea what it is you want from me. Am I to—"

"I want . . ." Dupin intervened, but he didn't get far.

". . . the truth." Madame Cadiou had emerged from her corner and was coming over to Dupin.

"I think the commissaire should have learned the truth a lot earlier, Monsieur Denvel."

Denvel stared at Madame Cadiou. Irritated, bewildered, unbelieving. For a moment he actually lost his aristocratic composure. He was about to say something but Madame Cadiou preempted him.

"The truth is . . ." She was standing directly in front of Dupin, and was speaking in a quiet voice, without fuss. "You're right, Monsieur le Commissaire. It's all exactly as you say. It's about the manuscript. The Source. A document from the ninth century."

Dupin was too taken aback to watch the faces of the others. He simply stared at Madame Cadiou. He couldn't believe it, and all of a sudden, now that it was finally happening, he felt as if it was surreal. Obviously he had hoped for a situation like this, but he hadn't really expected it.

"Gustave Laurent and my husband picked up on the trace of the manuscript in October last year. If it was really because of the momentum from last year's meeting, I can't honestly tell you. It had to do with a clue that led vaguely to this library in Wales, which was mentioned openly here in the group." She glanced around the room, but nobody reacted.

"Whatever. Then in July, my husband got hold of it. The manuscript ended up in our house. My husband took photographs of it."

There was still no sound from anybody.

"It was upstairs." Madame Cadiou looked Dupin straight in the eye. "In the dresser, in the first drawer. All this time."

A clear shrug of the shoulders. She seemed totally composed.

"My husband had told Paul Picard and me about the manuscript. Paul had given him an important clue to get him onto the trail. He had also taken a couple of photographs of a few pages of the manuscript." She turned around and looked them all in the eyes, one after the other.

"And yes, all this lot—the whole committee had an idea. No, more than that. They hadn't believed all that about the Cadbury excursion. My husband was asked a lot of strange questions. Guivorch had even told him to his face, a few times, that he was certain they had found it. And that it was an achievement for the whole group. Denvel knew too, my husband said. And Terrier. And certainly Madame Noiret too. No matter what they say now, they were all convinced. And yes, they were all focused on it themselves." She lowered her voice toward the end. Just to make clear this part of her performance was over.

She turned back to Dupin, waited briefly, then resumed.

"Paul Picard killed my husband."

"What?" Dupin felt as if he had been struck by lightning.

"He's the one who murdered my husband."

She remained cold and calm, keeping control over her voice even while making such a dramatic statement.

She had raised the possibility on the grounds of the abbey, but Dupin hadn't really believed her.

"That's what *you* say," he added soberly.

Madame Cadiou didn't react, but continued her story unperturbed: "My husband and Paul Picard argued with each other frequently, about what to do with their discovery. They were friends, but this divided them. Paul was in favor of giving it back to the library. And telling them what it was that for so long had lain unrecognized in their possession. My husband saw things differently. He no longer trusted Paul. He thought Paul wanted to twist things so that in the end he would have appeared to have discovered it. And putting himself forward as a noble character at the same time."

It was impossible to say which of the two positions Madame Cadiou preferred.

"They had both looked at it again in the kitchen. Paul wanted to take it away, but my husband didn't want to give it to him. In any case, Paul wanted to go public with it, which would have portrayed my husband as a common thief."

Which, taken literally, was exactly what Laurent and Cadiou were.

"How did it happen? How did he kill him?"

"Paul told me it was an accident."

This was getting ever more incredible.

"Picard himself told you that? You discussed it?"

"Yes, he came to see my husband yesterday about eleven thirty A.M. They argued more furiously than before, and it got worse. Paul threatened my husband, I'm sure, even if he played it down to me. My husband might have fetched the gun to defend himself. Maybe had it out even before the meeting, expecting the worst. In any case, Paul claimed my husband suddenly threatened him with the gun. It then came to a scuffle, which led to the fatal shots being fired. I came back home just before midday, I had left for the office early in the morning, and there—"

"Why?" Dupin had to interject at this point.

"I came back to eat and take a bit of a break. I do that most days. And there lay my husband on the floor, shot dead. I knew at once what had happened. I went straight to the site of Paul's dig in the wood. He was in complete dismay. He told me everything. At one stage he shouted at me, that I should go, leave him alone. He needed time to think. I went back to the office, to think it over myself. The rest . . ." She looked at Dupin. ". . . you know."

Dupin had so many questions he wanted to ask all at once, but which he reluctantly could only ask one at a time. He began with the most pressing.

"Why didn't you tell me everything yesterday afternoon?"

"I was too confused. I didn't know what to do." She hadn't looked in the slightest confused when Dupin had spoken to her. But in her case that meant nothing. Also by then more than two hours had passed, enough time for her to think up a strategy.

"Or was it that maybe you thought the manuscript might now also be yours, that you inherited it?"

She answered him with a sharp tone, and blank eyes. "After the murder of my husband, and then of Picard, it was clear to everybody on the committee what the motive had been. And all of them were purely interested in the manuscript. Nothing else."

"That's not answering my question. Was it the same for you? Were you not suddenly also one of those looking for the manuscript?"

She nodded imperceptibly. "You're right, yes, but I think I was acting on behalf of my husband."

"It was undoubtedly," Dupin joined in, "a remarkable find for the park. Financially as well."

Madame Cadiou said nothing.

"What did Picard do with the gun?"

The question was one of the most technically important for the investigation. They were going to need the gun and any fingerprints. And an immediate examination of Picard's fingers for powder residue.

"I don't know."

"You didn't see it when you came back home and found your husband lying on the kitchen floor?"

It spoke for itself that it was extremely unlikely that Picard would have made this fatal error, but if what Madame Cadiou had said was true, he must have been very distraught.

"No."

"Had Picard taken the manuscript?"

"That's what he said."

"And where did he put it?"

"He didn't tell me that, but as far as I know he had it with him."

"He could easily have hidden it."

"He had an old leather shoulder bag. But there was nothing in it."

Dupin hadn't heard a word about that until now. That meant the murderer had to have taken it with him.

"You looked into the bag?" It felt as if there were only two people in the room, the commissaire and Madame Cadiou.

"Yes. I just did it automatically."

Dupin thought that was quite possible.

"Did he go straight from your house to the wood?"

"At least that's what he said."

"But," Dupin resumed, "you didn't see either the gun or the manuscript in his possession?"

"Correct."

Dupin ran his fingers through his hair in frustration.

"You wouldn't tell me if it was otherwise, I assume."

It was a tricky situation. Should he believe her? In everything? Or just parts of her story? And which? One way or another she had been lying to him systematically since yesterday. The only possible witnesses for her story were gone permanently.

"You don't believe me?" Madame Cadiou didn't seem insulted.

"It could be a clever lie. Or a mix of truth and clever lies."

"I can't make you believe me."

"Kadeg!" There was one thing that might be proved right away. Dupin spoke without dropping the volume, so everybody could hear. "Call the pathologist. I want him to examine Picard's fingers for powder residue right away."

"Consider it done, Commissaire!"

"By right away, I mean right away."

"He'll do that, no worries. This is a special investigation." Kadeg made a friendly face and headed for the door.

Dupin turned back to Madame Cadiou.

"When you didn't find the manuscript what did you do? Kill Picard?"

She wasn't finished with her story by a long way yet.

"Maybe Picard and you scuffled, as was the case with your husband. Maybe he tried to physically prevent you from looking in his bag." Dupin took things calmly and factually, as if he were trying out a possible solution to a mathematical problem. And it was, as it happened, by far the most plausible assumption if—if—the first part of her account was true. She had a double motive, she had admitted it openly. Perhaps, as she had said, Picard really did have the manuscript on him. Maybe it was even true that he had tried to kill her.

"I was aware that you might think this, Commissaire. It's precisely for that reason that I initially decided to say nothing more. But then more people would die, believe me."

Dupin ran his fingers through his hair yet again.

"Madame Noiret and her husband, Bastien"—Dupin was still talking as if there was nobody else present—"somehow realized that you were in possession of the manuscript. And you therefore had to kill both of them. You have to admit that sounds plausible. Who else might have murdered Terrier and attacked Madame Noiret?"

"Auffrai Guivorch?" she replied without hesitation.

Everyone's eyes suddenly turned to Guivorch, who had maintained an indifferent face, and then rapidly switched back to Madame Cadiou. She had pronounced the last sentence with the same certainty as before. As if it was clearly and simply a matter of fact.

"He came toward me in his car. Just ahead of the parking lot close to the Fontaine de Barenton. There's absolutely no reason to park there, but people did."

The story was getting ever crazier.

"And you're certain who it was?"

"I am. It was his car and I saw him at the wheel. He saw me too."

"And so why didn't you at least tell us that earlier in the evening?"

"Because then I would have had to tell you everything."

"And your efforts would have ended abruptly without even mentioning the manuscript."

There was a short pause and then: "Yes, that too."

Dupin turned to Guivorch, and the other participants did the same thing.

"Very amusing, all of this." Guivorch shook his head. "I would have . . ."

Suddenly he stopped. That too was unusual for him. He seemed to have lost the plot.

"Yes! I'm listening. Speak to us at last. Or else I'll arrest you here on the spot." It was no empty threat.

"Okay, yes." A reluctant capitulation. "I drove there. I wanted to speak to Paul Picard."

He fell silent again. It was as if he regretted having even started to speak.

"What's that supposed to mean?" Dupin was shouting at him now, and couldn't care less. "What did you want to speak to Picard about? Did you actually speak to him?"

Guivorch had omitted everything that mattered in his answer.

"I wanted to offer him my help, examining the manuscript. Mine and that of everyone on the committee.

"We'd spoken together, all of us except Fabien Cadiou and Paul Picard. We were certain that they'd found it; there were too many indications. But without all of us working on it, they would never have got on the right track; the theory as to who was the author . . ."

". . . is all mine! Credit where credit's due!" It was Madame Bothorel, who despite her protest had remained there. She plowed ahead resolutely: "I told everyone at last year's meeting. The theory is mine, and it has to be stated loud and clear."

"And we all," Guivorch fired back, "settled on two libraries as possible locations. The Aberystwyth idea was mine. It was immediately clear to me that the journey to Cadbury was just a pretext to hunt down the manuscript."

"That's why all of you were, as if by chance, in England last year. I get it."

It wasn't the moment to rejoice, but from the start Dupin's instinct had been right. They had all known the story, yet had kept quiet about everything that mattered.

"We think," Denvel chimed in, "that the discovery should be presented as an achievement of the committee as a whole."

It was monstrous. That was what mattered to them primarily. The egocentricity, the narcissism of this collection of elite researchers had taken on hideous aspects. "We tried to . . ."

Dupin threw a monkey wrench into Denvel's boasting. "We've had three people brutally murdered here, four almost. Three people have lost their lives over the discovery of this damn manuscript. Do you realize that? And all that interests you is your own fame?"

He had never experienced anything of the kind.

"Monsieur Guivorch." He addressed the man in a commanding voice. "Tell us more. You got to the parking lot and went to the Fontaine de Barenton. What happened next?"

If it was really the truth, they had yet to find out.

"Paul Picard lay there, dead."

He had completely reclaimed his sense of authority.

"You say he was already dead?"

Guivorch's callousness was almost impressive.

"He was already dead. Yes."

"Why should we believe you?"

Even more important was: How was Guivorch going to prove this?

"All I can do is give you my assurance. I have no witnesses for this statement."

"How can that be? Madame Cadiou left Picard there when he was still alive. Shortly afterward, you turn up there, and he's already dead." Dupin turned abruptly toward Riwal, who was standing there with an amazed look on his face. "How long does it take to walk from the parking lot to the well?"

"About fifteen minutes at a quick pace."

"So. Monsieur Guivorch. This is ridiculous."

"Maybe the killer was already there at the same time as Madame Cadiou was there, and watched the whole scene from a hiding place. And then struck fast," Guivorch replied.

There was a pause.

"And the alternative?"

"That Madame Cadiou herself murdered Picard. That simple." He looked over at her calmly.

"Paul was still alive when I left him," she said, unperturbed. "And then you came, Monsieur le Commissaire." She looked over at Dupin, having given Guivorch a withering look. "Make your own judgment. I can only tell you how things were."

Dupin had started walking up and down again in front of the multicolored Excalibur scene. For a while it seemed he wasn't paying attention to anyone. A sinister silence ensued.

The complicated situation had gotten even more complicated. Everything was possible. Nothing could be ruled out. That Madame Cadiou was telling the truth and Guivorch a lie, or the other way around. But of course Dupin couldn't neglect a third possibility: that it was neither of them. That as far as this went both might be telling the truth.

"I am going to press charges," Dupin announced all of a sudden, "against all of you for giving false evidence, deception, and repression of information during an investigation into a triple murder. Inspector Riwal," he said with pleasure in his voice, "kindly begin the process immediately after we finish this conversation."

"Ludicrous," hissed Madame Bothorel, in a state of outrage. "You wouldn't dare."

"Oh, but I certainly would, madame."

And that was a fact.

"But . . ." Goazou spoke up for the first time. ". . . I knew nothing about this. And haven't withheld the slightest thing."

"Nor me," said the worried-looking forest worker.

"Just wait and see," Dupin added, unimpressed. They didn't know the whole story yet.

"Back to you, Monsieur Guivorch. You say you saw Picard lying there. Dead. How did you know that he was actually dead? According to you, the murder had to have just taken place. He could still have been alive."

"I felt his pulse."

"And you do that so well that you would have noticed a very weak pulse that even doctors would have had difficulty to spot? Along with giving false evidence to the police, we could add that you neglected to offer help in a precarious situation. That's to say," Dupin was relatively relaxed by now, "if you yourself aren't the murderer."

"He was already dead, believe me."

Dupin would add nothing to that.

"And then? What did you do then? Look for the manuscript?"

"I looked around a bit, yes. But it was clear to me that the murderer had taken the manuscript with him. If"—Guivorch grabbed his chin, and raised his thick eyebrows—"it had ever been there. If Paul Picard had ever had it there at the Fontaine de Barenton."

"If you"—Dupin suddenly grasped things—"had ever thought it was. I suspect that you believe it to be here in the castle. Which all the others think too."

Guivorch shrugged as if he played no part in any of it.

Dupin would put a large wager on it. Although each one of them had purely their own interest at heart, they were all prepared to make tactical alliances. At least in part and for a limited time. These alliances then fell apart for individuals when there were more advantages to going it alone. A concrete example: when one of them saw the chance to get hold of the manuscript without the others, then he or she grabbed it unscrupulously. The worst was: this seemed to be an unwritten law of the alliance. Nothing could be more cynical, brutal, and cold-blooded.

"Probably," Dupin was talking not so much to Guivorch as to himself, "you assumed Picard had hidden it away somewhere. Or maybe Fabien Cadiou had." Dupin felt a tingling sensation that normally overcame him when he suddenly thought he was close to something important. "You assumed he had hidden it in the castle. In the cellar, for example. And that's why, Monsieur Guivorch, you were studying the plans."

He had been convinced the whole time that they hadn't been extension plans he'd spotted on the houseboat.

"And that's what it was about when you came into the office early this morning. You wanted to search undisturbed. But the cellars were closed off by the police. However, there were other possible places."

An aggressive smile had appeared on Dupin's face. He made no effort to suppress it.

"But going back to the story as you've been telling it, Monsieur Guivorch. You had a look around the excavation site—and then?"

"I went back to my car, and drove to the castle."

"And immediately told the others, I assume. And also that there'd been another murder. You would have had to do that so as not to appear suspicious yourself. The others all knew that you'd gone to see Picard. You—"

Madame Bothorel intervened: "I didn't believe that he wasn't the killer. Quite the contrary."

"But you didn't think it was necessary to inform the police? Not even at a crucial moment like that?"

Madame Bothorel kept an indignant silence. Dupin tried to calm down.

"Of course not," he answered his own question, "because there was still a chance for you to get hold of the manuscript, you had every right to it, you had provided such an important clue. And even if you weren't interested in the professorship, you were certainly interested in the fame."

"Complete nonsense!" Madame Bothorel was frothing with rage. "I no longer need something like that. I don't need . . ." She paused for a moment.

"It wasn't for yourself you would have done it." Dupin concluded her sentence for her.

It was one of the rare moments in which the commissaire believed something one of the assembled had said.

"You would have done it for your stepson, isn't that right? You would have let him take the merit. At least that was what you figured. Then he would have taken over the professorship of your late husband. Relations between you aren't as bad as you implied, are they?"

It was a feeling he had had. But of course it was highly speculative. Dupin hadn't seen anything directly pointing that way.

Madame Bothorel's eyes bored into him with a withering look. Which only proved to Dupin that he had hit the mark.

"Whatever the truth is, you yourself had a strong motive to kill Picard and Terrier."

They all had strong motives, all of them, without exception. Least of all, admittedly, the two storytellers. But they could have been hired by Guivorch, to carry out the murders on his behalf. And paid richly for it. Even though Dupin was coming to think that less and less likely.

"I'm not going to reply to that," Sébille Bothorel said, and turned her head away in disgust.

"Who was it then . . ." Madame Noiret's voice was brittle. Like the storytellers, she had kept out of things up until now. ". . . that killed my husband?"

She looked at Dupin challengingly, still leaning against the wall. "Who was it?"

All of a sudden there was a lot more force in her second sentence. Aggressive force. She turned her eyes from Dupin and focused them on the others, one at a time.

"Who could have had a reason to kill you and your husband? Somehow connected to the story we now know. What do you know?"

"As we said earlier, we discussed them in the committee, when we were both present. And we learned from Auffrai Guivorch midday yesterday that he had seen Paul Picard lying there at the excavation site, dead. That's all. We didn't know anything more, and weren't in any way involved in the story." Even Madame Noiret was speaking as if it were just chicken feed. Of minimal importance. Each one of those present was now only trying to save his own skin in the most primitive way possible.

"Your husband and you were looking for the manuscript too, I assume. Maybe you already had it and were holding on to it. At least temporarily. Or knew its hiding place, if there is one."

Something occurred to Dupin. He pulled out the Citroën manual and made a note.

Dupin had been thinking again, as he, somewhat slowly and laboriously, noted down the point that had come into his head, along with a couple of other things from the conversation so far. "Since yesterday afternoon, you have all been lying through your teeth. And I don't expect you to stop now."

He paused for a minute.

"I believe that the manuscript exists. I believe you all knew about it and spoke to one another about it. I believe you were prepared, still are prepared, to stop at nothing to find it. But above and beyond that, nothing at all is clear for me. Not even that Picard," he glanced at Madame Picard, "was Cadiou's killer. . . ."

Dupin fell silent. He was frustrated.

"I am now officially declaring that *each* and *every one* of you is under acute suspicion. And I give all of you one last chance to contribute something toward the solution of this case. Otherwise from now on you will be under constant surveillance."

Dupin looked around at a sea of impassive faces.

"As far as I'm concerned"—Denvel opened his mouth again, speaking in his characteristic manner—"everything's been said. It is now up to you to identify the murderer. I don't think we can help you any further in that respect."

"Fine—Inspector Riwal will take care of listing the charges we're going to press against each one of you. And that'll be that, *au revoir.*"

Dupin headed swiftly out of the room.

"We have in any case officially ended the committee meeting, and will be leaving tomorrow," he could hear Madame Bothorel say behind him.

"Leaving?" Dupin turned round halfway to the exit. "You'll only be leaving when I say so. And not before."

A second later he had left the room, Riwal and Aballain on his heels.

Dupin was relieved to be back in the open air, even if the sky had turned as if from nothing to thick clouds and there was the smell of rain in the air once again. There wasn't a shred of the blue sky of a few minutes earlier. Even the gusty, blustery wind was back. When he had gone into the castle he could have sworn the summery weather would last the whole day.

Dupin turned left and walked down toward the lake. He stopped right at the water's edge. The water was turbulent, especially in the middle. Small whitecaps were forming. It looked wild. The water had also changed color. It had become a dark matte gray. An extremely troubling gray that no longer looked like a mirror.

Riwal and Aballain came over to him.

"Whom do you believe, Monsieur le Commissaire?" Aballain was visibly troubled. "Madame Cadiou or Monsieur Guivorch?"

"I don't know. I have to think about it."

The commissaire started moving again.

"I'll see you back here in ten minutes," he said, setting forth along the lakeside with no further explanation. "And stay together, don't split up! That's an order!"

Aballain gave Riwal a baffled look, to which Riwal replied with a routine shrug of the shoulders, as if to say "That's just the way he is."

"And Riwal," Dupin already nearly had to shout for the inspector to hear him. "Call Odinot, tell him to deal with the public prosecutor and the false evidence. We'll find out if this really is a special investigation."

* * *

There was no alternative. Dupin needed to be alone for a few minutes. He had to have a bit of calm, to think everything through. If he didn't have an opportunity like this on a case, it inevitably led to a poor result. What was equally important was that he had to put things in order, to distance himself, even just a little bit.

He left the path, the one they had taken the night before to reach the entrance to the tunnels, in order to stay close to the lakeside. He walked slowly, watching out for the stones, roots, slippery moss, and deep puddles. The wind was blowing in his face, which made him notice that his jeans and polo shirt were clammy still. He shivered.

Who was he to believe? Did he believe either of the pair? The unfortunate thing was that Dupin still hadn't gotten that special feeling, the intuition.

The vital question remained undiminished: Where was the man-uscript?

He had reached the long spit of land that stretched far into the lake. It looked as if it was regularly flooded. The vegetation was sparse, not a tree nor a bush. It felt almost like being on an island. It reminded him of the jetty into the lake that Madame Cadiou had planned for the park. The castle lay directly opposite. Under the dark, threatening clouds it looked like a ghost castle; the charm, aura, and magic had given way to a dark force. Large branches lay in the water the length of the spit, rotten and covered with moss. There were just a few twigs—his vision didn't extend below the surface of the water, making it impenetrable, impossible to say how deep the lake was here—sticking out of the water like withered fingers. Dupin's eyes had unintentionally stopped on a branch sticking astonishingly high out of the water at the end of the spit. All of a sudden the whole spit seemed as if it pointed to it. As if it were a sign. Surprisingly light, freshly cut wood. Its silhouette looked like a great sword. What was remarkable about it was the branch seemed to get narrower toward the end, and from a distance stood out against the matte gray back-ground as curiously two-dimensional. What was he seeing here? Was he really losing his mind? White mice, magic swords . . .

Dupin pulled himself together. All of a sudden his gaze fell on something beyond the branch, on the opposite side of the lake. It was moving strangely and was hard to make out in the gray light.

It was a while before he made out someone waving frantically at him. It was Kadeg! The inspector was gesticulating wildly. Then in the next minute he began to run along the lakeside. Now Dupin spot-ted Riwal and Aballain a few steps behind Kadeg.

Dupin took out his phone. What was going on? Why weren't they calling him?

No reception. Not a single bar. Obvious.

Something had happened.

"Damn!" Dupin had been planning to go a bit farther along the lakeside. What had happened now?

He turned around on the spot.

It was barely three minutes before they all met up.

"The doctor," Kadeg declared, panting, a few meters before he even reached Dupin. "The pathologist says there are clear powder marks . . ." He was still gasping for air. "Picard fired a gun not all that long ago."

That was a bombshell.

"That takes us one definitive step further. " It was Aballain who jumped to the conclusion, hardly short of breath at all. "We know about the manuscript, and we have the first killer. The second victim, in fact: Paul Picard. He killed Fabien Cadiou. But that means that for the second murder, that of the first killer, we need yet another murderer."

Aballain's statement illustrated the absurd complications following one after the other in this case.

"That means . . ." It was Riwal, who had breathed in and out deeply before speaking. ". . . we can safely speculate further." It sounded like: "We've reached the next resting point on the way to the summit."

Dupin put his head in his hands. He too was out of breath.

Picard had shot Cadiou. That much was clear. That said a lot, if not everything, in favor of Madame Cadiou for at least the first part of her account. Did that mean the rest was true as well? That when she left Picard he was still alive? Or was it precisely here that a cunning lie had crept in?

Riwal tried to take it further on his own. "Let's assume for a minute that Picard shot Fabien Cadiou and took the manuscript from him. He drives to his excavation site. That all fits together for him to be there before midday. Neither Madame Cadiou, who found him there still alive, nor Monsieur Guivorch, who saw him lying there already dead, found the manuscript." Riwal tried to conceal it, however with every mention of the manuscript there was a hint of emotion in his voice. "Maybe Picard hid it on his way to the dig site. Somewhere along the road! That's the only possibility!" His final summary.

"That's pure supposition," Dupin sighed.

"We shouldn't dismiss the possibility so easily though." Kadeg had taken Riwal's side. Dupin had already noticed a couple of times today an unusual unanimity between the two.

In this case it seemed to be quite different from normal. Maybe it was the result of their mutual experience of the hours shut in the blocked-off tunnel.

"It was Riwal who first of all got us onto the manuscript. Why shouldn't this theory be correct too?"

It was now starting to get uncanny: Kadeg plugging the work of others! Correctly, of course.

"Take a look here." Riwal pointed toward a stone. He took out a map that must have been in the pocket of his pants, unfolded it smartly, and laid it out on the stone. Aballain helped him.

"Here." Riwal now had a marker in his hand and noticed Dupin's impressed look. "All from the bookstore in the castle. So, look . . ." With a snappy circle he marked the Cadious' manor. "Paul Picard moved between here and . . ." He drew another snappy circle. "Here." The Fontaine de Barenton lay within it.

Dupin bent down over the map.

"The direct way," Aballain knew the region, "leads northeast along regional road D141 from Tréhorenteuc." He traced the route slowly with his finger. "Then along a couple of back roads. But you can also go directly along these back roads if you know your way about. In that case, it's slightly shorter, but also a bit more complicated."

"Where in particular are the Arthurian sites?" Dupin asked. "That would be the way Picard would probably have known best?"

Nobody contradicted him.

"The Maison de Viviane isn't far from Tréhorenteuc. But first of all you have to drive west for a stretch." Aballain had his finger on the map once again. ". . . Then turn north. That wouldn't be a major detour. Maybe two or three kilometers."

The points on the map made a flat triangle.

"The Maison de Viviane is the site of Guivorch's dig," Dupin murmured. "What else is there?"

They glanced down at the map again.

"The other Arthurian sites," Aballain resumed, "are quite a long way away." He pointed to a pair marked with illustrations on the map. "Picard would probably not have taken the risk. It was the middle of the day and his car could have been seen anywhere."

Dupin was thinking feverishly. "We need to know if there was one place in particular that he knew especially well. But how? We can't ask the others."

"It's likely," Kadeg sounded resigned, "they've all seen these places anyhow."

"Maybe," Aballain said, "Paul Picard was prepared to risk a larger detour. That could bring all the Arthurian sites into the equation."

Dupin sighed. It would be yet another major operation, but this time too, there was no more elegant way.

"We'll send cars to all of the Arthurian sites again. Including the site of Picard's excavation. The gendarmes need to examine carefully the route from the parking lot to the fountain. The woodland on either side of the road. Maybe we need to think a lot more simply. He might just have hidden it in the undergrowth," Dupin said without much conviction.

"The most probable," said Kadeg," would be the Maison de Viviane. Picard will have known the excavation site well, even if it was that of Guivorch."

That had been Dupin's first assumption, but his attention now fell elsewhere: "What about the Val sans Retour." The original target of their office outing. "It's right next to the manor."

"You can only get to such places on foot," Aballain reminded them. "He would have had to leave the car and then walk a good ten minutes each way. That could take him first to the 'Golden Tree' and the 'Mirror Lake,' neither of which have anything to do with Arthur. You can also get on foot from the valley to Maison de Viviane, but that would take significantly longer."

All of which sounded very unlikely.

"Then we should concentrate on . . ." Dupin faltered.

His eyes had fallen onto something else. A place they had, up until now, completely overlooked. Very close to the Cadious' manor. And was at least linked to Arthur by name.

"And the Church of the Holy Grail? What about the church?"

"As they've said, the researchers don't take it seriously," Riwal intervened.

"But it lies directly on the way, and moreover . . ."

Dupin stopped again, wide-eyed this time.

"I think I've got it. I . . ." A pause. Dupin headed off immediately without saying another word.

"That could be it!"

He had sprinted off. The three policemen were left bewildered.

"Right, let's go!"

Kadeg, Riwal, and Aballain ran off too.

* * *

It was almost noon by the time they arrived, during a strong rain. The weather seemed to be enraged again. The sky had gotten even darker, as if dusk were falling, and the clouds hung even lower than this morning. It almost seemed as if they had decided to settle on the ground. Strangely, the wind had dropped again and the gloomy towers of cloud moved only slowly.

Dupin parked the car directly in front of the church. The inspectors followed suit. Fender to fender. The rain was rattling loudly on the roof of the car: far removed from the sound insulation of modern cars, here there was a deafening noise when he turned off the engine.

He opened the car door, then leapt out and closed it behind him in one rapid movement.

In a few moments he was standing, soaked to the skin, in the semicircular stone entrance to the church. He didn't wait for the inspectors. Dupin hurried into the church. Even there he could hear the rain rattling angrily on the roof.

Was he in the right place? Had his instinct really led them to the object around which everything hung? Did Picard really hide the manuscript here? On his way from the Cadious' manor to the site of his excavation?

Dupin took a moment to get his bearings. The church was less spectacular in daylight, smaller too. Quite different from the way it had looked last night in the moonlight. Then he headed directly toward the wooden cabinet on which stood the statue of Sainte Onenne. The cabinet door had been ever so slightly ajar. A few more steps and he was standing right in front of it.

Meanwhile, the three policemen, their soaked hair glued to their scalps, were right behind him. "Do you think"—Riwal's voice oscillated between excited curiosity and a humble, almost frightened respect—"that the manuscript really might be here? The manuscript that could reveal sensational information about the Holy Grail?" Riwal had all but whispered the last few words hoarsely.

The commissaire didn't reply.

The door to the cabinet was closed tight.

It was a clever, almost ideal hiding place. Nobody would have any reason to get the prayer books out until the next mass.

Dupin opened it.

Great heaps of prayer books, at least ten to a pile, in a compact format, dark green, with a fine-dimpled, indestructible plastic covering that Dupin had known since his childhood; maybe fifteen rows next to one another. The cabinet was approximately one meter high and about two meters wide. There was a board inserted separating them into two rows with a narrow empty gap above the last prayer books.

Somebody had stacked the books meticulously.

"Here? You think the manuscript is in here?" Kadeg asked. "Near the prayer books?"

Instead of answering, Dupin knelt down and examined the last books in the piles. Even they had been fastidiously arranged; nobody seemed to have placed a single one in the wrong place.

"Boss, what makes you think that the manuscript would be precisely here?" Kadeg insisted.

Dupin got up, his forehead deeply wrinkled.

"Last night—" Dupin stopped to correct himself, since it sounded as if it had been days ago, and indeed it felt like that. "This morning, when I was here looking for you two, the left door of the cabinet was ajar."

"And so"—Kadeg still had a skeptical undertone—"it came to you that it might have been Picard who could have left the door partly open?"

Dupin felt he was suffering from a serious dose of sullen defiance. Not just against Kadeg—but anyone and everyone, including himself. Instead of answering he knelt down again and began taking out a few of the books from the top right.

Before long he stopped, to pull out his phone and turn on the flashlight app. He pulled out the other books in the row, then he pushed the pile next to it partly to the side, so that he could get a look behind the top row of prayer books.

"And?" Kadeg sounded excited.

Without a word Dupin moved over to the other side and began doing the same thing.

"Damn it." Dupin got up again. "Nothing!"

"It was perhaps a little over-hasty," Kadeg decided. And he was right. "We should have thought a bit first. Where might it be? One way or another we ought to send cars to the other Arthurian sites."

"Do that now," Dupin said, turning sideways to Aballain.

"Consider it done." Aballain was on the point of heading for the door.

"Wait a moment, there's one more thing. Give the order that our gendarmes watching over the murder candidates should pull back a bit. The guilty parties should get the impression that we've laid off the surveillance, or that they can escape from surveillance. We need the gendarmes to be completely invisible, do you understand?"

Dupin looked at the three quizzical faces.

"The gendarmes need to concentrate above all on possible ways for the suspects to escape. They need to be thinking about where they might drive to, and then follow them as inconspicuously as possible." Dupin rubbed the back of his head. "If they don't feel under surveillance, we might see where they're searching."

Dupin had not the slightest doubt that they would resume searching, all of them.

"It may well be that they know more than we do, at least one or another of them. One way or another if the killer doesn't have the manuscript yet he's going to get hold of it soon, not least out of worry that one of the others will get the right idea. One of them, or us."

"I would concentrate on Madame Bothorel. She considers finding the manuscript her duty first and foremost."

"Which means that we also need to keep an eye on Denvel. It's possible they're working together," Kadeg added.

There was utter silence for a few minutes.

"In any case," Kadeg hadn't finished yet, "I've got a funny feeling about Madame Noiret. There hasn't been much evidence so far of grief about the loss of her husband."

There was yet another short pause, then he continued:

"The funny feeling obviously also applies to Guivorch. In any case. And the storytellers aren't off the hook." He gave a deep, theatrical sigh. "But the most suspicious of all is Madame Cadiou."

Which brought them back to the beginning. Great!

"Aballain, let's try this another way. Tell the gendarmes to take their own private cars to the possible hiding places, and have someone on watch at the entrance to the various places, to be ready to report in as soon as one of the suspects turns up. They're not to notice that the police are there."

It was high risk. But it would be the simplest and most effective means, if they were right in their assumption.

"Right." Aballain headed speedily to the exit, his phone at his ear.

"I think the three of us should go to the Maison de Viviane." Seen objectively, it was the most probable site.

"Just one moment." Riwal had gotten down on his knees in front of the cabinet and was pulling out the prayer books from the lower shelf.

"Let's finish this off, boss. Just to be sure."

"The Maison de Viviane could—"

Riwal interrupted Kadeg. "Here's something."

For a moment Riwal stopped still, then began moving as if in slow motion.

Dupin and Kadeg watched him carefully.

Riwal dug deeper and deeper into the cabinet, so that he had to almost lie on the ground. In his other hand he held his phone with the flashlight app on.

"What do you see?" Dupin took a step forward.

"A brown envelope, a little bigger than A4."

Rather than asking another question, Dupin and Kadeg were in a second lying next to Riwal, shoulder to shoulder.

Riwal by now had the envelope in his hand. He pulled it out slowly. None of the three dared breathe.

Riwal got onto his knees, looked at the envelope from all sides without saying a word.

It was a normal envelope. Unsealed.

Riwal got up off the floor. Dupin and Kadeg did likewise.

He opened the envelope, looked inside extremely cautiously, as if his gaze alone might damage it.

"It's a document holder," Riwal said slowly.

"A professional archive holder. A sort of zipper-sealed bag that you can use to suck out the air through a little valve." His voice was getting ever thinner. "They're used," he was almost whispering, "for very, very old manuscripts and other documents."

He pulled the holder out.

Black. The edges of the objects inside were fairly clear. A rectangle with one side longer; maybe twenty-five centimeters long and twenty wide, four centimeters thick.

"That . . . could . . . be . . . it." Riwal had paused between every word.

"You . . . you mean really?"

Dupin pulled himself together. "Open it."

"But . . ."

"Open it, Riwal." They had to know for sure eventually.

Riwal squeezed the valve, and with a light hiss, the holder expanded a little. Then, very carefully, he began to slide open the zipper. His movements became ever slower.

"Can't we do this any faster?" Kadeg was exasperated.

The zipper was open now. Riwal glanced cautiously inside. And stared again.

"Come on!" Kadeg couldn't hold back any longer. Dupin felt the same.

Slowly, Riwal pulled out the contents.

"That's it! Ha! We've found it! The secret manuscript!" The emotion in Kadeg's cry was nothing compared with the momentous importance of the discovery.

Dark brown wood, scratched as far as the edges, copper clasps, in the center another metal fitting, a circle. And in between, irregularly cut brown pages.

"The circle," Riwal gasped. "The symbol of the Round Table. The eternal unity of the inseparable brotherhood. That, that . . ." Riwal was incapable of completing the sentence. "That has to be it: the Source."

Dupin tried to come to his senses. They had to keep cool heads, particularly when it came to what they did next. "Now we need to—"

"All orders carried out." Aballain came back into the church, speaking enthusiastically. "They'll . . ." He stopped. And stared with eyes wide open at the manuscript in Riwal's hands.

"The manuscript," Riwal said triumphantly, "that has been speculated about for almost a thousand years. It's real! Absolutely real, and I'm holding it in my hands. It's . . . fantastic."

Aballain seemed to have lost control of his senses. He stammered: "But where did you . . ."

"There, in the cabinet," Kadeg crowed proudly, though he had previously declared the cabinet to be an extremely implausible hiding place.

"Incredible," was all the stunned colonel could say.

"We need to have it examined as soon as possible," Dupin insisted. "But right now we have to concentrate fully on the question: Who is the murderer? That is all that matters right now."

That was a fact: despite their fascination, they had no time to lose, least of all in mythical fascination.

"We should lie in wait here." There were other possibilities, but this seemed the most urgent and easiest. The question remained, would the murderer think at all about the church as a hiding place? They had to believe it. It might be their only chance, to catch the killer in flagrante, to find him here.

"In that case"—Riwal was thinking purely pragmatically again; his internal thoughts could change as quickly as the Breton weather—"we should move our cars as soon as possible!"

Dupin was mortified he had not even thought of that. Not one of the suspects would come near the church if they saw their cars there.

Normally Dupin wouldn't let anyone touch his Citroën, but he would make an exception.

"Take my car and move it somewhere." He pushed his car keys into Kadeg's hand. "And then come straight back."

Riwal had put the manuscript back into the holder, and both into the envelope.

"It'll be safest if I hold on to it myself."

Dupin nodded.

"And I'll cancel the police action immediately," Aballain said.

"But I want somebody to keep an eye on the church inconspicuously, and let us know if somebody is heading this way."

"Obviously." Aballain pulled out his phone.

"And don't tell them anything about our find. For now, nobody is to know about it. Nobody!"

The strategy was not without risk. It was all or nothing. But that was the way things were. Sometimes that was the issue. To put it another way: sometimes a complicated situation had to be exacerbated in order to solve it.

Dupin began walking up and down the church.

The commissaire grumbled. Where could they hide so that they could see everything, the cabinet in particular, without being seen themselves?

If the killer came he would want to be sure that he was alone. It might become necessary for them to stay there a long time. The killer was going to have to feel more or less safe.

Dupin had walked up and down the church six times. In principle there were very few possibilities. Three little niches under the gigantic white stag he had seen the night before, and the priest's room in the extension, which—Dupin had checked—was closed. Riwal had been ordered to get hold of the key.

Despite the gray weather, and the minimal light, the white stag was shining. Just like the Grail in the church window opposite. Differently from the night before, however. Bright and clear, but somehow less mystical. The glass in the window must have been polished, and worked on to make the impression that luminous diodes had been built into every part of the glass. Dupin had to admit that for a brief second a sort of shiver had run down his spine when he looked at the image of the Grail. The whole story was crazy. They hadn't actually found the Holy Grail, but maybe a document that referred to it explained precisely what the Grail was, revealed, perhaps, where it was to be found. And if it didn't say anything about the Grail, then maybe, if Riwal was to be believed, it might refer to one of the other great secrets: Arthur's real historic identity. Which would be no less sensational. But Dupin had to abandon his fantasies; he had, after all, ordered his inspectors to do so.

"We're back, boss."

Riwal charged back into the church—the inconspicuous envelope under his left arm—Aballain and Kadeg trailing after him.

"I've got the key. And an idea. The little room would be an ideal hiding place. The killer will search everywhere thoroughly. We could lock the door from the inside. We place a mobile phone somewhere inconspicuous here in the room as a camera and use a second one to watch."

The next moment they were heading for the narrow door of the extension. Riwal unlocked it and the others went in one by one.

It was spartan: a big desk from the sixties, a single leather-bound prayer book lying on it, a few sheets of paper. A very wide, functional wooden desk chair. A shelf at waist height, books, files. A statue of a saint on a cabinet. Rough stone walls. A high window opposite the door, closed. A smell of dust, wood, and slight damp that had been there for years. Much worse than in the church. On the left side was a little toilet and a sink.

Riwal went straight over to the desk and silently held his hand up to Kadeg, who, not without a slight amusement, handed him his mobile.

Riwal set it down on the prayer book, carefully placing the envelope on the right-hand side of the desk.

Everyone gathered around him. Riwal had set his own cell phone down there too. Nolwenn and he had set up a Bluetooth network that would link all their cell phones. It didn't take long before he said: "It's working. I'm going to go out and position it. You tell me if the position and perspective are good."

Then he was gone.

"I'm leaving the door wide open. But you'll still have to shout."

"We will!" Kadeg yelled.

Dupin stared spellbound at the little screen. "Where are the cars?" he asked.

"Aballain helped me. We left them at the end of the big parking lot, where the road leads into the Val sans Retour. Both hidden well behind large bushes. In a few moments there will be two more cars there, with four men in each of them. Just in case we need backup. And, if we have to take prisoners."

"Well done, Ka—"

"Not bad!" Kadeg shouted. He had had to do a half turn in order to be able to call better into the church.

Both the cabinet and the figure were clearly visible from the front. Which, however, also meant that if somebody was standing in front of the cabinet it wouldn't be possible to see what they were doing.

Dupin went over to the door and yelled into the church: "It might be better to try a sideways view, Riwal. Maybe we could even see someone coming into the church."

"That'll be difficult with the light, but I'll try."

Riwal moved closer to the white stag. He was almost at the opposite end of the church, in the corner. He tried holding the camera up high to try it out.

"No, we can't see anything at all," Kadeg called out. "It's too far away and there's too much backlight."

Riwal came back a bit toward Dupin and changed sides. He set the camera on one of the huge picture frames amid the King Arthur scenario.

"That's not bad," Kadeg said.

The commissaire went back to the desk, and took a good look at the scene. "That's okay," Dupin cried out.

They would have been more likely to see the person from the side, and the door was barely in the screen. But nonetheless!

"All right!" the voice from the church said. "I'll stabilize the phone a little, then come and join you."

Kadeg had sat down on the big armchair by the desk, which seemed like a throne. Directly facing the phone.

Dupin stood next to him. He wouldn't have been able to sit still anyway. Aballain positioned himself on the other side so that there was still room for Riwal, who walked into the room at just that moment.

"Does anyone have to go out? If not, I'm closing the door."

Nobody answered. The tension was growing. They had no idea how long they would have to wait.

"We've put two of our best men on duty, but of course the murderer could come from the side, through the little park by the church, for example, or from behind, in which case we're only going to know at the last minute."

Riwal was examining the wooden door.

"We'll have to be fairly quiet," he said, shutting them up with a determined gesture and taking his own position.

It could take time. Hours at the worst.

Dupin took out his phone and went into the little bathroom.

He would bring Nolwenn and Jean Odinot up to date. Speaking as quietly as possible.

* * *

By now they'd been sitting in the small, muggy room with its high-up closed window for an hour. Of late, torrential rain had been pelting down on it, then, in a change of the weather faster than that morning, suddenly the midday sun had appeared, and impressively quickly heated up the stone walls.

Ever since his two phone calls Dupin had walked in hundreds of small circles around the extension.

Despite their long wait the tension was still rising minute by minute. For some time now they had experienced a tangible nervous angst, along with a simultaneous immense weariness. Dupin felt a leaden feeling in both arms and legs: a dreadful condition that was a mixture of deadly tiredness and exhaustion plus nerves and desperation for action. The only thing from the outside world they were aware of was what was shown on the eight-by-five-centimeter phone screen on the table. Dupin's mood had changed. He was tormented chiefly by the thought that this hadn't been such a good idea; indeed, might even have been a very stupid one, to get stuck in here, while the suspects were running free. With the legendary manuscript in their hands they could have made all of them face up to a hard confrontation, even harder than before. It might, after all, take days before the murderer turned up, before he felt that the air was clear. That was if—*if*—he even had the faintest idea where the manuscript was. It was also possible, it had just become clear to Dupin, that the murderer would send an accomplice.

He said abruptly, "Let's abort this mission and get the lot of them back together at the castle."

The commissaire had been expecting a protest; at the very least, questions. And some bitingly witty comment from Kadeg, a suggestion of something along the lines of "We could have decided that an hour ago."

But he said nothing of the sort. Quite the opposite—Dupin thought he saw relief on their faces.

"Fine"—Aballain already had his phone in his hand—"I'll notify them. I'll tell them to get together at three. In a quarter of an hour."

Dupin nodded.

Riwal went to the door. "I think—"

"Wait a minute, yes?" Aballain interrupted Riwal, as his phone vibrated just that minute.

"What's happened?"

The person on the end of the line clearly needed time to answer.

Dupin was impatient. "What's happened?"

"Thanks, see you later!" Aballain hung up. "A taxi!" He was jabbering so fast he garbled the words. "It stopped just outside the church. Someone got out. A single person. Whom none of the gendarmes recognized."

Before Dupin or one of the inspectors could say anything, they heard the loud squeak of the church door.

All four of them froze.

Within a fraction of a second, Riwal pulled out his phone, set it back on the table, and turned on the live feed again. Immediately the others gathered around the little display.

They waited tensely.

And waited. Nothing. Not a thing. They stood there motionless, slightly bent over, their eyes fixed on the display.

Still nothing.

The seconds dragged by.

The person seemed already to have entered the church—or had they?

And if so, was he or she staying clear of the area covered by the camera? What were they doing there?

"Maybe," Kadeg whispered, "it's just a visitor, who's got nothing whatsoever to do with the case."

"Or," Riwal murmured, "it's someone just come to take a look, to be certain that they're alone."

Riwal said nothing more. A large, dark shadow hung over the image. Whoever it was must have walked past, opposite the little cabinet. That meant he or she was heading for the stained-glass window. And in particular—toward the extension.

"We need to—" Dupin's voice was even more of a whisper than Kadeg's. A noise shut him up.

Somebody was trying to open the door. Of course, that was what they had expected; the person would look around to see if there was anybody there. Whether the door was locked. Yet more heavy rattling of the door handle. The commissaire, his inspectors, and the colonel held their breath.

This was no normal visitor.

Suddenly there were four pairs of eyes glued to Riwal's phone. Yet again there was nothing to say. Once again the seconds ticked by excruciatingly slowly. What was this person doing? There was nothing on this side of the church to inspect. And he or she could have glanced into the two transepts while walking by.

They waited. Waited longer still. They could hardly bear the tension.

Whoever it was still hadn't come near the cabinet. Had they

avoided this side? And if so, when? Had they noticed the camera phone? If they had, why hadn't they left the church immediately? Or had they left without being seen, because of the camera angle?

Dupin's thoughts were running through his mind at lightning speed, touching on every scenario.

He was trying to tell himself to be calm.

In vain.

Something here was wrong.

Without even thinking, in the next moment he charged toward the door with so little advance warning that the others jumped to the side in shock.

As he turned the key and threw open the door in almost the same second, he called out, "We're going in!"

With a mighty leap, Commissaire Dupin sprang into the church.

He ran into the middle, and stopped dead.

Empty! The church was empty. There was nobody there.

The next moment his inspectors were standing behind him.

"Where is . . . ?"

Riwal didn't finish his sentence. They could hear footsteps.

The next second someone stepped out of the small right transept.

Intuitively all four policemen reached for their guns.

Dupin recognized who it was immediately.

Denvel.

It was Marc Denvel. In a white shirt with his sleeves pulled up as far as his elbows. He must have been up to his room after the meeting in the castle, and changed.

"Stay where you are!" Kadeg was first to react. "And put your hands up. I want your open hands with the flat palm upward, facing toward us so we can see them, here and now, or else I will be forced to shoot."

Dupin moved away from the others and went up to Denvel, his gun at the ready.

He was the one! Standing directly in front of him. The murderer. After he'd sought after him so frantically. The one who had turned what was by now nearly twenty-four hours into a murderous nightmare. The aristocratic, smart Marc Denvel.

"What's your cause for having your guns out, messieurs?"

Denvel was master of the situation. He seemed in no way shocked, not in the least irritated. Even now he spoke with the same polite, natural superiority as every time they had met before. Dupin now noticed, for the first time, the professional-looking camera hung over his shoulder. With a huge zoom lens.

"You can't fool us, Monsieur Denvel." Dupin was in battle mode, fully under control. "You were the one. You murdered Paul Picard and Bastien Terrier, and you also were responsible for the attempted murder of Madame Noiret."

"What gives you that idea?"

He played his role well.

Kadeg and Aballain had positioned themselves to the right and left of Dupin. Denvel behaved as if he hadn't seen either of them. Riwal had remained at Dupin's side.

"Apart from Paul Picard, who else could have known where Picard hid the manuscript? You forced it out of Picard, threatening to kill him. Which you subsequently did anyhow."

"Here?" Denvel once again feigned surprise. "The manuscript is here? In this church? That's ridiculous. I came here to photograph a few details of the stained glass. I'm writing an essay in which this extraordinary picture will be mentioned in a footnote. I'm happy to let you see it. I had assumed we were going to be here longer, but now that we're leaving soon and I won't be back in the near future, I thought this would be the right—"

"I'm arresting you here and now, Monsieur Denvel. And will place you into investigative custody. We're putting you in handcuffs now."

He signaled to Kadeg and Aballain and put his gun away.

Dupin was quite certain Denvel was the murderer, but they had still made a mistake. They'd confronted him before he'd touched the cabinet. If he had, they'd have had more evidence. For any judge in the world. They'd lost that through Dupin's haste. Denvel was highly intelligent. When he realized he wasn't going to get away with his photography story, he would suddenly "admit" that, like all the others, he had been hunting for the manuscript, but that he, just like Dupin, had just tried his luck in the church. Obviously that was a lot of coincidences, but one way or the other, he would undoubtedly base his defense strategy on this. Dupin wished he hadn't just stormed out.

"Don't worry, Commissaire, I'm not going to resist." Denvel was almost grinning. "But I—"

Another rattling sound; the church door again. Somebody was coming in.

Riwal stepped toward the newcomer. "You can't come in here. This is an urgent police—" He suddenly broke off.

Madame Noiret had entered the church.

She was wearing a coal-black raincoat. Automatically Dupin thought of the Black Knight that Inwynn had talked about.

She reacted faster than all the others. She immediately pulled a pistol from under her coat. Dupin had taken an offensive leap forward and reached for his own gun, but paused the next second.

Her pistol was a Glock, most likely Fabien Cadiou's weapon.

"Madame Noiret, drop the gun!" Riwal stood just in front of Dupin: her gun was pointing directly at him, and his at her. "Immediately!"

"You're the ones who need to drop their guns, in my opinion." Madame Noiret spoke calmly and coolly.

"We aren't going to do that, not now or ever. And you know that." Dupin squeezed his words out harshly.

Madame Noiret aimed the barrel of her weapon straight at him, placidly. She had Dupin in her sights.

Then all at once, for a tiny moment, the fraction of a second, she swept her eyes past him to the left. Despite the speed with which she refocused on him, Dupin had noticed. He knew what was behind him: the cabinet with the prayer books. The books, but also the manuscript. That was what she had been trying inconspicuously to glimpse. She wanted to see whether they had already found it. To spot if somebody had been tinkering with the cabinet. She had undoubtedly not intended to look that way but couldn't help it.

Dupin lowered his voice, not letting Madame Noiret out of his sight. "It's gone. We took it."

Madame Noiret showed no reaction of any kind.

"It was you," he said, sounding absurd even to himself. Dupin had already spoken this sentence, addressed to someone else. "You are the one who killed Paul Picard, and Bastien Terrier. You feigned an attack on yourself as an alibi, inflicting a couple of serious but not life-threatening wounds on yourself." Dupin was rehearsing all this in his head. He had been an idiot. Why hadn't he seriously considered her?

"You have—"

"Drop your guns!" Madame Noiret interrupted Dupin.

Nothing happened. A ghostly silence arose.

Apparently she had no interest in denying it. There was, in any case, nothing left to deny!

"Messieurs, you're going to let me go now. Or else," she said in an icy voice, "I shall shoot the commissaire."

Dupin stared at her gun. He believed every word.

Only by escalating the situation to the brink did she believe she had any chance.

"I'll count to three."

She looked straight ahead. It was eerie. Her face was empty. Completely empty.

"One!" Madame Noiret paused; she sounded levelheaded. "Two!" She paused again, longer than the first time. "Thr—"

A shot was fired.

Followed by another, a split second later.

Dupin had thrown himself to one side at the first shot and was falling when the second shot rang out.

The first shot had been fired by Kadeg, who stood farthest away from Madame Noiret, who concealed Denvel partly.

The second shot was fired by Noiret. Milliseconds before Kadeg's went through her hand. An absolutely precise shot. Madame Noiret screamed and bent over in pain. She had immediately dropped the gun, and fell to the stone floor a few meters away.

Riwal, Aballain, and Marc Denvel too—who had watched everything with a pale face and in handcuffs—seemed as if paralyzed for a moment.

In the next moment their gaze turned to Dupin, who had fallen onto the stone floor with a muffled thud and collided with the wall, hitting it with his left shoulder.

For a while there was a grim, leaden silence.

The seconds ticked by.

Dupin lay there. Bent double.

Nobody could say how long it was before he moved. He turned

over and raised himself on his hands. Testing, uncertainly, whether or not he was shot or wounded.

"All okay" echoed through the church a second later, far too loud, and then—far too softly, as if he had to check out the volume—"I'm fine."

With those words he pulled himself finally back onto his feet, and in a second was next to Madame Noiret, who despite her serious wound was already looking for her gun again.

"It's all over now." He grabbed her hard by the arm.

She screamed again, then suddenly slumped. From one second to the next her body lost all its strength. It was a physical capitulation.

In the meantime, Kadeg, Riwal, and Aballain were by his side.

"How are you, boss?" Riwal sounded seriously worried.

"I wasn't touched."

The bullet had missed him, but only just. Nothing had happened to him, but he felt nonetheless in a strange state of mind.

Kadeg stared at the fiercely bleeding wound on Madame Noiret's hand.

"I'll fetch a towel," he said, heading over to the little extension. "Call an ambulance."

Madame Noiret's eyes were fixed directly on her hand. She had to be in serious pain, but still kept her composure.

Dupin took a deep breath. The last minute had seemed surreal, like a scene from a movie. A moment when anything could have happened.

"So, now we know the whole story, Madame Noiret." He stood directly in front of her. "And that's all I'm interested in."

His words were lost in the church.

Kadeg returned with a towel. Without a word he came over to

Madame Noiret and wrapped it tightly around the hand she had reluctantly proffered.

The ambulance would be there in a few minutes.

Dupin felt disgusted. He couldn't stand Madame Noiret's presence anymore. And he couldn't stand being in the church any longer.

He had already turned away when she began to speak. Thoughtfully, factually.

"Paul had promised me I'd be part of the team, the scholastic team that was going to examine the manuscript. He tried to win me back with that. It was all about me."

Dupin stood still.

"He called me a few weeks ago and told me everything. He had sensed my marriage with Bastien was over already, by the time of last year's meeting."

Dupin initially had difficulty understanding what she was talking about.

"What does that mean?" Riwal asked acerbically. "That Paul Picard wanted you back, and in exchange offered you a share in the expected fame?"

"And then suddenly he wanted to call the police. And admit everything. It had been an accident. He hadn't intended to kill Fabien Cadiou. Cadiou had threatened him. He didn't want to share the fame, didn't want me involved. If Paul had gone to the police, it would all have been over. Irreversibly. For all of us."

It had all been about narcissism, obviously. It was repulsive.

"Paul and I, we . . ."

Riwal said: "Paul Picard dragged you in without Fabien Cadiou knowing? That would have made you three official discoverers. At least from his point of view?"

She nodded.

"Then you arranged to meet him at the Fontaine de Barenton dig?"

Another nod, as mechanical as the first.

"And he told you where he had hidden the manuscript?"

"Yes, he did. He was completely beside himself, and just wanted to put it somewhere safe."

"And you killed him, after he changed his mind and wanted to surrender."

She was silent.

"And what happened to Terrier? Your . . . husband?" Kadeg asked incredulously.

"He realized that I had been back in touch with Paul. For some time already. Stupid, completely stupid. They were both idiots." She shook her head. "When he heard about the deaths of Cadiou and Picard, he immediately suspected me. He had put it together, the whole story. And told me he wanted to go to the police. Naturally, I denied it all, but he didn't believe me."

Monstrous. It sounded as if she was still disgusted by his reaction. Dupin was familiar with the upside-down, delusional ideas of murderers: a narcissism that was so boundless that they constructed a unique view of the world in which they then lived in total isolation. Where everything they thought, felt, and did was "normal" and "right." People like that didn't doubt themselves for a moment. Not even when they had committed a capital crime.

"And you thought your simulated attack on yourself would delude us all," Kadeg hissed.

"My husband wasn't convinced."

It was repulsive, simply repulsive. Dupin remained silent.

"And so you had to get rid of him," Riwal concluded. "All of a sudden there was only you left! And the manuscript. Which you still had to get."

"Not thinking," Kadeg gloated, "that we would find it before you?"

"And you had found a way to make it look as if you were the sole discoverer of the manuscript," Riwal said.

Dupin wasn't so sure about this point. There had simply been too many who knew, or at least guessed too much. Madame Cadiou, for example. Eventually she would have no reason left to remain silent. Obviously Madame Cadiou could suddenly die too. . . . However, even the most intelligent of people let their belief in their own grandeur outshine an everyday sense of reality. Particularly at crucial moments, which in the end settled their fate. But all that was irrelevant now. Madame Noiret would receive the punishment she was due. That was all Dupin wanted.

Dupin didn't want to hear any more. He set off. By leaving now he wouldn't hear any more of his inspectors' questions.

As soon as Dupin got out of the church he walked off wholly at random across the lawn in the little park that belonged to the church. In the glistening sunlight, endlessly reflected and refracted by the water, that not long ago had been pouring down as if in buckets from heaven. Once again the sky had turned back to a glorious beaming blue.

Slowly Dupin came back to his senses as to what had happened. It had all happened too quickly.

He wasn't interested in the slightest in the fact that a bullet had missed him by only a hair's breadth, and might have killed him. No, it wasn't that, it was the grim, lunatic story that had turned out to be the solution of the case. That and Madame Noiret.

Dupin couldn't have said if he'd been wandering about for three or fifteen minutes. He was befuddled. And exhausted. The lack of sleep had worn him out all of a sudden. It was always like this: it was only when the strain had worn off that he went to pieces. He had experienced fainting attacks, like the previous one in the tunnel, that unbearable feeling that the path in front of him was either falling away or rising, a complete loss of direction.

Dupin took his phone from his pants pocket.

"Well done, Monsieur le Commissaire!" Nolwenn answered the phone immediately and in the best of form. "The case is solved, the manuscript saved, the murderer under arrest. The other murderer already dead. *Ret eo Terriñ ar graoñenn—Evit kaout ar vouedenn.* You have to break the shell to get to the nut. All's well that ends well."

He smirked. "It would appear Riwal has already—"

"He has indeed. Briefly, but he's put me into the picture."

Dupin walked around a large fig tree, laden with fully ripe dark fruit, and the vista opened up to a phenomenal view of the wood. A dragon, very close, lying there on the flat hills.

"Aballain will take Madame Noiret personally to Rennes; he's really an excellent policeman." Nolwenn didn't sound in the slightest exhausted. "There we go, as ever, a cold-blooded monster, this woman, it has to be said. On top of that, one of the gendarmes brought Marc Denvel back to the hotel. He's still pale; the poor thing has had a bit of a shock."

Dupin had completely forgotten him. Even if his anger against the man had not diminished since Noiret's arrest.

"Riwal is going to take the manuscript with him to Concarneau for now. Odinot can deal with the rest."

Dupin didn't want to have anything more to do with it. It was, after all, Jean Odinot's case, a Parisian police case.

"You're bound to be worn out, Monsieur le Commissaire. Just take your time."

"Everything's in order," Dupin said, trying to calm her down.

"First," Nolwenn said buoyantly, "we'll sit down in the Maison des Sources and have something to eat. After that we'll drive home as calm as can be. To Concarneau."

It was just like last night again: after what they had just experienced, the idea that they should sit themselves down in a café sounded absurd, and Dupin wanted to object.

Instead of which he said, "I think . . . well, okay . . . very well then."

"Should I tell Odinot?" she asked.

"I should do that myself."

"Good, then discuss the question of the press and media in general with him. We are definitely going to have to say something, the editors have already been onto me."

"I'll do that."

"Then we'll all meet up at the Maison des Sources. It's just a couple of meters from you. You can go for a relaxing walk first, that'll do you good."

"See you soon, Nolwenn."

She had already hung up.

Dupin just stood there and took a few deep breaths.

Everything seemed more in touch with reality.

He took his phone out of his pocket. It was a while before Jean answered.

"Salut, Georges! How's things?"

"We're done here."

A confused pause.

"What?"

"The case is solved."

Dupin hadn't deliberately decided to answer cavalierly in monosyllables. He just wanted to save energy. "We've got the manuscript and the—"

"You've found this legendary manuscript? It really exists?"

"Yes. And the murderer too. Adeline Noiret. From your lovely Paris."

"Noiret? But she was a victim of an attack herself!"

"That's how . . ."

Dupin summed up in brief words the course of events and the results. He would go into the details later. When he was back in Concarneau.

"Madness! The natural death of Laurent set in motion a string of crimes," Odinot said.

"Just one more thing, Jean. You're getting on the next train and can deal with everything else when you get here. The press conference in particular. And whatever else there is to do." Dupin's mood brightened a little.

"I'm on it. I'll be there today."

Dupin was relieved to get a binding agreement.

"But first I'll call the boss. And then the minister of the interior. He'll be very relieved."

It sounded comic, and macabre. But Odinot made clear: "I mean he'll be at least pleased that the death of his brother was natural." The correction didn't make things much better.

Something occurred to Dupin. "The best thing for you to do would be to ring the prefect directly, talk it all over with him. I think he shouldn't have anything to do with the press."

He could almost hear Jean Odinot grinning through the ether.

"I'll do that. You can count on me."

"Thanks."

"You've done it again, Georges." Odinot paused briefly in respect. "You've won this game too."

Despite his exhaustion, Dupin almost grinned himself. That was how they'd always put it if they'd solved a case—back in the days when they had worked together in Paris. "Win the game." Dupin waxed sentimental briefly.

"The Parisian police department owes you a huge debt of thanks." That was the sentimentality over with.

"Good, we'll speak later, Georges."

This time it was Dupin who hung up. He'd been relatively successful since yesterday afternoon pushing the "special investigator for the Paris police" to the back of his mind most of the time. And that was the way it should stay.

Dupin was back at the bench in the little park. The most important phone call had still to be made. One that would relieve him enormously. Crazy as it might sound, it had been the strongest motive that had driven him to get the case over and done with as soon as possible, the real "game to win."

"It's me, Claire."

"That was quick, Georges. Have you solved the case?"

That wasn't a real question. More a statement to let him know that she had never had a doubt.

"Solved, yes."

It had been a brutal case, under brutal conditions. Dupin was relieved that he would be able to leave the wood soon. A magic wood, yes, and a unique location. Which had two faces. The endlessly beautiful forest, maybe even with some lighthearted elves—and the dark wood of the Celtic Otherworld. A place of shadows, black magic, and dangerous events. The sinister druids. The madmen. Drawing one into a world of ghosts and demons. A dark maelstrom. The story of Iwein had followed him. But Dupin had fulfilled the ultimatum, and the specter had gone. He would get home in time. To Claire. To the house they shared.

"Was it bad?"

"Later. I'll tell you later, Claire. We're having a brief meeting. Then I'll be on my way home."

What great words those were.

"To be honest, I wasn't quite expecting you. I had expected a couple of days on my own." She laughed. "But it's obviously better like this. When can you get here?"

"I think about seven o'clock."

"Then let's meet in the Amiral. We can get something to eat. And then we can get on with the unpacking."

One word had the effect of several dozen *cafés*. It was a magic word: Amiral.

"Excellent." He was back, back in the real world. With Claire. Back in his real life.

* * *

Up to a point it was a conciliatory parting. They had intended to start their office excursion in the Maison des Sources. But it didn't get that far because complete madness had broken out just before, and raged for the next twenty-four hours.

Now here they all were. All four of them. Overtired, exhausted, drained. Each and every one of them lost in their own thoughts. Dupin still felt disgust when he thought of the case, and Madame Noiret in particular. He tried to distract himself, looking around him.

The extremely comfortable room was dominated by an open fire, directly in the middle, for people to gather around in fall and winter. But even today there was a little fire, just two logs. The stone flooring looked to be as old as the house, itself from the Middle Ages. Old wooden tables, ancient wooden chairs, each of them an original. The thrown-together collection of ancient things made for a wonderful atmosphere.

Dupin had already drunk two *petits cafés*. And with them he had delicious tartine with mushrooms "straight from the wood, fried in bacon." The morning croissant on the go was by now nine hours ago, and it would be another three before he got to the Amiral. It gave him a little strength.

"*Hep stourm ne vezer ket trec'h!* There are no victors without a battle. And we've battled bravely." Nolwenn's euphoria met no reaction. "You've seen nearly all the Arthurian sites. Now you won't forget them very quickly."

Dupin closed his eyes a moment.

When he opened them again, his eyes fell on the envelope that Riwal had set in the middle of the little table. It was as if he wanted to have it permanently in view. On Dupin's serious advice they would have nothing more to do with it from now on. In so doing they had suppressed the sensational questions connected with it. Even now the thought of what had been linked to the contents was too monstrous.

"Riwal, don't you want to take a proper look inside?" Dupin himself couldn't believe his own words.

Riwal looked at the commissaire as if he had lost his senses.

"Go on then. Do it." He meant: "You've earned it."

Dupin himself didn't know what was driving him. But this wasn't something you came across every day. A legendary manuscript, the existence of which had until now been pure speculation. And which could contain something extraordinary.

"Do you mean that seriously, Monsieur le Commissaire?"

Even Nolwenn hesitated.

There was silence for a while.

Then, without saying a word, Dupin took the envelope, pulled out the protective sleeve with the manuscript, as if what it contained was some everyday article, opened the zip fastener, and reached for the contents.

Riwal moved back a little from the table intuitively; Kadeg and Nolwenn stared unbelievingly. Dupin now had it in his hand. It was lighter than it had seemed with its wooden covers and hinges. The copper circle genuinely did shine. Dupin set it down on the envelope, and opened it randomly in the middle, so that they could see all the pages lying open. Beautiful lines in curved letters written in black ink. The first letter of the page, an *S*, was three or four times the size of the others and extremely artistically formed, with fine ornamentation in green and red, like ivy. In the lower third was a box drawn with a fine line, within which was a drawing in glowing colors, looking as if it had only just been finished: a proud knight in armor, and a powerful lion—in gold—in a vast forest. Dupin couldn't believe it. That had to be him, the Lion Knight.

All of a sudden, Riwal exclaimed, "It's not old French! It's Ancient Breton. Celtic. The author was a Breton. Not English at all, and not even French. He was a Celt, a Breton. It all goes back to a Breton. He was the one to write down the story!"

Dupin wondered why this was such a surprise. Wasn't it the case—in Brittany—that it was *always* a Breton behind everything, at the end? A Breton or Brittany itself? Never mind what it was; a discovery, an achievement, or what the circumstance was. Dupin—as a layman—had expected nothing else.

Riwal studied the page further. Nolwenn, Dupin, and Kadeg had also gotten up and bent lower over the manuscript to see it better.

"Ancient Breton." Riwal's voice was laced with deep humility. "Not easy to read!"

He carefully turned over another page. He seemed to be in a trance. Nolwenn remained silent, but her eyes glowed.

"Difficult, difficult." All of a sudden Riwal sounded defeated. He seemed unable to decipher it. "Something for the experts."

He made as if to close the book again, but then stopped.

"Here! Here!"

He pointed to one short word, trying his best not to touch the parchment.

"*Tra.*" He raised his eyebrows almost to his hairline. "*An Tra!*"

"What does it mean?"

"*An Tra* is Breton. We still have the word today. It means 'the thing,' more or less."

"The thing?"

It was absurd.

"Precisely that, 'the thing,'" Nolwenn confirmed drily.

"But"—Riwal seized the word again—"it can also mean 'nothing.' Nothing at all."

"And what's that supposed to mean?" asked Kadeg, sounding skeptical.

Riwal scanned the text feverishly.

"Here!" It was a proper exclamation: "*Pesketaer ruoanez!*"

"The Fisher King!" Nolwenn translated, without further comment. Then left it to Riwal.

"The Fisher King! Don't you remember? In the story of Iwein! He's the one who guards the Grail."

A pause. Dupin recalled.

"The *Thing*!"

Yet another pause. Riwal was beyond himself.

"The Thing. Exactly how the great writers about the Grail put it. The Thing!"

Even this excitement went beyond Dupin. If this was really a reference to the Holy Grail—and not just to any old thing or even "nothing"—why would it be such a sensational discovery to hear that that was how the Grail was originally referred to, not only later.

"Don't you understand?" Riwal was giddy with excitement. Carefully now he turned the first page.

"Just no name of the author. Not the slightest clue. But that doesn't matter. In those days the name of the author was of no importance."

"I think we should put the manuscript away again. And let the experts deal with the whole question of deciphering it, translating it and sorting out the meanings."

"Couldn't we just—"

"We should leave now," Dupin interrupted. He now regretted ever having encouraged Riwal at all.

With a regretful look, Riwal packed the manuscript back in its holder. "You're right, boss. This is too banal a moment to unveil such a mystery," he sighed.

Nolwenn reached for her handbag.

"Just one more thing." Dupin hesitated, but he couldn't ignore it. It was like a little ghost that wouldn't leave him in peace. Even if it was a ridiculous detail. Riwal would probably be able to help him; he should have asked him earlier, the great flora and fauna expert.

"What white animals are there here in the wood, Riwal?"

It was now the inspector's turn to look helplessly at him. "White animals? How do you mean white?"

"Proper white, not light gray or something like that."

Riwal thought for a moment.

"Penguins?"

The inspector really had said "penguins."

"Penguins?" Dupin repeated in surprise.

"I don't know how or why it is, boss, but in every one of your cases, there's a penguin. It's extraordinary."

Dupin's favorite animal, for sure. But not one that had anything to do with this case. "You must have read about these monster penguins they've discovered, boss. The ancient penguins, that took over the earth after the extinction of the dinosaurs. They found bones. The ancient penguins were nearly two meters tall and weighed over a hundred kilos! The greatest hunters on the planet in their day!"

Of course, Dupin had been thrilled to read about them.

It seemed as if Riwal too had come back to reality now. "How big is the animal you mean?"

"Roughly the size of an overgrown cat, maybe a little bigger. A marten maybe?"

If he were honest, Dupin didn't really have a proper idea what a marten looked like; he was primarily interested in getting a possible—certain—identification of the thing he had come across several times on this case.

"You saw a white animal about that size?"

"Several times," Dupin revealed. As far as Riwal was concerned it was at the very least a relatively reasonable zoological question.

"Today?"

"And yesterday."

"As I said, if it were winter, you might have seen an ermine, even though they're extremely rare. And only ever come to the edge of the forest, not into the heart of the wood."

"An ermine?"

Dupin knew the ermine. Every Breton knew it. It was Brittany's most important animal. As early as the thirteenth century it was Brittany's heraldic creature, and was still today featured on the legendary Breton banner, the Gwenn-ha-du. Eleven black-tipped ermine tails, to be precise. Which also meant there were ermines to be seen everywhere, on beer mats, beer bottles, restaurant signs, cake boxes, T-shirts, car bumper stickers, soccer shirts. . . . Once upon a time it had stood for the proud Duchy of Brittany, and even today remained the most significant symbol of Breton independence. It was a synonym for Brittany. Later other duchies, principalities, and kingdoms throughout Europe had adopted it as their heraldic symbol. Even the pope wore clothing made from ermine. But it had had its origins, the insignia of power, in Brittany. Of course.

And the reason it was this animal, and no other, led deep into the heart of the Breton soul. An ermine, people said, would rather die than let its winter coat be besmirched with dirt. That in turn was the origin of the famed and renowned election slogan "Rather dead than defiled," the latter in the sense of "dishonored." In Breton consciousness it translated as "Rather die than submit." Occasionally, Dupin found himself humming the legendary seventies song, *La Blanche Hermine*, a proud battle song that for some Bretons had taken on the status of an unofficial national anthem.

"But as I said before"—despite the emotional theme, Nolwenn remained remarkably factual—"they're only white in fall or winter. The rest of the time they're brown and white."

"I get it. Nothing else occurs to you."

Dupin was disappointed.

"Unless of course," Riwal began, but then stopped.

"Unless of course, what?"

"In some legends there are ermines that keep their white fur all year round; unique, rare animals. But there are rare reports of encounters with these animals, though they more frequently belong in the realm of fables."

Dupin had had enough of fables.

"Apart from that—who knows? People say that an encounter with such a white ermine heralds something special."

"Such as?"

"That misfortune is imminent, but you will be lucky. A seriously difficult test, that one will only come through by a serious, difficult struggle. Without the ermine, it would be lost, that much is clear."

Dupin was silent. He felt wonderful.

Riwal continued, unfazed.

"Put it like this, for example. You have a car accident, drive into a tree. But not headfirst, and with no fatal outcome. Just damage to the bodywork. Or somebody shoots at you at close range, and the bullet misses. Something that ought to be impossible even for an inexperienced shooter."

Dupin remained silent.

"Things like that," Riwal added, "or even the whole case. We were lucky to have solved it, when you think about it."

Dupin still said nothing, even though everybody turned to look at him.

"That explains a lot," Nolwenn agreed.

"That'll do for now. We're leaving the wood." Dupin exited the room abruptly.

* * *

The *grande cocotte* had been fabulous. A dream. Alongside the entrecôte, one of his favorite dishes at the Amiral. Dupin had almost ordered the entrecôte—out of reflex—but then he had had one just a few hours earlier, for breakfast. Claire had suggested the *grande cocotte*. Eating it was always a celebration in its own right, which happened to fit the occasion. So simple, so refined, so delicious: a half lobster, various mussels, and langoustines in a finely matched sauce of shellfish, cream, and wonderful spices. For dessert, *soufflé au caramel* for Claire and *moelleux au chocolat* for Dupin, a heavenly warm chocolate cake with a molten center. Claire had ordered her favorite wine of the moment, a Chinon Blanc from Couly-Dutheil, a heavy mineral note with citrus aromas.

It had felt good to take time and leave the restaurant later than planned.

Astonishingly—and it was really like a miracle—Dupin's strength had returned. Not just a little—at least that wasn't the impression it gave at the moment—but completely, even though he had been on his feet for nearly forty hours. The trials and the insanity of the case had virtually disappeared. For every kilometer farther they had gotten from the wood in his battered Citroën, they had put behind them an internal distance in space and time. The past had receded farther and farther. If someone had told him it had all happened a week or even a month ago, Dupin wouldn't have disagreed. An objective sense of time was nothing but a lie.

They had gotten merry over dinner, if not exactly exuberant.

Dupin had begun to talk about the case. Claire said little in return. A few moments after the starters began to arrive—the *huitres sauvages au beurre persillé et gingembre* for Claire, wild oysters with parsley butter and ginger, and for Dupin the classic *terrine de foie gras*—he broke off in midsentence and said: "It doesn't matter. I'll tell you another time." He added a vague "maybe" and then asked: "How were the last few days in the clinic?" But Claire didn't want to talk about that either, so they switched to other topics that were a bit more relaxing.

When they got home, Dupin showered. Claire had opened more wine with some potato chips, her favorite, salt and vinegar, and made herself comfortable with a cushion and comforter on the living room floor, amidst all the boxes that still had to be unpacked. The light was romantically low, the sun would be going down soon.

Dupin sat down next to her and reached for a wineglass.

"To us, to our home, Claire."

He was overcome by an overwhelming feeling of happiness. Involuntarily he found himself thinking of the white ermine, however fanciful it was. Nonetheless. It wasn't obvious that he should be sitting here. That applied to everything. Above all that Claire was sitting here; that they were sitting here together. Even that had come about in a long and complicated way. One that could just as easily have ended in misfortune. Even back then he must have come across a white ermine at some stage or another.

"Yes, Georges: our home."

They drank the toast.

"Shall we get down to it?" Claire meant the box in front of her. She took a few more chips.

"Let's set to it."

She knelt down before him.

It was one of his boxes. His little collection of penknives that he had inherited from his father, and had been sacred to him even while he was still a boy. He had later expanded it: in Paris, on his travels, in Concarneau. In the big Fishing-and-Knife store next to the Amiral. In the knife store in the Ville Close, right next to the ice-cream parlor. To the side of the box, well packed, was the first painting Dupin had ever bought. In his first year in Brittany. By one of the great painters who had journeyed around Brittany in the nineteenth century, Maxime Maufra, a close friend of Gauguin. He had painted the craziest Breton sunsets, which was another way of saying totally realistic, just the way they really were. In the craziest, totally realistic colors. A master of light and colors, which brought the Breton magic into the soul. Paintings that made you drunk. Full of vibrant energy. Dupin had bought the painting at the Galérie Gloux, at the end of the *grande place*; from Françoise and Jean-Michel Gloux, the owners of the wonderful gallery that still looked exactly as it had at the end of the nineteenth century. Sometimes they would eat together of an evening.

"The sky, the sea, the colors." Claire had unpacked the painting and was holding it in her hand, then looked out the door onto the terrace. "But even so, tonight reality is outdoing art by a long shot!"

They had already been admiring the magnificent sunset on the way back from the Amiral in the car. Claire had left her car at home and come in Dupin's, which meant that she had seen the vehicle's battered left side, and was of the same opinion as Nolwenn: he needed a new one.

"Do you know what?" Claire set the painting deliberately to one side. "Do you know what we're going to do? We're going to watch everything live. The sunset. And we're going to watch it from *our* beach. And go swimming."

"I . . ."

Dupin said nothing more. It was magnificent.

"Let's go then. I'm going to change quickly." Claire ran up the stairs.

Dupin was just about to follow her, when the phone rang. He took a reluctant glance at it.

Jean.

Now that he had seen who it was, he had to pick it up.

"Yes? Are you home already? I won't trouble you for long, Georges. I'm arriving in Rennes in a few minutes. But I'm calling you about something else."

"Yes?"

Dupin ran upstairs. He needed his bathing suit too.

"I've just spoken to the minister of the interior and the head of police. At the end of the year, one of the highest positions in the service of the Parisian police is going to open up. With the rank of *directeur central*. They want . . ." a brief pause, ". . . they both want the job to go to you."

"Say that again."

Dupin had almost collapsed.

"They want you to come back, to Paris, where you belong."

"I . . ." Dupin didn't know what to say.

"And you're to bring Inspector Riwal with you, both inspectors even. And Nolwenn of course. They'll rearrange the position the way you want it and in accordance with your wishes."

"I . . . I'll call you tomorrow . . . thanks" was all that Dupin could bring himself to say.

Then he hung up.

For a while he just stood there on the stairs, then ran his fingers through his hair. Unbelievable. Disconcerting, but still, extraordinary, something of an event.

Had that really just taken place? Had that phone call been real?

If it had been real, then it was so absurd, that yet again he was facing something surreal.

* * *

The sunset was nothing like the gentle, mellow, peaceful sunset by the river the previous evening, beautiful as this one was.

If it had seemed during the day that the clouds and blue sky were going to fight each other for supremacy, it appeared by this evening that they had agreed on peaceful coexistence. With the sole intention to work out together which play of light, colors, and shapes was possible.

The clouds arrived in several layers, an endless chaos of fine, light, fleeting brushstrokes, thousands of them. Every stroke in its own different color variation. Light lilac, strong pink in all its intensities, white, dazzling white too, yellow, light blue, tending toward a greenish tone and particularly spectacular turquoise. The Glénan Islands to the south of Concarneau were acutely fine, especially the Penfret Lighthouse; where above the turquoise swam thick, plush clouds in a warm bluish gray, signaling danger. Their edges shone white and pink like a decorative fringe. Even these fleecy clouds built up into an extravagant formation above the lighthouse, a sort of crown with four spikes and four pearls, lit directly by the sun, with an unbelievable bright red shining through. A symbol dancing in the heavens.

The third layer, spread loosely and generously across the whole sky: white sunny-weather storybook clouds. And in the center the sun itself, a shimmering, gleaming orange ball, already half sunk in the sea. Glowing as if it would never fully be extinguished. An ancient power as beautiful as it was destructive.

Dupin and Claire had sat up front by the water, on the flat-washed concrete slabs that led a few meters into the ocean. Dupin loved the stones to lie on because they were sand-free. Claire, on the other hand, loved lying on the sand. For that reason alone the place was perfect. Sand and rocks together, they had both.

This evening they were sitting on the rocks close together, legs and shoulders touching. Claire's hair fell to her shoulders.

The water was peaceful, soft, a deep dark blue, seemingly unimpressed by the light-and-color drama in the sky, and kept its own shade of color untouched.

Claire had brought the bottle of wine with them, along with two glasses. Both just wore T-shirts over their swimsuits.

They were alone. As if the beach belonged only to them. Just like the sunset. To them exclusively.

The air was balmy, a perfect summer evening.

They hadn't talked much, just took a sip of wine occasionally. They had surrendered to the magic. Once or twice Dupin had thought about the call from Jean, with mixed feelings. He didn't think at all about the case anymore. All of a sudden Claire set her glass down and pulled her T-shirt off.

"Come on!"

Dupin did the same.

Claire put a foot in the water first.

They slowly went deeper and deeper. The water had kept its pleasant temperature despite the capricious weather. It had stored the summer.

Dupin stopped when the water reached his stomach. He always stopped at that point.

"There's nothing more beautiful, nothing else in the whole world."

Claire let herself slide into the water, and began to swim, with strong strokes. She was a good swimmer, an elegant swimmer. Dupin liked just to watch her. She dived, with her head under, and swam on.

Dupin supported himself on his toes, then dived under himself. Then he too swam on. He took a long diver's stroke. There was really nothing more beautiful. And with that he didn't just mean the Atlantic. He meant everything. Right at that moment, everything.

A Few Weeks Later

O bviously the discovery of the manuscript drew a lot of attention, not least in the academic world. There were reports everywhere about the "sensational historic find." That included the "adventurous theft" and the murderous fate of those involved, as well as how the Breton police had saved the day for their Parisian colleagues, all retold in numerous fabulous and fantastic elaborations. A "Breton commissaire" had had to help out in "the King Arthur Case," the reports said literally (giving Dupin a sobriquet he had fought for for seven long years—he was finally a "Breton").

Dupin was also called the "Brave Knight"—the sort of thing he hated—and the "Knight of the Grail," even the "Knight of the Round Table." It was ridiculous. But it was unavoidable for the King Arthur Case, as the whole world called it.

The decision about the famed Parc de l'Imagination Illimitée was postponed because of the "bloody events."

The manuscript was given back to the library in Aberystwyth.

Almost immediately, and as was due, a major "international special research project" was announced. The most famous scholars in the world—apart from those of the "discredited" French section of the International Arthurian Society—had set to work studying it thoroughly. Both the question of the author and the text itself.

The exact content would be revealed only after the conclusion of the studies. Then a translation would follow, into modern French and dozens of other languages. The various speculations went haywire. There was nothing that wasn't expanded on, up to and including the famed "sacred scripture" that would bring "eternal peace" because the find would lead to the "New Arthurian Age."

What was agreed was that apart from its content, the manuscript was indeed the sensation that had been expected. Not least because there was now without doubt an original text from the Arthurian legend: one that, according to the experts, had probably pulled together all the widespread oral—Celtic—stories of the time and put them on record. From which all the "Arthurian authors" who followed had derived their material. It was even suggested that Geoffrey of Monmouth had read the text, studied it, and that he himself had hidden it away in some monastic library under a false description, in the hope that it would never be found and he would be considered forever to have been the first author of the epic. At some stage the manuscript had ended up in Aberystwyth. The crucial factor in the discovery was simple: it was a Breton, old Breton, even ancient Breton text. Not that the Bretons of course hadn't always thought so.

A couple of scholars from the official illustrious circle who were allowed to study the manuscript had already leaked the fact that the regrettable use of the name "the Thing" for the Holy Grail would remain in place. And the hints about the "true Arthur," which were everywhere, but remained vague, were "extremely complicated" to interpret.

Dupin was happy enough with this present state of affairs, and for it to stay so. Maybe it was best if the Holy Grail remained forever just "the Thing," a glittering secret, something to be sought after and aspired to. And the same went for Arthur. An eternal ideal, an incentive to be striven toward, a challenge, a grand undertaking. Nothing was more powerful.

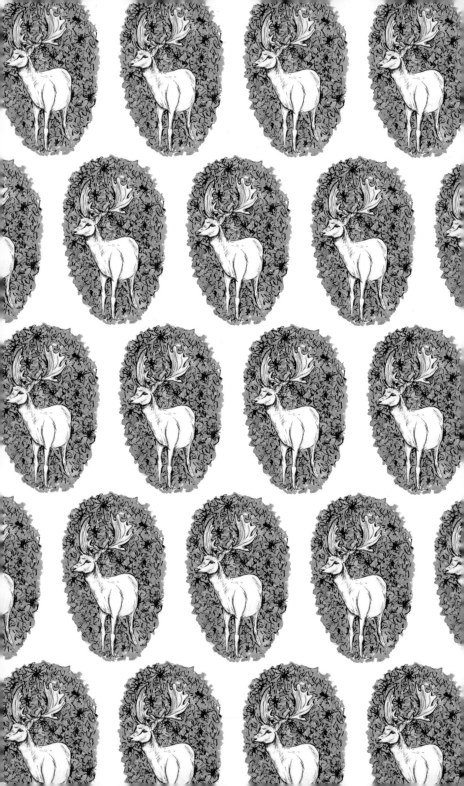